Praise f

"An enthralling, heartbreaking and thrilling courtroom drama that had me shouting out loud and gripped until the last page."
Nadine Matheson, author of *The Jigsaw Man*

"Brilliantly tense, this is another clever page-turner from Kia Abdullah. A nightmare scenario evolves into an engrossing human drama that I couldn't put down. Just superb."
Louise Hare, author of *This Lovely City*

"Amid the requisite revelations of resentments and secrets, Abdullah draws out the truth with compassion, charting with notable understanding the ever-changing currents in human relations."
The Times

"A stunning courtroom drama, taut, tantalising, deftly paced, with a denouement that will leave you reeling."
***Saga* magazine**

"Twists and turns aplenty . . . The author's greatest strength lies in her sensitive and relatable description of the relationship between sisters Leila and Max's mother Yasmin."
i

"A tense, brilliant read."
Bella

"Abdullah has handed us another gripping, brave and tense courtroom drama. *Next of Kin* is precisely observed, tense and guaranteed to enthral until the final, heart-stopping page."
***Platinum* magazine**

Kia Abdullah is an author and travel writer from London. She has written for *The New York Times*, the *Guardian* and the *Telegraph*, and is the author of *Truth Be Told*, which was shortlisted for The Diverse Book Awards, and *Take It Back*, named one of the best thrillers of the year by the *Guardian* and the *Telegraph*.

Kia frequently contributes to the BBC, commenting on a variety of issues affecting the British Asian community, and is the founder of Asian Booklist, a site that helps readers discover new books by British Asian authors. Kia also runs Atlas & Boots, a travel blog read by 250,000 people a month. For more information about Kia and her writing, visit her website at kiaabdullah.com, or follow her at @KiaAbdullah on Instagram and Twitter.

Also by Kia Abdullah

Take It Back
Truth Be Told

Next of Kin

Kia Abdullah

ONE PLACE. MANY STORIES

This novel is entirely a work of fiction. The names, characters
and incidents portrayed in it are the work of the author's
imagination. Any resemblance to actual persons, living or
dead, events or localities is entirely coincidental.

HQ
An imprint of HarperCollins*Publishers* Ltd
1 London Bridge Street
London SE1 9GF

www.harpercollins.co.uk

HarperCollins*Publishers*
1st Floor, Watermarque Building, Ringsend Road
Dublin 4, Ireland

This edition 2022

1
First published in Great Britain by
HQ, an imprint of HarperCollins*Publishers* Ltd 2021

Copyright © Kia Abdullah 2021

Kia Abdullah asserts the moral right to be
identified as the author of this work.
A catalogue record for this book is
available from the British Library.

ISBN: 978-0-00-853-832-3

MIX
Paper from
responsible sources
FSC™ C007454

This book is produced from independently certified FSC™ paper
to ensure responsible forest management.

For more information visit: www.harpercollins.co.uk/green

This book is set in 10.7/15.5 pt. Sabon

Printed and Bound in the UK using 100% Renewable Electricity at
CPI Group (UK) Ltd, Croydon, CR0 4YY

For my other little sis, Forida

PART I

Chapter One

It was a strange thing to be jealous of your sister, yet perfectly natural at the very same time. Perhaps it was inevitable. After all, weren't women taught to compete with one another; to observe, assess, rank and critique, which made your sister your earliest rival?

Leila Syed pondered this as she watched her husband lean close to her sister. Yasmin lit his cigarette and he took a drag with audible pleasure. Paired at the foot of the garden, the two seemed remarkably intimate. It coiled Leila's jealousy just a little bit tighter. It was a good jealousy though; a *healthy* jealousy. It reminded her of Will's appeal: his easy, raffish manner, his dark, contrarian humour and that magnetic confidence that only occasionally tipped into pride.

She couldn't blame him, really, for being drawn to her sister. Yasmin had an arresting softness that men could not resist. It was there in the sway of her long, dark hair and the lazy line of her Bambi eyes. Every part of her seemed to curve and curl next to Leila's hard edges: the strong line of her jaw, the thin purse of her lips. She was well aware of their respective roles: Yasmin the centre of gravity and Leila merely caught in the orbit.

She shifted in her seat, unsticking her thighs from the hard green plastic. The air held a tropical damp that felt heavy on her skin. It was unusually sultry for London; the hottest July on record. It gave the city a heady, anarchic feel – all that flesh and temper simmering in crowded places.

Laughter rose in the air and Leila closed her eyes, basking in the sound. What a surprising delight it was to hear her sister laugh. She wished she could pause this moment and gather all its details: the press of heat on her eyelids, the barely-there hint of wisteria, the bleed of a distant party close enough to bring life to the night but not too close for comfort. She sensed movement next to her and opened her eyes. Her brother-in-law, Andrew, watched the pair at the foot of the garden, huddled together like truant teens. He arched his brows at Leila and she returned a knowing smile. He sat down next to her, the lip of his beer bottle balanced between two fingers. They were quiet for a while.

'It's really helped her,' he said. 'Being here.'

'I'm glad,' said Leila with a cheerless smile.

'I appreciate it, you know. Everything you do for her. For us.'

Leila motioned with her hand, wrist still perched on the armrest. 'It's nothing.'

Andrew turned his gaze on her, his eyes dark and wistful. 'It's not nothing.'

She half-shrugged. 'She's my sister.'

'I know but still.' He tipped his bottle towards her, raised in a silent toast.

She clinked her glass against it and took a sip of the earthy red wine. She gazed across the expanse of grass, blue-green in the falling dusk. She watched Will brush something off Yasmin's shoulder: a fly, a spider, some unknown predator. Her bra strap slid off her shoulder and Will's gaze fixed on it briefly. The two red dots of their cigarettes waxed and waned in tandem until one burned out. Yasmin shifted in the dark and headed back to Leila.

'Will is hilarious,' she said with a scandalised shake of her head as if she *could not* believe his temerity.

'Yep. That's why I married him,' said Leila, her voice climbing high midway, signalling sarcasm or irony or some other bitter thing.

Yasmin paused for a fraction of a second before reaching for the wine. She filled her glass, the liquid sloshing generously, a single red droplet escaping the rim to stain the crisp white tablecloth. She didn't offer Leila a top-up. Rather than irk her, however, the casual act of selfishness reassured Leila. It meant that Yasmin felt secure here; unguarded and relaxed. It meant that Leila had succeeded in her task.

When their mother died two decades ago, just a year after their father, Leila, who was nearly eighteen, did everything to shield her sister, then only ten. She gave up her place at St Andrew's for a London polytechnic. She worked evenings at Marks & Spencer and weekends at a greasy spoon, stitching together pounds and pennies to eke out a meagre living. Her greatest success, she thought, was that Yasmin had grown into a happy, secure, well-adjusted adult. Until life came knocking of course.

'It's so nice here,' said Yasmin, stretching her arms

in a languorous yawn. She gestured at the conservatory. 'God, I wish we could get one of those.'

'We *could* if you want,' said Andrew, his face pinched in a frown.

Yasmin swatted the words away. 'You know we can't afford it,' she said a little sharply.

Andrew bristled, but didn't respond. Instead, he stood and headed over to Will. The two husbands had never quite gelled, but they made a valiant effort.

Leila glanced sideways at Yasmin. 'You know, you can always come and work for me. I could use a PA like you.'

Yasmin rolled her eyes. 'I've told you before. I'm not going to come and be your secretary, Leila.'

'You've always been too proud.'

'It's not pride, it's . . .' Her shoulders rose defensively. 'I don't want to be beholden to you.'

'You wouldn't be beholden to me. It's not charity. You'd be paid for the work you do. We have a training scheme too. If you wanted, you could study at the same time and work your way up.'

'I *like* my job,' said Yasmin.

'I know you do, but it's like you fell into being a secretary at eighteen and have stayed there ever since. Don't you want to do more?'

'No,' said Yasmin stiffly. 'I like my boss. I like my colleagues. I like coming home and spending time with Max. I don't need status like you do.'

Leila gestured with her glass. 'You were *just* saying you wish you could afford more.'

'That's your problem, Leila. You take everything literally.

I don't *actually* want your conservatory. I don't want *your* life.'

Leila fell silent. Will and Andrew were laughing, but the sound was forced and formal; the laughter of acquaintances.

Yasmin sighed. 'I'm sorry,' she said with a hint of petulance. When Leila didn't react, she poked her in the arm. When still there was no reaction, she leaned over and threw her arms around her. Then, she began to sing 'Father and Son', her voice laden with mock gravity. She chose the deeper register of the father, who lectures his son on life.

Leila tried to pull away, but a traitorous smile played on her lips. Yasmin always sang this song when Leila was overbearing. 'Okay, I get it.' She pressed a palm against Yasmin's lips, but she shrugged away and carried on singing.

'You're an arsehole,' said Leila, but she was laughing now, unable to resist her sister's cheer.

Yasmin stopped singing. 'No, I'm not,' she said matter-of-factly.

Leila's smile lingered on her lips. She reached over and neatened a strand of her sister's hair. 'No, you're not,' she said tenderly. They settled into companionable silence and Leila made a mental note to get a quote for a conservatory. Last year, she had lent Andrew some money so that he and Yasmin could move to the area. Perhaps she could lend him a little bit more. If Yasmin had more space, perhaps she would do more of the things she used to enjoy: make those silly giant collages with pages ripped from *Vogue* and *Vanity Fair*. She had even managed to sell a couple.

Will stubbed out his cigarette and walked back up the length of the garden. Andrew followed and made a show of checking his watch, prompting Yasmin to stand.

'We better get going,' she said. 'I have an early start tomorrow and Max will get cranky. He grizzled for hours last night.'

They drifted back into the house, the air inside still humid despite the garden doors slung open. Leila watched as Yasmin and Andrew moved in a domestic rush: she scooping up a sleeping Max, her shoulder hung low with the weight of her bag, while Andrew gathered all the books and toys needed to occupy a three-year-old. More than once in the past, Yasmin had lamented that Max didn't have a cousin to play with. Leila always laughed politely and said 'not yet' as if it were a choice she'd made.

'Thanks for dinner,' said Yasmin, scanning the room over Leila's shoulder to make sure that she'd packed everything. They swapped kisses and the two parents marched out, carrying Max to their house around the corner. Leila shut the door and felt the wash of relief that comes with departing guests, even ones you love.

'I'm shattered,' said Will, flopping on the sofa, raising a few motes of dust. He reached for her and pulled her onto his lap. 'You okay?'

She nodded.

He brushed his lips against her slender brown shoulder. 'Can I stay?'

She tensed. Things were complicated enough between them. 'Not tonight.'

'Are you sure?'

'I'm sure.'

'Okay,' he said reluctantly. 'Message received.' He kissed the fine knot of her collarbone and gently tipped her off his lap.

She listened to his footsteps echo down the hall and the

front door open, then close. How quickly their group had dwindled. That was the value, she thought, of building your own family. You were never forced to be alone. She felt an old, familiar ache and hung her head wearily. How many times would she have to do this?

Perhaps if she were more honest with Yasmin, some of the pain would ease. Her sister knew about the first miscarriage but not the three thereafter. She wanted to confide in her, but Yasmin carried her own trauma and Leila refused to add to it. When she and Will separated in February, she had downplayed it to her sister. 'It's temporary,' she told her. 'A chance to assess our priorities and stop taking each other for granted.' The messiness – Will staying over, their attending events together – made the break look superficial; a passing hiccup in a nine-year marriage. In truth, she wasn't sure that they would make it and the thought of growing old alone sometimes left her panicked.

Yasmin had told her once that parents who lost a child didn't have a word to describe themselves – like 'widow', 'widower', or 'orphan'. That was true but at least they could claim 'bereavement'. It was something to attach to. What did you call a parent who had never had a child?

You can't have everything, she told herself for the thousandth time. She had a highly successful business, a hard-won reputation, a comfortable home and lifestyle, a sister she would die for and a husband she still loved. Surely, *surely*, that was enough.

*

A breeze gusted through the open window but barely eased the heat. Leila dabbed her upper lip with a tissue, careful not to smudge her makeup. She was freshly showered, but sweat already lined the wiring of her bra, making her feel unclean. The day was set to break another record and London barely coped in the heat. Sure, there were ice creams in Hyde Park and boat rides on the Serpentine, but commuting on the Underground was like tightening a pressure valve. Leila preferred to drive to work: barely three miles from her house in Mile End to her office in Canary Wharf.

She scooped up her shoes, a finger hooked into each high heel, and dropped them into a plastic bag, its skin worn thin from repeated crumpling. She smoothed her white shirt and grey pencil skirt, then headed downstairs to the kitchen. This was her favourite room in her four-storey Georgian home: large and airy with raw brick and exposed beams dating back to 1730. She moved efficiently through her morning routine: a glass of freshly squeezed orange juice and a quick glance at her email, followed by a mental vow to finally start Headspace, the mindfulness app that languished on her home screen.

Leila ran an architecture firm and though she prided herself on discipline, time often seemed to swallow itself; a whole day gone in one glance at the clock. Today would be one of those days, she knew. Her partner at the firm, Robert Gardner, was pitching for a major project that would propel them into the big leagues. Leila had worked so hard for so long and this was her reward: financial security and lifelong protection from the shame of poverty. The thought of those early years left a hardness in her stomach. Sometimes, a memory would rise unbidden and wind her for a moment: Leila crouched in a campus bathroom stuffing her underwear with wads of tissue so that she could afford tampons for Yasmin, or keeping her bras meticulously clean so Yasmin would never know they were used. Leila had promised herself that she would never go back there again; had worked night and day to get to where she was. This project with Mercers Bank could be her biggest payoff. She had swallowed her pride and agreed to let Robert pitch, knowing that he – an upper-crust white man – had a better shot by default. She had to wait in the wings and see if all her prep paid off.

She drained her glass and filled it with water just as her phone vibrated on the counter. She saw that it was Andrew and felt a twist of anxiety. Yasmin's husband rarely, if ever, called her.

'Leila, are you home?' Andrew sounded breathless.

'Yes. What's wrong?'

'I'm so, so sorry. The office called and our entire bloody network's gone down. Is there any chance at all that you could drop Max off at nursery? It's practically on your way.'

Leila glanced at the clock, but was already saying, 'Of course.'

'You can say no,' he added, but the strain was clear in his voice. His employer, a web hosting company, was already struggling for profit. This latest outage could be catastrophic.

'I'll be over in five minutes,' she told him.

'I'm sorry,' he apologised again. 'I know we've been a pain since we got here.'

'Not at all,' she assured him, though they both knew it was true. Since moving there last year, he and Yasmin had repeatedly called on Leila, as if her *not* having a child meant she was always on hand to tend to theirs.

She was thankful that Will hadn't stayed over last night. Though he adored Max, he would surely launch into a monologue about Yasmin taking advantage of Leila – as if they should refuse on principle alone. Leila gathered her heels, keys, phone and bag, and headed out to her car, feeling her body slick with sweat. Inside her modest Mini, she tossed her bag on the passenger seat, then eased out of Tredegar Square, a leafy street that housed east London's nouveau riche: small-business owners, a couple of footballers, an actress from a comedy show that was successful in the nineties. Leila liked living here. There was none of the snobbery of better postcodes.

She drove round the corner to Andrew's house, a tidy double-fronted building with a mock Tudor facade. He was waiting outside on the path, pacing back and forth.

She parked behind his Toyota. 'Are you okay?' she asked, stepping out of her car.

'Yes.' He pressed a toe into his lawn and flattened a patch of grass. 'I'm sorry to do this to you.'

'It's fine,' she said briskly. She glanced at Max, who was peaceably asleep in his car seat, his brown hair plastered to his sweaty forehead. She picked up the seat, the handle hot and heavy in her palm. Andrew took it from her, the weight shifting easily on his muscular arm. He ducked into the back of her car and clipped in the seat with some difficulty. He leaned in and kissed his son's hair, then brushed his fingers against a soft cheek. 'It's really hot today.'

'I know,' said Leila. 'He'll be okay.'

Andrew stepped back with a grimace.

'He'll be fine, Andrew. Now go to work.'

'Leila—' he started.

'I know. You're sorry.' She tapped him on the arm. 'Go to work.'

'Thank you,' he said.

She nodded bluntly, then got in her car and moved off, sensing no urgency in Andrew's movements as he watched her go. She headed south towards her dockside office in Canary Wharf and switched on the air-con. As she sped down Burdett Road, her in-car phone began to ring. She answered it with a quick flick, careful to watch the road, though she had driven the route a thousand times.

'Leila?' It was Suki, her assistant at Syed&Gardner. 'We have a problem.'

'What is it?'

'It's Robert. He has to leave for the Mercers meeting, but he's misplaced the blueprints.'

'What do you mean he's misplaced them?' Leila asked sharply. 'Did he take them home?'

'No. He swears they were on his desk, but he can't find them.'

'Then they must be in the office somewhere.'

'We've looked everywhere,' said Suki.

Leila glanced at the clock on her dashboard. It was 8.08 a.m. and if Robert didn't leave immediately, there was a good chance he'd be late.

'Okay, well, I have proof versions in my office. They're not perfect but they'll have to do.'

Suki's voice held a note of panic. 'But your office is locked and no one can find the spare key.'

'Have you asked maintenance?' Leila asked calmly.

'We're waiting for them to send someone, but if they don't get here soon, we'll run out of time.'

'Could you run across the road to the printers?'

'They open at nine.'

Leila cursed. She rechecked the time and did a mental calculation. 'Okay, I'll be there in ten minutes, which gives Robert half an hour to get there. Make sure he has a car waiting and that he's ready to leave asap.'

'Okay. Thank you.' Suki was audibly relieved. 'I'll tell him you're coming.'

Leila hovered on the cusp of the speed limit as she raced towards the office, feeling flushed and stressed in the heat. Ten minutes later, she turned into the private car park. She plucked her heels from their plastic wrapping and slipped them on quickly, then grabbed her keys and hurried upstairs.

Robert spotted her and dashed out from his office. 'Leila—' he started.

She held up a finger. 'Not now, Robert. You need to get going.' She unlocked her office and rifled through a pile of prints, pulling out a set of three. She handed them to Robert along with her iPad. 'I know they asked for hard copies, but at least show them the latest version. I want them to know that we got rid of the portico.'

'I could have *sworn* they were on my desk.'

'It's fine,' she said, ushering him to the door. 'Go, go.' She watched him pause by the lift. 'Oh, and good luck!'

He turned and tossed her the Gardner grin – part Frank Sinatra, part elder statesman.

'Go!' she said as the doors pinged open. Back inside her office, she collapsed onto her leather sofa, jittery with adrenaline. *It'll be okay*, she told herself. All her efforts and sacrifices, the back-and-forth and meticulous planning would not be for nothing. She pressed her palms into the cool black leather as if that might steady her: a keel on a rolling boat. She rested there for a moment and listened to the ticking of her giant wall clock, calmed by its faithful pace. After a minute, she rose again, pulling on her poise.

There was a knock on the door. 'Coffee?' Suki raised a porcelain mug with the words 'Syed&Gardner' printed on the side.

'You're a star.' She accepted it gratefully and placed it on her desk. She switched her fan to full blast to stave off the smothering heat, then settled in for a busy day.

Chapter Two

Leila pinched the skin between her brows, hoping to ease her headache. It had throbbed for hours, tense and turgid behind her eyelids. She checked her watch – 11.25 a.m. – knowing she wouldn't have time for lunch. She gathered up the files on the conference room table, her gaze catching on the opposite building: a hulking brutalist concoction that Leila secretly loved. Sometimes, she would get lost in a building on purpose. She would wander its corridors, staring up at an intricate pediment or grand Diocletian window. Last year, a security guard had barked at her for straying into a room in Zimbabwe House to get a better look at its windows. Leila, usually so staid and serious, had channelled her younger sister. She had batted her lashes and pitched her voice a semitone higher, pleading dippy ignorance. The change in the guard had been instant and he'd led her gently to the exit. Leila couldn't believe it had actually worked. The memory made her smile despite herself as she picked up the last of her files.

She headed back to her office and found a sandwich, cereal bar and fruit smoothie neatly arranged by her keyboard.

'I don't deserve you,' she called to Suki through the open door.

Suki beamed and raised her hand in a self-conscious wave.

Leila unwrapped the sandwich, slowly, so not to stray from the perforations. Just as she bit into the soft white bread, her mobile began to ring. She swallowed quickly and answered.

Andrew's voice was worried. 'Leila. I got a message from the nursery. They said Max wasn't dropped off this morning.'

It took her a moment to compute the words – then they hit with a shrill and dreadful clarity. There was a clamping in her skull; an alarming pressure that made her blood pound.

'Leila?' Andrew's voice cracked as if he could foresee her lethal deed. 'Where's Max?'

Leila didn't answer. Instead, she left her office in a trance-like state, Andrew's tinny voice now clutched in her palm, growing increasingly panicked. She walked to the lift, but did not cry out or scream – quieted by a pulsing shock and the stunning effect of panic. She pressed the button for level zero, the blood in her ears now roaring. She walked across the foyer, heels clicking on the polished floor. It was only when she saw her car roasting in the silent square that she finally made a sound: a low whine of terror, for she could see the corner of a pale blue blanket reaching up the backseat as if it were asking for alms.

She instinctively backed away, commanded by an unknown impulse – self-preservation, denial, survival – before logic clicked back in. She forced herself closer and unlocked the car, her voice an unfamiliar whimper. Then, on seeing Max's limp body, finally she screamed. It was a wild, banshee wail – as loud a sound as she could make for it wasn't just a howl of horror but also a howl for help because she could not do this alone. She could not deal with the horror of what lay before her.

A security guard rushed to her aid and on seeing Max in the backseat, pulled her out of the way. He instructed a colleague to call an ambulance and began to check Max for vital signs.

Leila watched through a haze – as if the scene were filtered through gauze – and yet the details were startlingly clear. The lock of hair glued to Max's forehead, darkened by a pool of sweat; the deep texture of the paramedic's voice; the obscene glint of her hubcap as if there were something to celebrate.

She was mute with shock, so when the paramedics asked if she was related to Max, all she could do was nod. They bundled her into the ambulance and she sat there in a tense huddle, her feet raised on tiptoe to keep her thighs off the cold steel bench, a harsh contrast to the heat outside. She watched Max's tiny body as the paramedic infused him with cold liquid. He swayed to the rhythm of the vehicle, reacting to every rut and pothole. She reached forward to still him, but the paramedic waved her off.

At the hospital, he was rushed away, the staff ignoring her only question – *is he breathing?* – for they surely knew he was not.

'Leila?'

She turned to find Andrew at the end of the corridor. He strode to her and she dissolved into his arms, sagging so that he held her up. She grabbed his shirt, clammy in the palm of her hand. She wanted to scream at him, to blame him, to make it all his fault. If he hadn't asked this of her, she wouldn't have had Max in her car. She wouldn't have slipped straight into her turnoff with Max silent behind her. She wouldn't have left him to roast for three full hours.

Andrew held her wrist and tightened his grip until she released the fabric. He didn't shake her off, however; only trembled as she sobbed. 'Ssh,' he soothed her. 'Ssh.' But in his hand was a fistful of her hair, gripped so tight, she could feel the tension carry up the length of his bicep. She wished that he would hit her. She wished that he would pull back his arm and slap her: stun her or blind her to dull at least one of her senses because it was all too much, all too overwhelming. He held her and they watched the shift of figures in the room, working to save Max's life. It wasn't the heft and rush of action that left Leila shellshocked, but its sudden ceasing; the quieting inside the room because that's when she knew there was nothing to save.

A doctor emerged and corralled them to a corner. 'I'm sorry,' he said, his soft voice morphing into a blare. They had tried to resuscitate him for an hour, he said – an illogical thing to claim, for Leila could swear it was only an instant. They had infused him with cold fluids, packed him with ice and chilled him with fans to bring his temperature down – all to no avail. Max could not be saved.

Andrew stared, unblinking, as if the words had ruptured the circuitry in his brain.

'There'll be chances to say goodbye,' said the doctor gently. 'But you can see him now if you'd like to. If you wait just a moment, a nurse will take you through.' He retreated soundlessly, leaving them with their grief.

Andrew turned and pressed his forehead against the wall. For a moment, he didn't move. Leila watched the insistent dip of his throat as he tried not to cry. He bared his teeth, trying to force his pain into more manageable rage. But then his resolve gave way and he collapsed against the wall. His body shook, but his sobs remained soundless, teetering on the edge of a great gulf of grief. Finally, he made a sound: a dreadful drawing of breath that made Leila flinch. She reached out to comfort him, but he jerked away from her touch.

They remained like that – Andrew slumped against the wall, Leila close but separate – until the nurse arrived to take them to Max's room. Inside, there was a ringing in the air, like the silence after a loud sound. Leila approached Max tentatively. She took in the soft, round set of his jaw, the inky lashes against his cheek, the splay of his sun-lightened hair. She wanted to kiss him, to stroke a finger against his skin, to hold him to her chest and weep. She reached out to touch him, but Andrew stopped her.

'No,' he said, his grip tight on her forearm.

In that harsh syllable, Leila heard all the things he would not say. *You left Max. You killed him. You killed my son.* The crushing weight of that truth squeezed the air from her lungs. She closed her eyes, unable to confront his pain, for then she would have to face what else was about to break. She couldn't think what this would do to Yasmin or bear the thought of her anguish. She knelt over, elbows on her knees, to stop herself from retching. Andrew next to her offered no comfort. Instead, he watched his son, both of them as still as a photograph.

*

Yasmin sighed contentedly as she slipped her feet out of her heels. She kneaded the arch of her foot, wishing that she hadn't worn tights today.

'*I* can do that for you,' said Jason, his tone so neutral, it barely seemed suggestive.

For a mad moment, Yasmin considered letting him. She imagined stretching out her slender leg, resting her heel on his knee and letting his strong hands massage her skin. Instead, she rolled her eyes. 'Thank you for your generosity,' she said pointedly.

He broke into a wide grin and she noticed the upward quirk of his mouth. 'You've done really well,' he said. 'This morning went so smoothly.'

Yasmin leaned back, exposing her neck to him. She pressed languorously against one shoulder. 'Thanks. It certainly took a bit of conjuring.'

He looked at her as if she was something to eat and, for a moment, Yasmin let herself revel in the feeling. She liked to pretend that his attention was unwanted. In truth, he helped her remember who she used to be – before marriage, before motherhood, before endless discussions about postcodes and preschools. She felt guilty thinking it and she knew what people thought of women who cheated, but the slow-creep suffocation of domestic life surely wasn't unique.

'Do you want to get a drink tonight?' he asked.

She held his gaze. Jason represented everything that her life with Andrew lacked. How nice it would be to slip out after work and join him for a drink, the perfect way to counter this infernal summer heat. She was on the cusp of accepting, but felt her conscience prick. It was Andrew's day to pick up Max, but she couldn't just leave him to it. Bedtimes had become increasingly fraught and his day job was already stressful. She smiled instinctively as she thought of Max in his fireman pyjamas. How stupid she was to be tempted by Jason.

'Sorry,' she said breezily. 'I can't.' She stood and slipped her feet back into her heels. 'I'm going to grab some lunch before the afternoon rush.' She walked out, holding herself tall, knowing that he was watching her go.

Outside, she checked her phone and frowned when she saw the missed calls from Andrew. She called him back immediately, but it rang through to voicemail. She wondered if Max was sick. He'd been poorly once or twice recently and of course it was always *she* who had to take a day off work. She headed towards Pret and paused outside to try again. This time, Andrew answered.

'Everything okay?' she asked. She stuffed her cardigan into her bag. God knows why she had packed it. She paused. 'Andrew?'

'Yasmin.' His voice was strangely gruff. 'Can you meet me at the Royal London?'

She balked. 'Why? Is it Max?'

There was an audible intake of breath. 'I'll explain when you get here.'

Yasmin felt a jab of panic. 'What's wrong? Is he okay?'

'It's okay. Just come to the hospital and text me when you get here.'

'But—'

'I've got to go. Sorry,' he said and hung up.

Yasmin told herself to stay calm, for mothers did this to themselves all the time: talked themselves into panic, a knock on the head recast as concussion, a scratch becoming septic, rushing to A&E against their better judgement.

Andrew was logical and reliable, so if he said that all was fine, then surely it was true. Yasmin texted her boss a rushed apology and headed to the station. She gripped the phone all the way to the hospital, tethered by its bulk in her palm.

*

The hum of the fluorescent lights and distant scuff of rubber-soled shoes made Leila briefly wonder if they were in a psych ward. It had the same hermetic air, the same sterile decor, but the sign above the door clearly read A&E. Leila gripped her skirt in her clammy palms as if it might serve as an anchor. Her every vein felt engorged with guilt, pulsing and pulsing unforgivingly. A wild corner of her mind replayed the scenes again and again in a grisly reel: Max slumped in her car, her horrific banshee scream, the searing cut of sirens. This day, these indelible hours, had raised a tar-black feeling somewhere deep inside her; a feeling she may never escape.

As she sat there next to Andrew, she felt an urgent, childlike need for Will. She hadn't yet called to tell him. It was the logical thing to do, but she couldn't bear the thought of breaking the news. Will adored Max more than anything. With no child of his own, he poured his affections on Max, buying generous gifts like that little tweed suit from Liberty or the gigantic Tigger for his first birthday, which still stood by Max's bed.

Leila loved her husband fiercely in those moments of sincerity. He was usually so busy crafting his columnist image – the raffish provocateur, perpetually cool and unmoved – but when he was with Max, his yearning broke through. It was in the mournful way he would look at Leila as if he were saying sorry, or how he'd press his face to her shoulder at night as if that might stop him from crying. No, Will wasn't the person to call. Andrew was by her side and that was enough for now.

She turned to him on the long steel bench and roused him from his daze – one gentle hand on his knee. 'Please say something,' she ventured.

He didn't meet her gaze. 'What is there to say?'

Leila felt a churning anguish. Andrew was sitting there as calmly as if she had dropped his phone and cracked the delicate glass. She wanted to ask what he was feeling, but what words could possibly carry the volume of her question? *Are you okay?* How futile and insipid. Andrew tipped back his head and pressed it to the wall, splaying fine strands of blond hair against the bright white plaster. Leila heard a soft patter of footsteps hurrying down the hall and snapped to her feet when she saw who it was.

Yasmin paused just inside the double doors. She saw their faces and looked from one to another. 'No.' Her voice was breathless and her face did a strange thing: crumpled but then smoothed as if refusing to yield. 'Where's Max?' she asked, trying for an officious tone but cracking halfway through.

Andrew closed his eyes for a moment as if gathering strength for what came next. His breath trembled when he exhaled. He walked to her and pulled her into his arms, pressing his chin against her head as if to force her into place. She struggled but he held her tight. 'Max died this morning,' he said, barely audible.

There was silence: a contraction before a solar blast. Then, there was an animal sound so ferocious it made Leila step back. It seemed to ring on for minutes: a prolonged scream of anger and pain. Yasmin pulled away from Andrew and when he attempted to hold her, she pushed him away with such force, he stumbled against the wall. She bent over at the waist, a rag doll losing support. She clamped her palms against her ears and cried out in rage.

Leila watched with horror. Could she ever know a mother's pain? Her own torment pulsed blackly, but this animal show of grief spoke of something unknowable – a deeper plane of hurt. She fought the urge to go to her for she knew that Yasmin would be horrified to learn what had happened. Andrew had asked her not to speak. He would handle this part, he'd said. He approached Yasmin gently, but she pulled away from him, not yet ready to be comforted.

She turned to the wall and gripped fistfuls of her hair. 'No,' she screamed – a single, extended note of despair.

Andrew looked to Leila and there was a wildness in his eyes, as if they were on a precipice and he was about to lose his footing. Leila had asked if they needed a sedative on standby, but Andrew had declined. He needed Yasmin to believe that she had the strength to survive this; that they trusted her to do so.

Yasmin cried for a long time, curled in a ball on the cold steel bench, not letting Andrew or Leila approach her. Finally, after what felt like hours, she looked up at them. 'How?' she asked – a low, broken sound.

'It was me,' said Leila, her courage wavering; a creature caught between fight or flee.

Yasmin blinked. 'You? What do you mean?'

'Let me,' said Andrew. He had asked her not to be there, but Leila had insisted. Leaving would only make it worse and render their subsequent meeting far more explosive. Andrew sat next to Yasmin and laid a tentative hand on her knee. 'It was my fault,' he started. 'This morning, I got called into work. It would have taken me too long to get Max to nursery, so I asked Leila to do it instead.'

Confusion moved across her face. 'Was there an accident?'

He nodded. 'Of sorts.'

Leila forced herself to be quiet. She had promised Andrew to let him tell Yasmin in that gentle, measured way of his. It would be easier for her, he'd said.

He continued. 'I clipped Max into the back of Leila's Mini. He was fast asleep and didn't make a sound.' He paused. 'Leila drives that route every day. If it was a different route, then she would have remembered, but she drives it every day.'

The colour drained from Yasmin's face. 'What happened?'

'Max was asleep. He didn't make a sound and Leila . . .' Andrew reached out and gripped her hand. 'Leila forgot he was there.'

'Forgot?' she asked in a whisper.

'I'm sorry,' Leila cut in, unable to bear the silence. 'He was so quiet. I couldn't see him in the mirror. I . . . I forgot he was there.'

Yasmin stared at her. 'You forgot?' Her lips moved silently, unable to find more words. 'But you don't forget anything.'

Leila flushed with anguish.

'You . . . you don't forget anything.' Her tone took on a note of hysteria. 'You set alarms for *everything*.'

'I forgot him, Yasmin. I did.'

'No.' She panted as if struggling for breath.

Andrew tugged her hand as if to bring her back to him.

Her gaze darted from one to the other. 'What happened?'

Andrew dashed away his tears with the heel of a palm. 'The heat,' he said in a bark of a sound.

Yasmin's face was an open wound. 'My baby. He burned?'

'No,' said Andrew sharply. 'No, honey, no. He didn't burn. He didn't feel anything. He just fell asleep and he . . . didn't wake up.'

Yasmin began to wail. Her voice was a broken thing – cracked apart by pain.

Leila felt her own heart break, a slipping apart of something solid, a vertiginous freefalling. She stepped closer to Yasmin, but her sister jerked away.

'No. I can't.'

Leila stood there, immobile.

Yasmin shook her head vigorously. 'I can't look at you. I can't be near you.'

Leila swallowed her plea, for it was selfish to attempt to unburden her guilt.

'Please just go.' There was no venom in Yasmin's voice, only desperation. 'Leila, just go.'

She hovered in a state of limbo, then looked to Andrew for guidance. He nodded at her gently. Then, laden with the weight of crushing regret, she headed back up the plastic corridor, her shoes making small sticky sounds as she walked.

*

Leila pressed the can of Coke to her head and tried to cool the heat. It was 1 p.m. and the air in the ward was stifling even

27

with the fans on full blast. A loose leaf of paper floated to the floor from reception and she watched it inertly, unable to bring herself to retrieve it. The receptionist, a portly woman with a double chin, walked around the desk and picked it up, groaning with effort as she bent.

To her left, a set of double doors swung open and Leila strained to see the other side. Where was Yasmin? Was she with Max's body? Was she alone or with Andrew? Was he taking care of her? Did he need her help?

Leila pressed her hands to her face. Her heart hadn't stopped racing since Andrew's call this morning and as the adrenaline ebbed, she felt a profound exhaustion. The gravity of what she'd done was almost too great to bear. She thought of Max in the ambulance, swaying with the ruts in the road, lying mute and lifeless. Max was dead and it was Leila's fault. The knowledge raised something livid inside her and she realised it was bile. She retched, then quickly choked it down, tasting the yellow tang of acid. She folded forward and pressed her head against her knees as the room torqued around her, inducing her to vomit. She took a soggy gasp for breath as her body fought to betray her. Panicked, she hurried to the nearest bathroom and bent over the bowl. She retched again, but nothing came. With two hands pressed against the cistern, she swallowed and swallowed, wincing at the chemical aftertaste, until her nausea calmed. She stumbled to the sink and rinsed her mouth with water, now lukewarm in the heat. She waited until her hands stopped shaking, then dabbed at her skin with tissue. She took a bracing breath and giddily left the safety of the bathroom.

'Ms Syed?'

She turned to find a man waiting in the corridor. He was in his mid-forties, broad shouldered and with a roughness in his face that hinted at years of playing rugby or boxing.

'Yes?' she said uncertainly.

'I'm Detective Sergeant Christopher Shepherd from the London Metropolitan Police.' He showed her his badge and ID card, fixed to a cheap black wallet.

Leila stared at them blankly.

'I'm the officer in charge of Max's case.'

Leila felt a singe of anxiety. How should one conduct oneself in a moment like this? Should she rely on social norms? *Hello, nice to meet you, thank you for coming.* Should she act compliant? Or was it better to be defensive? Should she say the things she was actually thinking? *I'm guilty. I did it. Help me.*

'Can I have a moment of your time?' he asked.

Leila nodded. 'Of course, officer.' She could hear the tremor in her voice and knew that he noticed too.

'Call me Shep,' he said.

'Shep,' she repeated, the single syllable too glib on her tongue.

'I believe you're the last person to have seen Max alive?'

Her breath fluttered in her chest. 'Yes.'

'Do you mind coming to the station to answer a few questions?'

Leila faltered. 'Can't we do it here?' she asked.

'We would prefer to go to the station,' he said – kindly but not too kindly.

She looked at the double doors over Shep's left shoulder. 'Can I tell my family where I'm going?'

'We've taken care of that,' he said briskly.

Leila noticed another officer waiting at the threshold.

'We just want to have a chat,' he added.

Leila agreed gingerly and followed him out to an unmarked blue saloon. He opened the back door and she slid in, gracefully tucking her legs inside. As they drove, she felt a strange, amniotic calm, as if Shep had turned down the volume on life. The wend of passing traffic seemed unnaturally quiet and slow, and the blinks of sunlight between the tall buildings made her squint, un-squint, re-squint. Was this how it felt to survive a war? To come home to a strange land where everything was out of kilter?

As she sat there inertly, a vague question came to her. Should she be falling apart? Did she need to more clearly signal her horror? She caught Shep's eye in the mirror and immediately looked away, panicked by what she saw there: clear, explicit suspicion.

They arrived at Bethnal Green Police Station, a severe brown brick building adorned with two listless flags. He escorted her inside and though he held the door open, there was no gallantry in the action, only an abrupt efficiency. They marched along an austere corridor into a small interview room. It was stuffy and held a fruity smell: berries on the cusp of turning. Leila took a seat and pressed her palms against her skirt, wishing that she would stop sweating.

Shep ran through a list of formalities, but his words were strangely distant as if spoken through a tube. He leaned on the table, his sleeves rolled up to the elbow. 'Ms Syed, can you explain your relationship to Max Hansson?'

'I'm his aunt,' said Leila. 'He's my sister's son.'

He nodded in a patrician manner, hoping perhaps to put

her at ease. 'Can you tell me in as much detail as possible what happened this morning?'

Leila didn't answer. How could she grab the fragments of this day and arrange them in a logical sequence; a neat narrative to present to this unknown authority?

'Ms Syed?' he prompted.

Leila recounted her morning routine, starting with the glass in the sink, juicy bits floating in the cloudy water, for ease of washing later. She told him about the phone call: Andrew asking for help. 'He's a network engineer,' she said. 'So he's sometimes called into work in a crisis. Usually, it's okay because Yasmin is there in the mornings but she had to go in early for a conference. I agreed to help and drove round the corner to their house.'

Shep frowned. 'You run your own architecture firm, is that right?'

'Yes.'

He glanced over a piece of paper and raised an eyebrow. 'You restored the Whitechapel Synagogue. Impressive.'

She nodded graciously. 'Thank you.'

'It must be hard work.'

'It is.'

'Long hours?'

'Sometimes.'

'Arguably busier than a network engineer.'

'Sometimes.'

'How did you feel about being asked to collect Max when you yourself have just as busy a job as the father?'

Leila watched him, a creeping unease rising in her bones. 'It was fine. I was glad to help.'

'You were?'

31

'Yes.'

He made a sound as if to say *you're a better person than I am.* 'How often have you been asked to help them?'

Leila loosened her grip on the edge of her seat. 'Once a week or so.'

'That's a lot.'

'I'm happy to do it.'

He angled his head. 'How many times have you driven Max to school?'

'I haven't.'

He scratched his chin with a pen. 'Okay, what happened after you left with Max?'

Leila told him about her journey to work, the phone call she received from Suki, and how Max's rear-facing seat meant she didn't see him at all.

'How long did the call last?' asked Shep.

'Maybe five minutes.'

'And what did you talk about?'

She told him about the misplaced blueprints.

'Were you in a hurry?' he asked.

'Yes. Well, no. Not in a huge hurry. I knew I was only a few minutes from the office.'

'But not if you stopped at the nursery.'

Leila blinked. 'I didn't think about that. I . . . I forgot that Max was there.'

Shep leaned forward. 'I'm sorry, can you just repeat that? Your brother-in-law entrusts you with his child and you simply *forget* that he's in the car?'

'I couldn't see him,' said Leila. 'He was asleep. I was distracted. It was an accident.'

32

Shep did not respond; watched her coolly instead.

'You can't think I *meant* to do it.'

'What I think, Ms Syed, is that you were in a rush. You knew that Max was in your car, but you thought you would nip to your office and deal with the emergency – but you forgot that you had left him.'

Leila's face crowded with horror. 'That's not what happened. I would *never* leave Max in the car.'

'But you did,' he said coldly.

Leila faltered. 'Not intentionally. I've never left him alone on purpose. Not anywhere. Not even for a second.'

'The nursery. It's not actually on your way, is it, Ms Syed? It's actually five minutes further.'

She shook her head. 'It's practically on the way.'

'But not really.'

'I—'

'So isn't it true, that if there was an emergency, it would be easier to park up, run in, deal with the emergency and come back out?'

'That's not what happened.'

'Ms Syed, did you leave Max in the car intentionally?'

Sweat beaded on the nape of her neck. 'No.'

He studied her intently. 'Do you and your sister have a good relationship?'

Leila was disoriented by the change in subject. 'Yes.'

'I believe you raised her from the age of eleven to eighteen. Can you explain how this came to be?'

'What's that got to do with anything?' she asked defensively. Why should she have to share their ordeal with this hostile stranger?

'We're just trying to build some context.'

Leila felt a clenching distress as she thought back to that period. People spoke of happy childhoods and hers *was* happy in a way, but then their father died from a massive coronary attack. Their mother, already fragile by nature, suffered a complete breakdown. When Leila awoke in the mornings, she would find her mother sitting in the kitchen, staring at a wall. Leila had tried to get help, dragging her to the GP and then the hospital and then back to the GP, then being told that there was no funding. There was no support from the community or the so-called uncles and aunties. They had silly, reductive words for her mother – batty, quirky, cuckoo, doolally – but no one was moved to help.

One day, Leila came home and her mother was in the bath, in stone-cold water, eyes still open, hair floating like seaweed on the surface. Leila had pressed a fist to her mouth to stop herself from screaming. She had rushed Yasmin to their bedroom and commanded her to stay there. She remembered the police officers, kindly but official. The girls weren't allowed to stay in their home – everything they knew severed in a single swoop. She had felt so much rage at her mother. She barely did anything anyway. All she had to do was stick around.

Leila remembered their foster parents. A retired seamstress and her taciturn husband. They had a three-storey home in Gants Hill filled to the brim with trinkets and chintz: old chessboards, tuning forks and tweezers, an extensive set of glass beakers, a plastic model of a brain segmented into removable pieces – the frontal, temporal, parietal and occipital lobes, the cerebellum and brain stem. There was a mustiness in the house as if it had never been aired and when the sun hit it in a certain way, the dust motes were innumerable. Leila and Yasmin were never mistreated but the place lacked the warmth of a real home.

As soon as she turned eighteen, Leila applied for legal guardianship of Yasmin and they were able to rent a home of their own: a tiny one-bed flat just off Gants Hill roundabout. The genteel name of their road – Frinton Mews – was at direct odds with what it was: an ugly corner of the borough filled with discarded cigarette butts, plastic bags that swayed malevolently, the hum of a nearby generator and an awful industrial view.

How much of this could she tell the detective? How much of the stress, the sick feeling of hitting her overdraft limit, the relentless pressure and the grind of poverty would he understand as he watched her now, dressed in her expensive shirt, reinvented as successful?

'My parents died,' she said simply. 'I didn't want my sister to remain in care, so I gained legal guardianship.'

'So you lost out on some of your best years, is that right?'

'You could say that.'

'Was it galling that after raising your sister, you had to raise your sister's son?'

Leila glared at him. 'Not one bit. I loved that child more than anything and my sister will tell you the same.'

Shep watched her for a moment. 'Is that so?'

'That's so,' she replied tartly. In that instant, her mobile pinged with a message and she instinctively read the preview. *Have you called a lawyer?* read the text from Andrew. The words dropped a weight in her stomach, breaking the illusion that this interview was merely informational.

Calling a lawyer meant that Leila had something to answer for.

'Something important?' said Shep.

Leila met his gaze. After a moment, she spoke. 'I'd like to speak to a lawyer, please.'

He smiled as if he had won a bet. 'I thought you might,' he said. 'Please don't go anywhere.' He stood and left the room, leaving Leila to stew.

*

Yasmin sat in her cocoon chair and smoothed its lilac cushion, her hand moving against the grain to leave a dark column in the velvet. She had spent far too much on it, but it was so Instagram-ready, she knew she had to have it. It wasn't particularly comfortable – the rattan material too hard and knobbly – but she forced herself to use it to justify the cost. She chose it now because it was the only thing in the room with a back. She wasn't entirely sure that she could sit up on her own; feared that her body might fold to the floor.

Nothing in here knew of Max's death, not the soft yellow bumblebee with the dozy eyes – Humble, they had called him – or the pot-bellied rabbit that lay in the corner, ears still cocked expectantly. Yasmin brought the news to them like a pox, infecting them one by one. Who knew that absence could feel so solid? It wasn't an emptiness but a presence: a hard ball of something tumid.

It felt like a cosmic slap that this night should be so pretty: moonlight streaming through the window, painting the room in a silvery glow. The far wall was dotted with a child's handprints. First, the delicate palm of a newborn, then a red print from his first birthday, smudged by his moving hand, followed by a neater age two and then three. That there would be no others struck her as absurd.

There was a knock on the door and it made her shrink in physical pain. She only wanted to be left alone.

Andrew looked in. 'I brought you some tea,' he said, stepping inside tentatively. He had checked on her throughout the evening, eyes darting nervously, clearly not sure why she wasn't raging. She couldn't allow it all in yet, was busy with the scaffolding that would keep her mind from caving in. If she could just hold strong for a little while longer, then she could face her pain and let it wash away this narcotic state.

Andrew placed the mug next to her. It was black and glassy she noticed – not the shivery Paddington bear from the pair she shared with Max. The small kindness raised a swell of emotion and she dug her nails into her thighs to forcibly bite it back.

'Thank you,' she said, her gaze drifting to the handprints. She picked up the mug, blew on it briefly, then set it back down.

'Do you need anything?' Andrew spoke gently, as if talking to a child.

She looked at him numbly. 'A biscuit?' she said, only to give him something to do to make him think he was helping.

'Of course.' He returned moments later with three lots of three, spread in a spiral on a dinner plate. She took one and dipped it in her tea, watching it break off and sink, making no move to stop it. She looked up at Andrew, who hovered by the door, still afraid to leave her alone. 'I'll be okay,' she said. 'I promise.'

His face puckered for just a second, the pain like a wink of a bulb. 'I love you,' he said.

'I love you too,' she replied, but her voice was mechanical; a stock response to a common statement. *Knock, knock. Who's there? I love you. I love you too.*

Andrew closed the door but then, thinking better of it, reopened it several inches. His heavy tread traced down the stairwell and into the silent living room. Pain, even in a marriage, was sometimes best felt alone. He would do it his way and she would do it her own.

*

Leila traced her fingertips across the carving in the wood and tried to discern the letters. She already knew what they spelled, but was compelled to try regardless to keep herself engaged. J, E, A, N – an unlikely name for a former inmate, more suited to weekend bake sales and sensible M&S shoes. Was *Jean* also stunned to find herself in jail?

When Shep had led her here, Leila told herself that he was merely grandstanding. But as the hours ticked by, she realised that it wasn't a toothless show of aggression. She, like Jean, was truly a suspected criminal.

As she sat there, aghast, every surface in the room took on an air of indictment: the hardness of the narrow bench, the harshness of the walls. The window, which on first glance passed for tasteful sash, morphed into a lattice of bars. Who had decided that people caught in the worst day of their lives deserved no comfort at all?

There was a clanging at the door and Leila instinctively rose to her feet.

'Your brief's here,' said a uniformed officer, gesturing behind him.

She followed him across the corridor into the opposite room. On spotting her solicitor, Leila felt a sudden, overwhelming urge to cry. She forcibly bit it back and extended her hand in greeting, appalled to see it tremble.

'I'm sorry,' she said. 'I didn't know who else to call.'

Clara Pearson shook her hand. The elegant waif of a woman was a criminal solicitor and higher court advocate. She and Leila had met at a conference last year and stayed loosely in touch ever since. 'We have to talk,' said Clara, briskly taking a seat.

Leila felt the churn of nerves, for she recognised her tone: an official imparting unwanted news. *Sorry, but you have no recourse to public funds. Sorry, you're not eligible. Sorry, it's incurable.*

Clara steepled her fingers. 'The CPS have reviewed your case.'

Leila's throat felt razor dry. 'And?'

'They're charging you with manslaughter.'

Leila heard the rush of blood in her ears, blotting out all other sound. 'Manslaughter? They think I *meant* to harm him?'

Clara splayed her fingers on the table. 'They don't think you *meant* to kill him, but they *do* think you're responsible for his death. I know it's a lot to take in so it's helpful to think about it in smaller parts.' She drew an imaginary circle on the table. 'The charge is gross negligence manslaughter, which means the prosecution will try to prove four things.' She drew a stem from the circle. 'One: that you had a duty of care towards

Max and that you breached that duty.' She drew another stem. 'Two: that the breach of duty was so grossly negligent as to be worthy of criminal sanction. Three: that leaving Max in your car led to his death.' She drew a fourth and final stem. 'Four: that it was obvious to you that there was a reasonable chance your actions would lead to Max's death.'

She tapped the first stem. 'I don't think we can deny that you had a duty of care towards Max, but everything else we can fight. And this', she tapped stem two, 'will be key. If the jury believes that you *intentionally* left Max in the car, then the case could be made that your actions were grossly negligent. If, however, they can be convinced that you genuinely forgot him, then was that action criminal? I don't think so.'

Leila's own voice seemed distant when she spoke. 'So it all depends on whether I meant to leave him?'

'That's an important part, yes.'

Leila was quiet for a moment. 'I would never leave him on purpose.'

'I know.' Clara tried for tenderness but there was a clipped, efficient note in her tone that suggested they move on. 'You're going to be officially charged now and released on conditional bail. You will be expected to attend a Magistrates' hearing within twenty-eight days, but don't worry, I will be there with you.'

Leila listened as Clara spoke – *first magistrates, plea and trial preparation hearing* – but couldn't order the words into logical thought. Leila had known – *surely* she had known – that this was on the cards, but that it had happened so swiftly, so confidently, left her reeling in shock. Was this the default setting of the law? To assume the worst of everyone? To decide in a single day to tar an entire life?

'Can I still see my sister?' she asked, interrupting Clara.

The lawyer grimaced. 'I'm afraid not. Officially, it's the Crown bringing the complaint – not your sister – but she's a key witness in the trial and it will be a condition of your bail to stay away from her.'

Leila gaped at Clara. There was not a single possibility of her not talking to Yasmin. How could she commit such a heinous act and not beg for her sister's forgiveness? 'What will happen if I do talk to her?'

'If you're seen, you could be taken into custody.'

'Is that likely?'

Clara angled her head. 'As your counsel, I have to advise that you keep your distance from your sister.'

Leila understood the subtext. She had to be discreet.

'Do you have any other questions?' asked Clara.

Leila searched for something to ask her, if only to delay what was coming. 'No,' she said eventually.

'Very well.' Clara checked her watch. 'I'll let them know you're ready.'

Leila listened to the clang of the door. She exhaled as if she were slipping out of costume and able to breathe again. There were no tears and she struggled to put a name to this feeling. Guilt? Fear? Regret? It was a sensation of freefalling, a plunging to unknown depths, but instead of feeling scared, she somehow felt content in knowing there was no end.

Chapter Three

Leila winced at the smell in her room. It was muggy and medicinal, like unwashed bedding in a hospital. She tugged open a window, but the air outside was hot and still. She looked out across Tredegar Square, blinking at the shards of light that shone through the trees like dropped glass. The quiet beauty of the place was disorienting, starkly at odds with the panic in her chest. She had awoken in this state. There was no brief moment of ignorant bliss; as soon as she woke up, she remembered her crime with alarming clarity: Max's red cheeks, the limpness of his limbs.

Not yet, she told herself. She couldn't fall apart yet. There were things she had to do first. She had to tell Suki that she wouldn't be in the office this week. She had to speak to Will, who would be arriving any minute. And she had to reach out to Yasmin. Only then could she let herself break.

She went downstairs to the kitchen and was surprised to see that it wasn't yet eight. It was hard to believe that not even twenty-four hours had passed since that fateful call from Andrew. It seemed to her that she had lived a thousand lifetimes since coming home last night. She had collapsed into bed in a sobbing heap and dreamt of ghastly things: stop-motion monsters with gigantic jaws, dragons and gorgons and childish things. Her head was filled with it, swapping one horror for another more bearable. She startled when the doorbell rang and heard the clatter of Will's key in the lock. She braced herself against a counter, prickling with anxiety.

'Leila?' he called. 'I got your text.' His footsteps drew closer. 'Are you—' He stopped in the doorway as he caught sight of her. Her wet hair had inked dark patches on her T-shirt and her face was unnaturally pallid. He stepped inside, slow and cautious, as if any sudden movement might stir a nearby predator. 'What's happened?' His gaze dropped to Leila's stomach, a compulsion that clearly resurfaced from the handful of weeks that she had been pregnant. 'Are you okay?' He faltered briefly as his body remembered that, this time, there was no baby to check on.

'Something happened to Max.'

There was a lull in his eyes, a pre-emptive guess at her news. 'What is it?'

'An accident.'

'Is he okay?'

'No.' Leila's voice broke. 'He's not okay.'

Will crossed the kitchen in two long strides and grabbed her shoulders. 'Leila, what's happened?'

'Max is dead.'

Will stared at her, mute and uncomprehending. 'Max is dead,' he echoed, the words flat and tinny. 'Max . . . is dead?' His gaze darted around the room, searching for a tool that could handle the news. 'That's absurd,' he said, picking denial first.

'It's my fault.' Leila spoke in a breathless rush, desperate to confess. She told him about the heart-stopping call from Andrew, her panicked race to the car and the horror of the furnace inside, but she only got halfway before Will turned his back on her. He pressed a fist to his mouth, but made no sound, the slight displacement of air the only sign that he was crying.

Leila watched him helplessly. She had known that Will would take it badly, but not how this would manifest: the heartbreak of their first miscarriage, the wall-punching rage of their second, the wretched inertia of their third, or the stoic acceptance of their fourth and final. It broke her to see him like this: silent and rigid like a frightened beetle.

'How could this happen?' he asked, still facing the wall. 'To *us*? To *our* family?'

Leila wrapped her arms around him and pressed herself to the small of his back, but he squirmed away aggressively. He turned to face her again.

'Why didn't you call me?' he asked, his grief turning into something sour.

'I couldn't face it, Will. I had to get through the day.'

'But none of you thought to call me? Not you or Andrew or Yasmin?' His voice was harsh with disbelief. 'You know what he meant to me.'

'I know and I'm sorry,' she said in a plea. 'But I was in shock. I wasn't thinking logically.'

'You still should have called me, Leila.'

'Please, Will. Don't make this about you.'

He gaped at her in disbelief. 'That's a fucking low blow, Leila.'

She took a moment to compose herself. Will was the only

person in the world who could stir her temper and she was wary of saying something that she would later regret. What she really wanted to tell him was that as much as he loved Max, *his* grief was secondary.

'I'm not trying to make this about me.' Will cleared the choke in his throat. 'But Leila, he's the only child I've ever loved.'

It took her a moment to speak. 'I would have called you, Will, but there's more.' Haltingly, she recounted the rest of yesterday: her arrest, the long and exhausting interview, the official charge and subsequent bail. 'The trial starts in December,' she finished.

Will didn't speak for a minute, but she saw the way his body tensed, literally toughening up, setting aside his own pain to deal with this greater threat. 'I'll stay with you today,' he said. 'You shouldn't be alone.'

'Thank you,' she whispered, surprised by the force of her own relief. Leila had done the very worst thing in the world and still Will was there, bearing up despite his grief in order to share hers. He reached for her and in receiving this act of loyalty, she wished more than ever before that they could have built a family.

*

Yasmin cut around the green velvet boots and clipped them from her copy of *Vogue*. The last grain of paper still clung to the page and she tugged to gently detach it, leaving a speck of white on one heel. She placed the cut-out on the floor, next to dozens of others fanned around her like a peacock's plume. A single gust from the open door would send them all scattering, but Yasmin didn't care. The narrow utility room was *her* space and she felt safe in its cocoon. There was a washing machine at one end with an ironing board wedged beside it, but she had done her best with the rest of it. The wall above her desk was layered with her favourite collage: an ironic ode to motherhood. It was a garish barrage of pink booties and cardigans, frilly ribbons and pastel bibs. In one corner stood a snide-looking woman with a megaphone. A famous quote spilled out of it: 'There is no more sombre enemy of good art than the pram in the hall.' Yasmin had felt so smug pasting that onto the wall, her baby stationed outside the door, burbling away happily. *Look at me*, she'd thought. *Doing it all.*

She studied the collage now, hoping it would somehow stir her: with tears, anger, despair – anything but this bilious shock. It throbbed inside the walls of her gut, making her weak and nauseous. She imagined ripping the pictures from the wall in a fit of hysteria, but even the thought was exhausting.

There was movement behind her and Yasmin glanced up to find Andrew in the doorway. His face was shadowed with stubble and his eyes had a look so mournful that she had to turn away.

'Yasmin,' he said softly. He rubbed small circles at his temple as if he were soothing an ache. He waited and when she didn't speak, he came in and crouched beside her. 'Your sister texted. She tried to call you but couldn't get through.' He took the scissors from her hand and waited for her to look at him. 'They've charged her with manslaughter.'

Yasmin blanched with shock. 'They what?'

He laid the scissors down. 'They say she left Max on purpose.'

Yasmin stared at him. 'But that's crazy.'

'I know, but that's what they think.'

She was still for a moment. Then, gritting her teeth, she shoved away her materials in a single, violent sweep. 'How dare they do this?'

Andrew looked on with surprise.

She cried out in frustration for she couldn't explain the sense of injustice. She was mourning her child and she needed to rage against her sister. She *needed* to blame Leila, but fashioning her as a criminal forced Yasmin onto her side; forced her into solidarity when she wasn't *close* to ready. First, she needed to blame her before she could forgive her.

Andrew reached for her, but she pushed him away, making him fall on his seat.

'I need to hate her, Andrew. I can't just forgive her.'

'I know,' he soothed. 'That's okay.'

Yasmin coiled with anger. She opened her mouth, but only heard a strange whistling sound. 'I hate her, Andrew. I *fucking* hate her.'

'That's okay. You're allowed to.'

'She *never* forgets.' Yasmin's tone was bitter and accusing. 'She never forgets *anything*. How could she forget Max?' She crunched a glossy page in her fist.

Andrew pulled her to him more firmly and held the nape of her neck. 'I don't know, sweetheart.' He shook his head, his chin sweeping the top of her hair. 'I just . . . I don't know.'

She pushed out of his grip. 'Do they really think she left Max on purpose?'

Andrew looked at her solemnly. 'She was in a rush that morning. She got a call from the office. Maybe she meant to pop in and out.'

Yasmin digested this. She recalled an image of Leila with her phone tucked beneath her chin, ironing her clothes for an interview while pasta bubbled on the cooker in their studio. Leila was always doing three things at once and when she wasn't, she felt that time was wasting. 'Could she really do such a thing?' She searched his face for an answer.

'I don't think she did, but . . .' Andrew shifted uncomfortably. 'Haven't you ever been tempted to leave Max in the car when nipping into the petrol station?'

Yasmin balked. 'No,' she said vehemently. 'Have *you*?'

He bobbed his head guiltily. 'Yes.'

'And *have* you?'

'No, but I've come close,' he admitted.

Yasmin exhaled. '"Close" isn't the same as doing it.'

He was quiet for a moment. 'I don't think Leila left him on purpose.'

She looked at him forlornly. 'Where is she now?'

'I don't know.'

'In jail?'

'No, they charged her last night and let her go.'

Yasmin felt a clench of anxiety. Leila had been charged. With manslaughter. She pictured her sister in a prison cell, stripped of all her dignity. The thought made her feel giddy. How could she reconcile these two feelings: a beating pity with the strobe of fury? 'Is this really happening?' Her fingers grasped Andrew's sleeve, catching some of his skin. 'How could it be happening to *us*?'

Andrew started to speak, but the words broke off in his

throat. He pulled her into his arms again and they sat in a tangled heap, packed tight with horror and grief.

*

DS Chris Shepherd felt the moisture seep into his shirt. He spread out his arms, feeling the queasy unsticking of his skin. It was hot. Hotter than he remembered in his sixteen years on the force. The stifling heat in the station felt like breathing in jet fumes. He crouched over his notebook as if that might block out the sounds around him: the puttering of the coffee pot, the creaking effort of the printer, the clacking of a dozen keyboards. Shep worked best in silence, but there was no budget for private offices. This corner of the Criminal Investigation Department was all open plan: spindly grey desks crammed cheek by jowl, slipshod fittings and dying pot plants. Shep preferred to work at home, huddled in his cosy study, where, if he chose to, he could take out the wall clock's battery if the ticking got too loud. Time mattered less when you lived by yourself.

He stared at his scrawl on the notepad, tracing a thumb down the spiral spine. He preferred working with the space of an A4 pad. The other detectives laughed when he stuffed it into his 'man bag', and told him to switch to a tablet and stop being a Luddite.

He reviewed the rough timeline he'd sketched on the page. At 7.58 a.m. yesterday, Andrew Hansson placed a call to Leila Syed. The call lasted two minutes. At 8 a.m., Leila stopped at Andrew's home, at which point he strapped Max into the backseat. Leila said that Max was asleep.

Shep added a question next to this. *Already dead?* Leila didn't check that Max was breathing. She had no reason to believe he wasn't. Was there a chance that the father was responsible? That he offloaded his son to mask a mistake? Shep considered this for a moment, then drew a small note by the theory: *x* to mean unlikely.

He continued tracing the timeline. It was a fifteen-minute drive to Leila's office and twenty to the nursery. She received a call at precisely 8.08 a.m. in which she learnt that the blueprints were missing, and her phone showed that she arrived at the office ten minutes later. He made another note, *Speeding?*, for that would surely demonstrate that Leila was in a rush; more likely to decide to leave Max in the car while she ran in to fight the fire.

The father, whom Shep had yet to talk to properly, next called Leila at 11.27 a.m. to ask about Max's whereabouts. The ambulance was called seven minutes later. Max was pronounced dead at the hospital at 12.25 p.m. There, in the neat black lines of his A4 pad were the makings of a tragedy. But what really happened? And who was to blame? He turned a page and wrote the name *Leila Syed* in his angular scrawl. Beneath it, he listed his first impressions of her. *Calm, logical, practical*, he wrote. Then, next to it, *cold, distant, inscrutable*. Beneath it, he listed three options.

1. *She left him by accident.*
2. *She left him intentionally but meant to return quickly.*
3. *She left him intentionally and meant to harm him.*

Leila claimed the first. The CPS claimed the second. Was there a chance it was actually the third? If, in truth, she had *meant* to harm him, then it was up to Shep to find out. Next to the third option, he wrote a one-word question: *Motivation?* On the surface, it seemed absurd that a successful woman like Leila would intentionally kill her nephew, but Shep had been fooled by gloss before and swore to never repeat it.

He wished he'd had longer with Leila before she called her lawyer. Clara Pearson was an experienced advocate who was impossible to ruffle. He had worked with her before and was thwarted by her poise: sleek, practised, impermeable. Perhaps there was something about being a black woman in law that made her wary of showing emotion. Either way, Clara had curbed his progress.

He pictured Leila now: sitting in the witness room, eyes rimmed red but makeup intact, hair perfectly in place. Was there a devil hiding beneath the veneer? And if so, when and why had she planned this? Shep flipped back a page and glanced at the *x* by the father's name. Maybe *he* could offer some answers. Shep checked his watch. The parents hadn't even grieved for twenty-four hours, but he needed to see them. After the briefest hesitation, he grabbed his keys and left.

*

Shep drove up Tredegar Terrace, a picturesque strip of double-fronted houses set back from the road. Each had large bay windows with the occasional Tudor beam – original or mock, he couldn't be sure. He parked outside the Hanssons' house and studied it for a moment.

It had a sweep of decorative gravel and a tall line of hedges that shielded it from its neighbours. The house itself was well kept, with only a few signs of disrepair: the slight chipping of a window frame, the speckling of the brass doorknob, the box plants that had outgrown their shape. Mostly, it was like any other home. He noted that the unsightly recycling bins were kept in neat wooden housing. Was this Andrew Hansson's doing? He didn't strike Shep as the DIY type: all glasses and angles and the traits of an intellectual, the opposite of Shep, whose jug ears and deviated septum gave him the air of a reformed brute even when suited and booted. He approached the house, tapping a toe against a stray piece of gravel to nudge it into place. He rang the bell and stood back, knowing that his six-foot height would otherwise crowd the frame.

Andrew Hansson opened the door, blinking as if the sunlight was painful.

Shep could tell that he couldn't place him. 'Mr Hansson, I'm Detective Sergeant Christopher Shepherd. We spoke briefly at the hospital yesterday?'

Andrew's eyes grew clear – a lens slipping to focus. 'Yes,' he said absently. 'Of course.' He opened the door wider.

Inside, the home was warm and chaotic: paintings nailed up at jaunty angles; a footstall crowded with clothes; a pair of tiny wellington boots stuffed into a corner, one leg skewed against the other as if leaning in for support. The sight made something tug in his chest and he cleared his throat before speaking. 'Mr Hansson, I was hoping to have a few minutes of your time.'

'Please, call me Andrew.' He led Shep into the kitchen and gestured at the dining table. It looked out onto a garden, carpeted with grass that was approaching unruly. Andrew traced his gaze. 'Please excuse the state of things. We only finished the lawn in June and it's already a jungle.'

Shep batted away the apology.

Andrew hovered by a cupboard. 'Would you like some tea?'

'Only if you're having one,' said Shep. The tactic never failed. A witness with a cup of tea was always more responsive and this was his way to force them to have one. After all, no one ever refused. He watched Andrew move about the kitchen and waited until they were both seated. 'I'm very sorry for your loss,' he started. 'I know that this is an incredibly difficult time for you.' Over the years, Shep had tried different permutations of these words, but found that bland and insipid worked just as well as any other.

Andrew nodded briskly, the condolence being filed.

Shep gently pushed his tea to one side. 'I'd like to get a clearer picture of what happened yesterday morning.' He stooped in his chair, feigning a casual manner, but actually watching Andrew closely. 'Can you tell me what happened in your own words?'

'Don't I need to come to the station?' asked Andrew.

Shep noted this with interest. Parents were usually fazed by the prospect of going to the station, yet Andrew Hansson was volunteering. 'At this stage, we're just piecing together a picture. If we need more details, then of course we would appreciate a trip to the station.'

'I see.' Andrew smoothed his shirt self-consciously. 'Okay, well, um, I was called into work with an emergency. I didn't have time to drop Max off and my wife was already at work, so I called Leila, my sister-in-law, and asked her if she could do it. The nursery is practically on the way, so I thought it would be easy.'

'Can we back up a little?' Shep pulled out his notepad and flicked to his timeline. 'You were called into work for an emergency. Can I ask who called you?'

'It's not a physical call. It's an automated alarm that comes to my phone.'

'From who?'

'From our server system. If a server goes down, I receive an automatic text.'

'So it's a text, not an alarm?'

Andrew fiddled with his mug. 'Yes. We call it a page.'

'Can I see it? It might help me understand.'

Andrew hesitated. 'Well, yes, I . . .' He dug into his pocket, flicked through his phone and passed it to Shep. 'Here you go.'

Shep squinted at the screen, more for effect than anything. He wrote down the timestamp of 7.54 a.m. 'What happens if you ignore this?'

'I'd get sacked.' He caught the look on Shep's face. 'I know that sounds glib, but it's true. Every hour our server is down costs our customers around £20,000.' He explained the mechanics of this and though he spoke fluently, there was a practised quality to it.

'What happened after you received the page?'

Andrew shifted forward. 'Well, I felt a little panicked. It was twenty minutes to Max's nursery, then twenty minutes back so that's £13,000 just to drop off my son.'

Shep arched a brow. 'I wouldn't have thought of it like that.'

'In my job, you learn to.' Andrew fixed his gaze on the table, giving the effect of literally hanging his head. 'Sometimes, you forget the important things.'

Shep gave him a moment before pressing him on to Leila's arrival. 'Was Max asleep when you put him in her car?'

'Yes.'

Shep poised his pen above his pad, wanting him to be as precise as possible. 'Is that normal for that time of morning?'

'It depends,' said Andrew. 'There's not much "normal" when it comes to a three-year-old. Every day is different.'

Shep smiled tightly. 'Did Leila look stressed to you?'

'No.'

'Was she annoyed by your last-minute request?'

'No. She seemed happy to do it.'

'How would you describe her behaviour that morning?'

Andrew thought this over. 'She seemed normal. Not stressed or in a hurry. Just normal.'

'Okay, so after Leila left, you rushed off to work. When did you realise that Max wasn't where he was supposed to be?'

Andrew motioned at his phone. 'Just before eleven thirty when I checked my voicemail. I know because I was running a tracer program on the server and it was the first moment I caught my breath.'

Shep made a note. 'What did the voicemail say?'

'It was the receptionist from the nursery – Gina. She said that Max wasn't dropped off that morning. I started to panic and called Leila immediately.'

Shep murmured with surprise. 'You were panicked at that stage? Why? Did you not trust Leila?'

'I defy any parent not to panic when their child isn't where he's meant to be.'

Shep held his gaze, wondering how to ask this next question. 'Can you think of any reason why Leila might want to hurt your son?'

Andrew's eyes rounded into discs. 'No. Leila loved Max.

This was all a . . .' He shook his head, struggling to capture the magnitude. 'This was all a tragic mistake.' He cleared his throat to mask the choke in his voice.

Shep pretended to focus on his notes and continued only when he sensed that Andrew was composed. 'Can we back up just a little? You said you listened to the voicemail just before 11.30 a.m. Weren't you keen to know that he had arrived at nursery okay?'

Andrew looked at him blankly, mouth open a notch. 'I . . . He was with Leila. I didn't think there was a reason to worry.'

'And what about your wife? Did the nursery call her?'

'They usually only call one parent. I'm listed first – Hansson above Syed – so they generally tend to call me.'

'Did your wife contact you at all in the morning to check that Max got to school okay?'

Andrew bristled. 'Why would she? How many fathers check on their children during the working day?'

Shep bobbed his head. 'I take your point,' he said evenly. A brief silence settled between them. Shep glanced at the clock. 'May I speak with your wife?'

Andrew hesitated. 'I'd rather she rest, if that's okay.'

Shep grimaced in a show of sympathy, perfected by years on the force. 'I'm sure she's very fragile at the moment and of course I can come back when it's more convenient.' He paused, allowing Andrew a moment. 'If she *is* able to answer some questions, however, it would really help our investigation. She knows her sister better than anyone else.' Andrew considered this and Shep knew that he would crack.

'I'll check,' he said finally.

Shep watched as he left the room. Andrew Hansson was

clearly protective of his wife. Could it be that *she* – or the two of them – somehow harmed Max and pinned it on the sister? It was far-fetched, but Shep had seen worse in his time. He made a note to check the preliminary pathology report for any red flags: unexplained symptoms or a wonky time of death.

He waited to see if he could hear movement upstairs, then stood and looked around the kitchen. The bookshelf was stuffed with cookbooks. They were fans of Rick Stein, it seemed. A blocked-up fireplace served as a mantelpiece lined with various trinkets: a Chinese tea jug, a sturdy beer tumbler and a brass perpetual calendar next to an array of photos. Here was a young Yasmin looking sweetly over her shoulder, her long dark hair impossibly glossy. Could someone like her kill a child? In reply to his own question, Shep made a scoffing sound.

'Detective?' Yasmin stood in the doorway, dressed in black leggings and a loose grey T-shirt that hung halfway to her knees. Across the front, it read 'Imperial College London'.

Shep smiled warmly. 'Your alma mater?' he asked.

She glanced down at the T-shirt. 'No.' She gestured at Andrew who stood beside her. 'It's his. I, um, I didn't go to university.'

'School of life, eh?' said Shep, immediately cringing inwardly. Yasmin ignored this and took a seat. Shep noticed that she had a certain softness to her: a gentle, hypnotic appeal. He treated her like a fragile thing as he talked her through yesterday morning. Slowly, he charted her movements, from early breakfast to Andrew's call and the horror of the hospital. Then, he broached the subject of Leila. 'I'd like to ask a little more about your relationship with your sister. Is that okay?'

Yasmin nodded, her cheeks flushing pink.

'How often did you leave Max in her care?'

She took a moment to calculate this. 'Once a fortnight. Maybe once a week.'

'As often as that?'

Yasmin bristled. 'I don't think that's very often. Why? Did she say something?'

Shep didn't answer. 'Leila doesn't have children of her own. Did you feel she was equipped to look after your son once a week?'

'We always left instructions.'

'But leaving Max in her care never worried you?'

'No.'

'Did Leila ever indicate that she was having trouble with him?'

'No.' Yasmin was defensive. 'She wanted children of her own and thought this might be good training.'

'She said that?'

'Not in so many words but I figured.'

'So she never said this explicitly?'

'Well, she and her husband have tried to get pregnant, so I know that they want children.' Yasmin hesitated. 'They just haven't managed it yet.'

'Has that caused issues between you?'

Yasmin rubbed an earlobe. 'Not issues, no, but there was some awkwardness.'

'In what way?'

'Well, when I was pregnant, Leila couldn't really look at me or be near me. It was like it hurt her to do it. Afterwards, it was fine but during those months it was weird.'

'And things *are* fine now, are they?'

'Well . . .' Yasmin shifted in her chair. 'Sometimes, there's some friction. I see her looking at us sometimes – me and Andrew and Max – when we're laughing together or pushing him in his swing and there's this *look*.'

Shep waited. 'What sort of look?'

'Like . . . jealousy?' She stopped and corrected herself. 'No, that's not right. Not jealousy but a sort of wistfulness. You have to understand. Leila has always excelled. She's brilliant and disciplined and has always fought for everything. She thought it would fall into place for her and when she and Will couldn't have kids, it felt like a slap in the face. Seeing us with Max all the time made her sad, I think.'

'But also jealous?'

Yasmin tensed. 'No, that was the wrong word.'

Shep made a final note. 'Ms Syed, you've been immensely helpful.' He smoothed his tie and stood. 'I know this can't be easy for you.'

Yasmin nodded blankly, the platitude bouncing off.

'Thank you for your time. I'll see myself out.' He left his tea untouched.

Back in his car, he dialled the air-con to full, the frigid rush icy on his eyeballs. As he drove, his gaze flicked to the mirror and the soft depression in the backseat. Was it possible to forget a child? Shep wasn't a father and may never understand the constant stress of duty, but he simply could not imagine leaving a child accidentally.

Leaving it on *purpose* made more sense to him. A harried parent nipping into a petrol station to pick up a bottle of milk? It was logical, wasn't it? A decision made in the heat of the moment with some greater pressure weighing on your shoulders?

Shep was still reflecting on this as he parked outside the station and headed back to his desk. There, he found a slim black-and-white document: the pathologist's preliminary report. He snatched it up and scanned the text. The provisional diagnosis was that Max's death was unnatural and the cause of death was hyperthermia. Max had died from overheating. Shep dropped wearily into his chair. So it was certain then. Whether she meant to or not, Leila Syed had killed this child.

Chapter Four

Leila paced the length of her living room, pausing each time by the window to peer at the sky outside. It was strange. Charged with a serious crime, she assumed the whole world knew: the driver who took her home on Monday after she was released, the postman who knocked on the door yesterday, her neighbour in the garden this morning. Leila shrank away from them as if they could somehow tell. It was why she now waited for the cover of darkness before she ventured out. She scanned the length of the street, feeling the waltz of nerves in her stomach. She knew what she was risking by daring to visit Yasmin, but she could not see another option. She *needed* to speak to her, if only to receive her punishment.

She waited for the sweep of a headlight to disappear down the street, then hurried around the corner. She knocked on her sister's door, gently from habit, in case Max was sleeping. He was a loud child, prone to crying for hours when roused from a nap early. The doorbell often woke him, restarting the cycle of exhaustion. That there was no longer a need for this prudence made her throat clot with sorrow.

There was the turning of a latch and Yasmin peeked out. Her

face was unwashed and greasy and her hair lay limp against her scalp, exposing small patches of skin. Yasmin stared at her and the air seemed to distort between them, like tin warping in heat. Leila opened her mouth to speak, but Yasmin turned around, leaving the door ajar. Leila took a tentative step inside. How appalling that trauma could change a home overnight. Where before it was warm and cosy, it now felt cluttered and claustrophobic. Leila took off her shoes, pressing a palm against a heap of coats that stubbornly puffed back out. She walked to the living room and paused by the door. Yasmin pointed at the sofa, one of those hard-boned things from Ikea – bought with her first decent pay packet in a stab at being stylish. Leila remained standing, for she needed height to deal with this.

'Did you do it?'

Leila stared at her. 'What are you asking me?'

'Did you mean to leave him?'

Leila balked. 'I would never do that. *Never.*'

Yasmin's jaw was rigid. 'I know you didn't mean to hurt him, but did you mean to leave him? For just a moment?'

'No. Of *course* I didn't.'

Yasmin stepped closer to her. 'Were you on the phone?'

Leila blinked and it took her a moment to answer. 'Yes.'

Yasmin drew a breath. Then, without a word or warning, she slapped Leila's face: a crisp and clean breaking sound that ruptured the very air.

Leila was stunned. She let her cheek sing and remained as still as possible. 'I'm sorry,' she said, her voice deceptively calm.

Yasmin's chin dimpled with distress. 'You never forget

anything. You make a note of *everything*.' Her voice cracked. '*How* could you forget Max?'

Leila's guilt was searing.

'Who were you talking to?'

Leila flushed. 'The office,' she admitted.

Yasmin nodded as if it all made sense. 'Would you have left Max if you weren't on the phone?'

Leila grappled for an answer. 'I don't know, Yasmin. I can't say what would have happened.'

'We talked about this.' Yasmin gestured at the stairwell. 'Me and Andrew. We talked about a system when we got that car seat. I read that you should have a toy or a pair of shoes to put in the front seat whenever your child is in the car, so you don't forget, and I thought *that's a good idea* and I told Andrew about it but we never did it – like you do with a million things.'

Leila reached out to comfort her, but she jerked away from her touch.

'I can't.' Her hands fluttered as if shaking off nerves. 'I can't do this.'

Leila persevered. 'Yasmin, I need you to know that I didn't mean to do it. You *have* to believe that.'

Yasmin made a small bark of laughter. 'Don't you do that. Don't you tell me what I *have* to do.' She pointed at Leila. 'All my life, you've told me what to do – prodding me like a fucking piece of cattle – and then you go and do *this*. The worst fuck-up anyone ever did and it affects *me*. It affects *my child*.'

'Yasmin, please. I didn't do it on purpose.'

'Didn't you?' she cried. 'Ms CEO, always rushing here and there. Always on the run. I *know* that you resented looking after Max. Don't you think I know that telephone voice of yours when you're trying to be polite? I know how much you value your time; how you think that I, a lowly secretary, should be looking after my own child and not expecting *you*, high-flying CEO, to do it for me!'

Leila winced. She knew. Of course she did. Her sister, ever the empath, perceived Leila's true feelings.

Yasmin's voice grew low and deadly. 'I'll ask you again, Leila. I know you didn't mean to hurt him, but *did* you mean to leave him for a moment?'

Leila shook her head helplessly. 'I loved him. I didn't leave him.'

Yasmin made a wet sob of a sound. 'Was he awake, Leila? That's what I want to know. Was he calling for me? Did he know what was happening? Did he leave this earth feeling scared? Was that the last thing he ever felt?' Her voice broke and she folded into a chair.

Leila knelt down next to her. The thought of her nephew, alone in the backseat, crying out for help, made her heart crack in two. She hated herself. More than anything else, it was *hate* she felt and knew that her sister must hate her too; knew she may never stop.

'He was asleep,' she said. 'I promise you he was asleep.' It didn't matter that Yasmin would never know the truth. It was the only tenable answer Leila could possibly give.

*

Shep liked this hour of the evening when the constant rush of traffic outside slowed to a lulling hum and the station was still warm with the recent presence of others. He zoomed in on his screen and studied Leila's features. The CCTV was from inside the building; the car park not covered fully. It was grainy and did not reveal Leila's expression, her eyes reduced to shadowy pixels. The timestamp read 11.31 a.m. on Monday the 12th of July, the day of Max's death. Leila didn't seem panicked as she moved across the foyer, phone clutched in her right hand.

'What are you thinking?' he said, watching her. Her body language – squared shoulders and long strides – seemed tense but not agitated as she left the building and walked out of frame. If someone told you that you had left a child in your car, wouldn't you run to it? He rewound the footage and watched it again. The lift opens and Leila walks out. She heads straight for the exit and there's only a fleeting moment that presents as distress: her left fist presses to her mouth, but only for a second. Other than that, one might have believed that she was on her way to pick up a coffee.

Shep knew there were myriad ways to react in a crisis. Was Leila's composure an innocent sign of shock, or did it speak to something darker? He watched her intently and scanned for clues. In person, she seemed like a loving aunt, but Shep knew that people – especially those who inspired trust – could easily beguile.

He hadn't always been so cynical, but it was hard to do this job and not have your faith erode. Shep's disillusionment came from Cora, a two-year-old girl who was involved in a serious accident. When he and his colleague went to the house, they found a neat and orderly home. Julia, Cora's well-spoken young mother, was slim and elegant with fine-boned features and tailored clothes. A woman like that, he thought, would not be abusive. Now that he looked back, he could see the markers of manipulation: the well-timed hand on his arm and the pretty tears that speckled her face in a wholly pleasing way, never descending to the unsightly crying of other, lesser mothers. Even the gentle wringing of her hands was bizarrely attractive.

He remembered the last time he saw Cora. The school had called to report a new bruise and he had volunteered to visit Julia, making an excuse to be alone with her. He had no improper intentions; he just enjoyed the calming balm of her presence. She received him with a gentle smile and knowingly asked him inside. She stood too close to him and he remembered the heat rising beneath his collar, knowing that this was unethical; to allow himself so close to her. He remembered her perfume – a warm, sensual scent – and how desperately he wanted to reach down and kiss her.

He hadn't, though he knew she wouldn't complain. Instead, he had stepped away and backed into a cupboard. Julia didn't laugh; only gave him another sweet smile. He was entranced by her, blinded to the school's report. Shep had been thirty years old; old enough to know better. He left the house that day and sat in his car for fifteen minutes, willing himself to drive away. When he finally did, he wondered if she was watching through a curtain, perhaps hoping he would turn off the engine, walk back up the drive and knock on her door.

Three weeks later, Cora was dead. It was sixteen years ago, but that case would haunt him forever. He hadn't asked the questions he was supposed to. Instead, he'd accepted her coffee too readily and pretended they were in a café, speaking to her as he might when trying to impress a date. He had been tricked by her softness and grace.

Sometimes, he wondered if that case was why he was single.

He never quite let his guard down again. Leila Syed might act like a doting aunt in person, but that did not make her innocent. If she had *meant* to harm that child, then Shep would bring her down.

*

Leila sat in her semi-dark kitchen and stared at the garden outside. She studied the wilt of the grass, parched even in moonlight. It was Will's job to water it, but he had left five months ago and she was alone in their cavernous house. They had bought it after she won her first big contract. They were so happy, running in and out of rooms like children, Will swinging on a wooden beam, Leila telling him to stop, then creasing with laughter when he slipped and landed clumsily on the floor. They giddily designated rooms: a study-cum-library, Will's makeshift gym and the sunny spare bedroom for their planned firstborn. Leila had seen motherhood as a cleansing balm. If she could raise children of her own and give them all the comfort, love and security that she and Yasmin had lacked, then perhaps it would help her heal. She had done her best with Yasmin, but the pain of those early memories stained so much of what came after it. The image of their mother in the bath – bubbles beading her hair, the taut whiteness of her face – had haunted Leila for years.

When she got custody of Yasmin, she rented their flat in Frinton Mews, the cheapest she could find. She remembered their first night there, shivering in the winter, putting on every piece of clothing they owned. She worked evenings at M&S and weekend shifts at the café. Leila flushed hot when she remembered the shame of that time, for it *was* shame. Stuffing chips in her mouth from leftover plates; hiding red bills from her sister; poking a hole in her belt to hold up her jeans, a sickly new gauntness in her hips.

It helped when Yasmin was old enough to work and got a full-time job in an office. Slowly, they amassed some savings, but for Leila this was a surrendering; a stunting of her sister's future. She continued her shifts at the greasy spoon and inched towards her degree. After graduating, she secured a job through a diversity scheme at the architecture firm Farrell & White. She was taken under the wing of Eleanor Farrell, a stern whippet of a woman who fast-tracked Leila's career. She worked her way up to partner and, at the age of twenty-eight, left to set up her own firm. Eleanor was surprisingly blasé about their non-compete clause as long as Leila didn't poach any clients.

Over the next ten years, Leila built a successful firm. Meanwhile, Yasmin remained in the same office, working her way up to executive PA before hitting the glass ceiling for her lack of qualifications. She never seemed to mind very much. Life seemed easy for her little sister. She met a sensible man, got married and got pregnant while Leila toiled away.

In recent years, she had tried to convince herself that raising her sister was enough for her, but the truth was that she yearned for a family of her own; felt the absence like a hole, tiptoeing around it in every conversation. *Do you have kids? No? Oh, you must have so much free time! What do you even do with yourself?*

When Yasmin got pregnant, it was a joy – a real and genuine joy – but by then, Leila had already been trying for a year and her sister's relative ease felt like a punch in the gut. In the years that followed, she and Will went through five rounds of IVF and four miscarriages. Leila would lie in bed at night and make absurd bargains. *I'll give up my work for a healthy baby, I'll give up my money for a healthy baby, I'll even give up Will for a baby.* She wanted a child desperately and it hurt so much to see Yasmin – full and lovely and blushing – do it all so easily. It gnawed away at Leila that she couldn't have the same.

Could the police sense her desperation? Did it come off her like a stink? Did they think that she killed Max on purpose? Driven mad by jealousy? Maybe she *was* a little mad to have done what she did. Maybe she had fully lost her mind without even noticing.

Chapter Five

Yasmin sat in Max's bedroom, gripping a mug of tea that had long ago turned cold. The air had a dense, discomfiting feel – like sitting in a wet coat, her body steaming with moisture. She pressed Max's blanket to her face and inhaled, but it was recently laundered and smelled only of lemon: gentle but artificial. That small unkindness, that utter lack of mercy, made her curdle with fury. How could her fate be so thoroughly cruel? She threw the blanket across the room, but its feathery weight landed softly with none of the noisy catharsis she wanted.

She needed help and knew what would happen if she didn't seek it. She didn't allow herself time to think. Instead, she rushed from the room and hurried downstairs, calling out to Andrew. He seldom heard her in his study. Sometimes, she would call for him at the top of her voice and feel her temper bite when he failed to answer, even though it wasn't his fault.

In his study, she found him hunched by his laptop, frown lines etched in his skin. He glanced at her, and Yasmin thought that he'd see that something was wrong; that he'd spring to his feet and rush over to her.

Instead, he asked, 'You okay?' Insipid words he chanted like a mantra.

When she saw his gaze flick to the screen, she held in the words she was planning to say. *No, I'm not. I need help.* 'What are you doing?' she asked, walking round to his side of the desk. She read the words on his screen. *Statistics on infant car deaths.* Her features tensed. 'What are you doing?' she repeated.

He bit his lip. 'I was just doing some research.' He moved to close the lid of the laptop, but she promptly stopped him.

'What does it say?'

He hesitated. 'It says that dozens of children are left in cars every year.'

Yasmin scanned the text on the screen and pointed at a cluster of figures – *2019: 52.* 'Is that how many were left that year?'

He grimaced. 'No, that's how many died. In the US alone.'

Yasmin pressed her knuckles to her lips, her skin growing cold. The horror of that fact seemed too great to comprehend. All those broken families. All those dazzling futures whited out by a mindless act.

'I thought it would help her,' said Andrew.

'"Her"?'

He scrolled down the page. 'It says that fifty-four per cent are left by accident. If it's that common, then maybe it will help Leila's case.'

Yasmin stepped back. 'You're doing this for Leila?'

He looked up at her. 'Well, yes. She . . .' His face changed as he registered her anger. 'Should I not be?'

Yasmin made a sharp plosive sound. 'Andrew, Leila killed our son.'

'She was doing me a favour, Yas,' he said gently. 'I should have been the one driving him to nursery.'

She felt a flare of frustration. 'What does that matter? It doesn't matter if you were or were not meant to be driving him. *She* was the one doing it. *She* should have been paying attention. She was on the *phone*, Andrew. She was on the *fucking* phone.'

'Hon, we call each other from the car all the time.'

She shook her head vehemently. 'Not when Max is in the car.'

'Hon,' he said, a chiding in his tone.

'What?' she asked in challenge.

'You know that's not true.'

She narrowed her eyes. 'I *never* call when he's in the car.'

He looked at her pleadingly.

'I *don't*,' she insisted.

'What about last Tuesday on the way to the dentist?' The question landed like a slap.

Yasmin faltered and the frustration of losing her argument flared inside like a rash. She shoved the laptop, so hard that it skidded to the edge of the desk, then tipped over to the floor.

Andrew sprang up as if he'd been shot. 'What the hell are you doing?'

'You're a fucking arsehole!' Yasmin wanted to strike him. 'How *dare* you say that I put our son in danger?'

Andrew flexed his fingers. 'That's not what I said. I was saying we've both used the phone in the car and it isn't putting Max in danger.'

'It is,' she cried. 'Andrew, it *is*!'

He drew back as if preparing to shout at her, but then swallowed his anger instead.

'How dare you say that to me?' She pointed at the window in the direction of Leila's house. 'How dare you defend her over me?'

'That's not what I was doing.'

'It *is*.' Her voice grew shrill. 'You're saying she isn't to blame.'

'I'm not,' Andrew pleaded. 'That's not what I'm saying. I just—' He paused and clenched his jaw. 'Max was supposed to be with me. I was supposed to be looking after him and I palmed him off on her and . . .' He gestured powerlessly. 'If I really wanted to – *genuinely* wanted to – I could have told the office no. I could have said I have my son with me and sorry I can't come in yet, but instead I called Leila because it was easy and it's not fair to blame her. Not entirely.'

Yasmin felt the anger spark inside her. 'You don't get to do this,' she said. 'Neither of you get to do this. My son is dead and don't you *dare* plead mercy from me. If you're both to blame, then as far as I'm concerned, you can both go to hell.'

Andrew flinched and Yasmin took a perverse satisfaction from seeing him hurt, but in the moment immediately after, her pleasure burst into sorrow. She bent forwards at the waist and folded to the floor as Andrew stood agog, inert from the impact of what she had said. She pressed her head against a table leg, gripping it with both hands to keep herself braced. There, wrapped around the wood, she began to wail: deep, animal sounds that rang with anger and torment. When Andrew came to comfort her, she batted him back, not speaking but screaming because she didn't know how to contain her grief, didn't know that pain could feel like this.

*

Shep shifted in his chair and tried to adjust the backrest. He turned and scanned the room, then called out to Melanie, the team assistant.

'Who's been sitting at my desk again?' He scowled when no one answered and continued to fight with the lever. He was in a bad mood. He hadn't been able to sleep all weekend, partly due to the neighbour's dog who barked all the way to dawn but also because there was something on his mind but he couldn't pinpoint what.

He gnawed the end of a pencil, enjoying the woody taste in his mouth. He stopped when he felt the cold tang of lead on his tongue and set the pencil down. He had been on the force long enough to know that this spelled trouble. When they had already charged a suspect and packaged it up with a motive, it was a bad idea to go sniffing elsewhere, but something about the parents bothered him. He thought about his visit to their house last week and tried to recall what it was.

When he finally fixed his chair, he leaned back and closed his eyes and pictured walking through the corridor. His colleagues laughed when he did this – teased him about going into his 'mind palace' like a poor man's Sherlock Holmes – but it helped him to remember things with clarity and see what he'd initially missed. He had walked through the crowded corridor into the well-lit kitchen-cum-dining room. He had glanced at the garden outside, a neat little cat flap in the bottom-right corner of the door. He tried to recall if he had seen anything else that pointed to a cat: a scratching post, water bowl, or litter tray. Perhaps they no longer had one?

Then what? He had looked at the mantelpiece and its mementos and photos, all of a happy family. He had seen one of Max cradled in his mother's arms. Shep didn't have children but had worked with enough families to know that the boy was about two years old. It must have been taken last year.

Shep frowned and his eyes flickered open. In the photograph, Yasmin had a bob cut, a sleek, shiny halo that fell about her chin. When he met her last week, it was down to her waist. Was it possible for a woman's hair to grow fifteen inches in a year? His fingers flew over the keyboard, a lightning-quick query to the Google gods. The answer was clear: a woman's hair grew on average six inches a year. There's no way that picture was taken last year, but why hadn't Max grown?

A thought occurred to him and he felt the cold clench of premonition. He gripped his mouse and opened the general register, a database of all the births, deaths and marriages in England and Wales. He typed in the mother's name and date of birth. He scrolled down the screen, hoping there was a mistake, but then he saw it.

'For Christ's sake.' He scanned the record, stomach dropping like lead. Monday morning and it was already shaping up to be a bad week. The CPS wouldn't thank him for this, but now that he knew it, he couldn't ignore it. He rubbed a hand across his face, then grabbed his bag with a frustrated grunt. 'I'll be back later,' he called to Melanie, then headed out to his car.

*

Leila walked to the office from the bus stop, her Mini still with the police. Her feet felt sweaty in her ballet flats, the fabric of them wilting with heat. Her white shirt had a speckling of dirt along a cuff and she stared at it for a moment, remembering how filthy London buses could be. She felt it on her skin like a coat of grease, thickening in the heat.

Inside the building, she marched to the lift without pausing and changed into her heels discreetly. When it pinged open on the fifth floor, she held her head high and walked. A hush befell her colleagues as she strode to her corner office. A few valiantly tried to continue, but their chatter was stilted and unnatural. At her desk, she pressed the button that closed the blinds, muting the glare of attention. She fell into her chair and placed her head in her hands, careful not to smudge her makeup. It had taken so long today, getting it all right, her hand slipping with the mascara wand and leaving a splotch on her right cheek, the lipstick bleeding from her cupid's bow, her hair curling stubbornly into a cowlick. She had planned to arrive before everyone else, but had to take it all off and start again.

She switched on her computer. Suki usually logged in for her, but had clearly assumed that she wouldn't come in. She called her now and asked for a cup of coffee, then scanned the headlines as she waited, first the *Architectural Review* and *Metropolis* before switching to the *Guardian*. A story in the sidebar caught her eye: **London architect charged with killing nephew**. She felt her breath grow shallow. The words were so blunt, so lacking in nuance. She stared, reading them over and over until they bled all meaning. Finally, hand trembling, she reached out and clicked the link.

The details were sparse, but mentioned *the scorching shadow of a glass building in the middle of a searing summer.*

The words churned a well of yellow nausea in the pit of Leila's stomach. She reached for a tissue to blot the sweat on her upper lip and jumped at the knock on the door.

Suki walked in tentatively and placed the coffee on Leila's desk. She was competent and talented, but had a meek way about her that sometimes irritated others. She lingered there a moment too long and Leila glanced up at her. 'Was there something else?' she asked.

Suki shifted on her feet. 'No, I just wanted to ask if you needed anything else?'

Leila gave her a cursory smile. 'That will be all.' She waited until she left, then slumped in her chair. Could she really do this? Could she sit there and command a company and pretend she was okay?

There was another knock and Leila gritted her teeth, ready to bite, but saw that it was her partner. Robert Gardner walked in and gestured at a chair in query.

She nodded in reply. 'Would you like a coffee?'

His gaze flicked briefly to the decanter of whisky that she kept behind her desk. Leila didn't drink it, but it was part of her mise en scène. *I'm one of you,* it was supposed to signal to the men who came through her office. *You can trust me.*

'I'm fine, thanks,' Robert said with a dismissive wave.

She nodded sagely. 'It's nice of you to visit.'

He gave her a wicked smile. It was a running joke between them that he rarely made an appearance in the office, perfectly happy to let Giles, his deputy, handle most of his work. He wasn't lazy; he just didn't particularly enjoy working. He liked to say that forty-five was a perfectly acceptable age at which to semi-retire. 'I thought it would be prudent of me to pop in.'

He tapped the oak of her desk, deciding how to broach the subject. 'How are you?' he asked.

She gave him a dubious look. 'Is that what you really want to say?' Robert was the least sentimental person she knew.

He ducked his head obligingly. 'Should you be here?'

'What do you mean?'

He scratched the back of his neck – uncomfortably, for he struggled with sincerity. 'It's been a week since . . . what happened. Don't you need some proper time off?'

She caught the edge in his tone. 'Are you asking me or telling me?'

'I never tell you to do anything, Leila. You know that.'

'So what is this really about?'

He sighed, abandoning his stab at diplomacy. 'The Mercers project. I think it's a good idea to let Giles take over your side of things.'

Leila recoiled. Giles Salter was one of Robert's first hires at the firm. He was the sort of man who leaned a little bit too close when looking at her computer screen, or who would casually talk down to her despite her being a partner. She had seen first-hand how, when they walked into a room together, clients would turn to him first as if he were in charge, an assumption he did not correct. Over the years, Leila and Robert had clashed repeatedly about keeping Giles on.

He caught her dismay. 'Before you say anything, hear me out. I know you don't like him, but he's brought us over two million in billing this year and it's only July. Clients love him and he works harder than the devil.' Robert held up a finger, sensing her impatience. 'Now, as I understand it, your trial is scheduled for December – that's only five months away. If we leave Mercers in your hands, what happens next year?'

Leila's voice was brittle. 'We find a replacement when we need to.'

Robert clucked with impatience. 'You know how easily these legacy brands spook. One sign of trouble and we're out of the running.'

'But the contract will be signed by then.'

Robert tilted his head. 'Don't be naive, Leila. This seduction could last a year. If they catch wind of your trial, then they'll opt for one of the big boys. We have to protect the firm.'

'Well, what do you suggest I do? Play mother to the interns? Start a charity bake sale?'

He planted his elbows on her desk. 'I suggest you take a sabbatical – paid of course.'

She leaned forward and mirrored him. 'And if I say no?'

He studied her for a moment. 'If you say no, then I invoke the disrepute clause.'

She stared at him. 'You wouldn't dare.' Her tone was cool but she could feel the swing of panic inside. She couldn't believe that her long-term partner and confidant was threatening her with an ousting.

'I wouldn't want to.' He raised his chin defiantly. 'But I would.'

'Robert,' she started calmly, knowing that he had the upper hand. Given Leila's trial and the severity of the charge, Robert could easily demonstrate that she had brought the firm into disrepute and unseat her as a partner. 'How can you even consider this?'

He laced his fingers. 'Leila, I respect you more than anyone else I've ever worked with, but sometimes we have to protect each other from ourselves.' He paused. 'You remember year three? Where would I be if you hadn't intervened?' He nodded at the decanter of whisky. 'Didn't you threaten to do the very same thing?'

She flushed. 'So what is this? Payback?'

'No,' he said emphatically. 'This is me protecting the firm. All I'm asking is that you take some time off.'

She tried to think logically. She knew from experience that it was better to maintain a veneer of civility than set herself up against Robert. 'I'm not taking a sabbatical,' she said, 'but I'll agree to work from home.'

He considered this. 'Fine,' he acceded, 'but you'll stay under the radar?'

'Of course,' she said with an arctic smile.

He exhaled. 'Thank you. And I *am* sorry, Leila.'

'Are you?'

He stood and brushed off his trousers. 'More than you think.' He nodded at her grimly, then turned and walked away, gently closing the door behind him.

Leila wilted in her chair, her steel slipping away. For the first time in her life, she couldn't see a path to the other side. Her marriage had fallen apart, her family was in tatters, and now, the sole thing that she could still cling to had been cleanly snatched away.

*

Shep knocked on the door and fixed on a sorrowful smile. He listened for movements and, after a minute, heard footsteps in the corridor – sharp and efficient. Andrew Hansson opened the door and Shep caught the shiver of annoyance beneath his cordial mask.

'Detective?' His tone was polite but with a deliberate note of confusion to convey his bemusement.

'Mr Hansson.' Shep reached out his hand. 'Andrew,' he corrected himself. 'I'm so sorry to drop in on you like this. May I have a few minutes of your time?'

Andrew glanced over his shoulder. 'What do you need?'

Shep gestured towards the hall. 'I just need to ask you and Ms Syed – Yasmin – some clarification questions.' He waited, not wanting to spook him. Shep wanted both parents present so that he could study their reaction.

Andrew pulled the door ajar. 'Of course.'

Shep stepped in and, without invitation, headed to the kitchen table, knowing that that was where the picture would be. Yasmin stood against the kitchen counter in black leggings and an oversized grey jumper. He noticed that she was the better-looking sister but lacked the cool, inscrutable quality that made Leila so intriguing. He waited for the pair to sit, shoulder to shoulder as if heading to battle. He took his place opposite. Then, he twisted and pointed at a picture behind him.

'May I?'

Yasmin nodded, a light frown creasing her pretty features.

He plucked it from its place, leaving behind a clean strip in the dust. He set it on the table, to one side so that all three of them could see it. He pointed at the boy. 'Who's that?'

A shadow passed over Yasmin's face. She drew her arms across her chest, as if to hold herself in. Andrew stared at the picture and he swallowed once, then twice, his features in a strange contortion.

Shep watched and waited, letting the silence hang, far beyond what was comfortable.

Finally, Andrew cleared his throat. 'That's our son. Toby.'

Shep felt a thrum in his chest: the thrill of a hunch gone right. 'What happened to him?'

Andrew took a soundless breath. 'He died.'

Shep paused to even his tone, masking his suspicion. 'When?'

'Four years ago.'

'How old was he?'

Andrew shifted in his chair. 'Three.'

'The same age as Max?'

'Yes.'

Shep looked across to Yasmin. Her gaze was fixed on the hardwood tabletop, as if she were sitting alone. 'What happened to him?'

A vein tensed in Andrew's temple. 'It's all in his medical records.'

Shep winced as if his intrusion pained him. 'I know, but I'd really appreciate hearing it from you.'

Yasmin didn't move. There was a glazed, faraway look in her eyes as if she hadn't even heard him speak.

Andrew picked up an empty crystal glass and pressed it hard against his palms as if he were trying to break it. 'Toby was born in 2014. He was our first child and we were so unbelievably happy.' His lips twisted in a bittersweet smile. 'Broke but happy. We were in this draughty flat in Leyton, where we had the electric heater on all the time. You could hear traffic at all hours of the day, but we were happy. Toby was such a beautiful child. I know all parents think that, but he really was. Everyone said so. Our first few days were weirdly easy.' He glanced at his wife. 'Yasmin loved being a mother. She just . . . glowed. But then we noticed strange things: patches on Toby's skin where they rubbed against his clothes. They began to blister and . . . we found out that he had EB: epidermolysis bullosa.' Andrew moved a hand across his face. 'It's a severe skin disease. You can look it up. I can't . . .' He shook his head, unable to relay the details. 'He died from sepsis at the age of three so . . . that's what happened to Toby.'

Shep watched him carefully and felt a strange hollowing. He had hoped for a sign of guilt but found only innocent grief.

Andrew continued unbidden. 'When my wife fell pregnant again, the doctor said there was a one-in-four chance that our baby would have EB because Yasmin and I both carry the gene. We were terrified, but Max was . . . perfect.' There was a catch in his throat. Yasmin didn't react; only sat with her hands in her lap, silent and unmoved.

'I'm so sorry to have brought up these memories,' said Shep. He tried to find a delicate way to pose his next question. 'I wondered why you hadn't said anything about him.'

Andrew tensed. 'Were we supposed to?' His eyes darted to his wife and back. 'It's all in his records.'

Shep recognised the note of angst in his tone. It wasn't that of a criminal but an innocent man who worried that he'd somehow broken a rule. 'No, it's okay,' said Shep. 'Would you be willing to give us access to Toby's medical records?'

Andrew nodded and wordlessly signed the release forms. 'I'll give you fair warning, detective. There is a hell of a lot there and most of it is . . .' He searched for the right word. 'Horrific.'

'I understand,' Shep said gently. 'I just need to confirm the details.' There was a lull in the conversation and he saw that he had overstayed his welcome. He gathered the forms and patted them into shape. 'Please forgive my intrusion. I'll let you get on with your day.'

Andrew stood and led him down the hallway.

At the front door, Shep paused and gestured towards the kitchen. 'Is your wife okay?'

'She's fine,' Andrew answered a tad too quickly. He opened the door and waited for Shep to step out. 'Goodbye, detective,' he said with a note of finality.

Shep returned to his car, wincing at the heat. He tugged at his damp neckline to loosen the noose of his tie. He felt sodden with sorrow. Yasmin Syed and Andrew Hansson had lost two of their sons – through no fault of their own it seemed. He could scarcely believe the cruelty. He closed his eyes, calmed by the clatter of the air-con. It would be okay, he thought, to rest here for a moment or two.

*

Leila stacked the items on the conveyor belt: one ravioli ready meal, pre-cut vegetables for a stir fry, rocket chillies in red and green and a garish pasta sauce. She straightened each item so that the corners sat aligned. She had fought this compulsion all day: the need to rearrange things; to stop her hands from falling still. After her run-in with Robert, she had returned home, only to prowl the halls, feeling cut adrift.

There was a denseness in her body, as if she might start to sink if she lost momentum. She had ventured out on a run in the thirty-degree heat and though it had helped somewhat, the fix was only temporary. Growing restless in the evening, she had headed out to Waitrose for food she didn't need.

The woman on checkout greeted her warmly. She was portly with a halo of curly white hair, and smiled at Leila with each scan of an item, as if she could see a weakness and wanted to offer support. The gentleness in her manner undid something in Leila. She felt her skin flush and then it came: quiet, discreet tears that rolled soundlessly down her face. The woman stopped scanning and stared.

'Oh dear.' She looked around for assistance.

Leila held up a palm, mortified by this slip of composure.

'What is it, love?' she asked. 'Do you need help?'

Her motherly tone only made Leila cry harder. She brushed a finger along her lash line, skimming away her tears. 'I'm sorry,' she managed, hurriedly collecting her items. 'I'm fine.'

'Shall I call someone?'

'No, please.' Leila gestured at the last two items on the belt and the woman scanned them fluidly.

'It will pass, love,' she said. 'I promise you.'

Leila paid quickly and fled. Outside, she searched the concourse for somewhere to hide but it was a large, open space, flat in every direction. In the end, she turned to face a wall and broke down in sobs. She tried to be discreet but couldn't stop her shoulders from shaking. In that moment, she wished desperately that she had a mother or an aunt to call, but there was no elder presence in the family – just her and Yasmin.

This woman's kindness, fleeting as it was, had brought this to the fore.

'Leila?' said a voice behind her.

She turned to find Will on the edge of the kerb, his trainers half on and half off. He saw her tears and came to her instinctively.

'Oh, honey.' He wrapped his arms around her.

She burrowed into him and tried to quiet her sobs. 'What are you doing here?' she asked, hoarse with tears. She felt the roll of his shoulder as he motioned at the entrance.

'I was coming to see you. I was going to grab something.'

'Where have you *been*?' She realised that she was upset with him. She knew that she no longer had demands on his time but after their talk last week, had expected him to be around. Instead, he'd just sent a few cursory texts.

He tightened his arms around her. 'I'm sorry. I kept meaning to, but work has been nonstop.'

'Will you come over now?' Her voice cracked with need.

He kissed her hair, catching the curve of her ear. 'Of course I will.'

She leaned into him as they walked, her fingers wrapped around his cuff as if he might wander off. He stroked her waist and spoke soft words in her ear until they reached Tredegar Square. Leila gazed at the end of her street, to the corner that connected her house with Yasmin's. 'They're so close. It feels like I can't get away from it.'

'I know, sweetheart,' he soothed as he led her inside and through to the kitchen. He set down her sole bag of groceries. 'I'm sorry I haven't been round. My editor, he—' Will caught the expression on Leila's face, then waved a hand dismissively.

'It doesn't matter. I'm here now and that's what matters.' He drew her back into his arms and they stood there in that strange space of couples that hadn't yet parted properly.

She pulled back a little. 'I was crying in the supermarket. Just before you came.'

'Oh, honey.' He plucked a tissue from a silver dispenser, still holding her with one arm.

She gripped it in her fist. 'I just . . . I've been walking around as if this is something I know how to handle and then I walked in there and this woman was nice to me and it just made me . . . cave.'

Will brushed a knuckle under her chin. 'You've always tried to do things on your own.'

She looked up at him and felt a sense of yearning. 'I miss you.'

His eyes flicked to the floor. 'I miss you too,' he said. For a moment, they were still. Then, breaking the mood, he gestured towards a chair. 'Sit down. I'll make dinner.'

She obeyed gladly, soothed by the familiarity of Will in her kitchen. She watched him move around it fluently. First, he emptied the grocery bag, tsk-ing at the ready meal as he shoved it in the fridge. Then, he selected the vegetables that were nearly overripe and set them on the counter neatly. Will liked to cook and his dainty creations often belied his alpha image. Yasmin, who was also a foodie, would sometimes come over and cook with him, oohing and ahhing at the six-hob cooker and giant American fridge. On these occasions, Leila and Andrew would watch with amusement, catching each other's eye as their partners discussed a specific triviality: whether to cook the spiced salmon sous vide, or in the oven wrapped in banana leaf. Those evenings had been so easy and warm, but now seemed impossibly distant.

Will prepared a simple dish of pasta with crisped sage and truffle oil. He checked her wine rack and chose a white, then set it all out on the table. In the lull of candlelight, he looked at her earnestly.

'You're struggling,' he said, more a statement than a question.

'I . . .' Leila's emotions seemed raw and rapid, roiling beneath the surface of her skin. Just a light scratch and she would bleed. 'I can't stop thinking about that morning.'

'Do you want to talk about it?' he asked gently.

'I— It's like a blank page.' She gathered her napkin in pleats. 'I keep rifling through each moment and it wasn't even the call from the office. As soon as he was in the car, it was like a light switching off. I completely forgot about him. I was thinking all sorts of things: the blueprints, the meeting, if I had time for a run that evening. Not once did I think about dropping him off. I just blanked.'

Will took a sip of wine, studying her all the while.

Leila gestured helplessly. 'If he'd just stirred or made a sound or *something*, then I would have known, but he was so still, so silent, I just . . . I forgot.'

He reached out and took her hand, his grip as ever a touch too tight. 'How did you feel when you realised?'

Her hand began to sweat in his and she softly pulled it back. 'Just this loud white panic, like an alarm. I knew even before I opened the car door. Everything inside me was screaming.' She tensed. 'I still can't believe I did it.'

'It wasn't your fault, Leila.' He shifted his chair closer to her, the legs scraping on oak. 'Hey.' He waited for her to look at him. 'It *wasn't* your fault.'

She scoffed. 'Of course it was my fault, Will.'

There was something in his eyes now: a flicker of anger or something similar. 'It *wasn't*,' he repeated. 'You were doing them a favour, Leila. You can't see it but they took advantage of you.'

'No, Will, they—'

'They *did*, Leila. You know they did. God, it was endless. First, they move a street away so you're close enough to help – and they use your money to fund it. Meanwhile, Andrew's buying a car they don't need.'

'Will—'

He carried on talking. 'They ask you to babysit every week when they know how much it hurts you.'

'They don't know that.'

'Of course they do! We've been trying to have a child for *years*. How can they *not* know that it hurts you to look after Max? To see him cry out for his mother; to love her more than anything else in the world; to know that *you* will never be enough?'

'Don't,' Leila cut in. She didn't want to hear it, though she knew that he was right. There *were* times that being near Max was more painful than she could bear, but that wasn't Yasmin's fault. Perhaps they did take advantage sometimes, but that's what family was for.

Will brushed a strand of hair from her face. 'You were doing them a favour, Leila. Andrew didn't need to go into work straight away – he knows that – but he thought dumping Max on you would be easier than standing up to his boss. That's on *him*. Not you.'

Leila said nothing, for that was easier than explaining the truth. She *needed* to carry the blame. She needed to self-flagellate.

They talked for a long time and watched the last of the day slide down the kitchen wall. Even as it grew too dark in the room, neither stood to switch on the light. Will tipped the last of the wine into her glass. 'Can I stay tonight?' he asked.

Leila took a moment to answer. 'I don't think that's a good idea.'

'Please?'

'Come on, Will,' she said with soft reproach.

He angled his head in a plea.

It took all her restraint to say, 'Not tonight.'

He rose reluctantly. 'Okay, if that's what you need.' He lingered for a moment, then kissed her on the lips, one hand on the small of her back, the other lost in her hair.

She exhaled, feeling the swell of an old emotion. 'Will, when this is over, can we talk?'

He nodded tenderly. 'I'd love that.' He kissed her again and, then, he was gone.

Leila gathered the plates and cutlery, and placed them in the dishwasher. She picked up her glass of wine and moved to the living room sofa. She thought of the woman in the supermarket who had caused her to break down. In the moment, Leila had wished that her mother were still alive. Now, alone in her house, she reminded herself of the truth: her mother would not have helped. She'd been a flighty woman, taken to scams and schemes. When Leila was twelve years old, her mother told her that next year they would fly to Canada – *first class*, she promised. Too young to doubt it, she and a five-year-old

Yasmin spent months deciding what they would see and do: *polar bears, sledging, skiing.* They didn't know that she had signed up for a work-from-home opportunity, a front for a pyramid scheme. When she received a mere £3 in the post, she spiralled to a low. That was their chosen euphemism: a *low.* In its grasp, she would lie in the dark for days with the blinds drawn, shushing the slightest noise, debilitated by a migraine.

When she died, the coroner ruled it suicide. Leila remembered how the state-appointed therapist told her not to say that her mother 'committed suicide' for it made it sound like a crime. Leila had been so angry. What *was* it if not a crime to leave your children to survive on their own?

Leila drained the last of her wine. How tragic it was, she thought. They were children without a mother. And now, they were mothers without children. The thought induced a sort of paralysis and she slumped against the sofa, unable to find the strength to move. After a few minutes or maybe a few hours, she unclipped her skirt, pulled it off and folded it over the arm of the sofa. She pulled the decorative throw around her shoulders and sank into semi-consciousness. Tomorrow, she would book a therapist for Yasmin. She knew some good ones who could help. She would help her get through this. Her sister would be okay.

*

Yasmin looked at the prints on the wall: the delicate press of a newborn's palm, the red smudge of his first birthday, followed by ages two and three. It was the only sign of Toby that remained in the room. When she and Andrew had repainted the nursery before Max was born, it was the only thing of Toby's she couldn't bear to lose.

She stared at it now, as she had done for hours – ever since that detective left. She had heard him whisper in the hall and knew what he was really asking. *Is your wife okay? Or is your wife a nutcase?* She knew that this blank glaze of a state was unnerving, but there were moments when you had to set down the burden of social expectation and reroute your strength to yourself. How easy it was for that man to sit there and ask questions that put her entire world on a tilt. He, so strong and broad and sturdy that it was impossible for anything to move him, couldn't possibly understand. Andrew was better at it than she, packaging vast tragedy into a few neat sentences, leaning on the passive tense until it bowed beneath the weight of his pain. *It was announced that. It was stated that.*

In the crush of all her memories, Yasmin didn't know which son to grieve. Toby's life had been short and painful – almost inconceivably so. She remembered how the doctor who diagnosed him told them not to look up the symptoms. The urgency of his tone had filled her with a pulsing dread. At home, she had gorged on information, desperate to find the worst of it, but nothing – not the pamphlets or pictures, the forums or charities – prepared her for the truth. Toby's skin was so fragile, it blistered at the slightest touch. Even the seams of his underwear left him with open wounds. Yasmin would bandage him for hours, closing her eyes when his screams were too much. He couldn't eat normally for the merciless disease was internal too, causing his throat to blister. The corneal tears were the worst, blinding him for days so that he lay in his dark room, unseeing and untouched, unable to process his terror, never understanding why his mother couldn't comfort him. Those years were a waking nightmare and the horror was only tolerable because it became their new normal. It outlasted Toby's death, only really ceasing when Max was born healthy. To have him taken too and by a vagary of fate? She didn't know how to cope with it, succumbing instead to this sedative state.

Outside, Andrew was hovering, betrayed by a telltale creak. She knew why he was frightened. After Toby died, Yasmin had taken some pills before her Sunday bath. When he found her, she was unconscious in the stone-cold water. She remembered the next moments in snatches: the milky colour of the bathwater the very same shade as when they found their mother; Andrew clumsily blow-drying her hair, bawling over the noise; Yasmin's own pain that came from a place so raw, she just wanted it to stop. She awoke in a hospital bed and saw the hunted look in his eyes. 'I didn't mean to!' she shouted. 'I didn't mean to!' But Andrew didn't believe her. He gripped her hand so hard and urgently begged her not to do it again. And, then, he broke apart, crying into her abdomen like a chastised child. She wanted to scream, for she had no space for his pain and even as she reached out and dug her fingers into his hair, there was a rigidity in her body, a note of blame, that he was collapsing too. *She* was the mother, *she* had carried Toby in her body, *she* had ventured to that frozen ledge where life drops into death and returned with their son victoriously. It was *her* right to fall apart. It was *her* right to feel this pain.

After that, she began to resent him for the tremble and wobble of his lips. Once, she even lashed out – *you never used to be this girlish* – and took a sick satisfaction from the sting in his eyes. He had rallied after that, clenching his jaw whenever strangers skirted the death. They would catch each other's eye and instead of solidarity, there was only a sense of guilt.

Yasmin, naturally vivacious and happy, became cold and dismissive and their marriage threatened to implode. But then, joy – and also fear – with the news of her second pregnancy; relief when their son was healthy; and slowly a process of healing. In the years after Max's birth, Yasmin pieced herself together again, back to who she used to be: simple pleasures, simple dreams. And now? A new but familiar tragedy. How much, she wondered now, could one person endure before they decided to end it all?

Chapter Six

The sweep of grass in Victoria Park was parched in the summer heat. Leila slowed to a walk, feeling the scratchy blades bristle against her skin. The day was already blazing and there were children darting in and out of the old fountain, squealing with delight. It was a mistake coming here on a Saturday morning when the park was filled with families. Leila felt self-conscious; hyperaware of her sweaty T-shirt and greasy hair – a swift devolution from the sleek professional who left her office on Monday.

She wished she had let Will stay that day and maybe even this week. She knew that this halfway state wasn't healthy, but having him in the house again would surely ease her anxiety. Last night, she had tossed and turned until 5 a.m. before drifting to a turgid sleep, heavy and bulbous with forgotten dreams. She had forced herself out on a run, but didn't count on it being so busy. The volume seemed turned up: the harsh jingle of an ice cream van, the deafening screech of a child. She wanted to muffle the sound; to tune all the cheer out.

She drifted to the rose garden, which was usually quiet. Parents were clearly wary of letting their children loose among the flowers. She sat on a bench and tried to order her thoughts, which seemed to pull towards one thing, like moths to a lit window. She remembered leaving her car that morning. Her entire life had changed in the locking of that door. It made her clench with guilt and then a sickening fear. What if she was found guilty? A darker question followed on its heels. *Don't I deserve to be?* She *had* after all left Max in the car. She *had* after all killed him. She couldn't sit with that thought and rose to her feet again, hoping to shake it off.

She drifted towards Lauriston Road, past tidy storefronts of farmhouse delis and neat little cafés with stylish striped awnings. She continued down the street towards her favourite café, a cosy tearoom with only six tables. She paused in front and studied her reflection in the window between the yellow-gold lettering, the 'l' of 'Copper Kettle' bisecting her face neatly. She shifted to the right to check that she was presentable enough to venture inside. She stilled as a movement caught her eye. The corner table, a small bench strewn with cushions, was occupied by a couple: her brother-in-law, Andrew, with a woman. She was petite like Yasmin and had the same style of hair and softness of gaze, but was white, slimmer, and more toned – a good few years younger as well. She was dressed smartly in a rose-gold blouse and grey skirt and had a hand on Andrew's arm, touching it in a long, slow stroke, almost sensual in its motion. Andrew was visibly upset and drew away from her. The woman gripped his hand and squeezed it, her lips stretching in a joyless smile.

Leila felt the swing of disbelief. Could Andrew be cheating on Yasmin? He seemed so comfortable with this woman, so open and familiar. She searched for signs of indiscretion, but they sat apart now. The woman wrapped her hands around her coffee, her features in a grimace of sympathy. Surely, *surely*, this was innocent. The café was a mile away from their house and Andrew *knew* that Leila frequented it. In fact, she was the one who introduced him to it. There was no chance he would bring a mistress here.

She hovered in indecision, but when she sensed his gaze sweep towards the window, she spun around to avoid him. She retreated quickly, back to her corner in the rose garden. He couldn't be. *He couldn't.* Andrew *knew* what Yasmin had been through.

Leila recalled the endless, helpless days: Yasmin silently weeping as she wrapped Toby's wounds. He would scream with rage, not yet comprehending why his body felt this way – only reacting to a deep and carnal pain. Yasmin never grew used to it. It hurt her every single time to see him like that, shivering and writhing from pain. Leila would beg to take over, but this only made things worse. Toby wanted his mother and even in the last days, when he was anaesthetised beyond recognition, he was different with his mother: a little calmer, a little less confused.

When Yasmin was found unconscious in the bath a month after Toby had passed, it unhinged something in Leila. She rushed to the hospital, strafed with panic. The nerve-deep alarm of that half-hour was itself like a form of trauma. She remembered casting about the corridor wildly, which seemed to tilt as she searched. When she found the right room and saw that Yasmin was awake, she had turned around and walked out again, into the bathroom to bawl – with relief, with anger, with bone-deep gratitude that she hadn't lost her sister. Never had she felt the small size of their family so keenly. If Yasmin died, then Leila would be alone with no blood relatives.

After twenty minutes, Leila had returned to the hospital room.

'I'm sorry,' said Yasmin, her voice small and broken, her lips a bloodless blue.

Leila had wrapped her in her arms and bit down all the things she wanted to say. *How could you? After everything?* Below her anger was a vice-like fear. After what happened to their mother, could it be that there was something faulty in their genes? Some dark impulse or weakness?

That's when Leila decided that she couldn't take any chances. She had to take better care of her sister. She started to give Andrew money, knowing that Yasmin was too bullish to take it. She funded a new car and an expensive restorative holiday. She insisted on Saturday dinners together. Family was forged with traditions and they may not have inherited any, but they could build their own.

When Max was born, it felt like starting afresh. Though it set off a maternal pain in her brain, Leila vowed to be there; to nurture the shoots of their tiny family until it grew large and strong. It's why she swallowed her irritation when Yasmin requested last-minute babysitting in the middle of another week. She knew that Yasmin was complacent because Leila was there to pick up the slack. Sometimes, it meant staying up until 3 a.m. to catch up on her work, but Leila still agreed. She now realised that it was this very compulsion that had led them here. If she wasn't so close, always so involved, then Andrew wouldn't have asked her for help. She wouldn't have felt compelled to say yes. She wouldn't be the one to blame.

These past days, she had been worried sick that Yasmin would spin into relapse. To see Andrew sitting in a café, sipping coffee with a stranger like everything was okay stirred an irrational anger. She fought the urge to march back and yank him up by the collar. If he was cheating on Yasmin, then Leila would kill him. She would *actually* kill him, she vowed.

*

The wet towel lay on the bed and a dark patch bloomed around it. Leila plucked it up and folded it over the radiator. She blow-dried her hair roughly, leaving it in a cloudy halo. She checked her phone again, feeling jumpy and restless. She had sent Andrew a terse text to tell him they needed to talk, but he hadn't yet replied. She should have returned to the café earlier and confronted him then and there. Just as she started to text him again, the doorbell rang downstairs. *Finally.* She gathered her hair in a ponytail and hurried to the door. She flung it open, biting down her aggression.

On the steps outside stood Vivien Coombs. She was a stern-looking woman with an air of drab bureaucracy: a pewter-coloured skirt suit and mousy brown hair in a bun.

'Ms Syed,' she said, shifting her large brown bag in front of her torso, as if shielding herself from something. 'May I come in?'

Leila felt an instinctive anxiety about the state of the house: her scruffy outfit, her wet hair, the drift of unopened mail that had gathered on the hallway table, her shoes stacked askew. Then, with a clang of dismay, she remembered that these trivialities no longer mattered in the face of her larger crime. She held the door open and stood aside.

Vivien hovered in the hall, her gaze on the stack of mail.

'Please come in.' Leila's voice belied her stress.

In the living room, Vivien gathered her hands in her lap. 'This is a courtesy call,' she started. 'I received an alert and I didn't just want to send you an email. Which is why I'm here on a Saturday.' She twisted her lips in a show of sympathy. 'Ms Syed, your adoption application has been denied.'

Leila felt the swing of the sky outside and the weaving of her body with it. She had known that this was coming – of *course* it was – but to hear it out loud was stunning.

'I'm sorry.' Vivien looked as if she might reach out and touch her. In the end, she gave the lip of the sofa a little squeeze instead. 'I know how hard you tried, but given the circumstances . . .' She held out an envelope and when Leila didn't take it, she placed it neatly on the coffee table. 'This is the official letter for your records. I'm sorry I couldn't do more.'

Leila scrunched up her cuff in her fist. 'Is there anything that can be done?' She sounded pitiful, her voice cracking with hurt.

'Given the circumstances . . .' Vivien trailed off, for it wasn't necessary to finish the sentence. They would not give a child to a killer. 'I'm sorry. I know how much you wanted this.'

Leila groped for her tools of survival, but all the things she relied on – her drive, ambition, and intellect – were useless in this moment, like fending off rain with a plastic spoon.

Vivien gripped the strap of her bag, readying to leave. 'I'm very sorry for what happened.' She stood. 'I wish you well.'

Leila listened to the clop of her footsteps carry down the hall, taking with it her last hope of ever becoming a mother. Leila had wanted it so desperately. It was why she and Will had split, he unwilling to raise a stranger's child. Leila had resented him, knowing how hard it was for a sole parent to adopt. She had spent months preparing for the application: researching schools in the area, redecorating the house, looking at parenting courses online – everything to show that she was a valid mother; that she could and would love a child. And then this. She had spent so much time worrying about Yasmin, she hadn't fully processed how much it would hurt herself. Leaving Max that day had consigned her to a life of childlessness.

Vivien closed the front door and Leila couldn't even find the strength to cry. She walked upstairs and drew the blinds and collapsed into her bed. A tiny vigilant voice inside warned her not to despair for she knew where that road might end. She closed her eyes, the bright warmth of day still heavy on her lids. She curled into the foetal position, pulled the duvet over her head and blanked out the world in all its cruel entirety.

*

It was late afternoon when Leila stirred. She was groggy and her tongue felt thick and furry. With a start, she realised that it was 2 p.m. She had slept for four full hours. She heard the doorbell ring and realised that that must have made her stir. She sat up in bed, but then heard a key in the lock, its metallic clatter both strange and familiar. The door rasped open.

'Leila?' It was Will's voice – strong and warm and assured – and the relief of hearing something solid made her unduly giddy.

'I'm up here,' she called. Her voice was throaty and there was a dense, hormonal smell in the room. Will walked in and Leila could tell from his wince that she must look a state.

'Honey.' He darted to her side. His bulk tilted the mattress and made her reach for him. 'Are you okay?' he asked.

'They said no.' She gripped his sleeve in her hand. 'The adoption agency. They said no.'

'Oh, sweetheart, surely you knew they would.' He kissed a burl of hair just above her ear. 'What do you need?'

She wrapped her arms around him. 'Stay tonight.'

'Of course I will. I hadn't heard from you. I was worried.' He disentangled himself. 'How are you feeling?'

She shook her head. 'I don't want to talk.'

He kissed her on the lips tenderly. 'Do you want to . . .?' He trailed off, but there was no suggestiveness in his tone; only gentle compassion as if he were offering an act of mercy.

Leila felt the heat of him. 'Yes,' she answered solemnly. 'I do.'

Will leaned into her and traced his lips along her collarbone. He lifted her T-shirt, dipping a finger into her navel ever so slightly. He pulled the fabric taut across her chest, not yet undressing her. He put his mouth over the shape of her nipple and the fabric grew warm with his breath. Leila uncurled for him and her yielding made him aggressive. She lay back and waited for that loss of control that Will always evoked. He was an insanely fantastic lover, but as she lay there beneath his weight, she grew acutely aware of the great size of the room, of the slant of the sun on the wall, the roar of a passing plane. Nothing he did quieted the swell of her thoughts and, afterwards, as he collapsed in a sweaty, satisfied heap, she was left with a sense of vacancy.

He pressed her to his chest. 'Everything will be all right,' he said. 'I'll be there every step of the way.'

She shifted against his warm skin. 'What if I go to prison?' she asked, voicing her fear for the first time.

Will stroked the curve of her shoulder. 'They don't put people like you in prison.'

His words made her bristle, but beneath her feeble moral objection, she found a certain comfort. She was a respectable businesswoman. She had studied hard, raised her own sister, clawed her way to success. Wasn't it true that even in the throes of panic when she first found Max in the back of her car, she had never truly entertained the reality that she might go to prison? Was it naivety – an odious by-product of wealth and privilege – or was it reasonable logic? If Will believed it so, then maybe it was true.

Leila wrapped her duvet around her bare skin, cold despite the heat. 'Thank you,' she whispered.

Will kissed her temple. 'You're welcome,' he said magnanimously.

Chapter Seven

Sunday church bells rang in the distance. Leila glanced at the garden doors, chin angled as if trying to place a familiar voice. She had hoped that Will would stay today, but he had grabbed a piece of toast, kissed her on the lips and said, 'Sorry, gotta go. Deadlines.'

It was a wonder, she thought, that the two of them had wound up together. All her life, she had craved stability and yet married a man who was always rocking one boat or another. He often liked to say: 'If you're a journalist and you never regret anything you write, then you're not trying hard enough to be interesting.'

Perhaps that's what piqued her interest in the first place. They had met at a stuffy party at a high-profile conference in Switzerland. She was there on business and he was there to write a hit piece on how pointless it all was. He had smoothly snatched a martini off a passing tray and rolled his eyes insouciantly. *Do you buy it?* was the first thing he said to her. She tilted her head in query and he leaned in close, waving his drink at the room. *Do you buy it? All this bullshit?* She could see it was a conceit: a well-crafted gambit to catch her attention. Everyone there, including Leila, was professional and strait-laced, and he clearly revelled in being subversive. She laughed, but in a polite, restrained manner, letting him know that she wouldn't be seduced by this act.

'Ah,' he said. 'You're one of *those*.'

'One of what?'

A smile tugged at his lips. 'One of those women who sits in her ivory tower and stares down at us mere mortals, not allowing us to . . .' He traced the pad of his finger along the crease of her elbow. 'Touch you,' he finished.

The move should have raised her feminist hackles, but instead she felt a thrilling sense of momentum. His approach felt adversarial: a cynical battle of wits to see who could outlast whom. Leila played along, distant and aloof, but as they talked, everyone else faded away, leaving only the two of them, lit as if in spotlight, sparring with each other – a zinger here and a zinger back. It was utterly intoxicating. She didn't even notice how much she was drinking and when he asked her to go back with him, she said yes like it was the easiest thing in the world. He held her hand, lacing his fingers with hers, and led her out of the room. He kissed her as soon as the lift doors closed and for the first time in her life, her breathless desire was more than a mere performance acted out for a lover. She slipped her hands beneath his blazer to feel the heft of his body and it made her ache for him.

That night, she behaved in ways she never had before, thinking she would never see him again. The next morning, he asked for her number and she gave it to him with an exaggerated roll of her eye, signalling that she knew this was all a charade. She didn't expect him to call – but he did. For the next few months, they had an intense romance and the way he made her feel – light, carefree, even a little reckless – was addictive, so when he asked her to marry him only seven months after they met, she said yes.

Everyone around her was shocked, not least of all Yasmin who had never known Leila to be impulsive. Of course, Leila was secretly smug that she had landed such a catch – and in a manner so unlike her. She took pleasure in laughing airily when friends remarked that it had happened so fast. 'When you know, you know,' she would say, enjoying their bemusement. She threw a lavish party to celebrate the engagement: a public declaration that, *yes*, she was sure about Will.

Robert Gardner offered to host it at his townhouse in Chelsea and Leila accepted graciously. Will was on fine form and she could see that her friends were impressed. Everything was perfect – the tasteful lights in the manicured trees, the crispness of the Riesling, the unobtrusive breeze – which was why she was annoyed when Yasmin did what she did that evening.

With the guests settled and comfortable, the two sisters walked to the edge of the garden. They sat on a log-carved bench and watched the pleated surface of a pond. Leila nudged Yasmin's shoulder.

'Who'd have thought we'd end up here? Champagne and caviar and this ridiculous ring.' She splayed her fingers and admired the solitaire, an heirloom from Will's family. Yasmin was quiet and Leila sensed that something was wrong. 'Are you okay?' she asked.

Yasmin puckered her lips as if trying to decide whether to talk. 'Can I say something?'

Leila withdrew her hand. 'What?'

Yasmin shifted uncomfortably. 'Are you sure you want to do this so quickly?'

Leila laughed. 'I've never been more sure of anything in my life.'

'But it's so unlike you. *Will* is so unlike you.'

'So?' The humour in her voice faltered.

'Look, I trust your judgement, but Will is . . . He's a bit spoilt, isn't he?'

Leila startled. *Spoilt*. What an ugly way to describe him.

'I always imagined you with someone more mature. Like *way* more mature: a silver fox with his shit together. Someone who wears nice suits and pocket squares and drives a green Jag. Someone who doesn't have anything to prove.'

'Will doesn't have anything to prove.' Leila was defensive.

Yasmin scoffed. 'Yeah, okay,' she said sarcastically.

'Why are you being an arsehole?'

Yasmin flinched, realising that her words had landed poorly. 'Don't be angry, Leila. I just . . . You've spent your life taking care of me and I want someone to take care of you and I just don't know if Will is that person.'

'You don't have to know. *I* know,' snapped Leila. 'Jesus, Yasmin, it's my engagement party and you use it to bitch about Will?' She brushed her lap as if sweeping off a scrap of dirt. 'Okay, so no, Will is not what I imagined for my husband, but I don't need an older man to take care of me. In case you haven't noticed, I'm doing just fine on that front. What I need is someone who makes me forget *this*.' She motioned between her and Yasmin. 'Will makes me forget what we went through. He makes me live in the *here* and *now*; not ten years in the past when we were still hoarding coppers; not ten years in the future like I've been doing my entire life.'

'But is that enough for a marriage?' said Yasmin. 'You can't just live in the here and now. You've got to spend the next forty or fifty years together.'

'He makes me feel good, Yasmin.' Leila's voice softened then. 'And I've felt bad for *such* a long time.'

Yasmin fell silent and the two of them listened to the hum of the party. She hunched against the breeze, a long curl of hair sliding off her bare shoulder. 'Fuck,' she said under her breath.

'What?' asked Leila tensely.

'Now I know why you do it.'

'Do what?'

Yasmin smiled a little and began to sing 'Father and Son' in the deep register of the father who lectures his son on life.

Leila shook her head. 'And now I know why you hate it,' she said.

Yasmin carried on singing, coaxing Leila back into good humour. She slung an arm around her and kissed her shoulder. 'You love him?' she asked solemnly.

'I really do.'

'Then I will love him too,' said Yasmin. 'Come on.' She stood and pulled Leila to her feet. 'Let's do this thing.'

Six months after that, Leila and Will were married. Their first few years were fun as they sought to find a rhythm. Leila wasn't the sort of woman who would try to tame a man like Will. She knew he needed space and so she allowed him on his all-nighters and raucous boys' holidays, knowing that they were important to his sense of identity.

It was only when they started trying for children that he

truly matured. Leila was surprised by how receptive he was, thinking she would have to cajole and persuade him, as so many of her friends had done with partners. Instead, he looked up baby names and sent them to her in a neat little list. Leila could still reel them off now: Amelia, Isabella, Sofia, Olivia, Aisha, Hana, Safa, Rayla. Most men wanted a son, but Will was convinced they would have a daughter.

The first months passed without worry but as the spring drew on, they wondered if something was wrong. At six months, they went to see a doctor and so began the years of trying. It was an assault on her body: a years-long stress position, but she never lost hope. She had achieved everything she had set out to and this would be no different. After the fourth miscarriage, however, she couldn't do it anymore. That's when she mentioned adoption and Will had blankly refused. She had begged him and when that failed, pelted him with blame – *how can you be so cruel, how can you deny me this* – but it did nothing to move him and eventually, after nearly ten years together, Leila and Will split. She had been numbed to the pain of separation by her quest to become a mother. Now that it was no longer possible, she felt doubly robbed.

He had asked her once if he could write about their miscarriages and she had roundly refused. Will mined their personal lives sometimes for his weekly column, but this was far too raw. He argued that writing about trauma was akin to therapy and then sulked for weeks when she still refused. They clashed sometimes, but their affection for each other never waned.

As she sat at home alone now, the thought of him moving on, remarrying, maybe even having children made her sick with pre-emptive jealousy. She tried to shake it off and found herself stalking the house, opening and closing drawers and cupboards as if they might offer diversion. Finally, she decided to go for a run. Outside, the air was dry, and rasped against the back of her throat. The tower block in the distance seemed to warp in the heat, waves rising off it. Leila tightened her ponytail and was putting in her earbuds when she spotted a familiar figure. He was walking away from her and she jogged lightly to catch him.

'Andrew,' she called.

He spun and registered her guiltily. 'Oh. Leila.' He reached for something else to say. 'Sorry. I got your text yesterday and meant to reply, but . . .' He gestured vaguely. 'Time got away from me.'

'Can I talk to you?' she asked curtly.

He shifted his weight from right foot to left. 'About what?'

Leila gestured in the direction of her house. 'Can we go inside?'

He looked at his watch. 'Actually, I don't have very long.'

'I saw you yesterday,' she said. 'At the Copper Kettle.'

He looked at her blankly. 'Oh, sorry, I didn't see you.'

'Who were you with?'

He tensed. 'What were you doing? *Following* me?'

'Fuck you, Andrew,' she said with more acid than intended. She saw the flash of hurt on his face and groaned with frustration. 'Please tell me you're not cheating.'

He balked. 'How can you ask me that?' He turned away from her and stared at the horizon. 'You don't get to do that, Leila. You don't get to accuse me of something like that.'

She waited for him to look at her. 'You *know* what it would do to her.'

'Worse than what *you* did to her?'

His words landed like a slap. Leila stared at him, unable to process the shock. 'How can you say that?' Her voice was a hoarse whisper.

He thrust his face close to hers, menacingly close. 'It's not nice, is it? To be accused of something so shitty?'

She fought the urge to push him. 'I just want to know who she is.'

'It's none of your fucking business!'

'So it's true then?'

'No, it's not fucking true!' He took a ragged breath, and then another. 'If you must fucking know, she's a therapist.'

'Therapists don't *stroke* their clients.'

He looked at her as if she might be an alien. 'How long were you watching for?'

'I saw all of it,' she bluffed.

'Don't be an arsehole, Leila.' When she didn't respond, he threw up his hands. 'You remember our wedding in Denmark?'

Leila frowned. Andrew and Yasmin's wedding was eight years ago now. 'Yes.'

'You remember Ana?'

Leila was hit with a bolt of recognition. The delicate cheekbones and slender neck. 'It was your *sister*?'

'Yes, it was my fucking sister in the café. She flew straight here when she heard. Now back off, Leila. Stop being so fucking controlling.'

She flinched. It was the same accusation that Yasmin often made. Andrew using it now, after everything she'd done to help, filled her with resentment. She reached out a hand to bridge their distance, but Andrew batted it away.

'Don't,' he said sharply. 'Just leave us alone for a while.' He backed away and turned, leaving her mute in the middle of the street.

*

Yasmin looked on silently, masked by the bulk of a kerbside tree outside Leila's house. Her heart raced as she watched her sister and husband on the street. Leila was gesticulating wildly, which was jarring on its own. Usually when she was angry, she descended into a sulk like the martyr she liked to be. She reached for Andrew and he batted her away. Yasmin made a low gasp of a sound. She had never seen him so spirited.

She watched them remonstrate before Andrew turned away. But then, as if a cog had stopped in his brain, he paused, then turned to face Leila again. He looked at her with such intensity, it took Yasmin's breath away. She watched, transfixed, as Andrew closed the distance between them and pulled Leila into his arms.

The shock of it almost made her believe that they were entirely different people; that this was a cruel illusion. But no, that was her husband and in his arms was Leila, her head tucked against his chest and her hand gripping his shirt. She had barely seen them touch before, let alone embrace. To see them clinched together like this seemed like an obscenity. Their energy wasn't sexual but the sheer intensity was undeniable. Yasmin continued to gawk, physically unable to move. She marvelled at the caprices of fate that had led her there in that moment. At home, she had finished the last of the milk and forced herself to the shop on the corner, but then at the last minute, decided to dogleg to Leila's. The last thing she expected to find was this. She imagined marching over to them. What would she do? Coolly tap her sister on the shoulder? Or grip her hair and pull her back? Yasmin was mesmerised, as if watching a car upturn in slow motion.

Finally, they pulled apart and Leila seemed to wipe at her eyes. Andrew reached out and held her hand and even from a distance, Yasmin could see him press his thumb in her palm the way he did with *her*. With a nod, Leila stepped around him and broke into a jog. Andrew's gaze followed her until she turned the corner. He glanced over his shoulder and the look on his face was clear: guilt.

Yasmin gripped the spikes of the iron gate that fringed the small park in the square. Her thoughts clamoured and she tried to sort through the cords of them to work out what she'd seen. There was no single incriminating act: no kiss on the lips, no squeeze of the flesh, but the intimacy was unmistakable.

Yasmin looked at the gleaming facade of Leila's house. She had half a mind to pick up a rock and hurl it through the window. *Perfect Leila with her perfect fucking life.* Yasmin would never admit it – not even to her therapist – but a small delinquent part of her had been smug about Leila's breakup. Marriage and motherhood were the only things that Yasmin had over Leila. That she had taken Max felt like an act of vengeance. Yasmin knew it couldn't be true, but she needed someone to blame. Seeing Leila with Andrew gave her all the more reason.

Yasmin marched up the steps and plucked the spare key from a secret compartment in the ceramic plant pot. She let herself in and entered the alarm key code, knowing that the digits – 8093 – had no significance at all, typical of Leila.

Yasmin walked in and was angered to see zero signs of disarray. In the living room, she pushed over a pile of *New Yorkers*, letting the top two slip to the floor. She paused by the garden door and flexed her fingers, wanting to put her fist through the glass. She drank a glass of juice and left it on the counter. She wandered upstairs and was only gratified when she reached the master bedroom and saw that the blinds were drawn and the bed was still unmade.

She stepped into the bathroom and her gaze was drawn to the free-standing tub, its sublime lines shiny and white. How shocked would Leila be if she came home to find Yasmin in that bath? She was tempted to do it from spite. She sat on the lip and swung her legs inside, then slid down to the base, feeling the cold enamel on her calves.

In that white cocoon, the memories came rushing back. When Toby was diagnosed, Yasmin had sworn that she would bear it, that she wouldn't crumble like Leila expected, but the challenge was so hard, so *vast*, that no sane person could withstand it.

On the worst nights, when Toby's crying escalated to a sort of bleating, she thought she would lose her mind, that it would shatter apart and burst through the room like remnants of stars, but no – she was expected to keep on. When he died, Yasmin had cried for days and when after a month, the pain didn't fade, all she wanted was for it to end. To lose Max too after all of that left her feeling numb, as if she had spent all her sadness and sorrow and had nothing left to give.

She leaned her head on the hard ridge of the bath. She felt so tired, so overcome. She closed her eyes and, against the coolness and white, let herself drift off to sleep.

*

Leila kicked her front gate shut, flinching when it clanged against the latch. She secured it with her little finger and walked into the house. She set down the scant groceries, loose for want of a bag, and caught the two ripe peaches that rolled to the edge of the counter. As she put them in a bowl, she noticed a glass by the sink, speckled with the pulp of oranges. She frowned. Had she left it there before her run? She invariably filled hers with water to make it easier to wash. She inspected it as if it might offer an answer, then set it down and checked her phone. Had Will popped by without telling her? She saw that she had no messages. Perhaps she'd just forgotten. She washed the glass, then headed to the bathroom upstairs. She stripped off her yellow tank top and turned to toss it in the laundry basket. That's when she caught the shock of black hair strewn across the bath. She screeched in horror – a concussive howl of a sound.

Yasmin shot up in the bath and Leila's scream snuffed out, replaced by the vinegar jump of shock. The two sisters locked eyes – an electric rupture in the air. Yasmin winced as if caught in the sweep of torchlight. And, then, Leila was on the floor, folding sideways like a domino, knocked clean off her feet. She made a strange burbling sound and she wasn't sure if the words coming from her mouth were pleas or expletives. She trembled and the words took shape in the panting of her breath. *How could you? How could you? How could you?*

'Yasmin, what are you *doing* here?' she cried. 'How did you get here?' She noticed the glazed look in her eye. 'Oh, God. Did you take something?' She vaulted up and pelted to her side. She unfurled Yasmin's fingers, then searched the base of the bath. 'Did you take something? What did you take?' She cupped her cheek with a palm. 'Yasmin, what did you take?'

'No.' Her voice was hazy and disoriented. 'No, I didn't.'

'Tell me the truth.'

Yasmin shoved her hand away. 'I didn't take anything.'

Leila studied her, looking for signs of narcosis.

'I didn't take anything!'

Leila slumped against the panel of the bath. 'Then what are you *doing* here?' She reached for her but Yasmin jerked away. Leila exhaled, then leaned back on her heels. 'Yasmin,' she said softly. 'Please get out of there.'

Her lips twitched defiantly, but she clambered up and out. She sat on the lip of the bath and sneered at the lines of Leila's abs.

Leila noticed and pulled her top back over her sports bra, wincing as the damp fabric pasted to her skin. 'What the hell is going on?'

'You tell me. You're the one who's been out and about.'

Leila studied her. Was there something chemical in the slur of her words?

'So go on,' said Yasmin tartly. 'Tell me then. What's been going on?' She rose to her feet. 'Are you fucking my husband?'

Leila balked. 'What—'

'I saw you,' she said acidly. 'I saw you both together.'

Leila's mouth moved but made no sound.

'I saw you all over him.'

'When?'

Yasmin stared at her. 'When do you think?'

Leila groped for a way to placate her.

'So – *are* you? Fucking my husband? Is this house and your business and your fancy car and your fat bank account not enough for you? You have to take my husband too?'

'Don't do this.'

'Do what!?'

'Pit us against each other. I've always been on your side.'

'Oh, fuck off, Leila!'

'I was just comforting him.' Leila took a step back. 'Do you really believe I'd do anything with Andrew?'

The air grew taut in the room, stretching and stretching until it seemed that something would break. 'You might as well,' spat Yasmin. 'Everything you have, everything you do is perfect. Flying to New York for business meetings, champagne breakfasts, being courted by millionaires. Your career, your success, even your fucking body,' she said disgustedly. 'Everything is so fucking perfect.' Her voice broke. 'Max is the one thing I had that mattered.'

'Yasmin, you are so much more than me.'

'Don't fucking patronise me,' she snarled. 'I know you want a child, Leila, but you have *everything* else. I had one thing and now that's gone, so what am I meant to do?'

Leila watched her and her heartbreak was so acute, she had to look away. 'I'm sorry,' she said to the wall, her own voice freighted with tears.

'Tell me one thing, Leila. Just tell me this one thing. Did you mean to leave him?'

Leila exhaled sharply; a deliberate show of disbelief.

'I know you didn't mean for him to die, but did you leave him on purpose and go to the office?'

Caught in the blare of the question, Leila tried to find the best answer; the one that offered most comfort. 'No, Yasmin,' she said, her voice low and earnest. 'I didn't mean to leave him.'

Something hard flashed in her eyes. 'I don't believe you.'

'I would never . . .'

'But you *would*,' snapped Yasmin. 'You left me.'

'That was different. You were older. You could take care of yourself.'

'I was eleven.'

'I know, but . . .' Leila smarted. 'I was stuck.'

'And you weren't stuck when a multimillion deal at Syed&Gardner was at risk? You didn't think you had to go and deal with it?'

'That's not what happened.'

'Just tell me the truth.'

'I promise you.' Leila's voice was forceful, verging on the cusp of anger. 'That's the truth.'

Yasmin looked at her coolly. 'I don't believe you.' She raised a finger at her. 'I don't want you to talk to me until after the trial.'

'Yasmin, that's *five* months away.'

'I don't care. I don't want to talk to you.'

'Yasmin—'

'I swear to God, Leila.' Yasmin's voice dropped low and lethal. 'If you contact me, I will call the police and tell them you're breaking your bail.'

'You wouldn't.'

'I would. And I will.'

Leila felt her anguish build. 'Don't do this.'

Yasmin stared at her coldly. 'You killed my child, Leila. You'll be lucky if I ever speak to you again.'

'Wait.' Leila reached out to stop her leaving, but Yasmin smacked her away.

'Stay away from me.' Her face twisted in an ugly grimace. 'And stay *the fuck* away from my husband.' She stormed out of the house and slammed the door behind her.

Leila sagged against the cold tile wall. What a cruel limbo this was: to have her sister so near, but not be allowed to see her. She faced five long months like this. Five months to reckon with what she did. Five months to bear this grief and, beneath it all, tucked away in a dark place, the wet heave of guilt.

*

DS Chris Shepherd pored over the paperwork, checking the i's and t's ahead of the December trial. He trusted the CPS, but with multiple parties involved – the Met, the CPS, the barrister, the courts – wires were often crossed. Too many times he had seen a case collapse because no one checked a detail with a witness, or informed them of a change of date. CPS caseworkers were overburdened, as was his own team, and that meant not just cutting corners sometimes but skipping laps entirely.

They couldn't afford a mistake in Leila Syed's case. A successful prosecution was akin to building a wall: a brick-by-brick erection. Each brick was a piece of evidence that had to hold up in court. The defence had to take just a single brick to establish reasonable doubt, such was the burden of proof.

Shep leaned back and laced his fingers behind his head, certain that the pieces were all in place. He spun his chair to offer a round of coffee but realised that the office was empty. It was often this way, he the only non-parent on the team. He didn't mind the long hours and extra work; rather enjoyed it in fact. What he *did* mind was the constant reminders. *It's all right for you; you don't have three kids to put to bed* – a sort of performative martyrdom designed to show their selflessness. Shep in comparison had nothing and no one, such was the implication. What he hated even more was the suggestion that he couldn't possibly *feel* as deeply because he wasn't a father, as if he had an empathy deficiency that could only be fixed with offspring.

In dwelling on this, he was struck by his own hypocrisy. Hadn't he made the very same assumption about Leila Syed? Childless women were treated with even more contempt than men – a fact that would surely be used by the prosecution in Leila's case. It was no coincidence that femmes fatales in books and films were never shown to have children.

He heard the lift ping open as Karen, the cleaner, arrived for her shift. He took it as a sign to pack up for the evening. He piled up his files and shut down his creaky computer. The trial was in five months' time and everything was in place. Only then would they learn the truth. Only then would he know if Leila Syed was guilty of killing her three-year-old nephew.

PART II

PART II

Chapter Eight

The English winter was a dangerous thing. Even *sound* seemed to shrink beneath it. There was no jaunty birdsong or the crunch of leaves underfoot, only a sense of closing in. Leila wondered how Yasmin was coping. Her sister, like their mother, always struggled at this time of year as if the shrouding of sun also snuffed something inside her. Leila hadn't seen her in five months, not even by chance on the high street. Andrew had sent her weekly updates, but of course it wasn't the same. Today, in court, their paths would finally cross.

Leila had spent two hours preparing. She wore a navy blue trouser suit that tapered at the ankles, giving her a neat silhouette. As she paced her room, however, the suit felt stiff and unyielding – cinching her in all the wrong places. She had worked from home for the last five months with occasional weekends at the office. The sudden switch to business wear felt unwieldy and oppressive. She considered changing into something more casual, but knew it would tip her from being early to being just on time, and she couldn't risk being late. Besides, she needed to present the best version of herself.

In the cab en route to court, she felt a loping in her stomach:

the old, familiar ache of dealing with authority. All her life it had been something to battle; something to defeat. She remembered standing up in family court and applying to adopt Yasmin. The way she was treated, the shifting court dates, being told to go to Manchester at a moment's notice and then being sent back, the round robin of the justice system making her feel sick and helpless. And now it would decide her fate. This creaky, unsteady system would decide if she would go to prison or be presumed innocent.

She arrived at Inner London Crown Court and passed through security. It was a building of two parts. The front was grand and imposing with airy corridors, high ceilings and huge Diocletian windows that enchanted Leila. She wished she could get close to them, perhaps even sketch them. The rear was grey and plastic with austere schoolhouse stairs. It was there that she sat and waited, breathing slowly and deliberately to keep herself from shaking.

The usher approached and nodded: a grave signal that it was now time. Leila followed him to the courtroom and was led into the dock, an airless box fenced with bulletproof Perspex. On seeing the judge's bench at the opposite end, Leila fought the urge to cry. She had imagined this many times, but it was impossible to know how small she would feel when the moment arrived. She glanced around the room and built a mental blueprint. The witness box stood to her right and the jury box to her left, the two facing each other. In the middle were rows of benches for the barristers and solicitors. Leila's lawyer, Clara Pearson, sat closest to the jury box, calmly browsing a file. Above Leila, hidden from her view, was the public gallery. She wondered if Yasmin was up there watching.

'All rise!' called the usher.

Judge Warren entered the room. He was a fine-boned man with thin lips that were almost the same shade as his skin. His slate-grey eyes were beady and framed by thin-rimmed glasses. When he spoke, his deep, commanding voice seemed incongruous, like he might have borrowed it from someone else. He called for the jury, who filed in solemnly.

Leila instinctively scanned the women, looking for those who might have children and be predisposed against her. Sometimes, she felt awkward in front of mothers and their talk of an entire world to which she wasn't privy. She felt cold and rake-like next to them, her body too hard and thin. She thought back to a study that hit the headlines in 2019 for finding that unmarried, child-free women were the happiest in society. There was much cheering by these women and like always, it was 'us' against 'them', a pitting of the haves and have-nots who *also* happened to be haves because they *had* time, disposable income, free will and freedom, so of course they could never complain. Leila saw it play out again and again. There was that viral post by a woman who said she *hated* childless women because they swanned around Disney World in slutty shorts and dared to lengthen the ice cream queue. How scornful people were of childless women. *Women like me*, thought Leila. Would the jury judge her for this?

She watched them now: twelve jurors, five men and seven women with a balance of ethnicities. All the women were in their late thirties or forties with the exception of one girl, possibly in her late twenties. She had pale, catlike eyes and a cool demeanour that set her apart from the others. Might she be Leila's saviour? Courts preferred unanimous decisions but, at a push, would accept a majority of ten to two. The girl glanced over at Leila, who tried to smile at her – a discreet call for empathy – but the girl looked away, seemingly bored or disinterested. How awful it was to sit here at the mercy of strangers. They knew nothing of her and her life. They knew nothing of how fiercely she had loved Max.

The prosecuting barrister stood, dressed in a black gown and horsehair wig. Edward Forshall had a groomed American look: a slight tan and a strong jaw with the merest softening around his jowls, youth slipping into middle age. His brown eyes were deep-set beneath heavy brows that gave him a piercing stare. When he spoke, his voice was rich and warm; well spoken but stopping just short of plummy. He introduced himself and explained that 'his learned friend' Clara Pearson was the defending counsel – his opponent of sorts. Then, he segued to his opening speech.

'Members of the jury, you might describe what you hear today and over the coming week as a "tragedy". You will reach for gentler terms and euphemisms: "a shocking mistake" or "a lapse of memory" – but what happened on Monday the 12th of July this year was not a mere tragedy. It was the direct result of a wilful act.

'Here are the facts of the case: on the morning in question, the defendant Leila Syed agreed to drive her nephew to nursery three-and-a-half miles away. The nursery was a five-minute detour from her own office building and it was a fairly easy thing to do. However, en route, Ms Syed received a call from her office with an emergency. This emergency was so large, it threatened a multimillion-pound deal that her firm was pursuing.

'Ms Syed was ten minutes away from her office and, at this juncture, she had two options: make the detour to the nursery, meaning it would take her twice as long to reach the office, or go straight there, deal with the emergency, then drop Max off at nursery. We submit that Ms Syed chose the latter; that she drove straight to the office and *intentionally* left Max in her car while she dealt with the emergency.'

Leila felt the glare of the jury and dared not look up to meet it.

Edward Forshall laced his fingers. 'Now, members of the jury, many of you might be parents. You will have had scares. You might have briefly lost a child in a park or at a crowded beach. We all know the horror of what can happen in those situations. "There but for the grace of God," you might say – but this case is not about poor parenting or simple mistakes or losing a child momentarily. In this case, Ms Syed left a three-year-old child in a hot car. She left a child who was in her sole care in the back of a car with the doors and windows locked. She left him there for three hours. She did that on an extremely hot day; the hottest of the year in fact. As a direct result, Max lost his young life. Ms Syed claims that she completely forgot that he was there.'

Edward swept a dismissive hand at her. 'She claims that this emergency – which would have a staggering effect on her company – had absolutely nothing to do with what happened that morning. She would have us believe that she calmly and independently drove to the office and simply *forgot* that her nephew was there.' He jeered with incredulity.

'Ms Syed claims that she has never driven her nephew to school before by way of explaining why she forgot, but you will hear evidence otherwise. She claims that she was perfectly willing to look after Max but you will hear evidence that directly contradicts this – from Ms Syed's own acquaintances.'

He pressed his palms together. 'Ms Syed left Max in the car by her own admission. She claims she did it by mistake, but there was no mistake that day. There was a conscious, deliberate decision to leave Max in the car while she attended to her company. The act of leaving him on such a hot day was lethal and directly led to his death. Taken together, it is clear: Leila Syed is guilty of manslaughter.' He paused and looked at the jury gravely. 'I'm sure you will take no pleasure in reaching such a conclusion, but those are the facts of the case and based on the facts, Ms Syed is guilty. *Guilty* is the verdict we ask you to return.' He ducked his head in a humble flourish.

Leila's skin bristled as she listened. How appalling it was to be painted this way. How convenient to adopt the trope of a career woman in thrall to ambition. None of it was true. When Andrew had asked her for help, Leila had agreed because she always put Yasmin first. That act had cost her so much and to sit and watch them brand her as callous felt like a public flogging.

*

Edward Forshall called the first witness for the prosecution and Leila balked when she saw that it was Yasmin. She had expected Andrew, for it had all started with him. She watched the jury watch Yasmin and understood in an instant. For maximum emotional impact, you start with the mother. *Of course* you start with the mother.

Yasmin wore a pale pink shift dress, so light it was almost white. Her hair was in a chignon and she wore minimal makeup. Her large eyes had the finest slick of eyeliner and her lips were a pale plum colour. She looked like a receptionist at a high-end law firm or something equally inoffensive. A dark part of Leila was annoyed by this muting of Yasmin's beauty. Had she swapped out the red lipstick strategically to present herself more palatably? Yasmin, in full glory, raised the hackles of other women, something she found amusing. This makeup and outfit showed a different woman.

Leila strained to catch her eye but was studiously avoided. She wished now that she had made one last attempt to talk to Yasmin and find out what she was thinking. Was she seething with vengeance? Would she seal Leila's fate today?

'Ms Syed,' Edward started, his tone loaded with gravity. 'What kind of aunt was Leila Syed?'

Leila craned her neck, waiting for Yasmin to look at her but she only stared ahead, her gaze fixed on a point by the jury.

'She was a good aunt,' said Yasmin in a monotone.

'Loving?'

'Yes. I would say so.'

Edward angled his head. 'Forgive me, but I detect some hesitation.'

Yasmin smoothed her dress. 'Well, she wasn't affectionate if that's what you mean.' She sensed the shift of the jurors and backpedalled quickly. 'I don't mean that she wasn't affectionate as in she didn't feel affection; more that she didn't show it. She wasn't tactile or touchy feely.'

Leila felt a knot of anxiety. Yasmin wasn't wrong but how could the jury know that every time she held Max, it made her yearn for her own? The heft of him in her lap, his baby-soft palm on her cheek, his determined clumsy kisses unlocked fresh pain in some deep-down cavity.

'Would you say she was cold with him?'

Yasmin frowned. 'No. She was very . . . invested. She bought him lots of toys and books and always checked on how he was doing.'

'You moved home in 2020 to be closer to her. Did you rely on her for babysitting?'

Yasmin gripped the wooden rail of the witness box. 'Yes.'

'How often?'

'Roughly once a fortnight.'

Leila bristled. It was more like once a week.

'How did Leila react to this?'

Yasmin tensed for a second. 'She was largely fine. Sometimes I knew we were being intrusive.'

'What made you think that?'

'Well, she would sometimes make a point, like, "I've got a lot of work to catch up on so I might just have to stick on a DVD for him" – that sort of thing.'

'So, when she was looking after him, she would leave him on his own with a DVD?'

Yasmin gestured vaguely. 'Well, not on his own – at least I don't think so.'

'So she would work in the living room while there was a three-year-old child in it *and* a DVD?'

'Well – I don't know.'

'Does she have a desk in the living room?'

'No.'

'But she has a study?'

'Yes.'

'Leila is an architect. Do you think it's likely that she would spread out her work on the living room floor, or would she go to her study?'

'I couldn't say.'

Clara Pearson huffed pointedly and Edward soon moved on. 'Has Leila done anything to make you doubt her ability as a childminder?'

'No. If I thought that, then I wouldn't have left Max in her care.'

'As far as you know, Leila has never left him on his own for an extended period of time?'

'No.'

'Would you agree that that would be unacceptable?'

'Yes.'

'How old do you think a child should be before he or she can be left alone?'

Yasmin hesitated. 'Well, sixteen.'

Edward smiled indulgently. 'That's the socially acceptable answer, but I'm a parent too and I know that we've all done things we feel guilty about, like leaving a child on his own – so I ask you to answer honestly. How old do you think a child needs to be before you can leave him on his own?'

Yasmin shifted on her feet, eyes darting to the judge, the jury and then a spot on the far wall.

'Thirteen maybe.'

'"Thirteen maybe",' he repeated. 'Not twelve?'

'No.'

'Not eleven?'

Yasmin tensed. 'No.'

Leila watched and felt an acid-twist in her gut. How could they possibly know?

Edward drew out a piece of paper, but he did not read it; used it more for effect. 'Yasmin, is it true that you were in your sister's care from the age of eleven to eighteen?'

'Yes.'

'Do you remember what happened in January of 2002?'

Yasmin kneaded one hand with the other.

'Ms Syed, will you share this with the court?'

Now Yasmin did look at Leila but only for a second. 'We were living in a flat in Gants Hill. Leila got an evening job and had to go away for training.'

'Where did she go?'

'To the Cotswolds.'

'For how long?'

'Three days.'

'In whose care did she leave you?'

Yasmin coloured. 'I stayed on my own.'

'Ah, I see. And how old were you? Sixteen?' He waited. 'Ms Syed?'

'Eleven,' said Yasmin.

There was a shifting in the room: jurors craning forward and whispers in the gallery.

'Eleven!' said Edward, scratching his wig with feigned confusion. 'You were eleven years old and your sister – your legal guardian – left you alone in east London for an entire three days?'

Leila flushed. She remembered that week clearly. She had asked her new employers if there was access to childcare. She had even considered taking Yasmin with her and hiding her in her hotel room. She was completely stuck and wondered if Mr Horace across the hall might help, but that was even worse than leaving her alone. Finally, she had stocked up on groceries and left Yasmin with strict instructions not to go out at all. The three days passed in a blur of worry and she returned in a state of mania, convinced that she would unlock the door and find Yasmin gutted on the floor. When she saw her curled on the futon, their duvet heaped around her shoulders, Butterkist popcorn trailing to the floor, Leila almost cried with relief. Not wanting to scare her sister, she greeted her casually, then went into the bathroom and wept. Later, they had a blazing row when Leila spotted the chicken-shop box in the bin. She had shouted at Yasmin – half angry, half crying. *What if something had happened to you?* Tragedy could so easily have befallen then. Instead, it had lain in wait, striking two decades later.

'Ms Syed.' Edward's voice grew gentle, as if breaking bad news. 'Does that sound like the actions of a responsible adult?'

Yasmin's lips creased in a grimace. 'We were both young.'

'But it demonstrates something, doesn't it? About Leila Syed and her willingness to take risks?'

Yasmin shifted but didn't say anything or come to Leila's defence, realising perhaps that Edward was correct. It took a certain kind of person to do what she did, to take such a risk with the safety of someone she loved.

'Ms Syed,' said Edward softly. 'As a mother, do you think that was a warranted risk?'

Yasmin didn't speak until Edward pressed her again. Then, she answered honestly: 'No.'

Leila dug her fingers into her knees and pressed to the point of pain. *I'm sorry*, she wanted to cry. *I'm sorry, Yasmin, for everything I've put you through.*

'I want to turn to the morning of 12th July,' said Edward. 'Your husband asked your sister to drive Max to school. Was this unusual?'

'Yes. We try not to bother Leila in the mornings.'

'Oh? Why is that?'

Yasmin hesitated. 'Well, she's usually happy to look after Max but the last time I asked her to come over in the morning, she snapped at me.'

'Why?'

'Well, she packs her mornings so that the afternoons are free for thinking time. She schedules everything. It's called time-boxing.'

'So you were reluctant to ask for help in the morning? Did it surprise you to learn that your husband had called her?'

'Yes. I've told him not to.'

'You have specifically told him not to contact your sister in the mornings?'

'Yes.'

'Because she's exceedingly busy?'

'Yes.'

Leila could remember the morning that Yasmin referred to. It was five months before Max's death – a cold February morning. Leila had a meeting with a law firm who wanted her to bid for their Holborn office. It was a lucrative project but also good for her portfolio. The old boys' network of law firms was a difficult one to break into and she had used all her powers of persuasion to get a seat at the table.

But you're your own boss. You have flexibility where I don't,

Yasmin had whined. *He's not my child*, Leila had snapped. She remembered the tense silence in the moments after. *Sorry I asked. I won't again,* Yasmin had huffed and hung up. And she was true to her word. In the ensuing months, Leila was never asked to help in the mornings. Yasmin was nothing if not stubborn. Neither sister brought it up again and the next time Yasmin asked for help – on a Saturday evening – Leila readily agreed and that was that. She hadn't known that Andrew was under instruction not to approach her for help.

'So here are the things we know so far,' said Edward. 'Leila explicitly told you that, on occasion, she would leave Max to his own devices with a DVD; we know that she left you on your own for three whole days when you were eleven years old; and we know that she categorically did *not* like to look after Max in the mornings when she was most busy.'

Yasmin fiddled with a button on her dress.

'Do you think it's possible that your sister intentionally left Max in the car to attend to her emergency?'

Yasmin took a moment to answer. 'I don't know.'

In that moment, Leila saw that Yasmin truly doubted her; she truly thought it was possible that Leila had risked Max's life for a business deal. She shook her head in a stagey way to show the jury that she was appalled.

Edward probed further. 'Yasmin, I know this is painful but you need to answer truthfully. Knowing what you know – knowing that your sister has left a child alone before – do you think it's possible that she left Max intentionally?'

Yasmin didn't speak for a moment. Then, quietly, she admitted, 'Yes.'

'A little louder if you will.'

Yasmin cleared her throat. 'Yes, it's possible.'

Leila felt the yielding of strength inside her, a breaking of a dam. Her own sister had just condemned her. She fixated on this vital fact as the rest of Edward's questions played out on a distant stage. Yasmin didn't believe her, and if Yasmin didn't, what hope did she have with the jury?

*

After lunch, it was Clara's turn to examine Yasmin. She started with condolences but issued them in a clipped, efficient manner that suggested she wouldn't coddle the witness. Leila felt concerned for her sister. Usually, when Yasmin sparred with someone smarter, Leila intervened to smooth the sharp edge of debate. Yasmin would get caught in arguments about Palestine or gun control, of which she knew nearly nothing, and it was up to Leila to stop her from making a fool of herself. Here, pitched against a lawyer, Yasmin would surely struggle, a fact that worried Leila. She wanted Clara to be kind, but *needed* her to be harsh.

'Ms Syed, on the occasions when you left Max with Leila, and she warned you that she may have to occupy him with a DVD, did you object to this?'

Yasmin considered this. 'No.'

'Why not?'

'I didn't think there was anything wrong with it. I sometimes did it myself.'

'And did your husband ever leave your son with a DVD?'

'Yes. I mean, not for a long period of time but he might leave the DVD on and do some gardening.'

'As any parent might do?'

'Yes.'

'Isn't it true that Leila looked after you from the ages of eleven to eighteen, when she herself was aged eighteen to twenty-five?'

'Yes.'

'We've heard that at the very beginning of this period, Leila supplied you with a full kitchen's worth of groceries and strict instructions to stay at home while she fulfilled an important work obligation in the Cotswolds. Is that correct?'

'Yes.'

'Why didn't she leave you with another adult?'

'Because there was no one else to help.'

Clara clucked with surprise. 'You mean to say there was no one at all? No parents, no aunts, no uncles, no adults?'

'No. It's always been just me and her.'

Clara angled her head. 'So, Leila was truly stuck but if she didn't take that job, she wouldn't be able to provide food for you?'

Edward Forshall sighed and directed something at Clara. A trace of a smile tugged at her lips.

'That's right,' answered Yasmin.

'Did she ever leave you again after that occasion?'

'No.'

'Twenty years have passed since then. Is it fair to say that Leila developed as a guardian after that?'

'Yes.'

'Enough for you to entrust her with your son?'

'Yes.'

Clare nodded meditatively. 'Now, I want to move on to the

morning of the incident. You said that you tried not to bother Leila in the mornings and told your husband not to either. So it follows that Leila was busy that morning?'

'Yes.'

'Am I right that Max has a rear-facing car seat?'

'Yes.'

'Is it also true that you told Leila that you once considered establishing a system – like a shoe or toy on the passenger seat – to remind yourself that your son was in the car?'

'Yes.'

'Did you ever use this system?'

'No.'

'Did you ever tell Leila to do this?'

'No.'

'Okay, so if you – as Max's parents – considered using a system so that you would not forget your own son, doesn't it follow that a person like Leila who is not used to having a child in her car may make the same mistake?'

Yasmin batted at a strand of hair. 'I . . . Yes.'

'So you agree that it's perfectly possible that Leila – who was doing you a favour on a busy morning where she was preoccupied – may have genuinely forgotten that Max was in the car?'

'But she never forgets anything,' Yasmin said by instinct.

A juror looked over at Leila and she squirmed beneath her gaze.

'But if you as a mother were afraid of forgetting your own son – *so* afraid in fact that you even discussed a system with your husband – isn't it possible, likely even, that a person who isn't used to having a child in the car might tragically forget him; that it wasn't an irresponsible selfish act, but just pure, inexplicable tragedy?'

Yasmin grew flustered as she tried to decipher the question. 'Ms Syed?'

'Yes,' she admitted. 'It's possible.'

Leila felt the tension break, easing its grip on her ribcage. It did not undo the earlier damage, but it laid the seed of reasonable doubt and for that Leila was grateful. She tried to catch Yasmin's eye to acknowledge this small reprieve, but her sister did not look at her – then or at any other point during the rest of the afternoon.

*

As soon as the light waned outside, Judge Warren adjourned for the day. Leila watched the courtroom empty, feeling jumpy and wired, her nerves loud and jangly. She was grateful when Will met her outside and steered her through the courthouse, holding her elbow possessively as he guided her to his car.

At home, she collapsed on the sofa, caught in the white aftershock that follows funerals and natural disasters. She had survived her first day in court.

Will poured her a glass of wine and placed it on a stool beside her. 'How are you feeling?' he asked.

'Okay,' she answered by rote.

Gently, he brushed her chin with a knuckle. 'Hey.' He waited for her to look at him. 'Come on. How are you really feeling?'

She smiled weakly. 'Like I've been hit by a train.'

'You're doing great.'

Leila found his concern reassuring. Will usually silver-lined all her problems and peppered her with solutions instead of actively listening. She liked this more solicitous version.

He pressed the wineglass into her hand. 'Are you upset with Yasmin?'

'I don't really want to talk about it,' she said with a note of apology.

'Come on, sweetheart. Tell me what you're thinking. It can't have been easy hearing the things she said today.'

Leila lifted a shoulder weakly.

'Don't you think she should have defended you better?'

'I don't know, Will.'

'You're not angry at her?'

Leila motioned with her glass and the wine came dangerously close to spilling. 'I don't have the right to be angry with her.'

'That's not the point though.' He waited for a beat. '*Are* you angry at her?'

'I just want to get through the trial before I figure out what I'm feeling.'

He angled his head in doubt. 'It'll be easier if you talk about it.'

She set down her glass. 'I will. In time.'

He studied her for a moment, then tucked a panel of her hair to one side. 'Of course,' he said finally.

Leila felt herself relax. 'We don't need to talk. Just stay here awhile.'

'Of course,' he repeated.

Leila leaned against him and closed her eyes, feeling her mind quieten for one merciful moment.

Chapter Nine

Andrew Hansson stood in the witness box. He was cleanly shaven and his short blond hair had a wet sheen, teased into shape by gel or hairspray. He wore a pale blue shirt with a black suit, and looked handsome in a sombre, contemplative way.

Leila watched him, noting the signs of clear unease: the smoothing of his tie, the pocketing of his left hand, the twiddling of a button. How strange it was to see him, a comrade of sorts, harnessed by those who sought to imprison her. The two of them locked eyes and Andrew gave her a small, sympathetic smile. Leila flushed with gratitude, for it confirmed that he didn't want to be there, speaking against her when she had done so much for him.

Edward Forshall began. 'Mr Hansson, in your police interview, you said that you didn't want to ask your sister-in-law for help. Why was this?'

Andrew cleared his throat. 'Because I didn't want to impose on her.'

'Because she's exceedingly busy in the mornings; likes to "time-box" her day?'

Andrew frowned. 'Well, she already does a lot for us so I didn't want to take advantage.'

'Was she hesitant on the phone when you called?'

'No.'

Edward glanced up swiftly as if he was expecting a different answer. 'Not even a little?'

'Well, no. I mean, she . . . No, she was fine.'

Leila bristled. Why was he dithering? She had been perfectly willing to help.

'Okay, when she arrived at your home, how did she seem to you?'

'She was fine.'

'Not stressed?'

'Not any more than usual.'

'So she's usually stressed?'

Andrew was at a loss. 'No, I just mean that she didn't seem any more or less stressed than she usually would.'

Edward nodded, slowly, as if he had learnt a secret. 'Mr Hansson, how would you describe your sister-in-law?'

Andrew considered the question, clearly keen to get it right. 'She's a strong person. Formidable, actually. She's loyal and incredibly hardworking. She's achieved a lot in her life. She's . . . she's really impressive.' He looked at her now with the merest nod of solidarity.

Leila felt a knot in her throat: her profound need for approval met with heartfelt praise. For years, these were the things she had strived to be, but no one had acknowledged this. Hearing it here in open court made her well with emotion.

Edward made a curious expression. 'Would you say she's scatterbrained or forgetful or disorganised?'

'No.'

'Has Leila ever harmed Max?'

'No.' Andrew's voice was sharp and surprised. 'She would never do that.'

'Let me rephrase. Has Leila ever unintentionally hurt Max?'

'No.'

'Has she ever hidden from you an accident or incident where Max was harmed?'

'No,' Andrew repeated.

'Are you certain about that?'

Leila felt a hot coal of dread.

Andrew glanced at her. 'As certain as I can be,' he said unsurely.

Edward plucked a sheet from his thin blue notebook. 'So you are aware that, last summer, Leila took Max to the urgent treatment centre at the Royal London Hospital to treat a head laceration?'

Andrew squinted in confusion. It was clear to everyone watching that this was news to him.

Edward scanned the piece of paper. 'It says here that Leila Syed visited the urgent treatment centre on Friday the 24th of July. Did she tell you and your wife about this?'

Andrew craned forward in query. 'No. What happened to him?'

'The doctor who treated young Max will tell us next, but first, my learned friend has some questions for you,' Edward finished, pleased with this dramatic interlude.

Leila watched the cross-examination and grew increasingly hopeless. She had counted on Andrew to support her; to explain to the jury how much she had helped him with money, advice and last-minute babysitting, but the news of the medical visit had clearly distracted him. He kept looking over to her, his features tight with the disbelief that harm had come to his child and no one had deigned to tell him.

Leila wanted to explain that it had only been a precaution. If Max had been her own child, she wouldn't have even bothered, but in the same way that people were more careful with borrowed equipment – a neighbour's ladder, a friend's mower – so too was she cautious with Max. He had fallen off the jungle gym and landed badly. When Leila had checked him over and seen the tiny dab of blood, she had immediately called the NHS advice line. They had booked her a slot at the Royal London and she and Max had headed straight over. The whole episode had been slow and sedate, but 'urgent treatment' imbued it with outsize gravity. She wished she could explain this to Andrew. He was supposed to support her, but in his anaemic answers to Clara, his chance wasted away.

*

Dr Pritchard walked into the witness box and haughtily took the oath. Leila remembered her from last July: a stern-faced woman in her late forties, weak chin, tawny brown hair hooked back with a barrette and eyes that squinted like she needed glasses. Her bedside manner had been severely lacking.

Edward switched to a fulsome tone. 'Dr Pritchard, can you tell me what happened when Leila Syed came to see you with her nephew, Max Hansson?'

She nodded curtly. 'The lady, Leila Syed, was seen quickly. She said she wasn't sure if the child needed to be in A&E.'

'And how did she seem to you?'

'She was a bit jittery. She was talking fast and trying to explain what happened.'

'And what was it that happened, according to her?'

'She said the boy fell off the jungle gym.'

'Was his injury consistent with this?'

'I had no reason to doubt it. We examined him. It was a slight cut – nothing to worry about. She did the right thing not taking him to A&E.'

'So it was fairly routine. Nothing to worry about?'

'That's right.'

Edward frowned. 'Then why did you contact us about him?'

'Well, I saw her in the news last week and I remembered her from when she came in.'

'What struck you about this specifically?'

'The report I saw said that she didn't have any children.'

'And why was that strange?'

'Well, because when she came to see us, she said that *she* was the mother.'

A gust of noise rose in the courtroom. A juror shifted to look at Leila, her eyes wide in alarm. Edward was silent. There was something inexplicably dark about a woman claiming to be another child's mother and he was keen to let this diffuse.

Finally, he spoke again. 'Did you have any reason to doubt this?'

'No,' said the doctor.

'And do you know why she lied?'

'Presumably to hide the injury from the real mother.'

Leila forced herself to look neutral. She would not close her eyes, hang her head, or concede some other act of shame.

'To hide the injury from the real mother,' repeated Edward. 'Thank you, doctor. Please remain there for a moment.'

Clara Pearson stood to cross-examine her. 'Dr Pritchard, can you tell us more about the "laceration"? How deep or wide was it?'

'Not very. It didn't even need a plaster – just a clean and some antiseptic.'

Clara frowned. 'I'm sorry, I'm confused. My learned friend described it as a "head laceration", but it didn't even need a plaster?'

'It could be described as a small laceration, but really it was barely a cut.'

'"Barely a cut",' repeated Clara. 'But Leila Syed was concerned enough to bring Max in to be checked?'

'Yes. You often get that with parents.' She gestured outwards. 'Or family members. The slightest nick and they're off to the hospital.'

'So she was concerned about Max in the same way any responsible family member might be?'

'Yes, that's how it seemed.'

'You said it was "barely a cut". In your professional opinion, would this warrant a heart-to-heart discussion with the parents? For example, if it had happened at school, would you be shocked if the teacher didn't call a meeting with the parents to explain what had happened?'

'I suppose not. There must be hundreds of these things that happen every day.'

'So it was perfectly understandable why Leila might not have mentioned it to her sister? After all, it was an everyday occurrence.'

'Yes, but that's not the part that was strange. She was pretending to be the mother.'

Clara smiled. 'Ah, yes, but we are all familiar with bureaucracy. Might she have thought it was easier to say that than call in her sister for this tiny graze?'

The doctor frowned. 'Perhaps, but—'

'Do you have children, Dr Pritchard?'

She frowned. 'Yes, I have a daughter.'

'Would you be annoyed if you were called away from work because your daughter was grazed in a similar way?'

The doctor thought about this for a moment. Then, she sighed. 'Yes, I suppose I would.'

'Might Leila have wished to save her sister the trouble?'

'I don't know. You would have to ask her.'

'But do *you* think it's possible?'

'Well, of course it's possible,' the doctor said tetchily.

Clara smiled with arctic kindness. 'Thank you.' She turned to Judge Warren. 'Your Honour, I have no more questions for this witness.'

Leila realised that she was holding her breath and let it out slowly. She was utterly exhausted, and wilted with relief when the day finally ended. She caught Clara Pearson as the courtroom emptied.

'Did you know they were going to bring this up?' Leila asked in a stressed whisper.

'It was in the unused material. The document said that Max had seen a doctor but not that *you* were with him,' she said with reproof. '*Or* that you pretended to be his mother.'

Leila started to explain, but Clara glanced at her watch.

'I'm sorry, Leila. I have to go. Don't worry about what happened today. Try and get some rest.'

Leila watched her go, laden with all the things she needed to say but no one to whom to say them. She felt antsy and restless, in need of something to cut the tension. It sounded disturbing now – as if she had taken her sister's identity or claimed a piece of her life – but her intentions had been innocent. She had wanted to avoid the bureaucracy of having to call Yasmin and wait, when really it *was* just a little nick. When she had returned Max at the end of the day, he was bright and happy and Leila didn't want to worry Yasmin. After they lost Toby, every scratch or rash on Max would send Yasmin into a tailspin. Leila never imagined that her actions would be used in this way to imply something wholly darker.

She spotted Yasmin in the foyer, heading towards the exit with Andrew. It soothed her to see them together. In the past, she had worried that her sister would end up with a volatile lowlife. For years, Yasmin had judged Leila's boyfriends for being too 'establishment'. When she first met Will, she had rolled her eyes and called him bourgeois with his Oxford education and media career. When she met Andrew, however, she latched onto his fatherly appeal and Leila was relieved.

Sometimes, she wondered if her sister was jealous that *she* had the more interesting partner. Yasmin would never admit it of course; would only needle Leila about the 'boring' middle-class media parties that she was asked to attend. Perhaps the two of them were too close. Perhaps they were *all* too close: Will and Yasmin with their flirtations, Leila and Andrew with their solemn observations. The tension, the competition and the chemistry between the opposite pairs. Had some strange concoction led them to this moment: an unnatural entanglement of their four lives? Maybe they *all* needed some distance.

*

Yasmin used to think it was ridiculous, the way women would coo over a six-month-old child and claim it had a 'personality', but after she became a mother, she could see that it was true. Toby, at six months, was sombre while Max was loud and curious, always gurgling for this or that. He was a sunny, sociable child, oddly easy to reason with. If she explained to him why he couldn't eat another sweet, he, at three, would sulk for only a minute and then bounce back into laughter as if a bad mood simply wasn't worth the trouble.

She sat in his empty room and touched Max's toys, slipping a finger over each of them to check on their own grief: Humble the bumblebee and the pot-bellied rabbit who was still wide-eyed with the news. Yasmin felt the lardy weight of pain and tried hard not to cry, for Andrew would surely hear. He would rush to her side instead of leaving her to weep. She made herself sick from crying sometimes and just when she thought she was done and had reached the last rung of the ladder – reconciliation and acceptance – she went slipping back right to the start: anger and guilt. Guilt because she hadn't been there for Max, guilt because she'd so often felt relief when Leila agreed to babysit. Hearing the doctor in court today wasn't even jarring. It was *just* like Max to climb too high and come crashing off the jungle gym. Yasmin knew that if the cut wasn't serious, she would have been annoyed to be called away from work. She trusted Leila to deal with it.

No. She *had* trusted Leila. Past tense.

Yasmin recalled the question from court: 'Do you think it's possible that she left Max intentionally?' Yasmin's answer may have damned Leila, but she *had* to tell the truth. In this morass of pain and blame, she couldn't be the one who decided whether Leila was condemned or pardoned. All she could do was tell the truth as objectively as possible. Was Leila capable of leaving Max intentionally? *Yes.* Did that mean that she deserved to go to prison? Yasmin honestly didn't know.

There was a knock on the door and Andrew looked in. 'Hi,' he said softly.

Yasmin didn't meet his eyes. 'Hi,' she replied.

Andrew sat on Max's bed and traced the blue fleece of his blanket. He saw Humble in Yasmin's lap and, just like that, his composure slipped, exposing the anguish beneath. He shielded his eyes with a palm and began to quietly cry.

Yasmin froze. She knew that Andrew grieved, but he always tried to hide it from her. She watched as his broad shoulders shook, unable to contain his pain. Then, she went to him. She laced her fingers on the plane of his shoulder and pressed her mouth against it.

He drew her into him. 'I'm sorry,' he said into her hair.

'No.' She felt him tremble and realised how selfish she'd been, batting away his *are you okays* without realising they were not for her but for him because if she was okay, then maybe he would be too. '*I'm* sorry,' she said, his T-shirt gripped in her fist. They sat in a hot embrace, their pain like tape around them, binding them in a single piece.

She kissed his neck softly. He closed his eyes and his body relaxed, the crush of tension easing. She continued to kiss him, gentle and soothing at first, but then growing amorous. He opened his eyes in surprise as she pulled at his T-shirt.

'What are you doing?'

She paused. 'I thought we could . . .'

He grimaced. 'Here?'

She flushed at the note of accusation. 'I . . . I thought maybe we could try again.'

He blinked. 'Try again?'

She nodded and her voice was tender when she spoke. 'For another baby?'

Andrew balked so hard, it seemed to bounce off him and into her, making her flinch. 'No,' he said in a bark. He sprang from the bed and looked at her as if she were an alien. 'You seriously want another baby?'

'I do.'

He scoffed with disbelief. 'How can you even be thinking about that right now?' He pointed at Toby's handprints. 'Do you really want to go through that again?'

'But we could keep this one safe,' she said weakly.

'Could we?' he snapped. 'Could we really, Yasmin? After what happened to Toby, how can you say that for sure? How can you even *consider* it?' He clasped his palms together. 'Maybe this is a sign. Maybe you and I just shouldn't be parents.'

Yasmin was stung. 'You don't mean that.'

'I do.'

Yasmin was at a loss. She had always had an idea of her life: a husband, two children, a townhouse. She had had so many options when she was younger: the millionaire banker, the talented chef, the semi-famous comedy writer. She had chosen Andrew for his sedate, responsible manner and the way he never let her down. She had thought that money didn't matter in the face of his love and adoration, but then they began to struggle. She was okay giving up the townhouse – it was material anyway – but then the car began to leak and the drive couldn't get fixed. It had worn her down, but she still had joy in her life. Max was like a panacea, a healing for all her hurt. With him gone, she had nothing left, so how could Andrew deny her this? She was owed *something* for all that she gave up for him.

'I want another child,' she insisted.

'No way, Yasmin. There is absolutely *no way* I'm doing all this again. I'm done.'

'Don't say that. Please.'

Andrew knelt down beside her. 'Yasmin, my love. I will do anything and everything to make you happy. I will walk to the ends of the earth for you, but I *can't* do this. We can't have another child.' His voice crackled with hurt, like the shift of weight on leather. 'But we can still have a happy life – I promise you that.'

'How?' She pulled away from him. 'How can we possibly fix this?'

'We don't. We remember him and we feel the break in our hearts and we get up anyway and we live our lives – together.' He reached for her but she pulled away.

'No, Andrew. You don't get to just *decide* this.' She saw the defiant look on his face and felt her frustration build. 'You don't get to say no.'

'Actually, I do,' he said evenly.

Her anger flashed like neon. 'Then go.'

'Yasmin, please—'

'Just go, Andrew.' When he didn't move, she shouted, 'Go!' She watched him scrabble to his feet, angered even further by his meek obedience. That was the thing about grief: once the tears ceased, you were left with a hatred of everything.

*

Leila answered the door and was surprised to find Andrew outside. Her gaze darted behind him, scanning the street for witnesses. Quickly, she ushered him in.

'What are you doing here?' she demanded.

'I'm sorry to drop in. I wanted to see how you are.'

'You could have called. What if Yasmin saw you?'

He motioned dismissively. 'She wouldn't. She's . . . doing what she does.'

'Still holing up in Max's room?'

Andrew rubbed the furrow between his brows. 'Every night.'

Leila grew subdued. 'Listen, Andrew, I'm sorry I didn't tell you about Max that day. It was a tiny cut and—'

'I'm the one who should apologise, Leila. I was meant to do better in court and I let myself get distracted.'

Leila let out a long, slow breath. 'I *was* counting on you,' she said.

He ducked guiltily. 'I'm sorry. I messed up.'

She flexed her fingers. 'Well, there's nothing we can do now.' She gestured towards the hallway. 'Come on, I'll make you a cup of tea.'

Andrew sat at the kitchen table and cradled his head in his hands. 'I made a mistake,' he said gruffly.

Leila ignored him and busied herself with the tea.

'I shouldn't have asked you to help, Leila. You wouldn't be in this position.'

'For God's sake, Andrew,' she snapped. 'I've got my own guilt to deal with. I can't bear yours too.' The hurt on his face only irked her more. 'Look, I *chose* to help you that day. I could have skipped off to work but I came over. You didn't *make* me take him. You didn't *make* me do anything. It's not your fault, so don't ask me to play your therapist. I can't do that too.'

Andrew brought his palms together in a plea. 'What if she can't get through this?'

'She's doing better, isn't she? Than last time?' Leila couldn't keep the bite from her voice. It wasn't lost on her that Andrew had come to check on her, but had swiftly switched to Yasmin.

He gave her a sad, awful smile. 'She wants another baby.'

Leila reared. 'You cannot be serious.'

He shrugged but it wasn't a casual motion, more a shrinking into himself.

Leila abandoned the tea and darted to the table. She gripped his arm hard. 'Andrew, you're not considering it?'

'No. Of course I'm not.'

She noted his lack of conviction. 'Andrew, for God's sake, tell me you put her right.' Yasmin was fragile and clearly reaching for a quick solution. She needed time to heal and focus on herself.

'I love her so much and I wish I could just . . .' He made what looked like a strangling motion. '*Fix* her.' He dropped his hands. 'Do you remember what you said to me when you took me aside at our wedding?'

'I do.'

'You told me that if I ever hurt her, you would destroy me. The way you said it, I *really* believed you. But now it feels like – between us – we ended up destroying her.'

'Is that what you believe? That she won't come through this?'

'I honestly don't know.'

Leila squared her shoulders. 'Look, she's already doing better than last time, isn't she? She's dressing herself, feeding herself, talking in sentences. She's going to be fine, Andrew.'

'Do you really think so?'

'Yes, I do.' Leila had to believe it. After everything she had done for Yasmin, to have her fall apart now would be catastrophic. 'Andrew,' she said softly, trying to hide her shrillness. 'Are you really considering having another baby?'

He rubbed a hand across his face, the soft skin beneath his eyes stretching with the motion. 'I'm going to have a vasectomy.'

Leila sagged with relief. It was absolutely the right thing to do. 'Are you going to tell her?'

'No,' he said unequivocally.

She squeezed his arm. 'I think that's the right decision.' She stood and returned to the tea, mentally filing away this latest secret to be kept from Yasmin.

Chapter Ten

Suki Taylor stood in the witness box and fiddled with the button on her white silk shirt. It was stylishly dishevelled with one tail tucked in and the other trailing over her wide-legged navy trousers. She glanced over at Leila, lips curling in a joyless smile. She looked young standing there, blinking off her blunt fringe. She arranged her hands like a fig leaf as if she had something to hide.

Leila felt unduly anxious. She and Suki had a good relationship but she also knew that she was hard on her young assistant. It was conceivable that Suki might harbour a secret resentment for all the late nights and demeaning errands that Leila asked her to do: picking up her dry cleaning, getting her car washed, sorting out a speeding fine as soon as it was issued – not great use of her Saint Martins degree. But it was also true that while she expected a lot of Suki, she also stoked her ambition. She invited her to client meetings and made space for her to speak. Leila acted as an informal mentor and pushed Suki to succeed, but was their rapport mere window-dressing?

Edward Forshall stood and offered a weaselly smile. 'Ms

'Taylor, as Leila Syed's assistant, is it fair to say that you knew the ins and outs of her schedule well?'

'Yes.'

'In July of this year, what was Ms Syed working on?'

Suki pushed aside her fringe but it fell back into place. 'She was working on a project for Mercers Bank to redesign their headquarters.'

'Was this different to business as usual?'

'Yes. It was a stressful time for all of us. There was a lot of work to be done and so there were long hours and fraying tempers.'

'Including Ms Syed's?'

Suki frowned. 'No. Leila was always controlled.'

'So she wasn't prone to fits of emotion?'

'No. She was always calm. At first, I thought she was a bit of an ice queen, but I grew to admire her for it.'

Leila stiffened. She hated being called that.

Edward, in contrast, was pleased. '"She was always calm",' he repeated. 'Even a bit of an "ice queen". So she wasn't ever stressed or disorganised or scatterbrained?'

'No.' Suki shook her head. 'Well, she did get stressed but she was very good at hiding it. She was always professional and, no, not disorganised.'

'And not scatterbrained?'

Suki smiled affectionately. 'No, she's definitely not that.'

'You say she was calm in stressful situations. What do you mean by that?'

Suki waved a hand, her tasteful silver ring glinting in the light. 'Well, when there were deadlines or conflict, she always put out the fire calmly.'

'And was it only in work situations that she displayed this calm, or was it evident in her personal life?'

Suki fiddled with her button again. 'Well, I didn't spend time with Leila in personal settings.' She averted her eyes and there was something in the way she did it that piqued Edward's interest.

'In your statement to the police, you said that you often performed personal tasks for Leila: picking up dry cleaning, making salon appointments for her, and so on. Is that correct?'

'Yes.'

'So you *did* see her in some personal settings?'

Suki was visibly uncomfortable. 'Yes.'

Edward studied her carefully. 'In that case, you will forgive me for repeating the question: was it only in work situations that Leila Syed was calm, or was it evident in her personal life too?'

Suki rubbed her thumb and forefinger as if trying to make a decision. 'Well, there was this one time . . .' She grimaced at Leila by way of apology.

Edward pressed her to continue.

'Leila had a miscarriage at work.'

There was a shift in the courtroom, a rearranging of sympathies as if Leila recast as a mother unlocked the jury's empathy. She took no comfort from it, for she knew what was coming.

'I see,' said Edward. 'Can you describe what happened?'

Suki nodded gravely. 'I think it was a Tuesday. Leila's early week is always really busy. I saw her walk into her office and she called out to me a minute later. I, uh, I walked in and saw that she wasn't at her desk. I found her in her bathroom. She was . . .' Suki hesitated. 'She was bleeding. I started to panic but Leila calmed me down. I asked if she needed to go to the hospital but she said no. She said it was the fourth time it had happened and she knew what to do. She asked me to bring her a few things so she could clean herself up.'

Edward nodded.

'Then, uh, I waited outside. I felt upset and I remember telling myself not to cry. Leila sorted herself out, then came back and carried on.'

'Carried on?'

'Yes, she was on a conference call.'

A stunned quiet befell the courtroom. Leila shrank from the jurors' scrutiny. She remembered the day in question: the pulpy wetness in her tights and the collapse of something inside her. Her pragmatism took over, knowing that her bare tights would stain. She excused herself from the conference room and hurried to her office, making a beeline for her en suite and calmly calling to Suki. *Bring me my tights from the bottom drawer, please. And a tampon.* Suki in the doorway, eyes wide with shock. *I'm having a miscarriage. Let's keep it between ourselves please.* She had cleaned herself up quickly. It was her fourth miscarriage and what was the point of making a scene?

Edward angled his head. 'Can I just double-check that? Leila had a miscarriage while on a conference call and she just carried on?'

Suki tried to backtrack. 'I mean, it was clear that she was upset, but the call was really important and—'

'More important than tending to a dead child?'

A gust of surprise swept across the court. Clara Pearson leaned towards Edward and blasted him in a savage whisper.

'Please dial down the tone, Mr Edward,' said Judge Warren.

He bowed his head. 'Of course, Your Honour. I apologise.' To Suki, he said, 'Leila Syed had just experienced a monumental event, but she continued with her phone call?'

Suki swallowed. 'Yes.'

'Is it fair to say that her work was extremely important to her and that when she had to choose between a personal matter and work, she chose work?'

'I don't know if that's fair, but—'

'But on this occasion it was true?' He raised his voice over hers.

'Yes.'

Edward nodded bluntly. 'I'd like to move on to the morning of Monday the 12th of July. You placed a call to Leila Syed at 8.08 a.m. Can you tell us what that call was about?'

'Yes. Our team was heading out to an important meeting with Mercers Bank. One of the leads had misplaced his blueprints. They have to be specially printed and the printer wasn't open yet, so we couldn't make a copy last minute. I knew there was a spare in Leila's office but it was locked.'

'And who has the key?'

'Leila.'

'No one else?'

Suki grimaced. 'In theory, yes, but the reserve is rarely where it's supposed to be. Leila had to come in or we'd have to present the pitch without blueprints, which', she shrugged, 'would be ridiculous so Leila had to come in.'

'And you phoned her to tell her this?'

'Yes.'

'What did she say?'

'She said she was coming straight to the office.'

Edward's eyes narrowed. 'She said, "I'm coming straight to the office"?'

'Maybe not exactly, but something along those lines.'

'But she understood the urgency of coming straight to the office?'

'Yes.'

Edward tapped his lips in a show of contemplation. 'Given that Leila Syed is the sort of woman who has a miscarriage one minute and is straight back on a conference call the next, would it surprise you if she decided to leave her nephew in her car for a few minutes while she popped into the office to put out a fire?'

Suki shifted on her feet.

'You're under oath, Ms Taylor.' Edward waited. 'I'll ask again: would you be surprised to learn that Leila Syed left her nephew in the car on purpose to deal with an emergency?'

The silence grew tense and Suki looked like she might cry. 'No,' she said, a short pop of a sound that resounded like a gunshot.

Leila felt the pressure bloat in her chest. She did not look at Suki or reveal what she was thinking. The truth was that she didn't blame her assistant because even *she* would have answered the same. Leila could make difficult decisions that others were loath to do. Suki had worked with her long enough to know this.

'Thank you for your honesty,' Edward said indulgently. 'Please remain there for a minute.'

Clara Pearson stood to cross-examine Suki. 'Ms Taylor, I have just a couple of questions. How long have you worked for Leila Syed?'

'Three years.'

'Can you describe her working pattern? Does she work long hours?'

Suki shook her head. 'No, we try to follow the principles of a calm company: minimum late nights, no weekend emails. In the summer, we have the option of summer hours where we take Friday afternoon off.'

'Was the week of 12th July a typical week?'

'No. I mentioned that we were working on a big pitch so we were working long hours for a couple of weeks. Leila doesn't like to set a bad example but sometimes it's necessary.'

'Given that it was a busy time, did Leila send any emails on Sunday the 11th?'

'Yes.'

'Do you recall what time?'

'Well, when I woke up on the Monday, I had some emails waiting in my inbox, which meant they were sent very late on Sunday.'

'But this was extraordinary?'

'Yes.'

'Given that she was working so late, would it follow that Leila Syed would be more tired and distracted than usual the next morning?'

'Yes, that's very likely.'

'So tired in fact that she might have suffered a lapse of memory, uncharacteristic as that may be?'

Suki nodded emphatically. 'Yes, exactly.'

'Thank you.' Clara turned to Judge Warren. 'I have no more questions, Your Honour.'

To Leila's dismay, Edward stood to re-examine Suki.

'Ms Taylor, you said that it's extraordinary for Leila Syed to send emails on a Sunday. How rare *was* this?'

Suki lifted a shoulder. 'It's hard to say. Maybe once a month.'

'Not more often?'

'I don't think so, no.'

Edward nodded at the usher, who handed Suki a sheaf of paper. 'Ms Taylor, what you have there is a list of emails sent by Leila Syed in the six months preceding the incident in question. How many separate Sundays can you count?'

Suki regarded the pile in her hands. After a brief hesitation, she silently began to count. The seconds ticked by excruciatingly slowly as she worked her way through it. Finally, she spoke. 'Twenty-seven.'

'Twenty-seven Sundays, which in fact makes it *every* Sunday up to that point.' Edward neatened the cuff of his blazer beneath his black robe. 'Can you read out some of the timestamps from, say, January this year?'

Suki flicked to the first page. '11.57 p.m., 12.01 a.m., 1.07 a.m.' A pause. '2.20 a.m.'

'And what time was the last email sent on Sunday the 11th, the day before Max's death?'

She took a moment to find the right day. '11.53 p.m.'

'So – given that Leila Syed wasn't working unusually late, is it likely that she would be any less alert, cool, calm and calculated than usual on the following morning?'

'I . . .' Suki was at a loss. 'I suppose not,' she conceded.

'"I suppose not",' he quoted with an amused smile. 'Thank you, Ms Taylor, you've been very helpful.'

Judge Warren adjourned for lunch and Leila headed straight to the bathroom where she locked herself inside a cubicle

– a shelter from attack. She tried not to think of that day when Suki saw her bleed. It was true that Leila was calm, but she had learnt to be. How many times could she mourn a loss that had crawled into everything, large as a titan, small as a heartbeat? Leila had refused to fall apart. Now she saw that the very thing that kept her together might also be her undoing.

*

Josephine Allsebrook wore an olive suit that harked back to the eighties: broad shoulders and wide lapels on which she had pinned a brooch, a black gemstone with a gilded frame. She had dense curly hair cut so short, it almost looked like a flat top. The wrinkles around her lips – two deep lines from each corner to her chin – gave her a permanent scowl. She spoke in the straight-backed manner of a soldier as she confirmed her occupation: head teacher at Rosemont School.

'Ms Allsebrook, I presume that as headmistress you're usually in your office,' said Edward. 'Away from the hubbub of the school day?'

She smiled patiently, waiting for him to finish his question before she corrected him. 'Actually, I take a very hands-on approach. I'm there in the playground every morning, welcoming the children and ushering them in.'

Edward raised his brows in a show of admiration. 'I take it you get to know the parents quite well?'

She tilted her head in a hedging motion. 'Yes and no. My focus is on the children and many of the parents need to offload their kids and go, which of course is understandable.'

'Yes, but you *do* get to know faces,' said Edward twitchily.

'Oh, yes, absolutely.'

'Would you recognise Yasmin Syed?'

'Yes. She's Max Hansson's mother.'

'Would you recognise Andrew Hansson?'

'Yes, he's Max's father.'

Edward paused. 'And would you recognise Leila Syed?'

'Yes,' she answered. 'That would be Max's aunt.'

'Oh? But how is it that you would recognise her?'

Not having heard the preceding evidence, she answered without hesitation. 'She's dropped Max off several times.'

The jury stilled. This wasn't what they had heard before.

Edward frowned in a performative manner. 'Are you sure about this?'

'Yes.'

'But how can you be certain?'

'Well, as you said, you get to know faces. I remember thinking that she was very well put together; like a businesswoman in an advert.'

'So you even noticed what she was wearing?'

'Well, I couldn't say exactly, but it was very stylish. As I say, she was very well put together.'

Edward nodded encouragingly. 'And how many times would you say Leila Syed has dropped him off?'

The lines deepened around her mouth. 'I couldn't say.'

'More than once?'

'Oh, yes. At least two or three times.'

'Two or three times,' he repeated. 'When was the most recent time?'

She considered this. 'It's difficult to say, but I know she was there around Easter this year. I remember seeing her and thinking that her blouse suited the season because it was purple like our Cadbury Easter eggs.'

Edward was delighted by this specific detail. 'Easter would make it April?'

'Yes.'

'Only three months before the incident?'

'That's correct.'

'Are you certain it was Leila Syed you saw?'

'I'm absolutely positive.'

'But Ms Syed says she's never dropped Max off at school. What do you make of that?'

The teacher frowned. 'Well, that would be inaccurate.'

'"That would be inaccurate."' Edward's voice echoed across the open space. 'Thank you, Ms Allsebrook. You've been exceedingly helpful.' He inclined his head in a show of respect.

Clara stood now to cross-examine the witness. She spoke in a muted tone, knowing perhaps that women like Josephine Allsebrook did not respond to browbeating. 'Mrs Allsebrook, when you say that you thought Leila Syed was very well put together, was it because she was dressed differently to the other mums?'

'No, I wasn't comparing her with others. She was well turned out in her own right.'

'Can you picture her standing next to other mums?'

The teacher hesitated. 'No, but people come in and out at different times.'

'But you *can* picture her at the school gates, handing Max over?'

'Well, I don't know if she literally handed him over, but yes.'

'Is there a chance you might have seen Leila Syed elsewhere

and parsed this onto the school gates? A parents' evening or a school event? Maybe even a birthday party?'

Her lips puckered in thought. 'I'm fairly sure about that. I don't attend personal events and if she had visited the school for a parents' evening or event, her name would be on our system, which it's not.'

'I see,' said Clara meditatively. 'Ms Allsebrook, you said earlier that you remember seeing Leila Syed in April because of her purple shirt.' Clara gestured at a television screen which blinked to life with a picture of Leila. 'Was it this one?' The picture was cropped close, but her outfit was clear: a light-grey skirt paired with a blouse the colour of Cadbury purple.

The teacher nodded confidently. 'That's it exactly.'

Clara continued, leaving the picture on-screen. 'Can I ask: what ages does Rosemont School cater to?'

'We take children aged three to eleven.'

'And then they leave?'

'Well, we are attached to a secondary school, so you could say that we are an all-through school.'

'Where is the secondary school?'

'A five-minute walk away.'

'Do you ever go there?'

She nodded. 'Yes, all the time. They have better facilities so our classes sometimes go there and I often have meetings there.'

'How often would you say you go there in a given week?'

'Four, maybe five.'

'So almost every day?'

'Yes.'

Clara smiled. 'Do you share databases?'

'No, they have their own.'

'So if a visitor attended the upper school, it wouldn't be on your system at the lower school?'

'No.'

Clara asked the usher to pass a document to the head teacher. 'Can you see what this is?'

'It's a permission slip granting a visitor entry to the upper school.' She answered before she even received it.

'Can you read the date and name of the person being granted entry?'

Her features creased as she read it. 'It's for Leila Syed, dated the 1st of April.'

'What reason does it give?'

'An assembly.'

Clara frowned. 'An assembly? Why would Leila Syed be attending the school for an assembly?'

'Well, sometimes we invite visitors to speak at the upper school to inspire older pupils.'

'Ah, so as a successful businesswoman, Leila Syed was volunteering her time at the school?'

'I can't say for sure, but that is what this indicates.'

Clara pointed again at the television. 'Does this seem familiar?' The screen zoomed out to reveal the complete picture. Leila's photo was on the front page of a school newsletter. 'The Rosemont Monthly' was printed along the top. 'Is it possible that what *you* recall as Leila in a purple shirt dropping Max off at lower school in April was actually Leila giving an assembly at *upper* school in April?'

The teacher looked mortified.

'In fact—' Clara nodded at the usher, who handed the teacher a second set of documents. 'Leila Syed gave three assemblies in total over the course of twelve months. The dates are on those slips. On the larger sheet of paper is your schedule. What do you notice about the dates, Ms Allsebrook?'

A blush of pink laced up her neck. 'They match.'

'Ah ha!' said Clara. 'You're right. Leila Syed *did* come to the school "two or three times" but not to *your* campus and *not* to drop off Max. Rather, she was volunteering her time at your upper school on days that placed you there. Knowing this, Ms Allsebrook, isn't it likely that you didn't see Leila at the school gates at all? That, in fact, you only saw her at the upper school?'

The pinkish colour spread to her face. 'Oh,' she said and the single syllable was so effective that Leila could have laughed out loud.

'"Oh" indeed,' said Clara, her tone no longer respectful. 'For the record, Ms Allsebrook, do you now accept that you actually saw Leila at the upper school?'

'Yes,' she answered. 'It's possible – no, *likely* – that that's correct.'

'So your earlier assertion that Leila definitely dropped off Max isn't right at all, is it?'

'No, I fear not.'

Clara smiled coolly. 'Thank you.' She turned to the judge. 'I have no more questions for this witness, Your Honour.'

Leila felt a dangerous sense of hope as the judge adjourned for the day. Clara had masterfully undone the teacher's evidence. The detail of it was crucial. Leila had never dropped off Max at school, which meant that she lacked that mapping in her brain. Surely, any reasonable person could believe that she had driven to work on autopilot; that it was all a momentary slip – like telling yourself to put your toothbrush on charge but forgetting the moment you finish. A tiny, instant lapse.

Leila shot Clara a grateful smile and caught a juror watching, his eyes narrowed cynically as he tried to get the cut of her. She saw the snarl-like set of his lips and the creasing of his brow bridge and for one wild moment she wondered if this curious stranger had somehow divined the truth.

*

It was barely spitting outside and the wipers whined and juddered each time they swept the glass. Yasmin sat in silence, jaundiced by the sweep of a passing headlight. She had no idea that Leila had had four miscarriages. She knew there was one early on and remembered telling her not to worry, that one in four pregnancies ended this way and it really wasn't a big deal. Soon after, Yasmin had Toby and all her energy was spent on him, leaving no emotional capacity to monitor Leila's suffering.

Yasmin had thought that she and Will were having trouble conceiving; not that there was a problem carrying their child to term. She thought of her sister crouched in the bathroom at work, cleaning herself up and pretending it didn't hurt. The thought made Yasmin sing with guilt for all those times she felt self-satisfied for having something that Leila lacked. Her sister – educated, successful, rich, respected – did not have Max.

Yasmin remembered when Leila gave an assembly at the upper school. For days after, mothers with children at both campuses would stop her at the gates. 'Oh, isn't your sister Leila Syed? My Jorja was *raving* about her.' Yasmin couldn't escape her sister's brilliance even in her own domain.

This compulsion to compare herself to Leila made her nit-pick trivial things: dinner parties (*we would never blow so much on table decoration*), impromptu trips (*of course, with Max, there's just no way we could do the same*) and even her fitness regime (*it's easy for you because you never lost your shape to begin with*).

'There's an emptiness, isn't there?' she had once remarked to Andrew as they left a dinner at Leila's. And it was true: there was an emptiness in the unruffled tablecloth, the sleek white walls on which no one scribbled, the un-mussed pile of mail on the sideboard, even the sharp-edged letter opener. It was quiet and calm and . . . cold. And hadn't Yasmin felt superior? *Look at my busy, full,* peopled *life and accept that yours is empty.*

To know that Leila had struggled so much made Yasmin want to go to her, to hug her, to forgive her – and to ask for forgiveness too, but first she had to know the truth. She needed the jury to tell her: did Leila leave Max on purpose? She could forgive her sister if it was truly an accident. After all, how many parents – nay, *people* – suffered near misses every day? The driver who drank just a little too much with his dinner one night, the father who left a pan on boil, the mother who forgot to fix the smoke alarm. How close they all were to tragedy. Were those who tripped in the minefield any more evil than those who escaped it? If the jury ruled it an accident, then Yasmin could get past it. If, however, they said that Max was left on purpose, then she couldn't – wouldn't – ever forgive her sister.

*

Leila sipped her tea and felt the steam mist her skin. It was almost too hot to drink, just the way she liked it. She glanced at the clock – 8 p.m. – and realised that she hadn't eaten. She would finish reading her emails, she decided, and then order something in.

The first email was from her assistant: a message of apology for revealing her miscarriage. Leila wasn't angry with Suki, but hated that the details were harnessed against her. She thought of Edward's derisive tone: *more important than tending to a dead child?* Funny how men were lionised for bravely returning to work beneath the pall of tragedy, but women were expected to weep for weeks. That fourth miscarriage was the last straw. She had heard stories of women who had six, or seven, before they managed to carry to term, but Leila had had enough. She had felt a strange sense of calm and she hadn't grieved that final loss because actually she was relieved. There was a peace, wasn't there, in surrendering? In accepting you wouldn't have everything?

She archived Suki's message and clicked through to the next one. It was from Robert Gardner. 'What a TURD,' it said. 'Say the word and I'll slit his THROAT.' She felt a spike of unease. Robert was dramatic and she had trained herself not to react to his strops, but the lack of context made her worry. She reached for her phone and immediately dialled him.

'I'm going to gut that little prick,' he said, not bothering with hello.

'Robert,' she said breathlessly. 'What's going on?' She could tell from his tone that he'd had a few drinks.

There was a beat of silence. 'You haven't seen it?' He tutted. 'Your frog-prick of a husband.' A pause. 'He's written about you.'

Leila felt the strum of her chest. 'How bad is it?'

'It's bad.' He tutted again. 'Fuck, I'm sorry, Leila.'

The mere fact of his apology filled her with dread. She and Robert had a comradely relationship that never quite swayed to intimate. Instead, they traded in jokes and provocations, good-natured barbs and insults. His tone – serious, sympathetic – made her skin feel clammy. 'In his column?' she asked.

'Yes.'

Will's column was read by tens of thousands of people a week. She exhaled slowly and with the phone tucked beneath her chin, navigated to the website, then down to the list of columnists to Will Carmichael. There, she froze. The headline was a punch in the gut.

THE DAY MY WIFE WAS CHARGED WITH KILLING A THREE-YEAR-OLD CHILD

There was a gurgle in her throat and then the acid tang of bile.

'Leila?' Robert was asking. 'I'm sorry you married such a wanker.'

She felt the beat of blood in her ears. 'Thank you for letting me know, Robert.'

'Is there anything—' he started but Leila hung up the phone. She reread the headline to check that she hadn't got it wrong, then clicked into the article.

You don't expect to hear a confession like the one I did in July. My wife spoke in a glazed, mechanical sort of way like a soldier who had survived a shelling. She told me

173

*words that would change the course of our entire lives:
'Max is dead. It's my fault.'*

*Max is her nephew, or ours I should say (do you adopt
your spouse's nephews when you marry?). I knew him to
be a sunny, sensitive child, but not perfect as children
never are. He would sulk when he was angry, he found
it hard to articulate his feelings, and he was filled to the
brim with energy, which isn't always a good thing. He was,
however, sweet and generous and loving. At his last birthday, I dropped my piece of cake and he asked his mummy
for a knife so that he could cut and share his. I was looking
forward to seeing him grow into a young man, so when my
wife told me he was dead and that it was her fault, my world
stopped for a moment.*

Leila scanned the rest of the article, down to the final para-
graph.

*I ask her how she feels and she says, 'I don't want to talk.'
There is a vulnerability to her, a desperate need, when she
asks me to 'just stay' and cocoons herself against my body,
her delicate fingers gripping my T-shirt like a child clinging
to a parent. In that moment, I see the thing that exists in us
all: a scared and worried child, fearful of the world around
her. I hold her then and as she relaxes against me, I fall in
love with my wife – a potential convicted killer – all over
again.*

Leila pushed away from the desk, feeling the shock billow
inside her – a swooping, somersault sensation. Her vision

blanked for a moment, her rage like a cartoon villain sneaking up to close its cape around you. She wanted to lash out, to hit something with an open hand. Will was often reckless, but to co-opt this for his column was simply incomprehensible.

She glared at his picture on-screen: hair ruffled in a rakish way, three-day stubble and eyebrow cocked insouciantly. She was maddened by his expression; wanted to reach out and slap it off him. She gritted her teeth to the point of pain to keep her rage in a manageable package. *How could you, Will?*

She picked up her phone to call him, but knew that this wouldn't vent her anger. She made a snap decision and headed out to her car, a lease to replace her Mini. She drove towards Wanstead six miles away where Will was staying with an old school friend. It followed, she thought, that after they broke up, Will would head to a bachelor pad.

As she neared the address, she clung tightly to her rage, using it as a proxy for strength. She circled the street for parking, each revolution further stirring her anger. By the time she banged on the door, she was coiled with fury. Will opened it, his head still turned inward at the corridor as he yelled a joke or comeback. There was a bray of laughter inside. He turned and froze when he spotted Leila. He drew a breath as if gathering momentum to speak, but Leila didn't let him.

'How could you?' she said savagely.

He stepped outside, his feet bare beneath ratty jeans, and closed the door behind him. 'I tried calling you.'

'When?' She plucked her phone from her pocket. 'Because I didn't get any fucking missed calls, Will!'

He raised his hands in a peace-making gesture. 'Leila, please don't be angry. I wanted to ask you, but I knew you'd say no without even thinking about it.'

She felt a burst of something violent and it took all her self-control to not reach out and strike him. 'I don't get it, Will. I don't understand, so explain it to me: are you really so fucking obtuse that you can't see that this was wrong, or do you just not give a shit?'

He hunched against the cold and looked at her beseechingly. 'I needed to do this,' he said quietly. 'For me.'

She scoffed. 'I knew you were selfish, Will, but I never knew you were so fucking cruel.'

He was chastened but only for a fleeting moment. 'You always say that I don't deal with what I'm feeling. This was my way of doing that, Leila.'

She pointed at him, her finger almost touching his face. 'Don't you dare pretend this was noble. You used me. You wrote down my fucking words, Will!' She remembered his persistence – *come on, sweetheart, tell me what you're thinking* – and was humiliated that she mistook it for sympathy.

'Look—'

She cut him off. 'That's not even the worst of it. You *used* Max. He's not yours to write about!'

Will stiffened, a cold drain in his eyes. 'He was my family too.'

'No, he wasn't! To answer your cute little aside – *"do you adopt your spouse's nephews?"* – the answer is no you fucking don't, not when you exploit them for column inches.'

'I loved him too, Leila. Please don't say I didn't.' He twitched strangely, like a boxer shaking off a blow, keeping his hurt in check. 'It matters that you believe that.'

She regarded him with disgust. 'What I *believe* is that you're a hack, Will. A cheap, unoriginal hack.' She took a step back. 'Whatever this was, it's over. You don't talk to me again. You don't call me. You don't text me. You just collect your records and your fucking guitar and then I don't ever want to see you again.'

'Leila, can we talk about this properly? You're angry right now—'

'And *you're* a spineless weasel who's made a career of being a prick. Well, congratulations, Will! I hope that column gets you a fucking award since you haven't managed one so far.' His face flickered with hurt and Leila almost laughed at how that insult seemed to pain him more than her own anguish. 'Oh, and one more thing. If you *ever* mention Max's name in public, I will sue you. I will use everything I have to destroy you. If you don't believe me, then you're welcome to pit your "journalist's" pittance against me.'

He stared at her, open-mouthed.

She laughed, cruelly for effect. 'And good luck doing *that*.' She turned and stalked away, gratified by the look on his face. Back in her car, she smacked the steering wheel once, then again, and cried out in frustration. She felt overwhelmed, like a child who can't name his distress so resorts to a tantrum instead. Will was a thief, she knew, who picked over her anecdotes for fragments he could use, but to take this story wholesale without seeking permission was a betrayal she couldn't fathom.

She lowered her head to the steering wheel and let the tears come, her anger cooling to something bleaker. Friends had told her from the very beginning that Will was a narcissist, but she had put it down to a difference in personalities; to his overblown confidence and his abiding love for debate. Will would pontificate loudly on his subjects of interest – politics, media – but grow mute and dismissive when the conversation swayed to something unfamiliar. Sometimes, when dining with mutual friends, she would steer the subject back to politics if only to mollify Will. They were a team and his betrayal now felt like a physical injury.

She told herself that she needed time away from him: not these fragments of absences but actual time away to grieve the end of their relationship. She vowed that when the trial was over, she would travel somewhere peaceful. There, she would design a beautiful building purely for the pleasure of it. She had worked so hard at Syed&Gardner, grinding away for profit, that she'd lost touch with what she loved about her job: the striking lines of a unique building, grand flying buttresses straight from a Grimm fairy tale. She would make her building tall and Gothic, akin to the gems of the Black Forest: a complex castle of traps and corridors.

As she pictured the lines of her building, a dark thought crept in. *Do they have graph paper in prison?* The question left her winded, for she could not confront a guilty verdict. In her heart of hearts, she simply could not believe it. If the jury could be convinced that it was all a tragic accident, then surely they wouldn't punish her. *Surely* they'd set her free.

Chapter Eleven

Jennifer Li stood in the witness box with the relaxed demeanour of the naturally confident. Her long black hair was tied in a ponytail and she wore a dark blue jumper with tapered grey trousers. Her high cheekbones were free of makeup, giving her a fresh-faced look.

Leila watched from across the room. She and Jennifer, Max's babysitter, had a good relationship. They listened to the same podcasts and swapped notes on the same sort of shows: *The Good Wife*, *The Newsroom*, *The West Wing*. Sometimes, when Leila relieved her in the evening, Jennifer would hang around and they would chat over a glass of wine. She was only nineteen but had the manner and taste of someone older.

Edward Forshall began with some basic questions: Jennifer's name, age and job, how well she knew Leila and how often she saw her. Then, he turned to her relationship with Max.

'What was Leila like with him?' he asked.

Jennifer smiled warmly, as if recalling a nice memory. 'She was great. She was really interested in his development, always buying him educational toys, giving him books to read.'

Edward squinted at her. 'Aside from buying him gifts, how was she in terms of actually interacting with him?'

'Max loved playing with her. I always thought that Yasmin was lucky to have such a supportive sister. Between the three of us and Max's dad, it was kind of like he had four parents who loved him.'

Leila swallowed, feeling a hard knot in her throat. She had loved him so much and was grateful to hear someone say it. She wanted the jury to know that she wasn't a so-called ice queen.

'It's natural that parents sometimes grow impatient with their children, isn't it?' asked Edward.

'Yes,' said Jennifer.

'And given that Leila was like a parent to Max, is it fair to say that she was sometimes impatient with him?'

She frowned. 'Not really.'

'"Not really", meaning yes?'

She half-shrugged. 'Occasionally maybe.'

'Can you give us some examples?'

Jennifer seemed less sure now. 'I mean, maybe once or twice, when he was playing up.'

'Can you give us some specific examples?'

'Well, there was one time when Max wouldn't tidy up his toys and Leila raised her voice at him. He didn't like that and started to cry and when I started to go to him, she stopped me and said that he needed to learn to do what she told him.'

Edward arched his brows. 'So she stopped you from offering comfort to him when he was in clear distress.'

Jennifer's lips puckered in doubt. 'Well, I wouldn't put it like that. He was behaving badly.'

'But not so badly that *you* thought he deserved to be comforted?'

'Well, as a babysitter, you sometimes feel that you have to be more forgiving with a child than a parent might. As Max's aunt, Leila acted more like a parent would.'

'I see.' Edward nodded contemplatively. 'Ms Li, has Leila ever threatened to hurt Max?'

'No. Of course not.'

'You're sure about that?'

'Yes.'

Edward directed the usher to hand Jennifer a piece of paper. 'Ms Li, that is a transcript of your interview with the police. In it, did you say that Leila once told you that she could "throttle" Max?'

Jennifer blinked. 'It . . . it was just a figure of speech,' she said, stumbling over her words as Leila looked on in horror.

Edward made a small scoffing sound. 'Leila saying the words "I could throttle him" was just a figure of speech?'

'She didn't mean it. I was trying to explain that she never threatened Max; only made a throwaway comment like any parent might. Max was a bit grizzly at night recently and that was frustrating for everyone.'

Leila watched with mounting dismay. She remembered the occasion clearly. Max had been acting up, running about the house on a sugar high, barrelling into the room when she was on a conference call. Perhaps she *had* been a little impatient when she forced him outside, but she was doing Yasmin a last-minute favour and did it really matter if she was a little harsh with him? He had played up all day and when Jennifer came to pick him up, Leila had been frazzled. When she heard something break upstairs, she groaned and said *I could throttle him*. Jennifer had kindly headed up to try and defuse his mood. It was just an offhand comment, a way to let off steam. Leila couldn't have known that it would be recalled in the cold light of court to imply something sinister.

Edward continued. 'Ms Li, did Ms Syed ever complain about her sister, Yasmin?'

Leila squirmed, knowing that Jennifer was under oath and legally bound to tell the truth.

'Yes, all sisters moan about each other,' she answered.

'What specifically did she complain about?'

Jennifer's gaze slid up to the public gallery where Yasmin was presumably watching. 'Well, sometimes, she felt that Yasmin didn't realise how important her job was.'

'What do you mean by that?'

Jennifer shifted, now visibly uncomfortable. 'Well, Leila runs her own company and Yasmin is just—' She caught herself in time. 'Yasmin is a secretary and I guess Leila used to think that Yasmin didn't appreciate the difference. Like she would call up Leila and say that Max was ill today and could she work from home and look after him? Leila said that just because she's her own boss, it didn't mean that she didn't have to work; that it was far less damaging for Yasmin to take a day off work.'

Edward nodded, pleased with what he was getting. 'And what was Leila's tone when she shared these grievances? Was she angry? Bitter?'

Jennifer's features tensed in thought. 'She seemed angry.'

A pause. 'Well, more annoyed than angry; fed up. She couldn't do her job while looking after Max.'

'"She couldn't do her job while looking after Max",' he repeated. 'And her job was her priority?'

'Generally speaking, yes.'

'I see,' he said with a satisfied smile. 'Thank you, Ms Li.'

Clara Pearson stood to cross-examine Jennifer. 'Ms Li, you mentioned that Leila would buy Max educational toys and books. How often did this happen?'

'Oh, all the time. Fortnightly if not weekly.'

'What sort of things?'

'A mini chemistry set, puzzles and brainteasers, mazes and other strategy games. Basically, anything that would make him think.'

'So she was interested in his long-term development and seeing him grow into a happy, healthy child?'

'Yes.'

'Did they ever play with these toys together?'

Jennifer smiled. 'Yes. He loved the science experiments, would cackle with delight every time they tried something new. He would always involve her too. Normally, children want to dominate and be in charge of the experiments, but he made sure that Leila got her turn.' Her smile broke into sorrow. 'He was a really happy child.'

Clara moved swiftly on. 'I want to rewind a little to your conversation with my learned friend. You said that any parent might have made that comment. Have you ever heard Max's mother, Yasmin Syed, threaten to harm him?'

Jennifer stilled. 'Well . . . yes, but again it was a figure of speech.'

'What did she say?'

Jennifer shrugged as if it was trivial. 'Things like "I'm going kill him" but . . .' She trailed off, noting the jurors' expressions. 'Not in a serious way.'

'And what about Andrew Hansson, Max's father? Did you ever hear him say anything like this?'

'Sometimes.'

'Like?'

'Well, the same sort of thing. To be honest, I've heard all the parents I work for say things like this – and worse.'

'How many parents have you worked for?'

'About fifteen families, so thirty or so in total.'

'And how many of those have you heard say things like that?'

'All of them.'

'Have you ever feared that these parents would actually cause harm to their children?'

'No.'

'So this is just a normal, healthy expression of frustration?'

'Yes. Absolutely.'

Clara nodded meditatively. 'You mentioned that "generally speaking", Leila's priority was her work. Does that mean in specific situations, she had other priorities?'

'Yes.'

'Like when she was looking after Max?'

'Yes.'

'In that instance, Max was her priority?'

'Yes.'

'Thank you,' Clara finished.

Leila could see that Clara was satisfied, but she herself was deflated as the judge adjourned for lunch. She felt as hopeless as she ever had since that day in July. It was an intangible anxiety, not borne of a specific thing. It was broader and deeper than what she had done, or the looming threat of prison. It was a dark, unsettling feeling that made her skin itch. There was a dryness in it and she felt a sudden compulsion to take off her jacket, roll up her sleeves and rub something soothing, like lotion or cream, into it. Everything seemed to fit her poorly and chafe in the wrong places.

Outside, she retreated to a solitary corner. Clara often checked on her at lunch, but Leila didn't want to talk to her, or anyone. She bit into her sandwich and chewed the soggy pellet in her mouth. All the things that Edward was trying to prove – that Leila valued her job more than Max, that she was cold and inscrutable, that she had threatened to throttle a child – was just lurid theatre. These strangers didn't know her. They didn't know how much she loved Max or how deeply she felt his loss.

In this state of desultory angst, she slowly picked through her lunch, flinching a little each time she heard the approach of footsteps. Before court resumed, she nipped to the bathroom to wash her hands. She wished she could splash her face but was wary of wrecking her makeup.

A door behind her opened and Yasmin froze in the cubicle. Their eyes met in the mirror and all sound seemed to magnify: the rush of the drier next door, the plink of water from the dodgy tap, the clanking of an ancient radiator.

Leila turned to face her. She seemed thinner and her skin had an unhealthy pallor. 'Hey,' she said gently. 'How are you?'

Yasmin hung there as if trying to decide what to do. For a second, it looked like she might spit something angry, but instead she nodded softly. 'Fine.' Her mouth twisted, but she smoothed it down, forcing herself not to cry. 'You?'

'Oh, you know,' she said, trying to keep her voice from breaking. 'It's good to see you.' It felt so strange, caught in this blank formality after so many years of jokes, fights, laughter and candour. She shifted uncomfortably. 'What Jennifer said in there . . . about what I said about Max, it wasn't serious. I was just letting off steam.'

Yasmin nodded. 'It's okay. I . . . I've said far worse.' The hand-drier next door stopped, leaving behind a palpable vacuum. 'Leila,' she said softly. 'I didn't know.' She twisted a hand towards her torso. 'About the miscarriages.'

Leila held herself determinedly still. 'It's fine,' she said curtly, not wanting to talk about it – not here in this draughty bathroom with its leaky sink and chipped mint wall.

Yasmin kneaded one hand with the other. 'I thought you were having problems getting pregnant, not that you were losing them.'

'What's the difference?' Leila sounded more bitter than intended.

'Just stop for a second,' said Yasmin. 'Stop pretending that you're okay with this. Leila, you lost four pregnancies. That's not the same as never conceiving.' She pressed a hand against her belly. 'I've been there. I know what it does to you: the hormones, the emotions, the joy and stress. You did all that on your own?'

'I don't want to talk about it.' Leila's voice was hard and cool.

'Of course you don't.' Yasmin scoffed. 'Leila the super-woman can handle it on her own.'

Leila wanted to respond but sensed movement outside the door. She turned to face the mirror, wary of being caught with her sister. She smoothed her blazer and tucked a stray hair behind her ear. 'It was nice to see you,' she said to Yasmin's reflection. Without waiting for a response, she walked out and strode back to the courtroom.

*

Dr Robert Morgan was clearly at ease in the witness box. He held himself tall despite his height and there was a looseness in his manner. He was stocky with the sort of meaty frame that came from building muscle without first shedding fat. His hands seemed oversized and Leila wondered how they could be delicate enough to do the work he did.

'Please call me Bo,' he told Edward, revealing Hollywood teeth.

'Bo.' Edward obliged but seemed uncomfortable – the single syllable too dainty in his mouth. 'Can you start by explaining what you do?'

'Yes, of course.' Bo steadied his gaze on the jury. 'I am a forensic pathologist. I work with police and the coroner's office to determine the cause of death when a person dies suddenly, unexpectedly, or violently. I perform post-mortem examinations and, when asked to, I may also attend the death scene and work with police officers to determine the best approach to the scene, the removal of the body and so on.'

'You did the post-mortem examination of Max Hansson, is that correct?'

'Yes.'

'And how many post-mortem examinations have you done over the course of your career?'

Bo puckered his lips. 'Easily over ten thousand.'

Edward raised his brows in a show of surprise. 'That's very impressive.'

Bo accepted this with an obliging nod.

'Now, doctor.' Edward paused and corrected himself. 'Bo. Much of what you deal with is highly complicated so I'd like to start very simply: what is a healthy temperature for a human being?'

Bo spoke clearly with none of the dithering of previous witnesses. 'A healthy temperature is 37°C. Adults that are fit can tolerate temporary changes in internal temperature by plus or minus 4°C. This is narrower for susceptible populations such as elderly people or children.'

'And why are children more susceptible?'

'For various reasons. They have a higher metabolic rate, a reduced capacity for sweating and a larger body surface-to-volume ratio. What this means is that they can overheat at three times the rate of adults.'

Edward nodded slowly as if he needed time to digest this. 'Most of us know that leaving a car in sunlight warms up the interior – sometimes to unbearable levels. Exactly how hot can it get?'

'Well, it's difficult to say exactly, but studies that have shown that temperatures in the UK can rise as high as 66°C.'

'Sixty-six?' Edward repeated.

'Yes. What most people don't understand is that for every ten minutes of time, the heat in a car can rise ten degrees.'

Edward plucked up a piece of paper. 'On Monday the 12th of July, the temperature in east London was 36°C. In these circumstances, would the interior of a car get as hot as 66°C?'

Bo angled his head. 'We couldn't say for certain. There are myriad factors that might affect the temperature.'

'But it *would* be lethal?'

'Oh, yes.'

'Would you expect a reasonable adult to know this?'

Bo's gaze flicked to Leila, then back to the jury. 'Yes, I would.'

'Earlier, you said that a fit adult can tolerate a 4°C change in internal temperature, which puts the tolerable range at 33°C to 41°C. Is that correct?'

'Yes.'

'What was Max's temperature as recorded by the paramedics?'

Bo smoothed his tie. '42°C.'

There was an audible drawing of breath as the jurors absorbed this detail.

'Is this what caused Max's death?'

'Yes,' said Bo with no hesitation. 'Max suffered a form of hyperthermia. His heat-regulation system became overwhelmed, causing his internal temperature to rise, eventually leading to organ failure.'

'How can you be sure that hyperthermia was the cause and not an underlying illness?'

Bo dipped his head, conceding that this was a reasonable question. 'Well, firstly, his temperature was 42°C, which is well within the high-risk hyperthermic range. Secondly, our blood samples showed that he was severely dehydrated. Thirdly, we found stress ulcers in his stomach, which is typical in a case like this. Taken together, I'm confident that the cause of death was vehicular hyperthermia.'

'In that case, is the person who left Max in the car responsible for his death?'

Bo nodded grimly. 'Yes,' he concluded.

Leila blinked and flashes of light burst in her lids. For a moment, she felt herself sway. Fearing she might actually topple, she pressed a hand against the Perspex screen. The clerk noticed and scowled, and she immediately removed it. She dared not look at the jury, for she knew what they were picturing: Max in the backseat, his apple cheeks red with heat.

Edward spent the next hour combing the details of Bo's report. By the time he finished, the jury was visibly flagging, but Clara was undaunted. She stood, as sleek as a shark in water, and peered at a piece of paper.

'Bo, you said that "what most people don't understand is that for every ten minutes, the heat in a car can rise ten degrees". So, in your experience, most people do not know this?'

'That's correct.'

'Including reasonable adults?'

'Yes, but—'

Clara cut him off. 'You also said that there are "myriad factors" that might affect the internal temperature of a car. What are some of these factors?'

Bo swallowed his annoyance. 'Well, for starters, the position of the car, whether it was in direct sunlight or in the shade, the strength of sunlight that day, the angle at which it was hitting the car.'

'So there are many variables and uncertainties at play?'

'Yes.'

'Would you expect a reasonable adult to be aware of the scientific intricacies of ambient temperature inside a vehicle?'

Bo considered this. 'No, I wouldn't—'

Clare moved on swiftly before he could add a *but*. 'Bo, you mentioned that in the course of your post-mortem examination, you found stress ulcers in Max's stomach. What exactly are these?'

'Literally speaking, they are superficial red marks in the lining of the stomach. When you look at them under the microscope, you can see that the lining of the stomach has been lost in these little areas. In terms of their significance, they show that the body has been under severe physiological stress.'

'And in Max's case, how many stress ulcers did you find?'

'Lots.'

'How many is lots?'

Bo sighed. 'Well, tens or twenties, but this doesn't matter because just *one* would be sufficient. Twenty doesn't mean it's twenty times as stressful. The key thing is that they exist whether it's one or ten or twenty or fifty. What it shows is that this child was severely stressed.'

Clara seemed pleased that he was losing his patience. 'Are stress ulcers always caused by high temperatures?'

'No, they are nonspecific.'

'Meaning they could have been caused by some other illness?'

'Yes, but in this case, they were acute. They weren't caused the day before or the week before, but on the day itself.'

'But how do we know that Max wasn't suffering from another illness that stressed his body?'

Bo huffed impatiently. 'We have a standard battery of tests for children that looks for infections and other disease processes. We do blood tests, bacteriology tests on urine and sputum, and microscopic examinations. None of our tests showed any evidence of a pre-existing illness.'

Clara picked up a piece of paper. 'In your "battery of tests", you found traces of promethazine in Max's system. Is that right?'

'Yes.'

'Promethazine is used to treat allergies, insomnia and nausea, is that correct?'

'Yes.'

'Did this not raise suspicion?'

'No. Max's father confirmed to the police that he gave Max some promethazine on the morning of his death. If you look at Max's medical records, you will see that it was medically prescribed a month earlier to treat his hay fever.'

'But promethazine is a heavy-duty drug for a child, is it not?'

'It depends on the child.'

'Does it cause drowsiness?'

'Yes.'

'Does it cause low blood pressure?'

'I believe that's one of its listed side effects.'

'And can low blood pressure lead to organ failure?'

'In severe circumstance, yes.'

'So is there's a chance that the promethazine caused Max's organ failure?'

Bo frowned. 'The pattern of organ damage would be different.'

'But you do agree that Max's father gave him a drug that morning that could cause organ failure?'

'That's not what killed him.'

'But, theoretically, it could have?'

'Theoretically, lots of things can kill you: an anvil falling from the sky, a boulder flattening you mid-stride, but that's not what happened here.'

Clara looked at him coolly. 'Are you patronising me, sir?'

The air seemed to chill. Bo was chastened, realising perhaps that talking down to a woman wouldn't rouse the jury's sympathy. 'I apologise,' he told her.

She nodded wearily, as if she had dealt with a thousand men like Bo. 'Apology accepted.' She turned to the judge. 'I have no more questions for this witness, Your Honour.' She sat down solemnly with only the faintest trace of a smile curling on her lips.

*

Yasmin and Andrew headed to their SUV and slipped inside in silence. She glanced at the backseat, motherhood still in her muscle memory. It was a wonder to her that they, the parents, didn't have a designated place in court. She had expected to be treated with kindness, but they weren't even seen as victims. Instead, they were mere witnesses, left to brave the public gallery. Yasmin had already lost one child and naively assumed that she could navigate this system, but the courts were conducted in a different language. With Toby, she had become an expert by proxy, reeling off *prognoses* and *prophylactics* in everyday talk. Being the parent of a sick child had a culture of its own: loud commiserations and louder advice, sometimes even a sliver of competition as to who had suffered the most. Beneath it all, though, was empathy. Whether it was fair or not, beleaguered doctors and nurses also acted as therapist, teacher and priest. The law in comparison was unforgiving. Yasmin did not want to be infantilised – she balked at the babyish tone used on bereaved parents – but she *had* expected a gentler system; some sort of insulation from the cruelty of the courts. After what they had heard today, even the act of driving home seemed unduly heroic.

In their driveway, they sat for a minute in silence, calling up the energy to confront their empty house. Andrew got out first and Yasmin followed passively. She didn't thank him when he stood aside to let her in first. Instead, she walked to the radiator to toast her icy fingers. When Andrew stepped towards her, she detached herself quickly and started up the stairs.

'Yasmin,' he said hesitantly.

She stopped, one foot poised on the next step. 'What?'

'Do you think that maybe we should spend an evening downstairs?'

Her shoulders grew rigid. She knew what he was really saying. It was a ritual for her now to go up to Max's room and curl up in her chair, secure once again. Andrew monitored her carefully, like a particularly invested nurse. A month ago, he had gently suggested that they start clearing the room, causing yet another fight. Perhaps he was confused. After Toby died, Yasmin had insisted on clearing the room immediately, leaving only his handprints. It was a form of catharsis – a purging of her pain – but she had had time to prepare. This time, the loss was so sudden, so unexpected, that she needed time to process it.

'I'd rather not,' she said, continuing up the stairs.

'Okay,' he said quietly.

She could feel his eyes on her back, but did not turn around.

'I might go for a walk,' he said. 'Clear my head.'

'Fine,' she replied.

She twisted the handle of Max's room, her gaze catching on a blemish in the doorframe. They had use Polyfilla to cover etches in the wood that had charted Toby's height. These traces of him had been tolerable when the room was alive with Max, but now they filled her with residual horror. She sat in her cocoon chair and stared at a shadow in the pale-grey carpet, a fist-sized patch that had been stained with Toby's blood one night. She closed her eyes to blank it out. There was something inside that a mother had to deaden to look after a seriously ill child; some part that could no longer hurt or ache if she hoped to stay sane. It was the part of her that refused help from Andrew; the part that believed that in order to be a good mother, one had to be a martyr. She remembered feeding Toby one day and the skin around his lips just flaked away, making him look ghoulish, and even as he reached for her, she shrank away, unable to comfort him, closing her eyes to him, wondering if this was punishment for some long-forgotten sin. Now, she could see that it had broken something inside her. That was why she had run a bath that day and sank into oblivion.

All she wanted was to know if Max was asleep when he died. If she could know that for sure, then maybe she could find some peace. Maybe there was even joy to be found in other corners of life. But, she wondered bleakly, what joy could be found in an empty house? Was it really so grotesque to want another child? Andrew had been adamant despite her tears and pleading. Maybe they'd have a daughter this time. They would cherish her and keep her from harm. This time, they would do it right. But Andrew had refused, voice edging to something hard.

She felt an icy resentment that he would so baldly defy her. For the entire length of their marriage, Andrew had given her whatever she wanted, fully aware that *he* was the chaser. That he would refuse her now raised a destructive flare in her gut. She fingered the bulk of the phone in her pocket and gingerly took it out. She scrolled down the chats in her WhatsApp and opened the one with her colleague, Jason. Their flirty exchanges were infrequent but went back years.

What if?

The suggestion unfurled deliciously in her mind. She thought of him and all their near misses: the brush of his hand on the small of her back, his warm breath on her neck, the time she was pressed against his chest on that packed lift in Covent Garden. And then there was that office party when they both got blind drunk. If Andrew wouldn't give her another child, maybe Jason would. She could seduce him. It would be easy. A late evening at work, a few drinks, a pre-booked hotel. The prospect grew solid in her mind, tipping from fantasy to the realm of reality. She twirled it around, toying with it like a criminal mastermind. The possibility made her calm, a heavy weight finally lifting. It was possible that she would never act on it but knowing it was an option – a last resort if Andrew refused – made her feel light. She heard the front door slam shut and somehow it felt like a sign.

*

Leila heard the doorbell and recognised the one long note followed by a short, sharp trill. It was how Will used to ring the bell on the nights he forgot his key. She considered ignoring it, but knew he would only let himself in.

Sure enough, she heard the door whine open followed by his tread in the hall. She crumpled up her takeout bag, wincing at the smell of stale grease mixed with the chilly whiff of the fridge. She threw it in the kitchen bin, not wanting to give him the satisfaction of seeing her like this, surrounded by disposable plastic. He appeared at the threshold, the dark circles beneath his eyes ageing him five years.

'I take it you've come to collect your records?' she asked tartly. 'When you're done, leave the key on the counter.' She moved to sweep past him, but he stepped into her path.

'Do you remember the day we took Max to the museum?'

Leila met his eyes. 'Don't you dare.' Her voice was cool and hard. 'Don't you fucking *dare*, Will.'

'You think I was just pretending? You think it was all for column inches?' His hand curled in a half-claw. 'You don't remember how it fucked me up for days?'

Leila said nothing, but of course she remembered. It happened last year on a bitterly cold October morning. They had agreed to watch Max while Andrew and Yasmin attended a wedding. They wrapped him up in his dark blue duffel coat and red mittens on a string, and traipsed to the Natural History Museum on the other side of London. While they were standing in the queue, something caught Max's attention and he absently grabbed Will.

'Daddy, look!' he cried with glee.

Will and Leila locked eyes, an electric pain passing between them, a reminder of the life that they wanted so badly. Will crouched down next to Max and spoke to him brightly, but later, at night, he clung to Leila in bed, his chest quaking funnily. Leila tried to turn to face him but he held her so tightly, she couldn't move. She lay there in his arms in the dark and let him weep in semi-private.

The next day, she suggested adoption for the first time, but Will staunchly refused. He wanted a child of his own, he said, and raising someone else's would never be enough. Leila couldn't accept this, and so began their months of conflict. In some ways, that moment, Max's mittened hand in Will's, was the beginning of the end for them.

'I remember,' she told him now. 'But then why not be honest? If you're hurt, then be hurt! Why spin it into that snide, cynical tone of your column?'

Will flinched. 'I didn't mean to do that.'

'Yes, you did, Will. You *did* because the very worst thing that could happen to you is that you let your image slip for a minute and your media friends see that there's a *human* underneath.'

'Come on, Leila.'

'Let me ask you this: knowing what you know, knowing how much it hurt me, would you go back and write that column again?'

He exhaled slowly. 'That's impossible to answer.'

'No, it's not, Will,' she said acidly. 'It's actually really simple and if you can't see that, then what the fuck are you doing here?'

He clasped his hands in a show of penance. 'If I knew it meant I could lose you, then of course I wouldn't write it, Leila. Come on, we're a team.'

'We're not a team, Will. Not anymore.' She started to move past him and he reached out and gripped her wrist. That gesture, the casual show of ownership, raised a current of anger. She turned and pushed him away with force. 'Understand this, Will. This house is not your house anymore. You don't get to walk in any time you want. And *I* am not your wife anymore. You don't touch me unless you're invited.'

He held her gaze. 'I may not live here, Leila, but this is still my house and you are still my wife.'

She raised her chin in cool defiance. 'Then maybe it's time we got a divorce.' The words were like a death knell, demanding silence from all those who heard it.

'You don't mean that,' he said, his voice so low it was almost a whisper.

'Then touch me, Will, and call my bluff.' The air crackled with warning. Will stood a single pace from her and for a dreadful moment, she really believed that he would reach out and touch her. But then his pride gave in and he backed away resolutely.

'Don't give up on me, Leila.'

'You know your way out,' she said. She sidestepped him and strode upstairs. She felt a buttery satisfaction, but flinched all the same when the door slammed shut, as quick and mean as a hunter's trap.

*

Shep had had a bad feeling all day: a tight somersault sensation in the pit of his gut. It had throbbed through the morning briefing, roiled throughout the day and dogged him into evening. As daylight ebbed in the windows and the station emptied of staff, he sat at his desk tensely, viewing and reviewing the evidence to make sure that nothing was missed. He took a sip of coffee and absently moved the mug so that it wouldn't stain the photo of Leila. Earlier, a colleague had paused at his desk, drawn there by the photo.

'*Who* is she?' he'd asked suggestively.

'*She* is an offender.' Shep had shooed him away. He knew that his colleagues thought him a bore but he rarely engaged in banter. When he first joined the force, he became aware of an unofficial index, the WILF – or 'witness I'd love to fuck' – that officers discreetly used. Most would share it verbally, 'a ten out of ten on the WILF scale', while a few cavalier officers would scribble it innocuously on official notes. If questioned, they would say it stood for 'witness interview largely futile'. The force had since undergone a dramatic shift, but officers still crossed the line: looking up a witness on Facebook, or casually dropping by to check a trivial fact, as he'd done with Cora's mother all those years ago. He had learnt his lesson and vowed to never trip up again.

He picked up Leila's photo and slipped it into the bottom of the folder. All the evidence was in order, but the case was far from open and shut. The prosecution had excavated certain damning facts: Leila had left Yasmin alone for three whole days when she was only eleven, she had taken Max to the doctor and pretended to be his mother, she had carried on with a conference call straight after her miscarriage. All this was designed to paint her in a certain light: cold, calculated, non-maternal, *unnatural*. But they'd also seen another side of her: the generous aunt who took an active interest in Max's trajectory. She was a busy, successful businesswoman and still made time for her nephew. Yes, she occasionally left him with a DVD, but this was hardly damning. They needed something more.

Shep scoured the interview with the babysitter, Jennifer Li, for something he could use. They had the reference to *throttling,* but any parent on the jury would commiserate. They needed something stronger. He spent the next hours looking through transcripts and video evidence. Finally, he picked up the box of unused material and spread the contents on his desk. The prosecuting team would have already been through this but he knew how overworked they were. Though he would never say it to their faces – not as a *lowly* cop – they were known to occasionally miss things.

He sifted through reams of paperwork: Leila's phone bills, the URLs she visited, the emails she sent, the photos she uploaded – hundreds and hundreds of pages of data. He picked up another photo. In this one, she was standing on a stage, her hands raised in a stately gesture as if she were commanding a country. Everything about her signalled power, from the deep-red shade of her dress to her neat hair and trim figure. Shep wondered if she frequented a gym. He flicked through her data and saw that she was a runner. He examined her Fitbit data; daily workouts stacked on top of each other: five minutes of warm-up, five minutes of cardio, thirty minutes of HITT and five minutes of warm-down. She really was an overachiever. He examined the location data and noted the places she visited most often. Her top five stops in order were her home, her office, her sister's house around the corner, the Waitrose close to her home and Siam Eatery, a restaurant near her office. He scanned the location data connected to Yasmin's house. The sisters saw each other more or less every weekend, the only interruptions in the pattern were when Leila visited midweek presumably to babysit Max: a mishmash of weekdays and late evenings. Contrary to what Yasmin had said in her police interview, based on this data, Leila looked after Max at least once a week. Wasn't there anything, in all those days and in all that time, that put a dent in her armour?

Shep reached for his coffee cup and realised it was empty. He surveyed the wreck of paperwork strewn across his desk and tried to decide if he should call it a night. He needed to be fresh for court tomorrow and this was almost pointless. All the evidence was ready to go and he was being obsessive. He leaned back in his chair and rubbed a knot beneath his shoulder. Maybe one more hour and then he would give up. He stood and walked to the grotty kitchen to make himself a coffee, black and bitter the way he liked it.

Back at his desk, he closed his eyes for a moment, warmed by the glow of his amber desk lamp. He flexed his shoulders to ease the ache. When he picked up his coffee mug, the ring on the paperwork perfectly circled a date and time: a stop at Waitrose in the early hours of a Thursday. It seemed so out of kilter with the rest of the beats of Leila's days. A vague thought took shape in his head and he snapped to attention, realising that this could be significant.

'Please,' he said to himself. 'Please please please please.' He sifted through the files and eagerly plucked up the one he was after. He scanned it rapidly, then let it fall back to the desk. He curled his hand in a victorious fist and pumped it in the air.

Chapter Twelve

Leila had worn the wrong thing today. In her effort to look professional, she had chosen a white silk blouse, but it was sheer in the harsh court light and the outline of her bra was visible as well as the shape of her nipples. The prosecution had tried so hard to render her unfavourably – a cold-hearted career woman with overtones of femme fatale – and here she was, playing into their hands. Given the choice, she would rather be grouped with that other cabal of childless women: barren, lonely and sad. At least *they* inspired empathy. She pressed her arms against her torso to create some slack in her shirt and mask the line of her bra, keeping her movements small and subtle.

Edward Forshall stood and called his final witness: Detective Sergeant Christopher Shepherd of the London Metropolitan Police. She had met him before of course and found him aloof and abrasive, despite his winsome nickname: *Call me Shep*. She noted with satisfaction that his ill-fitting suit and tie did little to neutralise his brutish appearance.

'DS Shepherd, thank you for being here today,' Edward started unctuously. 'How long have you worked for the Met?'

'Coming up to eighteen years now.'

'And how long have you been with the Criminal Investigation Department, or CID?'

'Fourteen years.'

Leila did a quick calculation. If he was about forty-five, it meant he had joined the police at twenty-seven. She wondered if he had served in the army before that. There was something about the tension in his spine that implied a military background.

Edward spent a while establishing Shep's expertise before moving onto his interview with Leila. He picked over parts of the transcript but there was nothing overly damning other than Leila's fluency, which she now regretted. Perhaps it would have been better if she had channelled a hysterical mother. Edward inched through the timeline of the day, piecing together what had happened. Then, he said something that made Leila squirm.

'DS Shepherd, we've heard evidence that Leila Syed was a bit of an "ice queen". What is your opinion of this?'

Shep hesitated. 'I can see why some would think that.'

'The sort of woman that might leave a child alone if it suited her to do so?'

Clara was on her feet. 'Your Honour, my learned friend knows that the witness can't possibly answer that question.'

The judge sighed. 'Mr Forshall,' he said as admonishment.

Edward ducked his head obsequiously. 'Of course, Your Honour.' He turned back to the witness box. 'Detective Shepherd, did Leila Syed say in her statement that she has never intentionally left Max in a house or car alone?'

'That's right,' Shep confirmed.

Edward directed the jury to the relevant page in their bundles. 'Detective Shepherd, based on the data you received from Leila Syed's phone, are you able to share with us the top five places she frequents?'

Leila stared at him. How could this be relevant? She knew there was nothing incriminating – a lover's home, a secret addiction – so why was it important?

Shep reeled off a number of addresses: Leila's home, her office in Canary Wharf, her sister's house, her local Waitrose and an eatery near her office. Leila felt a sense of unease, the hairs on her nape bristling. Why had he said the store's name like that, stretching it into two syllables – *Wait Rose* – as if he wanted to imprint it on the jury?

'And what about infrequent places?' asked Edward.

'Well, there were myriad locations: Rich Mix cinema in Bethnal Green, a restaurant in Bank, an actual bank, a printer's near her office, lots of cafés and bars.'

'So a normal urban professional life, one might say?'

'Yes.'

Leila shifted in her seat, not knowing where this was going.

'You were able to analyse the times she attended these places. Did they tend to follow a pattern?'

'Mostly.'

Edward feigned sudden interest. 'Oh? Did you find something unusual?'

'Yes. On one evening, the timestamp on her location shows that she was at Waitrose at 1 a.m.'

Three screens at the front of the room blinked on, each with a map of Mile End. Leila sensed a frisson in the air: jurors no longer slumping, a rustling in the public gallery.

'The red route is Leila Syed's Fitbit,' said Shep. 'You can see that, based on the speed, she walked from Tredegar Terrace to Waitrose. She spent seven minutes there, from 12.58 a.m. to 1.05 a.m., and then walked back.'

Edward frowned. 'And why is this significant?'

'Because Leila lives on Tredegar *Square*, not Tredegar Terrace. The address shown is her sister's house. Leila was babysitting Max that night.'

'Leila was babysitting Max, but headed out to Waitrose?'

'Yes.'

'How do you know that Max wasn't with her?'

'Because we know that he was at home.'

Leila took a shallow breath to try and calm herself; to show no visible sign of stress. They couldn't prove anything. It was in February, nearly a year ago now. The store would no longer have CCTV, so how could they know for sure?

'How do you know?' Edward echoed her thoughts.

'Yasmin Syed had a nanny cam system installed last year.'

Leila's mouth parted in shock. Yasmin hadn't told her this.

Shep went on. 'It's a discreet filming system that's popular with parents who leave their children in others' care. In Max's case, it wasn't on all the time. The parents simply choose which days they will be out and the nanny cam system records the home. This is more cost-effective in terms of the pricing, and the footage can be kept for longer.'

'How long?'

Shep held the pause. 'A year.'

Leila closed her eyes as alarm bells blared in her mind and even though a cold, practical part of her told her to look up and act nonchalant, she knew that it was futile. How could she possibly recover from this? She felt a heave of disbelief. It strafed through her senses, like a swill of milk that's gone to rot – pungent and overpowering. How could Yasmin not have told her this? Leila was her sister; not a stranger to be spied on.

'We have the footage from the nanny cam,' said Shep. The screens switched to a fuzzy grey image that looked like CCTV. The timestamp at the bottom read: *20/02/2021 01:00:00 SAT*. Max was asleep in his bed. Juxtaposed with the video was a map, which showed Leila's location a quarter of a mile away. The time was circled with a thick red line: *01:00:00*.

The mood in the room hardened and Leila knew that the tide had turned. As far as the jury was concerned, Leila had left Max alone while she went out to Waitrose. The frames on the video ticked by while next to it, the red dot on the map came closer to home. It whirred on like this until 1.10 a.m. when Leila could be seen coming into the room. The red dot on the map now hovered over the home.

Leila felt a sinkage in her chest as she watched her double on the screen. She was peeking at Max and carefully fixing the blanket. Then, she placed two bottles on the dresser next to him. You couldn't see the labels from here but Leila knew that one read Gripe Water and the other, Aveeno Baby Calming Comfort Lotion. She was desperate to explain; to tell them how Max had behaved that evening. It was true that he was a naturally sunny child, but there were occasions he was unbearable – and that night had been one of them. He had screamed and screamed in frustration and she hadn't known how to help him. She had called Yasmin and got angry that unlike other mothers, when she went out, she was able to switch off completely and ignore her phone. Leila remembered

thinking those words – *what sort of mother is she* – completely
unironically, judging her sister for something she wasn't faintly
equipped to be. Leila had given Max a bath, gripping his
hands harshly when he began to smack the water and scratch
at a scab on his skin, reopening a wound, then rubbing at it
as if to spite her. She dried him, fed him, swaddled him, took
him to the garden for fresh air and then searched through the
cupboards in desperation for something with which to soothe
him. She knew that gripe water might work, or a massage with
calming lotion, but there was nothing in the cabinets. She tried
to find the baby bag that Yasmin kept stuffed with medicine,
then grew increasingly frustrated when she couldn't find it.

She spent two hours soothing him and when he finally went
to sleep, she nearly wept with relief. She remembered Yasmin
saying *if in doubt, give him gripe water, it works a treat*, so
she did another sweep of the house. She found a few droplets
at the bottom of a bottle. She knew from past experience that
Max wouldn't sleep through the night and so she made a snap
decision. She could run to the shop nearby. It would only take
ten minutes. She would lock all the doors and set the alarm so
if something went wrong, the neighbours would immediately
know. It was completely low risk. What was the alternative?
Go through a night of war while Yasmin blithely enjoyed her
birthday weekend?

Leila locked up and left before she could change her mind.
What was the worst that could happen? That Max would
wake immediately and bawl for a full ten minutes? That
hardly made a difference. It will be okay, she told herself.
And, of course, it was. She returned minutes later and Max
was mercifully still asleep. He woke an hour later, fussing and

crying, and she had fed him the water and rubbed some lotion to soothe him and it had worked a miracle. When Yasmin returned on Sunday night, Leila pretended that it was all fine. She didn't know then that the consequence of that snap decision would one day prove disastrous.

Edward Forshall didn't dwell on the discovery. Instead, he let it sit and steep, knowing he had won the jury. He turned to Judge Warren and ducked his head submissively. 'I am finished with this witness, Your Honour.'

'Thank you, Mr Forshall,' said the judge. 'This might be a good juncture to break for lunch.'

Leila was released from the dock into Clara's grasp. The lawyer ushered her outside and into a witness room. She pulled off her wig and sat down opposite Leila. There wasn't anger in her stare but a chill disapproval.

'You have said several times that you have never left Max alone. Was there someone else with him when you went out to Waitrose?'

Leila started to speak, but caught the strange expression on Clara's face: a narrowing of her eyes, almost like a warning. 'I . . .' She trailed off.

'Did you ask a neighbour to pop over? Or call your husband? Wasn't he only five minutes away?'

Leila's lips parted but she didn't speak. It was in February and she and Will had already separated. 'I . . .' Leila was mute with confusion. In that moment, she felt an acute desire to break down and cry; to tell Clara that she deserved to go to prison; that she wanted to change her plea; that she couldn't do this a moment longer. Instead, she tamped down the compulsion and said, 'I don't remember.'

Clara pursed her lips. 'Well, think about it,' she said pointedly. 'You're an intelligent woman, Leila. I'm sure you know how key this is.' With that, she stood and stalked out, a cool column of ice.

Leila felt the clamp of panic. She needed to fix this as soon as possible – but she *hadn't* asked a neighbour to help. The only person who could have conceivably been there was *Will*. Only *he* could get her out of this. She groped in her bag for her phone and scrolled down to his number. Before she could change her mind, she typed out a message. Can we talk? Over dinner at seven tomorrow?

To her relief, the reply came almost instantly, split over several messages as was typical of Will.

I'd love to.

I'm so sorry, sweetheart.

I'll make it up to you.

Leila wilted with relief. She made a mental note to pick up a bottle of Jura, Will's favourite whisky, on her way home. She had a decision to make. How far was she willing to go to prove that she was innocent? Her fingers hovered above the keypad. I hope so, she typed. Then, she deleted it and tried again. I look forward to finding out how. She cringed and deleted that too. Finally, she sent see you soon.

She felt jittery and realised that she hadn't eaten since yesterday evening. She couldn't face the thought of venturing out. The constant scrutiny of the dock had left her feeling paranoid. Timidity was so unlike her, but being accused of a crime had eroded her sense of dignity. In court, she swerved from the paths of others before they got too close and kept her gaze fixed to the floor to avoid drawing contact. Faced with the prospect of being watched, she decided to stay in the room. One missed lunch was easy after the hundred she'd skipped at work. She drew her arms around her to stave off the crypt-like cold and counted down the rest of the hour. Finally, with five minutes to go, she headed back to the courtroom and the goldfish bowl of the dock.

Detective Shepherd re-entered the witness box. He greeted Clara with a smile, but there was a telltale tension in his shoulders. Leila also noticed a new wetness in his hair, as if he had slicked it with water before coming back in.

'Detective Shepherd,' started Clara, her tone cool and businesslike. 'You gave evidence earlier that you thought Leila Syed was an "ice queen". Can you explain your thinking behind this?'

Shep's gaze flicked to Leila in what seemed like an involuntary tic. 'Well, it's a combination of her body language and what she said.'

Clara waited for more. 'Can you elaborate? What do you mean by "her body language"?'

'She had a cold manner about her.'

'Yes, we understood what you meant by "ice queen". I'm asking what specifically about her body language made you think that?'

He shifted uncomfortably. 'Well, for one, she didn't cry. When we normally question witnesses about the death of a child, they cry, but she was completely composed.'

'What else?'

'She was very still. She would sit with her arms across her

chest and a . . .' He frowned, trying to find the right word. 'Superior look on her face.'

Clara made a contemplative sound as if his answer had revealed something. She picked up a piece of paper. 'Detective, is it true that you invited Ms Syed to have coffee with you?'

He balked, clearly surprised by the question. 'Not in the way you suggest,' he said.

'What is the way I suggest?' she asked innocently.

'It wasn't a romantic thing.'

A smile tugged at Clara's lips. She seemed pleased with his use of the word 'romantic'. 'Oh? Then what was it? Is it normal procedure for the officer in a case to ask the prime suspect out for *coffee*?'

He squirmed. 'It was a casual thing, like "if you remember anything else, please let me know and we can discuss over coffee".'

'A *casual* thing?' She spat the word as if it were dirty. 'So – not *professional*?'

'No, it *was* professional – in a professional context – but it was a casual invitation, as in, take it or leave it.'

Clara angled her head. 'And she chose to leave it, didn't she? Is that why you think she's an ice queen? Because she rebuffed your *casual* invitation to coffee?'

He scowled. 'You're making it sound like something it wasn't.'

'I don't think I am,' she said mildly, as if it were a simple observation. 'Detective, you have made a meal of this one trip that Leila took to Waitrose. How do you know that she left Max alone?'

'We saw it plain as day on the nanny cam.'

'Yes, but how do you know there wasn't another adult in the house?'

He stalled. 'Because we didn't see one on the nanny cam.'

'Yes, but that doesn't prove there wasn't another adult in the house.'

'Like who?'

'Leila's husband perhaps.'

'She's divorced,' he said with a smirk.

'Actually, she's separated,' said Clara smoothly. 'I would have thought you would know that given how much time you've spent poring over her data.' She waved a hand at the dock. 'Did you ask Leila if she's ever intentionally left Max alone?'

'Yes.'

'What did she say?'

'She said no, she hadn't.'

'Did you ask Leila if she's ever left Max alone with her husband?'

Shep's jaw was a hard line. 'No.'

'So you don't actually know if her husband was in the house or not?'

'I think we would have seen him on the nanny cam.'

'You "think"?' Clara was indignant. 'We don't deal with *thinks*, officer. We deal in *certainties*. Given the evidence, are you *certain* that Leila left Max alone that night?'

'I think we can—'

'Please, sir.' Clara's voice was a bark. 'I'll ask the question again. Are you *certain* that Leila left Max alone on the night in question?'

A cuff of pink wrapped around his neck. 'No,' he admitted.

'Thank you.' Clara angled her body away from the jury so that they wouldn't see her smile.

Leila swallowed, finding the answer to her earlier question. How far was she willing to go to prove that she was innocent? She was willing to go all the way.

*

Leila slid her fingers into her hair and shook it vigorously, aiming for a youthful, tousled look. She wiped a tissue around a smudge in her lipstick and frowned when it raised a ruff of dry skin, which she tried to cover with makeup. She undid another button and positioned a lock of hair so that it skimmed her cleavage. She stood back from the mirror and felt a slick of nausea at this attempt at manipulation. It's strange: all your life, you could believe one thing about yourself but find that you were different when it really mattered. Leila was not a rule breaker. She believed in order, fairness and justice. She believed that she was the sort of person who would tell the truth under oath. But now that her fate was at stake, she had abandoned her morals. She did not want to go to prison; would do everything she could to escape it. If that meant leading Will to believe that they could be together again, then that's what she would do.

She heard the doorbell ring – one long note followed by a short – and headed downstairs to let him in.

'I thought I had better not use this.' Will held up his key sheepishly. He placed his phone on the sideboard like he always did. 'You look great,' he said.

She stood a little awkwardly, never adept at seduction, not

like Yasmin, who stopped men in their tracks with a passing glance from beneath her lashes. Leila was all angles and edges. She led him to the kitchen but didn't offer a seat. 'Will you be writing about this?' she couldn't help but ask.

Will flushed. 'No, of course not.'

She swallowed her retort, knowing that this needed delicacy.

'Leila, I fucked up, but this can't be it, can it?' He waited. 'Come on. *Divorce?* We promised never to say that word unless we really meant it.' He braced himself. 'Did you?'

She held a palm to her chest. 'You hurt me, Will.' She knew that word would unstick something inside him. He always did like it when she showed vulnerability.

'Oh, sweetheart, I didn't mean to hurt you. I just needed to work through the tangle in my brain and this was the way I knew how.'

I bet all the clicks and shares didn't hurt, she was tempted to say. Instead, she frowned prettily. 'I'm sorry if I overreacted.'

He rubbed the nape of his neck. 'These last few years have been so fucking hard. On both of us. I've ignored it for so long and this was my way of dealing with it and I tried really, really hard to be sensitive. I mean . . . did you even read it all?'

There it was. His insecurity. His neediness beneath the bluster. 'Of course I did,' she said. 'It was . . . astounding.' She let that hang for a moment. 'But I was too close to it, too raw to see it for what it was.'

He beamed with pleasure, preening beneath the praise. He leaned on the counter and cupped his chin. 'It wasn't baggy in the middle?'

She smiled indulgently. 'Not at all. You've always said that the writer's job is to make the reader want to read the next sentence. That's what you did in that piece. It was . . .' She shook her head as if struggling to find the word. 'Special.'

'You really think so?'

'Yes,' she said emphatically.

He exhaled. 'That is so good to hear.' His relief folded into laughter. 'But, wow, I've never seen you so angry. What you said about the prize and the pittance.' He made a *woo* sound. 'That was harsh.' His voice was breezy but she saw that he was serious.

'You deserved it,' she said, trying for a playful tone.

He smiled impishly. 'Perhaps.'

There was a brief lull in the conversation and Leila laboured to fill it. 'Do you want a drink? I have some Jura somewhere.' She had deliberately tipped out a third of the whisky to make it look coincidental. She poured him a measure and added a splash of water. When she handed it to him, she let her fingers brush his. It felt strange to play at seduction with her husband of nine years.

Will took a sip and winced a little. 'Leila, I *am* sorry,' he said, growing serious. 'I know I should have talked to you about it and I swear I was planning to, but the words came so easily and I was excited for my editor to see it. He loved it and the next thing I know it's up on the site.' Will's eyes grew bright. 'It's had nearly a million views, can you believe?'

Leila forced a smile. 'That's amazing.'

'*You're* amazing,' he cut in. 'No, no,' he said, catching the cynical shift of her eyes. 'You *are*.' He set down his glass. 'You've made me a better man and, Jesus, I know that's a lazy cliché but you *have*, Leila. You . . . you made me fit to be a father.' He swallowed. 'I know it doesn't matter because it's all gone

217

to shit, but that counts for something.' He reached out to touch her, but then dropped his hand. 'It does.'

Leila felt a heave of emotion. She took a sharp breath to stave it and pretended she was still pretending. Will noticed her distress and took a tentative step towards her. When she didn't protest, he drew her into his arms.

She felt the tension uncoil in her muscles. 'I miss you,' she said, her breath hot against the blue of his shirt, and though she said it as a gambit, a vigilant corner of her mind warned her that it was true. Leila missed her husband's body: the solid mass of it against hers, the beat of his footsteps in the study upstairs, the sound of his voice calling from a strange direction: the attic when he was exploring or the basement where he stored his files.

'I miss you too,' he said. He pressed his lips in her hair. 'Do you think we can find our way back?'

Leila closed her eyes to calm the squall of conflicted feeling. *This is just business*, she told herself. This is purely transactional.

'I always thought we would,' he said. He tightened his grip but spoke gently. 'Now that adoption is off the cards, maybe we could figure things out?'

'There's so much going on right now.' Leila spotted her segue. 'If I'm found guilty then there won't be a "we" to go back to.'

'That won't happen,' said Will, conviction making him loud.

Leila pulled away from him. 'Something came up in court yesterday.' She wrung her hands helplessly. 'And I can't figure out what night it was.'

'What do you mean?'

She pressed the glass of whisky back into his hands and explained what happened in court yesterday, specifically with her trip to Waitrose. 'You know how we've babysat together sometimes?' She didn't wait for his answer. 'I can't remember if that was a night you were with me.'

Will frowned. 'When was it?'

'Twentieth February.'

He fished out his phone and scrolled through it.

She carried on talking as he searched. 'We've spent a couple of evenings together since then and I think that might have been one of them. If I left Max alone, obviously it would stick in my mind – but it doesn't so you *must* have been there.'

He continued scrolling. 'But 20th Feb was after we—'

'I know,' she cut in sharply.

He looked up at her and the change in his face meant he knew what she was suggesting. Twentieth February was three weeks after they broke up, when things were still too raw for their cosy evenings together. But if Will had been with her, then Leila hadn't left Max alone. He blinked, then glanced around the house as if there might be spies. 'Are you . . . are you saying we spent that night together?'

'I'm saying we must have,' she said, her voice neutral.

He ran a hand through his hair. 'I . . .' He looked at his phone again, at the calendar, which Leila could see from where she was standing had only one appointment in the late afternoon. 'I suppose I must have been,' he said.

Leila watched him carefully. 'We're married so they can't ask you to give evidence against me.' She gestured at his phone. 'I just wanted to check that date with you to make sure I remembered correctly.'

He nodded, uncertainly at first, but then more conclusively. 'Yes. You're remembering correctly.'

Leila felt a shoot of relief. Will knew what game they were playing. 'You won't write about this?' she asked, her eyes sweetly wide.

'I won't. I promise.'

'Thank you,' she said, hoarse with gratitude. With Will on her side, no one could prove that she had left Max. Knowing this, she felt herself relax, ignoring the question posed by her conscience: a grave and confused *who are you?*

*

Yasmin took in the overwrought décor of the restaurant and regretted everything about this. It all felt wrong: her tight black dress, the plump upholstery, the garish green floor lit from beneath. It was jarring, like a song two beats behind its music. She checked her reflection in the window and noticed the bags beneath her eyes that she had tried and failed to conceal and the split ends in her hair. She quickly tied it up but the hasty arrangement of it exposed her scalp in unsightly places, so she let it down again. She snapped her hands away when she noticed him walk in the door. She stood to greet him and allowed his eyes to wander to her cleavage. They gave each other an awkward kiss hello and he slid into the booth opposite her.

'I was surprised to hear from you.' His voice was strangely foreign without its usual note of flirtation.

'I thought you might be,' she said. She let herself notice how handsome he was. In the office, Jason was always shaved and coiffed with starched collars and polished shoes. Now, with two days' stubble, jeans and a casual shirt, he looked uncommonly handsome. She gripped the base of her glass of water, disoriented in his gaze. She was used to holding the power, knowing that if she arranged her body just so, she could keep his attention for as long as she deigned to. Now, she felt frayed and ugly.

'How are you?' he asked.

She waved a hand, unable to muster an answer. 'How are *you?*' she countered.

He fingered the crease of his napkin. 'I'm fine.' They sat in silence for a moment longer than comfortable. He ordered a bottle of wine, then launched into a monologue, mainly about work. He must have seen her eyes glaze over because he reached out and took her hand. 'Do you want to talk about it?' he asked gently.

She shook her head. She wondered what he would say if she came right out and said it: *I want something more.* The words fizzed on her tongue and she willed herself to say them. It would be so easy. They could go to the hotel across the street, pay in cash and head upstairs. He wouldn't say no. Even with Yasmin in this state, with her hair dull and skin sallow, even caked in the stink of grief, he would gladly take off her clothes and put himself inside her.

'So what do you want?' he asked, and there it was: the hint of suggestion. The probing of possibility. He stroked her palm with the pad of a finger. 'You don't have to answer that. I think I already know.'

She held his gaze. 'And?' She parted her lips, pulling on seduction like a favourite jacket.

'And I don't need to spell it out, do I?' His eyes traced her cleavage.

She sat there suspended in space, clinging to her sense of integrity. She knew that if she surrendered, she couldn't blame the alcohol or the heady mood of a party. This was an intentional submission to him. The indecision felt exquisite, like a silk dress on naked skin. No one would know but the two of them. He had already proven he could be discreet. She took a deep breath, pushing out her chest with the motion, and just as the words formed in her mouth, a waitress stopped at the table, tension breaking like a cloudburst.

'May I take your order?' she asked, her teeth as shiny as a wineglass.

'Yes,' said Yasmin, light with relief. 'Yes, please.' She ordered the biggest meal on the menu: beef sirloin cooked with crispy shallots and a side order of fries. If they sat here and ate, it meant that they wouldn't be elsewhere, doing something else. And if she could prove to herself that she could sit here in his presence calmly and intentionally without running away, then perhaps she wasn't all the things she feared: selfish, weak, deceitful.

'And you, sir?' The waitress hovered patiently.

Jason tensed with annoyance as he placed his order. When the waitress left, he turned his gaze on Yasmin. 'So I guess we're doing lunch,' he said, a hard edge in his voice.

'I guess we are.' She smiled, falsely bright, and reached for her glass of wine.

Chapter Thirteen

Leila had chosen her outfit carefully this morning: a tasteful navy dress that stopped just short of fashionable; a sedate Kate Middleton affair with a calf-length hem. She had worn her hair loose in an effort to soften her angular jaw, but regretted it now as it sat flatly on her scalp, making her want to shrink. She felt shaky with the effort of holding her poise, like a weightlifter locked in position – one slight give and it would all crash down. It occurred to her that if it all went wrong today, then she might be in prison by Christmas next week. The thought filled her with dread, for she knew what she was lacking. She was many things – strong, resilient, ambitious – except the one thing she really needed: *likeable*. She needed the jury to like her and as she sat there, waiting to be called to the witness box, she realised she was unprepared. She should have practised all those things that were endearing in her sister: the rounding of innocent eyes, the flush of bashful cheeks, the quivering, whimpering style of speak that sparked a protective instinct. It was far too late now, she realised, as Clara stood to give the defence's opening speech.

'Members of the jury, this case is about the death of a child.' She surveyed each juror gravely. 'I'm going to repeat that: this case is about the death of a child. I want to give you a moment to absorb that because I know how hard it is to talk about this. I know the visceral gut punch of those words and I don't want to soften them with euphemism or platitude. What we're talking about is awful and serious and tragic. There is no denying this.'

She smoothed the cuff of her sleeve. 'Now, you might wonder why I – the defence counsel – want to highlight the gravity of what we're dealing with.' She pressed her lips in a grim line. 'Well, because I want you to understand what you are feeling. I want you to acknowledge that you feel pain and anger and shock and sorrow because of what this case involves. I also say it because I know that what I'm going to ask of you next requires extraordinary strength and skill.'

Clara steepled her fingers. 'I want you to *feel* that pain and sorrow, and then I want you to set it aside because what we need from you is clarity of thought. You were chosen because the law believes in your ability to think rationally; to examine the facts with the cool head needed to deal with the matter at hand. I know that this will be hard, but I – like the law – trust you to do that.'

Clara pointed at Leila, who tried not to shrink from the glare. 'Leila Syed is a loving aunt and professional business-woman. She runs her own firm and is a trusted member of the community. She lives close to her sister, Yasmin Syed, and her brother-in-law, Andrew Hansson. On Monday the 12th of July, Andrew called Leila and asked if she could drive Max, her nephew, to nursery as he had an emergency at work. They live close to each other and Leila is used to stepping in last minute to help with babysitting. We've heard from several witnesses that Leila took an active interest in Max's development and was happy to look after him.

'On the morning in question, Leila drove to Andrew's house and waited while Max was strapped into the back of her car. It is a rear-facing seat and Max was asleep, which means that he did not make a peep for the entire journey. Now, had he woken up, the tragedy of what happened that day would have been entirely prevented. Or if the father had had the foresight to place an item in the front seat as many parents do. Or had the nursery been on the way to Leila's office rather than five minutes beyond it. One or all of this could have jogged her memory.

'Instead, Max remained asleep and Leila, lulled by her morning routine, switched to autopilot as so many of us do on our way to work. En route, she fielded a phone call from work as she often does as the head of the firm. She even has an adapted phone so that she can do this safely.

'As she drove, she saw her office building and, as she has done a thousand times, she turned in and parked in her designated spot. She walked into the building, took the lift upstairs and began her working day. Now, some of you will be wondering how on earth she could forget a child.

'I'm a parent as I'm sure some of you are. Can you think of *one* lapse? One moment where you lost sight of your child? Maybe you were at a picnic and he escaped your periphery, or in a supermarket aisle and he was drawn away, or at the beach when he got too close to the water. All those would-be tragedies averted in the nick of time. "There by the grace of God," we say, for we know that their safety was down to serendipity, not some foresight or skill. In Leila Syed's case, that momentary lapse – that single, fleeting moment – bloomed into tragedy and here we are; all because she agreed to help her brother-in-law who found himself in a bind. That act of decency ultimately led us here, to this juncture. Leila Syed is not guilty of a crime. She is a loving aunt who has suffered a great tragedy. Please do not punish her further.'

Leila listened, her tears just a breath away. Goosebumps pocked her arms and when she blinked, she felt her lashes dampen. She skimmed a finger along her lash line to dash away her tears – discreetly, for she feared they would seem on cue. She didn't know how to arrange her features to elicit the jury's sympathy; to signal that she wasn't guilty. And then it was too late. Leila was called to the box.

She took the oath and marvelled at how such familiar words could also feel wildly foreign: *the truth, the whole truth, and nothing but the truth.* She felt like a comic actor suddenly tasked with gravity. What was the correct behaviour when you were accused of being a killer?

Clara spoke gently, her sharp edges in soft focus. It was a gambit no doubt to show that Leila was worthy of sympathy. 'This is going to be a long day or two, Leila. We have a lot of ground to cover, so if you need a break, please say so.'

Leila nodded, knowing that she would not. She dared not waste the jury's time.

'Let's begin on the morning of 12th July. What was your state of mind when your brother-in-law called to ask you to help with Max?'

Leila thought back to that fateful phone call. 'I . . . My state of mind was fine. It was a normal day.'

'A busy one?'

'Yes.'

'Were you annoyed with him at all?'

'No,' Leila lied.

'Okay, well, we know from the police transcripts—' She paused to direct the jury to the correct page in their bundles. 'That Max was asleep when you picked him up. Can you describe the car journey? What happened during the drive?'

Leila remembered how she drove extra carefully as if it might forestall tragedy. 'Nothing remarkable.' She modulated her voice so that it sounded softer. 'He stayed asleep and I drove to work. I received a phone call from the office while driving.'

'Why?'

'A colleague had misplaced some key blueprints for a meeting and the only other set was in my office. I needed to go and let him in.'

'How did this affect your state of mind?'

Leila considered this. 'I was worried,' she admitted.

'Were you dwelling on the missing blueprints?'

'Yes. I was annoyed that he had been careless and lost such an important resource. I was wondering whether the printer across the road might open early for us, or if we could show the blueprints digitally even though the client asked for printed ones.'

'So there was a lot going through your mind?'

'Yes.'

'What happened next?'

Leila wiped her palms on her dress, hoping the jurors wouldn't see. 'I drove to the office, parked in my spot and hurried upstairs.'

'You "hurried" upstairs. Were you in a panic?' Clara narrowed her eyes.

'No. I wasn't running. I just wanted to get there quickly.'

'Did you think it would be more efficient if you popped into the office first and dropped Max off afterwards?' Clara asked this casually as if it might be a logical, perfectly acceptable thing to do.

Leila squirmed. 'No, I didn't do that.' Her voice held a hairline fracture and she was grateful for the way it made her sound: honest, genuine, contrite.

Clara continued. 'Max's headmistress, Josephine Allsebrook, said that she has seen you at the school gates, which we established wasn't likely, but can I double-check: have you ever dropped off Max at school?'

Leila shook her head firmly. 'No, I have not.'

'What worries me, though, Leila, is that Detective Shepherd says you have a history of leaving Max. Did you leave him alone to go to Waitrose?'

Leila had wrestled with this question for days. She had wondered how many defendants lied in court. The pomp and grandeur would have you believe that witnesses told the truth, but surely this couldn't be right. What power could a holy book wield if you were intent on being deceitful?

'No,' said Leila, forcing herself to remain neutral.

Clara tilted her head. 'But you *did* go to Waitrose at 1 a.m. on the 20th of February?'

'Yes.'

'So where was Max?'

'At home.' Leila saw the jurors shift uncomfortably.

'Alone?'

'No.' Leila knew she could not hesitate. 'He was with my husband, Will Carmichael.' She hoped that his familiar name might lend her some second-hand gravitas.

'And you're sure about that?'

'Yes.' Leila desperately hoped that her face wouldn't slip. Standing there, in front of twelve ordinary men and women, it was harder to lie than she had thought possible.

Clara nodded. 'So all of Detective Shepherd's grand conclusions were a mere confection?'

Leila swallowed. 'Yes.'

Clara looked at the jury in dismay. 'So this whole Waitrose business was much of a muchness, it seems.' She sighed heavily, then righted her robe with a tug as if it was time to get serious. 'Now, Leila, what *is* true is that your sister was left to look after herself for a few short days in youth. Can you tell us about this? What prompted the decision?'

Leila didn't speak as she tried to formulate what she wanted to say. Then, she forced herself to look at the jury. 'So often, we hear about the "hardworking family": on TV, in newspapers and every political speech. Our whole society is built around it, but usually it means a very narrow thing: a mother and a father, two children, and grandparents who can help out when needed. This leaves out so many other families: the single parent, the orphaned children, the carer and her partner, the teenager and her younger sister. There were only two of us and I worked *hard*. Does that mean we're a "hardworking family" or not?'

Leila tried not to clench her fist. 'I did everything I could. And that was one time – *one time* – when I didn't have a way out. I thought about leaving my sister with neighbours, but they had three boys and I thought she'd be safer at home.' Leila flexed her fingers wide. 'People who have support find it hard to believe that others do not. They think that *of course* there's someone to help, but there *isn't*. We talk of people falling through the cracks as if they're collateral damage: an acceptable sacrifice in a system that works for the large majority, but when *you're* the one who's falling, it's *so* . . .' Leila paused to steady herself. 'Lonely.' She took a quivery breath. 'I did what I had to do to keep me and Yasmin together.'

There was silence in the courtroom as Clara let the words settle. She waited a beat before she continued. 'I'd like to talk a bit more about Max. We've heard about his scrape in the playground and the throwaway comment you made to his babysitter, but I want to get to the heart of your relationship with him.'

Leila felt herself bristle. She and Clara had disagreed on this vehemently. Leila was keen to expand on Max's injury to try to explain herself, but Clara insisted that they skate right past it. There was no point in dwelling on details, she said.

'Tell us about Max,' she prompted.

Leila wrestled with the question. How does one sum up a young child's life?

Clara noted her difficulty and swiftly adapted the question. 'Tell us about a fond memory you have of him.'

Leila tried to smile, but it cracked into sorrow. She did not look at the public gallery, but was sure that Yasmin was weeping. 'Max was such a sunny child. Last year, I asked him what he wanted for his birthday and he thought about it for a while and then said that he wanted five blue buttons.' Leila drew a breath to compose herself. 'Max looked at me and said, "But Auntie, they all have to be different."' Her tears spilled over, but she continued speaking. 'I spent the next week snipping blue buttons from outfits and of course I bought him some other presents, but when he got those buttons, his face lit up like it was the best thing he ever got.' She swallowed. 'I loved Max. I loved him more than I could possibly say.'

Clara nodded and segued smoothly to Andrew's phone call. She spent the rest of the morning combing over details: how hot it was in the car, how hot it was outside, whether Leila turned on the air-con, what about the heater, how many layers was she wearing, did she take anything off, was she sweating, did she crack a window. Leila knew what Clara was trying to prove: that even if she *had* intentionally left Max in the car, she couldn't have reasonably known that it was hot enough to kill him. Leila answered each question with a soft-focus stoicism: stiff upper lip but not heartless.

Finally, Clara arrived at her final question. 'Leila, one thing that got lost in all this talk is that *you* yourself have lost someone you loved. Can you explain how this has felt to you?'

Leila felt her energy leave her, like the dot in the middle of an old TV just before it blanks. She knew what Clara wanted, a grand show of sorrow, but Leila couldn't lay claim to this grief, for it belonged to Yasmin. She couldn't stand in front of her sister and mourn for Max so brazenly. She couldn't tell the jury that death had altered the weight of gravity so that she was always close to tipping. Her pain was a private, wordless thing – a secret, silent creek that sometimes flowed imperceptibly and sometimes at alarming speed. She couldn't describe the wrenching pain of the day that Max had asked that question – *is there a baby in your house?* – and knowing that her answer was also now Yasmin's. *No.* There was no baby in her house because Leila had killed him.

'It is the worst thing that's ever happened to me.' Leila looked at the jury. 'Grief is heavy enough, but when you're the one who caused it, then it's . . . overwhelming.'

Clara nodded solemnly. 'Thank you for being so honest.' She studied Leila for a moment, then nodded decisively, choosing not to push her further. She turned to the judge. 'I have no more questions, Your Honour.'

*

Edward Forshall stood and fixed his gaze on Leila. She was surprised by his demeanour. So far, he had played the elder patrician, patiently asking questions, trying to uncover the truth. Now, he held himself aggressively: eyes narrowed and shoulders squared, like a viper about to strike.

'Ms Syed, do you have a bit of a superwoman complex?'

She blinked. 'I'm not sure what you mean.'

He wheeled his hand impatiently. 'A superwoman complex. A woman who has it all. A woman who is infallible; who can achieve all things effortlessly; who never drops the ball. Do you see yourself like this?'

Leila tried to ignore his tone: haughty, cutting, critical. 'No, I don't,' she answered. Clara had told her to keep her answers short and polite; to ignore his attempts at drama.

'No?' he asked sceptically. 'So you don't go to schools and conferences purporting to be a successful woman?'

Leila tried to work out the best way to answer without seeming conceited. 'I do give talks at schools and conferences.'

'And during these talks, you project yourself as a successful woman, yes?'

'Yes, but I—'

'You can make hard decisions, can't you, Ms Syed?' he cut in. 'That's why you left Max alone the day you went to Waitrose?'

Leila's skin blushed hot and she prayed they couldn't see it. 'I didn't leave him. My husband was with him.'

'If that's true, then why isn't he here to confirm this to the jury?'

Leila swallowed her retort. *Talk to my lawyer.* 'I'm sorry, I don't know.' She had been relieved to learn that if Clara didn't call Will as a witness, the prosecution could not question him given that she and Will were still married. He had agreed to help her, but he was a showboater and could not be trusted in a forum like this. He would try too hard to hold their attention.

Edward raised a doubtful brow. 'I guess we shall never know,' he said pointedly. Then, he changed direction. 'Do you have children, Ms Syed?'

'No,' she answered neutrally.

'So, in fact, you don't "have it all" in the traditional sense of the term?'

'No, but I never—'

He interrupted. 'So, even though you project yourself as a successful woman – a woman who "has it all" – you in fact, *don't*. Does that bother you?'

Leila tried to unpick the question. 'I don't know if anyone has it all.'

'*Yasmin* did,' he cut in. 'She had a warm and sunny child, a loving husband, a nice house, an interesting career.'

'She hated her job,' said Leila. She immediately regretted the bite in her tone.

'Ah,' said Edward knowingly. 'So *there* it is. Yasmin had everything except one thing: a job that she loved. And that's one thing you could hold over her, isn't that true?' He didn't wait for Leila to answer. 'Your job is the one thing you could use to say, "Look, I'm better than you."'

'That's not true.'

'But it *is* true,' he snapped. 'Tell me, does your husband live with you?'

She blinked. 'No.'

'Why?'

'We're separated.'

'Why?'

Leila wanted to tell him it was none of his business, but Clara had specifically told her not to get drawn into conflict. 'For various reasons,' she said.

'Such as?'

'We couldn't have children and that pushed us apart.'

'Oh?' said Edward as if he didn't already know this. 'How long were you trying?'

She pushed a fingernail into a cuticle and sawed it back

and forth. 'Seven years.' She heard an intake of breath and made eye contact with a juror, a thirtysomething woman with brittle blonde hair. She saw not empathy but fear there, as if just being in the same room as Leila might infect her with the same misfortune. 'We failed to conceive naturally,' she said, 'so we tried IVF.'

'How many rounds?' he asked glibly.

'Five.'

'So you failed at marriage *as well* as motherhood. The only success you *did* have was your career. Is it fair to say that that career was important to you?' When Leila didn't speak, he prompted, 'Ms Syed?'

'Yes.' Pressure grew in her chest. Edward Forshall was exposing everything she felt in the dark of night. Despite her spacious house, sleek car and glossy, glassy office, people clearly perceived the emptiness in her life.

'You felt inferior as a woman, which is why when it came to your career, you did everything you could to keep the balls in the air. So when it came to a choice: drop Max off at nursery and lose a monumental business deal, or leave him in the car, you chose your business, didn't you?'

'That's not true.'

'It bothered you, didn't it, that Yasmin kept asking you to help when you had so many other responsibilities?'

'No.'

'That's why you chose to prioritise yourself that day?'

'No.' Leila felt the sweat pool in the crease of her knees.

'The fact is clear: you're a woman who can make hard decisions.' He swept an arm across the courtroom. 'We've heard all about them: how you had a miscarriage right there

235

in your office and five minutes later you were back on the phone. You left your sister alone when she was a child. You did things you knew were wrong because you needed to get on with work, isn't that true?'

'I—'

'You left Max in the car on purpose, didn't you?'

'I didn't.'

'You knew it was burning hot that day and you left him in the car.'

'I didn't.'

'You knew – as any reasonable adult would – that if you left him, there was a chance that he might die and you left him anyway.'

'No.'

'Yes.'

'No!'

'Yes, you did!' he thundered. 'Yes, you did. You left Max intentionally knowing he could die – and he *did*. That makes you *guilty*, Ms Syed. You are *guilty* of this crime.'

Leila blistered in the raw, ruthless exposure of the truth. A primitive part of her mind called on her body to act: to crouch down, raise a shield with her arms, deflect this merciless salvo. Instead, she closed her eyes, blanking out the spotlight, catching the thick sob before it spilled out. 'No,' she said feebly. 'I forgot.'

'You did not forget,' he said cruelly. 'A woman like you does not *forget*, Ms Syed. A woman like you makes a deliberate decision and that's exactly what you did. You left Max, knowing full well how risky it was. You are guilty of this crime, aren't you, Ms Syed?'

Defeat coiled like a rope round her neck because she knew that he was right. A woman like Leila Syed who snapped back onto a conference call after suffering a fourth miscarriage did not forget. A woman like that was able to coldly compartmentalise and make hard but deliberate decisions. She knew how the jury saw her and in that moment of electric panic, she was certain that her fate was sealed.

*

Will sat on the top step looking out onto Tredegar Square. His hands were wedged in his underarms and his skin was flushed with cold. Next to him was a cotton bag, its base stained dark by the wet stone.

Leila paused on the bottom step. 'Will, what are you doing here?' She narrowed her eyes in query. 'How long have you been here?'

'Oh, about half an hour,' he said casually.

'It's three degrees! Why didn't you go in?'

He pushed his scarf down with his chin and gave her a sardonic smile. 'My wife told me I wasn't allowed to.'

Leila heard the creak of her leather glove as she balled her hand in her pocket. It was a marvel how that word, in his mouth, and the claim it laid to her, still filled her with a sense of security. *My wife*. It meant that Leila belonged somewhere, and to someone.

He stood and brushed the seat of his coat. 'Can I come in?'

Leila tried to keep things light. 'You'll get frostbite if you don't.'

Inside, he slung his coat on the heater and followed her to

the kitchen. He unpacked his bag of groceries – two parcels wrapped in paper, a fat bulb of garlic, a bunch of rosemary and a bottle of wine – and then picked out a knife, moving with a blithe industry.

'Will, we said we'd take things slowly.'

He crouched down and rummaged inside a cupboard. His hand snaked up and placed a griddle on the worktop. 'I'm just making dinner, Leila.'

'I can see that, but we didn't talk about this.'

He straightened and met her gaze. 'I was there in court today. I looked for you afterwards, but they said you were talking to your lawyer.'

Leila stiffened. Will had seen her lie to the jury.

'I saw how they treated you and I didn't want you to be alone tonight. I know you need time. All I'm asking today is that you let me cook for you.'

Leila shifted uneasily. 'Will, it's the last day of the trial tomorrow. I don't know what's going to happen.' This was her way of curbing false hope, not just his but hers.

He looked at her with tenderness. 'Then shouldn't we be together today?'

Leila knew that 'yes' would be the easiest thing in the world to say if she were still pretending, but the nearness of him, the sheer force of his presence punched cleanly through that illusion. She thought about the vastness of their years together and though she didn't know what the next days would bring, or if she could even forgive him, there was only one thing she wanted to say: 'Yes.'

'Okay, then,' he said a little hoarsely. He rolled up his sleeves and got to work.

Leila settled on a stool and watched him, finding comfort in the familiar pattern of his cooking: oil so hot that it tinkled, salt dashed in so liberally that grains skittered to the floor, and Will – her brash, unyielding husband – steadfast in his love for her. In that moment, she felt a sense of fearlessness about the days ahead. Will was here and he didn't care that she could lie to a jury, or that she was an "ice queen". He didn't judge her for rejoining that conference call after her final miscarriage. He didn't care that she could be logical even in the face of death. Will loved her regardless.

Chapter Fourteen

Dr Bell was a sinewy man with short grey hair and delicate hands that he used to punctuate his points. He was the final witness of the trial and though his evidence was necessary, it had the flavour of an afterthought. There were two prongs to Leila's defence: first, that she did not intentionally leave Max in the car. This the jury had to take on word. There was no hard evidence to prove that she had done otherwise. Second: that even if she *had* left Max intentionally, she could not have reasonably believed that this might have killed him. To Leila, this second prong was moot. Surely, any reasonably intelligent person knew that you could not safely leave a child in a car, but Clara had told her that she'd be surprised. Still, it seemed too much of a tangent, like a flimsy safety net as if to say, Leila didn't mean to leave Max *but even if she had* . . . If the first were true, why were they concerned with the second? Clara had explained that this might be the thing that saved her, so Leila had acquiesced.

'Dr Bell, can you explain in the simplest terms possible what "vehicular hyperthermia" is?'

'In the simplest terms possible, it's when a child suffers from heatstroke when left in a car.'

'How many children die from vehicular hyperthermia every year?'

He pinched his lower lip in thought. 'It's difficult to say because the official cause of death may be recorded as dehydration or cardiac arrest, or any of the complex interweaving factors that result from hyperthermia. I can say that in the US, it's about thirty-seven a year.'

Clara raised her brows. 'And how many happen in the UK?'

The doctor waved a hand in the air. 'Oh, far, far fewer.'

'How many? One or two a year?'

He looked horrified. 'No, no. More like one or two a decade, if that. The Royal Society for the Prevention of Accidents doesn't collect data on hot car deaths because it's so exceedingly rare.'

Clara exhaled in relief, more for show than anything. 'So it's not common at all in the UK?'

'No.'

'Is that because parents are more vigilant here?'

He frowned. 'No, no. That's a profound misinterpretation. Parents forget their children by the dozens, but due to the cooler weather in the UK, this rarely leads to death.'

'"By the dozens",' repeated Clara. 'Is that an exaggeration?'

'No.' He waggled a finger in the air, like a teacher rebuking a child. 'In fact, these are just the cases reported to the police, usually by a passing stranger who spots the child in the car. There are likely dozens of other cases where the parent returns to the car with no recorded consequence.'

'I see. So parents in the UK commonly forget their children in the car, but this rarely leads to death?'

'Correct.'

'Huh,' said Clara as if surprised. 'So in your expert opinion, is it reasonable to believe that a child left in a car for a short period of time in the UK would not die from vehicular hyperthermia?'

'Yes, that's reasonable.'

'Dr Bell, we heard from pathologist Dr Robert Morgan that an infant's body can heat up at three times the rate of an adult's. Is that correct?'

'Yes.'

'Would you expect the layman to know that?'

'No.'

'He also mentioned that there were myriad factors that affect the temperature inside a car. Do you know what some of these are?'

'As you say, there are myriad factors. The position of the car, the built environment, the interior material. Even the colour of the vehicle makes a difference.'

Clara cocked her head in surprise. 'Is that so?'

'Yes, studies have shown that a dark-coloured car heats more quickly than a white one.'

'So there is a huge variety of variables that affects how likely a child is to suffer from hyperthermia?'

'Yes.'

'Would you reasonably expect the layman to know this?'

'No, I would not.'

'So let me sum up: it is reasonable to believe that a child left in a car in the UK for a short period of time would not suffer vehicular hyperthermia?'

'That's correct.'

'So Leila Syed may not have reasonably known that leaving Max in her car could lead to his death?'

'Correct.'

'Thank you, doctor.' Clara nodded at the judge. 'I have no more questions, Your Honour.'

Leila let her breath out, glad that she'd trusted Clara. Somehow, Dr Bell's cool, surgical demeanour had lessened the sting of Leila's crime; made it seem less awful even if intentional.

Edward Forshall stood for the final cross-examination of the trial. 'Dr Bell, you've spoken a lot about whether a reasonable person might know that a child's body heats at three times the rate of an adult's, or that white cars heat less than black cars.' His tone was snappy and impatient, as if none of this was important. He cracked a sheet of paper as if it were a whip and made a great show of checking it. 'Would you expect a reasonable adult to know that leaving a child alone in a car for *three hours and twelve minutes* places that child at risk?'

'It's not clear that the—'

'A yes or no will do, doctor.' Edward was testy.

'I . . .' There was a yielding in his shoulders. 'I would, yes.'

'Do you know how long Ms Syed left her nephew in her car?'

Dr Bell raised a brow. 'Three hours and twelve minutes?' His tone was sarcastic but the effect was grave.

'Indeed,' said Edward.

And just like that, the last witness of the trial was released.

*

Leila sat alone and sifted through her cold pasta salad. The balls of tasteless mozzarella were cold on her teeth when she bit them. The rocket was too vinegary and the sundried tomatoes too sharp and chewy. She forced herself to swallow, feeling her stomach churn with nerves. Today was their last chance to address the jury, their final try for innocence.

Leila grew still when she felt the cast of a shadow. She turned, expecting Yasmin, and was flustered to find Detective Shepherd instead.

'You did very well in there,' he said.

She couldn't discern his tone. Sarcastic? Suspicious? Or could it be that he was genuine? She ignored the comment and took a sip of water.

He sat down beside her, angling his body so that he could study her. 'What really happened, Leila?'

She took a mouthful of penne, glazed with runny liquid.

'Come on, it's just you and me here.' He patted his pockets to show that they were empty. 'I'm not talking to you officially, so go on.' He nodded encouragingly. 'Tell me. What really happened that day because I know it didn't play out the way you said.'

Leila swallowed the soggy pasta, then steadied her eyes on him. 'Why are you trying to intimidate me?'

He pulled back, offended by the question. 'I don't wish to intimidate you. I'm impressed by you.'

She braced herself for an insult. *I'm impressed by your cunning and deception*. But he did not follow up.

'I think you're an impressive woman and I can't figure out how something like this could happen.'

'I'm so tired of hearing that.' Her voice was brittle, ready to snap. 'People make mistakes. People forget.' She pressed a hand against her chest. 'Why am *I* expected to be perfect?'

'Because you *are*,' he said.

'You don't know that,' she spat. 'You don't know *me*.'

'Which is why I'm trying to.'

She searched his face, not knowing what this was. A threat? Or a genuine plea for the truth? 'Are you even allowed to talk to me without my lawyer?'

A corner of his lip curled in regret. 'No. I could get into trouble for this.'

Leila blinked. 'Then why are you here?'

'Because I owe it to Max.' The hard nut of his face softened into something warmer, more fatherly, and Leila felt an urge to tell him what he wanted to hear. Instead, she gathered her plastic spoon and tray and gripped them together in her hand. 'I'm only trying to help you,' he said as she stood.

'Sure you are,' she said unkindly and strode away from him. She tipped the rubbish in the bin and saw that court was reconvening. It was time for closing speeches.

*

Edward Forshall righted his gown and greeted the jury with a respectful nod. Leila expected fireworks, but he launched his speech sedately.

'Members of the jury, no one is saying that Leila Syed did not care for her nephew. Much of what she did for him was commendable.' He folded his palms together. 'The problem is good intentions do not and should not excuse a serious act of negligence. In this case, Ms Syed's actions had devastating consequences that deserve to be examined carefully.

'These are the facts of the case. Leila Syed was meant to

be looking after her nephew that day. She had a duty of care towards him, but left him in her car. She does not contest this. Two: leaving him in her car directly led to his death. We have heard from an expert pathologist that Max's temperature was 42°C, beyond the limit of what most humans can withstand. He was dehydrated and had stress ulcers in his stomach. The cause of death is clear: vehicular hyperthermia. Her counsel has bombarded you with a glut of unnecessary detail. We've heard about the colour of a car, the shape, the position and the many intricacies of ambient temperature to try and excuse Ms Syed's actions that morning, but ask yourself this: can we expect a reasonable adult to know that leaving a child in a car can lead to its death, *especially* in the height of summer? I think we all know that the answer is "yes". So, taken together, those things mean that Leila Syed placed her nephew in a potentially lethal situation. This *by definition* is gross negligence. She claims that she simply forgot, hoping perhaps that you will chalk it up as pure tragedy, but let's review what we've heard.'

Edward raised an arm in Leila's direction. 'There are four pertinent things that we know about Leila Syed. One: when her sister was only eleven years old, she left her alone for three whole days.' He punctuated each word. *Three. Whole. Days.*

'Two: Leila Syed lied when Max sustained a head injury in her care, an injury that was severe enough that she had to rush to hospital. Leila Syed lied to the doctor who treated Max in claiming to be his mother. Later, she lied to Max's *real* mother, actively concealing the injury.' He shook his head as if struggling with the scale of deception.

'Three: on one occasion, Leila Syed said that she could "throttle" Max. Now, I'm not suggesting that she meant this literally. I'm the first to admit that parents say this sort of thing sometimes.' He raised a finger, asking for pause. 'What this *does* tell us, however, is that Leila Syed was struggling. What this *does* suggest is that she wasn't coping perfectly well with having to help out with Max.

'Four: Ms Syed presents herself as a successful woman, but she failed at marriage and motherhood. In the void left behind, it was her *career* that mattered most. In fact, we've heard how, on one occasion, she suffered a miscarriage and carried on with her *conference call*.' He made a sneer of a sound. 'It is clear that Ms Syed places immense value on her work, so when she was lumbered with her nephew yet again and found herself in a jam, she made a decision that most of us would not. She decided to leave him in her car so she could tend to an emergency at work.'

He pursed his lips regretfully. 'Now, you may be reluctant to find Ms Syed guilty. You may think, "Well, it's not as though she *intended* to kill him." Well, no, but what she did was just as lethal. She left him in her car on the hottest day of the year and that was a *deliberate* choice she made. Leila Syed is responsible for the death of Max Hansson. What she did was an act of gross negligence. That act led to Max's death. Therefore, she is guilty of gross negligence manslaughter. She is guilty of the charge. I am sure you will make this decision more in sorrow than in anger, but find her guilty you must.' He gave a little bow as he finished.

Leila exhaled to ease the pressure in her chest, wringing and wringing like a piece of wet cloth. She risked a glance at the jury, but they sat impassively, giving away no clues. It seemed absurd that these twelve strangers who didn't *really* know the truth, only a refracted version of it, were tasked with deciding her fate. How could they possibly know?

Leila had no time to dwell on this for Clara Pearson now stood for the final word of the trial. She frowned at her blue notebook and for a moment it seemed she had forgotten her speech. But then, she closed the book with a grave flourish and fixed her gaze on the jury. The implication was clear: *what I have to say is more important than rehearsed lines.*

'Members of the jury, at the beginning of this trial, I asked you to think of one lapse that you've made at a point in the past. Perhaps you realised that you left the oven on, or your front door unlocked at night. If a person accidentally burns down their building, they are branded a villain. But what if they remember to turn it off in the nick of time and everything turns out fine? Morally, is the person with the close call really any better than the other?' She tilted her head in query.

'All of us can name a lapse. "There by the grace of God," we say.' Clara's tone grew grave. 'God didn't show up for Leila that day. *God* or luck or chance or serendipity didn't show up for her. Leila suffered one lapse of memory and it changed her life forever.

'Now ask yourself this: is Leila Syed a danger to society? Is it likely that she will do this again? The answer is no and no, and so we have to ask ourselves: is she here purely for punitive reasons? What and who is this serving? If we put her in prison and she closes her company and her fifty-seven employees are made redundant, who are we protecting? Who are we saving?' She stressed each 'who' with a jab of her hand.

'Leila's sister and brother-in-law deserve some peace, but are they likely to get that from us sending Leila to prison? They seek *peace*, not retribution.' She pointed towards the dock. 'Leila Syed has had to sit here in court and watch every piece of her character be questioned, but here's the truth about Leila. One: she raised her sister and worked two jobs throughout her degree in order to keep them together. She could have handed her over to the state, but she raised the girl herself under an immense amount of pressure.

'Two: despite having huge responsibilities at work, Leila frequently and happily looked after Max. She was a conscientious carer, proven by the fact that when Max fell in the playground as millions of children do every year, Leila took him to hospital even though – in the words of the doctor who treated him – he "didn't even need a plaster".

'It's true that Leila values her career and my learned friend Mr Forshall has made much of the fact that she is childless. Do we despise and pity these women so much that we're willing to paint them as killers? Is that what we think of women? That they become crazed beyond reason if they can't reproduce? This is profoundly insulting.'

Clara shot Edward a look of contempt. 'It's true that Leila returned to work straight after a miscarriage. We revere men who do this! When the Prime Minister returned to work two days after the death of his son, we praised his dedication, but God forbid if a woman does the same.' Clara raised a finger at Leila. 'This woman doesn't fit the labels applied to her. She's not a superwoman or an ice queen as the Crown suggests. She's not a femme fatale or boss babe like the media say. She is an ordinary woman who has suffered extraordinary tragedy. Leila had never driven Max to school before. He was in a rear-facing seat. He was asleep. It was *so* easy to do – a perfectly human mistake. Please don't find her guilty because "someone has to pay". No. This was a genuine tragedy – devastating and awful but blameless. It is one of those tragic turns of history. Please don't ruin her life over this. Leila Syed isn't guilty of this crime. She is not. The only right and just verdict in this case is one of not guilty. Members of the jury, you *must* free Leila Syed.' She brought her palms together and dipped her head. 'Thank you,' she finished.

Leila felt overcome. She bent forward and braced her elbows on her knees. There was a chemical tang in her mouth and she swallowed thickly to clear it. Something – fear, panic, relief – strummed inside and she breathed deeply to calm it, the curve of her back rising and falling. All the fight had left her and now she felt exhausted. The practical voice inside her told her to sit up for she looked like she was guilty curled in a ball like that. Shakily, she straightened and looked at the men and women who now held her fate in their hands. She caught a juror's gaze and tried to telegraph a message: *I'm innocent, please believe me*. The woman's eyes swerved away and it felt like an omen. *This thing isn't going your way.*

*

Shep watched Leila from across the foyer. He had hoped to be in court for closing arguments but was waylaid by a separate case. He'd arrived just as the courtroom was emptying and loitered outside for a while, wondering if he'd somehow missed her. He was on the cusp of giving up when he heard the familiar click of her heels. He straightened, as if she might spot him in the corner of the hall. Instead, she headed straight to the exit. Out of an inexplicable instinct, he followed her, not knowing what he was looking for. He got into his car three bays away from hers. Journalists gathered around her but she slid into the driver's seat and moved smoothly off, seemingly unfazed.

Shep followed, compelled by intuition. There was something else to Leila Syed and he wanted to find out what it was. He trailed her onto the A11, careful not to get too close. This wasn't official business and if Leila happened to spot him, she could report him for harassment. They approached Tredegar Square and Shep parked discreetly. He stayed as still as possible as Leila walked to her door. He noticed that a figure was already waiting and wondered if it was her husband. Shep got out of his car, careful not to slam it shut, and crept a little closer. He saw a flash of blond hair. With a jolt, he realised that it was Leila's brother-in-law. What was *he* doing there?

Shep squinted in the darkness, trying to glean her reaction. Was she angry? Happy? Relieved? She flung an arm outwards and it looked like they were arguing. After a moment, she unlocked the door and led him inside, their silhouettes framed in a column of light. The door closed, leaving only a sleepy street. Shep could feel the drumbeat of his heart and the sharp surge of adrenaline, telling him there was more to this. He crossed the road, nimble on the balls of his feet. For a big man, he was surprisingly agile. His father always told him off for that. *Creeping around the house like a mouse.*

He stopped just to the right of Leila's gate and tried to peer in. The front room was empty. He glanced up the street and realised that he could skirt around the row of houses and approach them from the back. He moved quickly, for there was something about this street that gave him the heebie-jeebies. The tall silhouettes of houses and the pervasive silence around them seemed like the set of a horror film. He turned left towards the rear of Leila's house. *Bingo*. There was a light on in the kitchen, low and romantic. He approached, but the boundary wall was much too high, even for his height. He scouted the street opposite and saw a bank of dark houses. He crossed and hauled himself onto a stranger's front wall. He hunched between two trees, knowing that if someone saw him, they were sure to call the police.

He saw movement in the kitchen. Leila was pushing Andrew away and he gripped her hands in his. Shep held his breath, waiting for slow-motion to kick in as they leaned forward to kiss – a movie moment caught in real life. Instead, Andrew pressed her hands to his chest, holding them over his heart. He seemed to be crying and she embraced him now. His shoulders shook and Shep felt a twist of guilt at the extent of his trespass. This didn't seem like an illicit rendezvous but an innocent snapshot of grief. But why was their body language so intense?

Eventually, Leila peeled herself away, her hand still on his chest. She gripped his sweater in her fist, spoke a few words and then released him, pushing him back a touch aggressively. This was not mere grief. Something else was happening. If only Shep could hear. He wondered if there was any way he could get closer, but knew that that would irreversibly cross a line. Instead, he watched for ten minutes longer until Andrew stepped away and headed down the hall. Shep waited to see what Leila would do. What could he glean from her moments alone? Instead, the light switched off and Shep was left perched on a wall in the dark.

*

Leila heard the doorbell and groaned with frustration. She had told Andrew to go home for she needed some time alone to think. She headed back down the stairs, the buttons on her blouse left half undone. She threw open the door, preparing to reproach him. Instead, she froze. There, on the doorstep, was Yasmin. She had lost half a stone and it had tipped her into scrawny. She seemed weak, her verve dulled to a dark sobriety. Strangely, she had made an effort with her appearance. Her lips were painted red and her hair curled into loose swirls. It gave her an eerie look, like a wartime widow still harbouring hope.

'Yasmin?'

'Is it a bad time?'

Leila searched the street behind her. Had she seen Andrew leaving? 'No,' she said casually – too casual. She opened the door wider. 'Come in.'

Yasmin seemed light on her feet, as if the case had corroded her very being. Together, they moved to the kitchen as they had done a thousand times. Yasmin sat by the fireplace and Leila made tea – Earl Grey for her, green for Yasmin. She placed a plate of Waitrose shortbread on the table, knowing they were Yasmin's favourite. Then, she sat down opposite.

Yasmin wrapped her fingers around her mug. 'I wish you'd talk to me,' she said, her voice so soft it was almost a whisper.

'I'm always here,' said Leila. 'You know that.'

'Last week, you literally ran out the courtroom toilets when I tried to talk to you.'

Leila didn't reply. She fixed her gaze on her tea and watched the light refract.

'You should have told me about the miscarriages,' Yasmin said more gently.

'I didn't want to burden you. Toby was ill and . . . whatever I was going through seemed trivial.'

Yasmin looked wounded. 'You still could have told me, Leila. You *should* have told me.'

'It's not just that.'

'Then what?'

Leila wanted to lie, to bluffly bat it aside, but it was time to tell the truth. 'I didn't want to admit that I wanted it so badly because it only makes it worse that I failed.'

'You didn't *fail*,' Yasmin said emphatically.

'I *did*,' countered Leila. 'It's baked into the very language. "Failure to respond to drugs." "Incompetent cervix." I *did* fail and I didn't want you to see that.'

'But why? You tell me everything!'

Leila smiled sadly. 'No, I don't, Yasmin. I don't tell you a lot of things.'

'Like what?' she demanded.

Leila took a moment to answer. 'Like how sometimes I look at you and I am overwhelmed by jealousy.'

Yasmin's mouth was agape. 'Jealousy? Why?'

'All my life I've tried to make things easy for you, but I've also begrudged you for having it so easy. When you were being bratty, sometimes I wanted to slap you or shake you and make you understand what I went through even as I shielded you from it. And then you got married and pregnant and everything seemed so . . . easy.'

'But I was always jealous of you!' cried Yasmin. 'You've always been the successful one. Everyone looks up to you. I'm a fucking *secretary*. Why do you think I always sniped at what you have? I was jealous. I . . .' She gestured helplessly. 'You should have told me, Leila. I had no idea what you were going through.'

Leila took a long sip of tea, buying the time she needed to brace herself for this. 'The first time it happened, I did tell you and we agreed it wasn't a worry; just one of a million chemical pregnancies. The second time, I felt embarrassed. I didn't want to say anything until the problem was sorted. By the third, Toby was born and diagnosed and you were under so much stress. By the fourth . . .' Leila trailed off.

'When Toby died?'

'No. Before.' She didn't want to bring them there, to the darkest stretch of Toby's life: the long nights of howling, his skin flaking at the gentlest touch.

Yasmin flexed her fingers, splaying them wide to expel her pain. 'Do you remember that night you came to see me?'

Leila nodded. How could she forget? Toby had been upstairs screaming and Leila had wanted to go to him, but Yasmin had tugged at her arm; told her he had to wear himself out. Yasmin had sat on the kitchen floor, hair lank and stringy, collarbone jutting out, and held out a letter, sweaty from multiple reads. It was from the council passing on complaints from neighbours even though they knew. They *knew* what she was going through.

'Do you remember what I said to you?' she asked now.

'You said . . .' Leila paused to swallow the choke in her voice. 'You said that no one told you that children like Toby still have basic human needs; that they *need* touch even though it hurts them.'

'And?'

'And you spoke of the Greenland shark that lives in darkest ocean. You said that parasites dangle from its eyes and that similar things were growing inside you.'

'And?' pressed Yasmin, her voice edging higher.

'And you said . . .' Leila drew a fractured breath.

'"Sometimes I wish he would die",' finished Yasmin. Her tears spilt mascara on her cheek and it cut such a straight, dark line it could have been drawn by ink. 'And you were so calm and so non-judgemental, but you don't *know*, Leila. You don't know how I meant it.'

Leila reached across the table. 'I do know.'

'You don't!' Yasmin pulled away from her. 'You think I meant it in a motherly way, like I wish his suffering would end, that my baby would find peace and go gently into the night.' She shook her head bitterly. 'No. I meant it in a vicious, vindictive way. I wished he would just die and be done with it. I wished he would just shut the fuck up!' Yasmin's rage was still there, deep beneath the surface. 'I don't blame you for saying you could throttle Max; I've said the same a dozen times, but with Toby, I *meant* it. I meant it, Leila, and what hurts now is that I hated him. On nights like that I really, truly hated him.'

Leila shook her head. 'You didn't hate him, Yasmin. You were going through something no mother – no *human* – should ever be expected to.' She moved to Yasmin's side and drew an arm around her.

'I deserved it. I deserved to have Max taken.'

'No.' Leila kissed Yasmin's hair. 'No. You were a brilliant mother.'

'I wished my own child dead.'

'It's okay. He's at peace now. They're both at peace. I promise.' She rocked her sister in her arms. 'I promise.'

Chapter Fifteen

Leila stood up and fastened the button on her blazer in one fluid motion. She had been twenty-six years old when she had learnt that this was etiquette. Until then, she had always kept it buttoned, even while she sat. A motherly interviewer had whispered it to her as she escorted her onto the street. *By the way, if you want to convince them you're one of them, undo your suit button when you sit down and redo it when you stand,* she had said with a wink. Leila had burned with shame, taking it as admonishment. She had since learnt that men like Robert Gardner noticed small flourishes like this, using them as markers to identify who was and who wasn't initiated. Leila had fooled him enough so that he overlooked her polytechnic degree and judged her on her work. Now, with her expensive suit and haircut, few could tell the difference.

In the hallway, she slipped on her heels and examined herself in the mirror. There was a certain relief in knowing there was nothing else she could do: no more masks to wear, no more lies to tell. Her fate lay with the jury.

Will joined her in the hallway. He had shaved and put on a suit and though he hated to follow convention, he looked uncommonly handsome. He held out his hand and she took it like it was the easiest thing in the world. After their dinner on Monday, he had asked to spend the night but Leila had refused. She needed time, she'd told him, but when he turned up on her doorstep this morning, she felt a ringing relief. She had no time to analyse the meaning. Whatever they were, whatever they might be, had to wait until after the verdict.

Together, they walked out onto Tredegar Square and were met by a cluster of photographers. They slipped into her car, Will in the driver's seat, still covered by Leila's insurance. They headed to Inner London Crown Court and Leila waited until they turned the corner before checking herself in the mirror. She fished out her light berry lipstick and touched up one corner of her lips, keen to do it now before they arrived at court. She didn't want to be photographed touching up her makeup, the act seemingly callous.

Will glanced over at her. 'Nervous?'

She nodded.

'You'll be okay.'

'You don't know that.'

'I promise you, Leila. Women like you don't go to prison.'

'Women like me are hated.' The acid in her words surprised him and she felt compelled to explain. 'I don't know if the jury got to see who I am. I tried to show them, but I just don't think they liked me. I—' Leila hesitated, still wary of sharing too much.

He sensed her mistrust but said nothing, letting her decide whether to confide in him.

'You don't know what it's like, Will,' she continued after a beat. 'I've spent so many years feeling scared. Scared

I'd lose Yasmin or have her taken away; scared that in ten years' time, we would still be struggling; scared that she might suffer from the same thing our mother did. It felt like a constant clenching and something inside me just stayed that way – permanently on alert – and that makes it hard to be the things that people admire: warm and funny and carefree. Those things don't come naturally to me and I . . . I just know they didn't like me.'

Will frowned in doubt. 'I think you're too hard on yourself, Leila. People are drawn to women like you.'

'Being drawn to someone is not the same as sticking around.' She looked across at him. 'You should know that.'

He was quiet for a moment. 'I never wanted to leave. You know that.'

She watched the road in silence, remembering her cruelty towards the end: the shrill accusation, the scathing blame for daring to want something different from her.

Will kneaded the steering wheel. 'When you brought up divorce last week, I imagined what that would be like and there was just this sense of . . . goneness.' He cleared his throat. 'I want us to work things out, Leila.'

She held out a hand to cut him short. 'Let's talk about it after, Will.' She couldn't contemplate the future right now; wanted to think as little as possible of everything she stood to lose. She turned on the radio and fiddled with the dial, chopping up snatches of song. It did nothing to ease the sense of foreboding as they approached the court.

Will pulled into the car park and gently touched her knee. 'Ready?'

She gripped his hand to stop her own from shaking. 'Yes,'

she said in a low croak. They left the car to the flash of cameras and walked side by side to the courthouse.

*

Yasmin reread the text from Jason. When can we do it again? She grimaced, then swiftly deleted it. She had ignored his last two messages, but he wasn't the sort of man to quit. She placed the phone on her dresser, face down so that the green flash of new messages wouldn't draw Andrew's attention. She tried again to lace an earring through her lobe and cursed when she couldn't do it.

Andrew turned around, his tie half done. 'Do you need help?'

She tossed the earring onto the dresser. 'No,' she said, defeated. Her nerves felt unnatural, like a perverse excitement. Today would bring some form of closure and she had told herself over and over that she would trust the court's decision. If Leila was acquitted, then Yasmin would forgive her. If she was guilty, however, then their relationship would never recover.

She checked the time and saw that they were running late. She gathered her makeup, keys and wallet in her bag, a charge of hysteria in her actions. What sort of mother turns up late on a day like this? She saw that Andrew was waiting and snapped at him for standing there, placing more pressure on her.

'I'll wait in the car,' he said quietly.

She wheeled around the room, swapping the long cardigan that made her look frumpy for a shorter one riven with creases.

She stuffed some tissue into her bag and then hurried downstairs. She scrabbled around for her heels and then, finally ready, joined Andrew in the car outside. They passed Leila's house on the way, a full two storeys bigger than Yasmin's. She had known for a long time that Leila secretly helped them financially, but she never acknowledged it. If she pretended that she didn't know, Leila couldn't bask in the credit.

Yasmin first found out at a dinner one day when she walked into the kitchen. Andrew reared away from Leila and she could see from the tension in his shoulders that he was hiding something. She saw him slip a piece of paper in his trousers and she smiled at them both, widely and dumbly, despite the pace of her heart. It was only later when she searched his pockets and found the cheque for £5,000 that she understood what was happening. The only reason they could suddenly afford a nice sofa was because Leila was financing it. She didn't feel guilt or anger. If anything, Leila *should* share her wealth; she had so much of it. From then, she grew attuned to their clandestine gatherings, the whispering in her direction, and she took a certain satisfaction in knowing they were outwitted. The only thing that had jarred was when she saw them embrace on the street. Leila had claimed it was innocent, a mutual offering of comfort, but something about it still bothered her. Until then, Leila and Andrew had moved around each other as delicately as dancers, only ever touching briefly. On that day, however, there was *such* intensity, it left her feeling breathless.

No, Yasmin. I don't tell you a lot of things. Leila's words rose in her mind along with a complicated mix of emotion. Yasmin was haunted by the knowledge of her sister's miscarriages. She felt guilty that Leila hadn't felt able to confide in her.

Beneath those feelings, however, was something uncharitable: *You don't have to be such a martyr, Leila.* They were no longer children and Yasmin was impatient with all this protection.

A horn beeped behind them and she looked across at Andrew, feeling a resentful flare as he hovered on the edge of the junction. He always drove too timidly. When Max was alive, she appreciated it, but what was the point now?

She looked pointedly at her watch. 'We're going to be late,' she said, her voice snapping on the t.

Andrew finally inched forward and joined the swarm of cars heading along the A11.

She noticed that he hadn't said a word during the drive. 'Are you okay?' she asked curtly.

'What do *you* think?' he bit back. Before his words could settle, he immediately apologised. 'I'm just stressed,' he said. 'I just . . . I'm worried they'll find her guilty.'

The depth of his concern for Leila compared with Yasmin's own forced her to confront an uncomfortable truth: if Leila was found guilty, a part of her would feel relieved, for it would give her someone to blame. It would mean that there was some sense and system in the weaving of a tragedy. Human error could be prevented, mitigated, corrected; not so with the whims of fate. If Leila was freed, then where could Yasmin put her pain and how could she stop it repeating?

'Leila will be fine,' she said stiffly as they approached the court. 'She always is.'

Andrew turned into the parking lot and switched off the ignition. The silence was like a cold pocket in the ocean, sudden and bracing, leaving her scrabbling for warmth. She stepped out of the car and flinched as photographers gathered around her. Andrew was by her side in an instant. Together, they strode through the revolving doors to learn of Leila's fate.

*

The diligent clang of the heating did little to offset the chill in the courtroom. It was raining outside and the dank smell of pavement had filtered through the walls, filling the room with a sense of disquiet. Leila shivered as she sat in the dock. She fought the urge to crane towards the public gallery, knowing she couldn't see up there given the angles of the room. Clara Pearson had explained what would happen in the moments after the verdict. If Leila was found guilty, she would be led to a prison that had space for her – a prospect that left her breathless. She had had months to prepare but the reality of having her liberty stripped was simply incomprehensible. Leila had tried all her life to escape the system and here she was, teetering over its jaw, waiting for it to snap.

'I believe we have a verdict, jury, please,' said Judge Warren.

Leila balled her fists and felt the dry texture of skin on her fingertips.

'Will the defendant please stand?' asked the clerk.

Leila stood, fingers jittery as she fastened her button.

'Mr Foreman, have the jury reached a verdict upon which you are all agreed?'

A balding man in a green jumper stood. 'Yes,' he said. He cast a glance at Leila and her stomach churned at the look in his eye. *Pity.*

'On count one, do you find the defendant guilty or not guilty of gross negligence manslaughter?'

Leila held her breath and time seemed to slow, stretching into a vacuum that thrummed with something primal. Her heart wrung in her chest and she wondered if the foreman had already spoken and she had somehow missed it. She looked to the judge then back to the foreman, panic like tin in her mouth.

'Not guilty,' said the foreman.

'You find the defendant not guilty and that is the verdict of you all?'

'Yes,' the foreman confirmed.

The walls swung around Leila. *Not guilty*. Her face crumpled but there were no tears, only the strum of relief. Clara was on her feet speaking to Judge Warren and she heard him say *you're free to go*. The dock was unlocked and she stared at this passage to liberty like it was an alien thing. For a mad moment, she refused to leave the safety of her Perspex box. A guard ushered her forward and she stepped out gingerly. Clara swept up to her and squeezed her shoulder.

'You're free to go, Leila.'

She nodded dumbly. 'But how?'

Clara smiled broadly. 'We don't ask the jury why. We take their verdict as it is.'

Leila groped for the words to express her gratitude, but Clara nodded briskly, as if she understood. She held out her hand to Leila. 'If you have any questions, call my office.'

Leila shook it. 'I will. Thank you.' She stood in a daze for a minute. When she turned, she saw that the jury box was already empty. Her liberators, to whom she owed so much, had swiftly taken their leave. Could it really be over so quickly? Shakily, she left the courtroom and found that Will was waiting outside. She leaned into his chest and, then, the tears came: relief, release, gratitude. The jury had absolved her of blame.

Will stroked her hair and over his right shoulder, she spotted Yasmin watching them from across the hall. Leila had lost her footing in their relationship, no longer elder and wiser. *Yasmin*, she mouthed desperately.

Her sister held out a palm and shook her head. Leila tried to divine its meaning. *No, not now* or *no, not ever*? But then she caught the word on Yasmin's lips and it filled her with soaring relief. *Soon*.

Leila nodded, fresh tears now falling. Yasmin turned and walked through the exit, her hand gripped in Andrew's. So much pain had befallen their family, but now it was time to heal. In time, Yasmin would come to accept that it was all a tragic accident. That's what the jury believed so Yasmin had to believe it too.

*

Yasmin peeled off her socks and tucked them into her boots. Next to them stood Max's green wellingtons and she stared at them for a moment. She knelt and traced a finger over a speck of dried mud. She remembered when they went out with his yellow Paddington raincoat and he had stamped in the water. A young couple walked by and Yasmin had apologised – *sorry, it's his first puddle* – and they had bubbled with laughter, thoroughly charmed by the prospect of a child's first encounter. That, she supposed, was the delight in having a child – experiencing everything through his or her eyes: the joy of a tickle, the shock of a pop-up book. Max's life was full of promise, and the knowledge that he would never grow up, never find his friends for life, never fall in love filled her with torpid grief. What did you call a mother who was twice bereaved?

Yasmin picked up the charity sack that she'd cast aside with the junk mail and rubbed one corner of the plastic to separate the slippery film. Carefully, she set the green boots inside. Next, she picked up his trainers – still Velcro – and placed them with the boots. She sensed Andrew behind her and heard the small pocket of air as he opened his mouth to speak, then closed it again. After a moment, he turned and walked out to the garden. This was the part he found the hardest. With Toby, he had been desperate to keep everything: his half-filled bottle of shampoo, his gripe water, his baby formula. She couldn't understand the compulsion. How could you hold onto so much when all it did was pulse with grief? She took comfort in knowing that some other little boy might wear these boots; might laugh as he played in his very first puddle.

She vowed to be strong as she packed his life in bags and boxes. She remembered the last time she had had to do this and a memory rose like a shock: sitting in a cooling bath, hair plastered against her collarbone, kneecaps reduced to perfect circles as they breached the tepid water. The despair of what she felt that day came to her in sharp relief and, for a moment, it seemed to wind her. She sank onto her knees and groped for her phone. Then, not knowing if it was a kindness or cruelty, she sent a text to Leila.

I'm packing Max's stuff away. Will you please come and help me?

Minutes later, there was a knock on the door. Yasmin opened it to find Leila on the doorstep, trembling from the cold, her hair haloed by the streetlamp. They studied each other for a moment. Then, Yasmin reached forward and Leila stepped into her arms. She could tell from the quiver in her chest that she was trying not to cry. Yasmin held her hard, as if she could press her pain into storable size.

Leila faltered when she spotted the green boots in the plastic bag. Then, like jelly holding its shape, she grew still and silent. Without a word, the two of them knelt on the floor and started to sort through the piles of shoes. They moved down the hallway, collecting the remnants of Max's young life: a drawing in purple crayon, a stray nub of plasticine, an abandoned square of Lego, a collar and bell from a Lindt chocolate rabbit, and as they worked, it was a cleansing in more ways than one.

*

It was gone midnight by the time Leila left. Yasmin sat on the deck in the garden, wrapped in a duvet with a glass of wine resting by her fingertips. She took a sip and winced. It was a day past its best but the bitter purplish taste felt good. It was a clear night for December and the delicate dusting of stars seemed designed to stir nostalgia. Leila had taught her as a child that the longer you stared at the sky, the more stars you would see, as if you could magic them into being. What a privilege it was, she thought, to have an older sibling. They were the unsung heroes of childhood. Parents, teachers and best friends were lauded as most formative, but it was older sisters and brothers who often made the biggest difference.

A lazy smile spread on her lips as she teetered on the edge of drunkenness. Andrew padded over and joined her. He pointed at the duvet. She fanned it out to him and he arranged a corner across his legs.

'It's cold tonight,' he said, tipping his head to the sky.

'A perfect night for a cigarette,' she said wryly. He made a conciliatory sound. Yasmin had quit when she fell pregnant with Toby and only smoked occasionally.

He placed a hand on top of hers. 'How are you feeling?'

She set down her wine. 'Strangely relieved,' she said. 'I thought I wanted to hate her, but I . . .' She waved as if batting off a fly. 'I need to forgive her.'

'Can you?' he asked gently.

'Yes, I can. In some ways, I already have.'

Andrew watched the sky in silence.

'I don't want another one,' she said quietly. 'I don't want another child.'

He squeezed her hand. 'I think that's the right decision.'

Yasmin shifted in her seat, creating soft peaks in the duvet. 'Andrew, I need to tell you something.' She felt his hand stiffen on hers. 'When you said you didn't want another child, I texted my colleague Jason. You know the one with the curly hair. We had lunch together.' She saw the stricken look on his face.

'And?'

'And nothing. We had lunch and he's texted me a few times and I thought that I should tell you.'

'Texted you what?'

'That he wants to see me again.'

Andrew flinched. 'Romantically?'

'No, well, I don't know.' She laced his fingers in hers. 'I told him no. I'm going to tell him tomorrow not to contact me again.'

He shook out of her grip. 'But why did you text him to begin with? Did you want to . . .' He trailed off, unable to complete the sentence.

'No, I didn't want *anything*,' she lied. 'I was lashing out. I was angry that you didn't just,' she clicked her fingers, 'fall in line and I was in a foul mood and wanted to get back at you. I promise I didn't intend anything.'

He exhaled, breath misting in a faint white cloud. 'God, Yasmin.'

'I'm sorry.'

He steadied his eyes on her. 'I never liked that guy. He thinks he can flirt with other men's wives because it's clear that they're taken, so *of course* it must be innocent. What the hell were you doing texting him?'

'It was a stupid thing to do, but I promise you it was nothing.'

'Then why are you even telling me?'

'I just felt that I should.'

He scowled. 'Fine,' he said, but Yasmin could see the knot in his brow.

She poured him a glass of wine. 'Promise me,' she said.

He took the glass but set it on the floor beside him. 'Promise you what?'

She waited until he looked at her. 'Promise me that we're going to do something with our lives. We're not going to be that childless couple that fills their time with gardening and Netflix. We're going to go places, see things and live lives that are full.'

His features blanched with sorrow.

'Promise me,' she urged him.

'I promise.' He gripped her hand again. 'I promise you everything, Yasmin.'

She leaned into him and felt him tighten the duvet around them – just him and her, the newest, smallest version of their family.

PART III

Chapter Sixteen

It was Will's idea, but where Yasmin would once agree, she now stood back unsurely.

'Come *on*,' he pressed. He hovered next to her, but didn't grip her arm in that overfamiliar way that used to perturb Leila and Andrew. He pointed at the hot tub. 'It's the perfect weather for it.'

Yasmin winced. 'It's February!'

'But it's perfect,' he said with aggressive cheer.

He was right, Leila noted. It was a crisp evening but not too cold; perfect for a dip.

'I don't have any swimwear,' said Yasmin.

'Like that's stopped you before,' he said, trying for a playful tone. Yasmin hadn't entirely forgiven him for writing about Max and he tried every time that he saw her to force his way back into her favour.

Leila watched them from across the lawn. She pitied him in a way for believing that the strength of his effort could distract them all from death. 'He's trying so hard to take us back to before.'

Andrew rolled his beer between his palms. 'I can understand that. It all feels so complicated now.'

Leila murmured in agreement. It had been six weeks since the verdict and the few times that they had all met had felt stilted and awkward, as if they'd forgotten how to be a family. Will, for all his faults, had helped Leila cope: fending off reporters until they lost interest, doing all the shopping and admin, allowing her to refocus on business. She hadn't given him enough credit for it. He had come through and was genuinely trying to reknit the family, plying them all with drinks and retelling his best war stories, like the time he shadowed a famous footballer for a profile in a magazine.

'So the police pull him over and they ask him why there's five grand in his back pocket.' Here, Will would narrow his eyes wickedly. 'And Mario looks him straight in the face and, cool as anything, he replies, "Because I'm rich." You should have seen the copper's face!' Here, he would crack up with laughter, buoying everyone else with it.

Now, he cajoled Yasmin to the edge of the tub and threatened to push her in.

Leila watched and felt a well of affection. 'Push her!' she yelled and the two of them looked up in surprise. Emboldened by Leila's blessing, Will shoved Yasmin and she fell ungracefully into the water. When she yelped with shock and delight, Leila couldn't help but laugh. *There* was her younger sister.

Andrew looked on. 'I think she's going to be okay,' he said.

Leila squeezed his hand. 'I think so too.'

He leaned over and kissed her cheek. 'Thank you,' he said. 'For taking care of her.'

'Are you guys coming in or what?' Will yelled.

Leila arched a brow at Andrew. He rolled his eyes in good nature. Together, they stood and headed to the hot tub, he stripping to his boxers and she to her bra and pants. In the water, the four of them shared a bottle of wine. Yasmin sidled closer to Leila and rested her head on her shoulders. The act made Leila feel light. In the six weeks since the verdict, their relationship had lost its tactile edge. Yasmin was a hugger. She would touch an arm to make a point, use a stranger's shoulder if her heels made her wobbly, hug Max so fiercely that he wriggled away from her grip. She was a people person and the physical distance between them had begun to feel like a chasm. Having her here, her sleepy head resting on Leila's shoulder made them feel whole again.

Yasmin straightened and held her glass towards Will for a top-up. 'Max used to love this tub,' she said. 'Do you remember? Every time he was here, it was clothes off and straight into the water. He loved it.'

Leila shifted nervously. They hadn't spoken of Max since the night of the verdict.

Yasmin brushed a strand of hair aside. Lit from underneath, her face looked ghostly blue. 'I think what breaks my heart is that Toby and Max never met. They each had such a big part in our lives, but they both lived and died without ever knowing the other one.' Andrew reached for Yasmin, but she shrugged him off. 'No, I'm okay. I'm not upset. I just . . . I want to remember them, you know?'

'I know,' said Andrew. His eyes shone and it wasn't clear if they were tears or simply a reflection of the water.

'Do you remember how Toby would always chew on the right side of his mouth and Max did the same thing? Was that inherited? And, if so, what else would they have shared?'

'Or how they could both sleep absolutely anywhere,' said

Andrew. 'You remember when I almost stepped on Max curled up on the bottom stair?'

Leila smiled. 'They would come up with the silliest things. Like when I said there was something in my eye and Toby said, "Maybe it's a dinosaur bone."'

They all laughed. And, like that, with shared memories, they slipped from no man's land back to familiar territory, realising that little lives could live on in spirit.

*

Shep listened to the gentle clink of mugs as Karen, the cleaner, placed them in the sink. It wasn't her job to wash up, but Shep had given up apologising on behalf of his colleagues. He glanced into his own cup gloomily. The coffee was cold, but he didn't want to get under Karen's feet to fix himself another. They worked in respectful silence. Even their greetings were quiet: arched brows and a nod. She didn't judge him for being at his desk long after everyone else had gone. It was the only time he allowed himself to pull out the file from his bottom drawer: a thick wedge of paper forced into a manila folder. He knew he should let it go. It had been six weeks since the verdict and everyone had moved on, but Shep was still stuck on Leila Syed.

He had seen all sorts of things in the line of duty, but the fact that Leila was freed had genuinely surprised him. Juries hated child killers, especially when they were women and especially ones like Leila: smart, smooth, professional. At times, he'd wanted to advise her himself: you can't sit like that or brush your hair like this. You can't be calm and unknowable; you need to break down, you need to cry – but none of it had mattered. The jury had set her free.

Shep drained his coffee and grimaced, feeling the cold wash of it go down. He leaned back in his chair and surveyed the file on his desk. He should put it back in his drawer. He should lock up and leave, but he felt comfortable here, cocooned in the warm halo of his lamp, the soft rustle of Karen in the background. His eyes caught on a postcard, a lonely shepherd in a field. It was from a long-past girlfriend of his. On the back was some cheesy message he couldn't quite remember. He reached forward and plucked it from its blue tack, the whites around the side yellowed by the musty air. He flipped it over. *When I am lost, you shepherd me home.* When she gave it to him, he'd rolled his eyes and gruffly dismissed it, but now he recalled the warm feeling that had overcome him. He'd pulled her into his arms and had really thought then that things would work out for him: that they would get married and have kids and he would be the father picking up daughters from violin lessons or football practice, *shepherding them home.* Was forty-five too late to start a family?

He watched the clock creep past eight. Then, with a sigh, he started to lay out the contents of the file. Once again, he combed through statements and transcripts, trying to find the cipher that would unlock everything. He reread the toxicology report. *Promethazine.* It was the only drug found in Max's system, but it was explained away innocently, prescribed to treat his hay fever. Shep did a quick search online, then, frustrated with medical jargon, he snatched up the receiver and dialled the pathologist who had worked on Max.

'Bo speaking,' he answered, a slight laugh in his voice as if he'd been caught in the wake of a joke.

'Bo, it's Detective Shepherd here from the Met. I'm sorry to call so late. I had a query I'm hoping you can help with.'

Bo chuckled. 'Eight p.m. is like dawn over here, detective. What can I help you with?'

'I was just looking over the final pathology report in Max Hansson's case. I believe promethazine is a sedative. Is it odd that the father gave it to Max in the morning when he was on his way to school?'

'No. If a child has a flare-up in the morning, it makes sense to administer it then.'

Shep pushed up a sleeve over the nub of his elbow. 'But wouldn't the child be sleepy?'

'Yes, but if it's a choice between a screaming child and a sleepy child, most parents would choose sleepy.'

Shep considered this. 'And we're sure that none of his allergies were life threatening?'

There was a short pause. 'What's this about, detective? Do you think we missed something?'

'No,' said Shep firmly. 'No, I don't. There's just something about this case that I can't put my finger on.'

Bo spoke patiently. 'Look, his allergies didn't kill him. The promethazine didn't kill him. Being left in the car for three hours is what killed him.' Another pause. 'My advice? Go home. Crack open a beer and put this case behind you.'

Shep sighed. 'Okay.' Then, more certainly: 'Yeah, I will. Thank you.' He said goodnight, but instead of packing up, he stood to get a coffee and readied for another long evening.

*

Robert Gardner perched on Leila's desk and picked up her paperweight, a brass rendering of the goddess Hestia, an early gift from Will. *Fitting for an architect,* he'd said.

'So! It's been an interesting few months.'

'It has,' said Leila.

'Are you and Will back together?'

'Why?'

'Because he's an arsehole and I want to know.'

Leila angled her head in reproach. 'Not that it's any of your business but yes. Sort of. We're still working things out.'

He groaned. 'Does that mean I have to see him at the Mercers party?'

'Actually, I wasn't sure I'd come.'

Robert screwed up his face in a theatrical frown. 'Leila, we've won the biggest contract in the history of our firm and you're "not sure" you'll celebrate?'

'Well, after my "sabbatical", I wasn't sure you'd want me there.'

'Come on, you don't have sour grapes, do you?' He replaced the paperweight and nudged it just so. 'That was purely a business decision.'

'I know. I just . . . I don't know if I'm ready to face everyone.'

'Why? You didn't do anything wrong.'

Leila flinched a little. 'I did do something wrong, Robert. I just wasn't found guilty of it.'

'You know what I mean,' he said with a glib flick of the wrist. 'You're not a criminal and it's important that we demonstrate this – publicly.'

She sighed.

'So . . .' he said in a persuasive drawl. 'Will I be seeing your arsehole of a husband then?'

Leila smiled. 'No. I might bring my sister instead. It would be good for us to have a night together.'

'Excellent. Excellent,' said Robert. 'That would make a statement. All is well between the two of you.'

'God, you're so cynical. That is not why I'm inviting her.'

He tapped his nose as if promising to keep a secret. 'Well, I'm off for a while. I'll see you at the party next Friday.'

Leila watched him go. She leaned back in her chair and allowed herself a moment to breathe. The past six weeks had been a learning curve, but things were finally settling. Leila no longer felt others' eyes on her when she arrived at the office each morning. She could walk down the street without thinking that everyone knew she was guilty. What happened to Max would always be on her conscience, but she could see now that there were pockets of peace, and even happiness, to be found in the aftermath. Andrew and Yasmin were slowly healing, she and Will were working things out and Syed&Gardner was thriving. Maybe with enough time and therapy, they would all be okay. Leila pulled off her blazer and slung it on her chair. *Time to get to work.*

There was a knock on the door and she glanced up to find a woman she did not recognise. She was blandly pretty and wore an artfully dowdy dress with Dr. Martens boots.

'Katie Borough.' She strode in without an invitation. 'I'm sorry to drop in on you like this, but you weren't answering my emails and so I thought I should try to explain in person.'

'How can I help you?'

'I'm an editor at *Visor*. We're working on a seminal series about motherhood and I wondered if you would be interested in writing something for us.'

Leila stood up smoothly. 'No, thank you.'

The woman held out her hands defensively. 'Please just hear me out, Leila. It will be a sensitive portrayal of all aspects of motherhood. You've been through so many guises of it: playing guardian to your sister, infertility, adoption, caregiving. You could add so much to the conversation.'

Leila ignored her. 'Suki!' she called out, but her assistant wasn't there.

'Please, Leila. Women need to hear your story.'

'No.' Leila's voice was brittle. 'Please get out of my office.' She pressed a firm hand against the woman's back and ferried her out of the room.

'If women could—'

'Please don't contact me again.' Leila shut the door in the woman's face and waited until she heard her leave. She shook her hands to ease the tension. She told herself to be logical and poured herself a calming whisky. Attention made her jittery. It felt like a loose thread that could undo her entire life if someone thought to tug it.

Her phone chimed with a message. I'm sorry to have startled you. Please can we meet and talk? Katie. Leila immediately blocked the number. She dropped her phone on the desk, feeling a sense of disquiet. She needed to clean. That's what she did when anxious. She gathered all her loose paperwork in one tall pile and methodically sorted through them. Next, she cleared out her filing cabinet, ducking out briefly to return the spare key to Suki's desk. She wiped down her keyboard and screen and then started on her digital files. First, she emptied the trash can, then sorted through her inbox, whittling it down to zero. Then, she worked through her bookmarks. It felt cathartic to delete her folders. First, the 'CVAA' folder with its links to adoption sites and resources. Next, she deleted 'CPS' with its dozens of links: *being charged with a crime, when you are arrested*. Finally, she arrived at 'EB' where she had collected information on Toby's condition. There was a charity, a foundation, various medical sites with long lists of symptoms and treatments. She right-clicked it and, weighed by a sense of finality, she pressed 'Delete'. Maybe, she thought hopefully, all their bad luck had worn out and all that followed would be better than the past.

*

Yasmin watched her husband rifle through their mail. He had got into the habit of opening letters addressed to her. After Max died, she had let it all pile up and after nagging her for weeks, he had delved in himself. For some reason, he had kept up the habit. *I should tell him to stop.*

He frowned as he looked one over, then crumpled it and tossed it in the bin.

'What was that?' she asked.

'Just some junk,' he said absentmindedly. A knock on the door made him start. He set down the mail and left the kitchen.

Yasmin darted over and plucked out the piece of paper. It was a letter from a publisher offering them a book deal. Weren't people paid *thousands* for that sort of thing? She folded the piece of paper. Andrew shouldn't make these decisions without her. As she slipped the letter in her pocket, she heard the echo of a familiar voice and it made her stomach curdle. She walked out to the hall.

'Detective Shepherd. Is something wrong?'

He smiled at her, but on his weathered face, it looked more like a grimace. 'No, nothing's wrong.' The words came out like a threat. 'It's just a courtesy call – to see how you're both getting on.'

'Oh, I see.' She gestured towards the kitchen. 'Would you like a cup of tea?'

'I'd love one.' He rubbed his hands together like a stallholder in a soap opera.

'Two sugars and milk I seem to recall?'

He nodded, impressed. 'That's right. Well remembered.'

'I make a lot of tea,' she said sardonically. 'It's basically my job.'

'Ah.' He hovered awkwardly for a moment. 'Are you back at work then?'

She gestured at the kitchen table and waited for him to sit. 'Yes, I returned last week. They're easing me back in.'

'I see.'

She noticed him glance around the room. 'We cleaned out the house,' she admitted. 'It just got too hard.' She pulled her cardigan tight around her and waited for the tea to brew.

'I understand,' said Shep. He accepted his cup with thanks.

Andrew joined them at the table. 'We weren't expecting a courtesy call.'

Yasmin noted his chilly tone.

'Ah, yes, I'm sorry to drop in on you like this. I wanted to see if you had any unanswered questions about what happened.'

Yasmin lay her hands flat on the table. 'I don't think so.' She glanced at Andrew. 'Did you?'

'No,' he replied briskly.

She noticed that he was studying Shep carefully.

'I'm so sorry about what happened to you both. I've worked with many parents and it's never easy to lose a young child.' He paused and took a casual sip of his tea, but there was something contrived in his actions. 'Max was *three*, wasn't he?' He smiled warmly as if reminiscing.

'Yes,' said Yasmin.

'It's a difficult age.' He took another sip of tea. 'Did you notice that at all? A change in Max?'

Yasmin frowned. 'I don't think so.'

'I just wondered because your babysitter mentioned that he had grown grizzly in recent months.'

Yasmin waved a delicate hand. 'He was playing up at night a little.' She glanced at Andrew. 'That's why you took over, remember?'

Andrew was still watching Shep. 'But you don't have children, do you, detective?' he asked.

Shep scratched his stubble. 'Sadly, no.'

'Oh, because when you said, "It's a difficult age", I thought you were talking from experience.'

Beneath the table, Yasmin placed a palm on Andrew's knee. She didn't know why he was being so frosty.

'No, that's what I *hear*,' said Shep. He leaned forward on the table. 'So you had to take over the night-time routine. Why do you think he was grizzly? Could it have been his allergies?'

The two men watched each other for a moment. 'To be honest, detective, we're trying to get on with our lives and we'd rather not have to revisit the death of our son, especially with such scant warning on a Saturday morning.'

Yasmin balked a little. Andrew was usually so mild mannered.

'I'm sorry. I didn't mean to upset you,' said Shep.

'You haven't, but . . .' Andrew cleared his throat. 'Remembering our son is difficult, especially when we're not mentally prepared.' There was an awkward pause before he stood and patted his pockets. 'Anyway, I'll let you finish your tea and then Yasmin and I were planning to head out.'

Yasmin smiled politely in the face of Andrew's lie. 'Thank you for dropping by, detective.'

Shep drained his tea. 'Thank you for letting me stop in and I'm sorry to have disturbed your morning.' He followed Andrew out, but hovered on the doorstep.

Yasmin heard them exchange words, but struggled to hear what they were. When she stepped into the hall, Shep fell silent. He raised a hand in parting, then turned and strode to the gate.

Andrew leaned against the door and closed his eyes for a moment, not seeing that she was watching.

'Are you okay?' she asked.

His eyes flew open. 'Yes, I'm fine.' His face was pinched with tension. 'Just . . . they should warn people about this sort of stuff.'

'Why were you so rude though?'

'Was I?' he asked absently.

'Is something going on that I don't know about?'

'No.'

'Then what's this?' She held out the letter from the publisher.

He recognised the cream paper. 'What about it?'

'It's offering us a book deal. Shouldn't we discuss it?'

He stared at her. 'You can't be serious.'

'Why not? Lots of people do it.'

'You seriously want to write a book about this?'

'No, but . . .' She lifted one shoulder. 'Maddie's parents did it.'

His face was an insult. 'And you want to be like them, do you?' He walked over to her. 'Sweetheart, it's best that we put this behind us. Why on earth would we want to write a book about it? Let's look ahead. We can travel: go on the Trans-Siberian like we always wanted, eat at Michelin restaurants, watch the Monaco Grand Prix. We shouldn't dwell on the past.' He drew her into his arms. 'Okay?'

She leaned into his chest. 'Okay,' she said and wondered why his heart was racing so scarily fast.

*

Leila took in the view from her office: the wend of the River Thames behind the gleam of skyscrapers. As much as she fostered a culture of work-life balance, she loved being at work on a Saturday when London fell into slumber, sinking into peace after the wildness of the working week. She was dressed casually in jeans and a jumper, her feet bare, her toes pressed into the ball of one foot, relieving a tiny ache.

She watched the figures amble below, their gait far more relaxed on the weekend. There were no stuffed shirts or suits testily queuing for their morning coffee. As she watched, something caught the corner of her eye: a flash of panicked movement – a worker on deadline perhaps. As her gaze focused, she noticed that he was familiar. She squinted, then felt herself run cold for she recognised the figure. She watched him dart across a road without even looking and then scurry up to her building. Moments later, the phone on her desk was ringing. Terry from the front desk told her she had a visitor.

'Send him up,' she said. She slipped into her heels and began to pace the office. What was he *doing* here? Whatever this was, it couldn't be good. She saw him emerge from the lifts on the opposite side of the office floor. Too anxious to wait, she marched out to meet him.

'What are you doing here?' she hissed.

'They know,' he said, his voice tinny with panic.

Leila tensed. 'Andrew, just calm down a second.' She ushered him into her office.

He paced to the window and scanned the horizon, searching for an unknown malevolence. His long canvas raincoat gave him the air of a beleaguered fisherman. 'They know, Leila. Or *he* knows.'

'Who?'

'Detective Shepherd. He came to our house this morning.'

Leila felt a vinegar tang in her throat. 'Sit down,' she instructed.

He drew a hand across his face, voice edging into hysteria. 'Oh, God. How did they find out?'

'For fuck's sake, Andrew. Calm down.' She pointed at a chair. 'Sit down!' She took the seat next to him, then reached across and gripped his hands, hard enough to startle him. 'Tell me what he said.'

Andrew took a jittery breath and pulled out of her grip. He relayed the morning's conversation, startling as he spoke: at the clink of a bee against the window, the motor in Leila's fridge. He finished with a sharp intake of breath as if surfacing from a depth.

Leila stared at him. 'Is that all?'

'What do you mean? He was asking about Max, about whether he had grown grizzly recently, why he was struggling at night-time, whether he really had allergies. He *knows*, Leila. He *knows* that Max had EB.'

'Andrew, you need to calm down.'

'What if he knows that we planned it?' He pressed a hand against his temple as if to keep a vein from bursting.

'He doesn't know,' said Leila.

'She couldn't do it again.' Andrew paled with anguish. 'It was too hard the first time round. The hours and hours of bandages, the tears, the tantrums. Toby screaming *I hate you, Mummy. I hate you.* Yasmin just took it and took it and took it. It would have broken her to do it all again with Max. It would have broken us both.'

'I know,' soothed Leila. 'I know.' She leaned forward. 'Listen, you're not the one to blame, okay? You didn't do it.'

'It was my idea.'

'But *I'm* the one who did it. *I'm* the one who left him.'

Andrew shook his head defiantly. 'But I'm the one who gave him the drug. That's what put him to sleep.'

Leila felt her patience waver. 'And *I* left a fucking child in the back of my car. A child I loved more than anything.' Her voice took on a strange, abrasive texture. 'I took a look at him and I walked the fuck away, Andrew. I closed that door and I walked away – and you don't know how fucking hard that was, so don't cry to me about it now.'

He looked at her with wide-eyed hurt. 'I thought it was over.'

She laughed cruelly, hating him for what he had asked her to do. 'You think this will ever be *over*, Andrew? You think we'll ever just move on from what we did? We ended a child's life.'

'Out of mercy!' he shouted. 'And love.'

'So what? Mercy and love. So fucking what?' She realised how much anger she harboured. All these months, she had kept it on a simmer, never letting it boil, never letting it out of control. 'It doesn't change what we did,' she said, a cold malice in her tone.

'Of course it does!' Andrew blinked fast to keep his tears from falling. 'Do you remember what Toby's hands were like? Do you remember his screams when we parted his fingers so they wouldn't fuse? Do you remember what he went through? I couldn't let that happen to Max. My baby boy went peacefully.'

Guilt hummed inside her. It was easy to blame Andrew for he was the driving force, but deep down she was grateful for she knew that it was true: a second child with EB would have broken Yasmin.

'What are we going to do?' Andrew looked lost and Leila felt it too: an unhinging of something solid, like a bridge parting beneath their feet.

'You shouldn't be here,' she told him. 'What if someone saw you? You'll be on the CCTV.'

'I had to talk to you. You weren't answering your phone.'

Leila tried not to snap at him. 'Look, don't worry about that detective. I've been acquitted and you and Yasmin have moved on.' Andrew moved to speak, but she cut him off. 'What if he just dropped by innocently?'

'What if he didn't?'

'Then I'll take the fall,' said Leila.

Andrew clasped his hands together. 'I couldn't let you do that.'

'Oh, but you *did*.'

He flinched, stung by Leila's words. 'That's not fair. You *know* that I planned to do it myself.'

Leila slumped against the backrest. 'I'm sorry,' she said but there was still a sting in her voice. She stood and poured them each a whisky. 'We agreed not to talk about it again and now you barge into my office on a Saturday morning cawing with paranoia.'

'*You* agreed not to talk about it. I never did.'

She motioned at him with her glass. 'What do you want to do, Andrew? You want to go over it all again? You want us to convince each other that we're not bad people? That what we did was noble?' She made a harsh jeer of a sound. 'I can't say all that to you.'

Andrew's voice was a plea. 'You're the only person I can talk to about it.'

'But what is there left to say?' She regarded him with cool distaste.

'You didn't see the full horror of it, Leila. I know you think you did, but you didn't.' Andrew pressed his lips together, creating ugly creases. 'Just after he turned three, there was a Halloween party on our street. Toby went in costume as a mummy, covered in bandages. During the evening, some of the blood from his wounds began to seep through the gauze, and those who didn't know that this child had EB were remarking how realistic the bloodstains were and we . . . we just had to smile because we couldn't break down and sob.' Andrew's voice trembled. 'Max died peacefully. He died with his favourite blanket and Poppy the penguin beside him and he was safe and loved. *That's* what we gave him. That's what *you* gave him and I can't not talk about that because it was the bravest, most selfless thing anyone has ever done for me and my family.'

Leila's shoulders bowed with the knowledge of what they did. As fate would have it, they had noticed it at the exact same time: a thumbnail-sized sore on Max's right shoulder when he stripped off to play in Leila's hot tub. Yasmin was mixing some potato salad, pausing only to take a generous swig of the white wine she liked. Leila was under the parasol and could sense that Andrew next to her saw it on Max's shoulder too. Their eyes met and immediately they knew what the other was thinking – but it couldn't possibly be true. Max had been tested before and after birth and was mercifully found negative.

Andrew had rushed over to Max and whisked him inside with the promise of ice cream. Leila had made a beeline for Yasmin, determined to hold her attention. It was a rash. *Of course* it was just a rash.

'What are you watching on Netflix?' she'd asked, reaching for the first inane thing that came to mind.

Yasmin had spent a good ten minutes telling her about a new show – something charming with Anna Kendrick. She never did like the dark stuff about internet cat killers or kidnapped teenagers. Throughout the entire conversation, Leila's heart had revved in her chest. *Let it be a rash. God, please, let it be a rash.* It seemed an age before they returned, Max slung on Andrew's shoulders. He had winked at Leila and she'd almost crumpled with relief.

Almost exactly a month after that, Andrew turned up at her door, pacing like a madman.

'What's wrong?' she demanded, fear making her terse.

Andrew sat on her stairs, as if he'd lost the strength in his legs.

Leila watched him anxiously. 'Is it Yasmin?'

He looked at her, broken. 'No. It's Max.'

A drumbeat snared in her heart. 'What's wrong?' If something happened to Max, Yasmin would not survive.

'He's got it, Leila. He's got EB.'

Something clicked apart in the room, a rupturing of normality. 'No,' she said blankly.

'Yes.' He spoke fast, trying to outrun his dread. 'He's been getting sores at night. I've tried to keep it from Yasmin. I do his bath times now and change him in the morning when I know he's got one, but it's only a matter of time.'

Leila felt the room swing around her. 'No. Yasmin had the test. They said it was okay. It's not EB. It would have appeared at birth,' she babbled in denial.

Andrew closed his fist as if clinging to a mooring. 'There's so much they don't know about EB. It's a vicious, vicious thing.'

Leila whirred through their options. 'What did the doctor say?'

'Doctor?' He gaped at her. 'I haven't gone to the doctor.'

'Then how do you know?' she cried.

'I *know!*' His voice rose to a shout. 'I lived with Toby for three years. I know what it looks like. It even has a smell and he . . . he smells like it.'

'Andrew, you need to get him tested.'

'And then what?'

'Then we—' Leila knew then what. *Years* of agony.

Andrew looked at her – *really* looked at her – and tried to find a way to couch what he needed to say. 'What you saw, Leila, was only half of it. You saw the bandaging and the screaming, but you weren't there when we held our newborn son and his skin came away in our hands, or when the doctor gave us the diagnosis and told us not to look it up because it was all so awful.' He gestured bleakly. 'Some days, Toby would wake with corneal tears that would turn him blind for days. He was *terrified* when that happened. His throat was starting to close up and we were told he'd need a fucking balloon inside him. And if his tiny body survived all that, he had skin cancer to look forward to. We lived in a state of constant horror and we only learnt to survive because it was so relentless. We had no time to stop and think.' He looked up at Leila as if asking for mercy. 'I can't do it all again – and neither can Yasmin.'

'Well, what choice do we have, Andrew? We can't *hide* it from her.'

He was quiet for a moment. 'I've been looking into a clinic in the Netherlands.'

'What kind of clinic?' Her voice held a dangerous quiver.

'They've euthanised two babies with EB.'

She blinked dumbly, caught in a form of paralysis. Then her brain completed the loop and she grasped the full implication. She physically jerked away from him, a strange gurgle in her throat. She opened her mouth to shout at him, but something cool and sober kept her rooted still. 'You want to . . .' She couldn't finish the sentence.

He shook his head dejectedly. 'I've already looked into it. They don't treat foreign nationals.'

Leila exhaled.

'But there's another way.'

She stared at him. 'What way?'

'I read an article last year about a man in Florida who accidentally left his child in the car.'

Leila felt the seep of ice in her chest. 'Andrew, what are you saying? This can't be what's in your head right now.'

'I've mapped it all out.'

Leila crouched on the floor next to him, an urgency in the action. 'Andrew, you've got to go to the doctor. You've got to get Max tested and treated. Treatments get better all the time.'

'You *know* EB's incurable.'

'But there may have been some developments.'

'To preserve life, yes, but not the *quality* of it.'

'You don't know that.'

'It's not enough,' he snapped. 'And I don't mean for *me*. I would do it, Leila. I would spend the hours and days doing the work, but Yasmin *can't* see him in agony – not Max. With Toby, it was all he ever knew, all he ever was, but to have Max degrade like that . . . It will be the end of her.'

Leila slipped to the floor from her haunches, needing the support. 'Andrew, what you're proposing. It's murder.'

'It's mercy.'

She dug her nails in the flesh of her palm, forming deep white grooves. 'You have to stop this right now.'

His face took on a strange composure. 'You know, it's so fucking weird. We're so sentimental about human life. We kill deer when they begin to overpopulate, but we can't imagine this fate for ourselves, even as an act of mercy. We hold so *tightly* to the sanctity of our lives, that it drives us to inhumanity. If an animal suffered as Toby has – as Max *will* – we would immediately end its misery, but we don't give humans the same mercy.'

'Andrew, *think* about what you're saying.'

'I have, Leila. It's all I've thought about.'

'For how long?'

His Adam's apple dipped in his throat. 'Two weeks.'

'Two weeks? For two weeks, you've been thinking about killing your son?'

The line of his jaw hardened. 'Don't say that.'

'But that's what it is!' Her voice shook. 'Andrew, this is madness.'

'I've thought it through.'

'Stop this. We'll take him to the doctor, we'll get him tested, we'll figure out the next steps.'

'It will kill Yasmin. You know it will.'

A memory lurched in Leila's mind: careening down a hospital corridor to find Yasmin in bed, her lips a bloodless blue. What if they couldn't save her this time?

'Andrew, if you're feeling like this, if you're *considering* this, then I think you need to see a doctor.' She reached for him. 'I think you—'

He batted her hand away, teeth bared in a sudden snarl. 'No, Leila! Doctors can do nothing for me. Doctors can do nothing for *him*. I will not let my family break apart again. I can't. I will do this and if you want, you can call the police and tell them, but I'm doing this.' He flung an arm at the window. 'They're like third-degree burns, Leila. On his skin. Every day.' His voice cracked. 'How can he live like that?'

Leila recalled an earlier memory. Yasmin on the kitchen

floor, Toby crying upstairs. *Sometimes I wish he would die.* She felt a swell of adrenaline pulse through her veins. 'Andrew, can you seriously be considering this?'

'I can't think of another way,' he said brokenly.

'You wouldn't get away with it.'

He clasped his hands together. 'I've read about these cases. They happen when there's a break in routine: when the father instead of the mother takes a child to school, or you take a different route. They're very rarely prosecuted.'

'You couldn't do it, Andrew. Not in the moment. You couldn't leave Max.'

'I could give him something. Promethazine would knock him out and it's easy enough to get if I say he has an allergy.'

'Yasmin would hate you.'

'She would forgive me. Eventually.'

'She wouldn't,' said Leila. 'She couldn't.' She grew still, quieted by an idea that spread in her brain like an ink stain. She steadied her gaze on him. 'It can't be you,' she said.

And that was how it started.

Chapter Seventeen

Leila's bed was strewn with clothes: a wine-coloured McQueen dress with a bustier top, a white floor-length gown with an asymmetrical neck, an ill-advised red taffeta affair. Yasmin had opted for a canary-yellow mini that skimmed her figure just so. She studied herself in the mirror.

'I love it,' she said, breaking into a wide smile.

Leila beamed at her. 'You look stunning.'

Their eyes met in the mirror. 'Thank you for asking me to this.' Yasmin neatened a lock of hair. 'I know things have been weird between us, but we're going to be okay, Leila. I promise.' Her gaze dipped to the floor and back. 'You do know that I forgive you?'

Leila's smile was falsely bright. 'I know.' Forgiveness meant little if Yasmin did not know the truth. It was easy to forgive an accident, to blame a cruel twist of fate, or assume some grander plan. For Leila, there would be no absolution because she and Andrew had made a pact to take this to their grave.

Yasmin smoothed her dress and took a deep breath to calm her nerves. 'Okay, I'm ready.'

Leila walked to her closet and picked out a tan Celine bag.

'Take this. It will go well with the dress.' Sometimes, when Leila bought a designer item, she ordered two in different colours and casually lent one to Yasmin, then waved it away upon its return. 'Keep it,' she'd say lightly. 'I have another just like it.' In this way, she furnished her sister with the same luxuries without denting her pride.

Yasmin clutched the bag and admired it next to her dress. Leila joined her in front of the mirror and was pleased by the way they looked together. Her own dress, a wispy sea-green, was cinched at the waist and gave her a deceivingly generous chest.

'You look stunning too,' said Yasmin.

'Thank you.' Leila kissed her, aiming it in her hair so not to ruin her makeup. 'We're gonna be okay, kid.'

Yasmin nodded, a shine in her eyes. 'Yes, we are.' She squeezed Leila's hand and together they headed out.

*

Shep rang the bell and hoped that this was the last time he would see this family.

Andrew opened the door. His face fell, but he made a valiant effort to hide it. 'Detective,' he said. 'It seems you can't keep away.'

Shep wiped his feet on the mat. 'May I come in?'

A muscle twitched in Andrew's jaw. 'Yes, of course.'

Shep followed him to the kitchen, but instead of taking a seat at the table, he leaned against the sink. 'Is your wife here?'

'No, she's at a . . .' He paused. 'She's out with her sister.'

Shep felt a sliver of relief. It would be easier on his conscience with just the father here.

'So, to what do I owe this pleasure?' Andrew asked sardonically.

'I owe you an apology.' Shep held out his palms in a mea culpa. 'I'll be honest with you. When I dropped by last Saturday, I asked about Max's allergy because I couldn't find proof that he actually had one.' He shifted awkwardly. 'I wondered if you were actually using the drug to sedate him on difficult nights.'

Andrew fixed his statue gaze on him. 'You thought I'd dose my own son?'

'You would be surprised by what I've seen,' said Shep. 'But then it clicked.' He gestured towards the garden. 'I remembered that you said your lawn was finished in June, the same month that Max's allergy flared.' He nodded at the cabinet above the kitchen sink. 'May I?' He opened it and plucked out a big green bottle. 'I'm guessing you started using pesticide in June?'

'Yes.'

Shep read the label. 'Neem oil can cause allergic reactions. Once I put all that together I realised I'd been unfair to you.'

Andrew blinked. 'Well, I hope that satisfies you, detective.'

'It does. And once again, I apologise. There was something that didn't sit well with me, but sometimes a copper's intuition can lead him astray.'

'Yes, well . . .' Andrew looked at him expectantly. 'I appreciate the visit.'

It was obvious that Andrew was keen for him to leave. Shep wondered if in another life the two of them might have been friends. Would they spend evenings together, with or without their wives? Might he grab a drink with Andrew instead of heading back to his empty flat? He waited, not wanting to leave yet.

'So are Leila and Yasmin having a girls' night out?' he asked.

'Something like that,' said Andrew absently.

Shep waited to see if he might ask him something. The silence grew awkward so he gestured at the hall. 'Anyway, if you ever need anything, please give me a call. You have my number.' He patted his pockets. 'I'm very sorry about what happened to you, Mr Hansson.'

'Thank you,' said Andrew, not getting up.

'I'll let myself out.' Shep left him alone in the empty house and headed out to his own.

*

Leila was pleased that they had hired a space in central London, far away from the office. Here, perched high above Embankment, they could trace the River Thames all the way to the horizon. Lights blinked on all across the city and, for the first time in months, Leila felt truly hopeful. She laced her arm with Yasmin's and introduced her to all her colleagues. She made a beeline for Josh, a confident Canadian guy she knew Yasmin would like. These parties often started a little uptight and she was keen for Yasmin to have a good time. She left the two of them talking and picked up another drink.

Robert Gardner approached her. 'Well, she's *lovely*,' he said. 'I can see why you've kept her hidden away from us all these years.'

Leila smiled. 'I haven't. She's been in the office plenty of times. Perhaps if you were there more, you'd know that.'

Robert laughed. 'Well, perhaps I will if she continues to make a habit of dropping by.' He took a sip of champagne, then steered Leila to one side. 'I don't want to talk shop all night, but I wanted to mention that Eli at Mercers said he could set up a meeting with Coutts.' Robert raised his glass. 'I'm telling you. It's all going to happen for us this year.'

She clinked her glass with his. Over his shoulder, she saw Yasmin laughing with Josh and felt a sense of contentment. This was what life was meant to be. She and Robert making big plans for the company; Yasmin nearby, happy and laughing; a new start with Will. Things would be okay, she thought. Things might really be okay. She leaned forward and kissed Robert's cheek, surprising him.

'Let's have a night off, eh?' she asked.

Robert laughed. 'Let's.' He whirled around and rejoined the bombshell he was currently dating.

Leila decided to let her hair down – as far as bosses can. She knew her limit was four drinks. After that, she tipped towards unpleasant drunkenness, too giddy on her feet. Including the drink she had had at home, this was her third. She had better keep an eye on it.

She did the rounds, checking in on Yasmin to see if she needed rescuing from the band of men surrounding her, but she seemed to be enjoying herself, slipping back into familiar ways, prepared by a lifetime of attention. Leila left her to her audience and headed out to the balcony, stepping through the low window. It was cold but clear and the alcohol warmed her. She watched a barge steam downriver and winced as it passed beneath an arch, sure that it would graze it. It passed safely to the other side and Leila closed her eyes. She needed to stop worrying about things she couldn't change.

'Hey.'

Leila turned. 'Hey.'

Yasmin climbed through the window and joined her.

'Are you having a good time?'

Yasmin nodded, then sat on the thick concrete ledge that bordered the length of the balcony.

'Tired?'

'No.' Yasmin smiled lazily. She was one drink past tipsy.

Leila joined her on the ledge and snaked an arm around her waist. 'I'm so glad you came tonight.'

'I am too.' She gazed out across the Thames. 'God, March is going to be strange.'

Leila squeezed her waist. Max would have turned four in March.

Yasmin cupped her glass like a crucible. She focused on a light winking in the distance. 'You know, sometimes I think I deserved to lose him.' Her voice was low and perfectly calm.

Leila turned and stared at her. 'Why would you say that?'

'You think I'm a good person but I'm not.' She gestured outward, her bracelets sliding down the length of her arm. 'The way I treated Toby sometimes. I used to scream at him when he cried, begging him to stop.'

Leila made a low consoling sound. 'Yasmin, that's natural. I'm sure every mother's done it.'

'Not like me. Not like that.' She kneaded the stem of her glass. 'I'm not a good person, Leila. I never told you this but in the middle of the trial last year, I met up with Jason.'

Leila squirmed. 'That sleazy guy from work?'

'Yeah. I texted him, pretending it was just innocent drinks, but the truth is . . .' She hunched a shoulder defensively. 'I was planning to sleep with him.'

Leila shifted so that she could look at Yasmin head on. 'Tell me you didn't.'

'No, but I was planning to. I was just so lost and *angry*.'

Leila started to speak, but Yasmin interrupted.

'There's more.' She took a breath to brace herself. 'A few years ago, not long after Toby died, I had to go to our summer party. Do you remember the one you were meant to come to? In 2017?'

Leila nodded guiltily. It was a grand affair at the V&A, but she had had to bail out for work at the very last minute.

'I was still feeling so low and I just needed *something*. I drank way too much and I . . .'

Leila studied her. 'Oh, Yasmin, you didn't.'

Glassy tears now welled in her eyes. 'I did.'

'Oh, God. But you said he was so sleazy.'

'There's more.'

'Does Andrew know?'

'No.' Yasmin flushed with guilt. 'It's not even like we were unhappy. We were in love – we still are – but things changed between us after Toby. It was like we'd gone through a war together. How can you be sexual with someone you've been in the trenches with? When you've seen them covered in blood and pus and . . .' She trailed off. 'I just needed to reset, to feel something other than rage. I needed to feel good about myself.'

Leila smoothed away her disbelief and gestured philosophically. 'Look, lots of people have affairs. That doesn't mean you're a bad person or that you deserved any of this.'

'You don't understand.' She shrugged away from Leila's touch, like a cat resistant to petting. 'I got pregnant.' The wind tore up from the Thames and hit them with an icy blast.

Leila grew still. 'When?'

'With Max.'

'That can't be right,' said Leila, dread lining her stomach.

Yasmin gestured at the river as if it would bear witness to the truth. 'It's right,' she said. 'Andrew's not his father.'

Leila instinctively dropped her glass and flinched when it broke apart, fragments skittering across the stone. Yasmin spoke rapidly to allay her judgement, but Leila wasn't listening. Andrew wasn't Max's father. Max wasn't Andrew's child. Which meant that Max did not inherit his genes. Which meant that Max did not have EB. The knowledge blared like a siren, bouncing off the walls of her skull. *Max did not have EB*. She didn't know that she'd said the words out loud until Yasmin responded.

'No, and that's why I was so adamant to keep him. When you and Andrew both told me to consider aborting him given the chance he'd have EB, I kept refusing. It was my one shot, Leila. I didn't plan it but I fell pregnant and it was my one shot to have a healthy child.'

'Max didn't have EB,' Leila repeated. 'But . . .' Her horror was thick like treacle. 'I . . .' She was dangerously close to falling apart, like a balloon one breath from bursting. She shot to her feet, her palm sweaty on the windowpane. 'I . . . I need another drink,' she blurted and stepped back into the building. She skirted around the crowd into the silent corridor. She bypassed the first set of bathrooms and found her way to another. She locked herself in a cubicle and, then, she dissolved in one corner. She pressed a fist against her mouth to stave off her scream. Max wasn't sick. He did not have EB. Leila and Andrew had conspired to kill a healthy child.

For a moment, her body refused to absorb this fact in an effort to preserve her sanity. Then, she felt a caving inside her. She flattened her hands against her mouth and let out a silent scream: a low rush of sound. There was no act of mercy. There was no selfless sacrifice. Leila had killed a healthy child.

The tears came in hard, staccato sobs that convulsed through her body. The logical, dependable part of her – the part that was calm in crisis – collapsed entirely. She slid down into a corner and wept with shock and tar-like horror. The walls around her seemed to warp and distend, leaving her exposed to the ruthless truth. Hours passed and from deep in the murk of grief, she worried that her mind might click apart. Madness, after all, was in her blood.

Chapter Eighteen

Victoria Park was nearly empty on the foggy Saturday morning. Obscure figures took shape in the distance: the churning spokes of a passing cycle, the black filigree of a lantern. Leila sat on a rain-soaked bench and repeatedly scanned the horizon. The air was dense and her skin was clammy as if it had pruned for hours beneath a damp swimsuit. She freed her hair from her woollen scarf, feeling the crackle of static. Andrew had asked her to meet him there and she wondered if Yasmin had told him the truth in a fit of conscience after last night's party.

She spotted him in the distance; could tell it was him from his purposeful gait and the angular shape of his chin. As he approached, she saw the circles beneath his eyes and the grey-blue of his skin. There was a stunned, vacant quality to him and Leila realised with a charge that he knew. She almost started to cry – in dismay but also relief that he could share her burden. She instinctively rose to meet him, but he stopped a few steps away from her.

She scanned his face. 'Andrew?'

'Leila.' He caught his bottom lip in his teeth to try and

stop it quaking. He closed his eyes for a moment, gathering the strength to speak. 'Something happened.'

Leila said nothing, unable to grant him what he needed: a second chance, a time machine.

'Detective Shepherd came to see me yesterday.' Andrew clasped his fingers around his neck: an act of contemplation that looked like he was trying to choke himself. 'He . . . he said it was the pesticide. We normally use the organic version, but Yasmin bought the wrong one. I checked the label. Neem oil can cause rashes and sores. I didn't know. I couldn't have known.' His voice was a panicked babble. 'Leila, do you understand what I'm telling you?'

The two pieces clicked together. It seemed that Shep – not Yasmin – had led him to the truth.

'It might have been the pesticide that caused Max's rashes.' Andrew tensed as if Leila might strike him. 'We pretended he had an allergy to hide his EB, but what if he actually had an allergy that just looked like EB?'

Leila watched the nervous dart of his eyes and felt a sudden and visceral hatred of him for getting it so wrong. She remembered what he had said: *it even has a smell and he smells like it*. That was what had convinced her to help; to coolly plot out that morning: the scripted phone call, the server crash at Andrew's workplace that he had secretly scheduled, the missing blueprints at Syed&Gardner that Leila had stashed in her boot, the spare key slipped from Suki's desk to create the perfect emergency – all of it timed to the minute. To find that Andrew's conviction was actually mere conjecture devastated Leila. And the worst thing? Andrew didn't yet know for sure. Unlike Leila, he could still cling to ignorance.

He began to pace, crunching delicate frost underfoot. 'They were the same sores, the same rashes, the same rabid way that he would scratch at them.' He looked at Leila imploringly as if she might redeem him.

'Why are you telling me?' she asked.

He stopped. 'Because . . .' He motioned with his hand as if it should be obvious, then spluttered a jumble of words. 'Because I *had* to,' he said finally.

'Why?'

'I needed to talk it over.'

'*You* needed,' she said coldly.

He searched her face. 'Leila, why are you being like this?'

She felt a cruel impulse to tell him; to lash out and inflict ruin. *This is all your fault*, she would scream. *You said you were sure. Well, guess what? Max wasn't even yours.* She would barrel forward and slam his chest with both her hands, shove him to the ground, kick him in the gut.

'Leila?'

Venom pooled on her tongue and she desperately wanted to spit at him. She opened her mouth but stalled when she saw his torment; that of a father broken. She swallowed her anger and spoke calmly instead. 'Andrew, that two-bit cop is toying with you.'

Hope rose in his face like a fever. 'Do you really think so?'

'Of course.' She spoke quickly, like a stone skimming over water; pause for too long and she'd sink. 'That detective is trying to get into your head and make you admit to things you didn't actually do. You were certain about Max. You said you knew the *smell* of it.'

Andrew nodded.

'So you have to trust yourself.' She spoke more gently now. 'Andrew, you need to go to Yasmin and you need to treat her with love and care and devotion. You need to rebuild your life together. You could adopt if you wanted to. You and I can't change the past. What you did, the decision you made, was altruistic. It came from a place of love. Don't let anyone undermine that.' She held a hand to her chest. 'What we did was an act of mercy. You *have* to believe that.'

Andrew covered his face and made a low growl of a sound. 'You're right.' There was a small catch in his breath. 'Of course you're right. I'm sorry. God, I'm such a fucking mess.'

She smiled benevolently even as her heart broke. 'Just keep it together from now on, all right?'

He nodded. 'You're right. I just got into a head spin.'

'I know, but it's over, Andrew. It's time to look ahead.' She gestured outward. 'Now go home to Yasmin.'

'Thank you.' He reached out and squeezed the nub of her shoulder. 'For everything.'

She tipped her head graciously. She watched the fog envelop him, one hand clamped to her mouth to silence the howl in her chest.

*

The forceful rap on the door startled Leila and she immediately knew who it was. She strode over and opened it and Yasmin stormed straight in.

'You can be such an arsehole,' she said angrily.

Leila sighed. 'I don't have the energy for this.'

'Yeah, well, I didn't have the energy to spend a fucking hour looking for you at your own party!' She put on a silly, high-pitched voice. '"Oh, sorry, I got waylaid by work." Well, you could have told me that before I spent an hour asking everyone if they'd seen you. God, you can be so *selfish* sometimes.'

'Not now, Yasmin.'

'You think of yourself as a martyr. *My long-suffering carer.* Well, guess what? I didn't *ask* you to look after me, Leila. You could have put me in care and gone off and enjoyed your life and got your architecture degree without working three jobs like some fucking Mother Teresa. That's what the state is there for.'

Leila was momentarily struck mute. 'Are you saying you would rather have gone into care than stay with me?'

'If it stopped making you into such a frigid, judgemental bitch, then yes.'

Leila flinched. 'I wasn't judging you.'

'Don't patronise me, Leila. I know you were. Perfect Leila would *never* cheat on her husband, though I bet he cheats on you!'

'Oh, fuck off.'

Yasmin flinched with shock, but then almost smiled, taking it as licence to be nastier. 'Be real, Leila. You've seen the way he sniffs around anything with a double D. You don't think he plays away at all his conferences and press trips?'

'Why are you being like this?'

Yasmin was in full flow now. 'He's always been such a prick. Maybe it's a blessing that you couldn't have kids!'

Leila stepped back as if physically punched. The air seemed to leave the hall and everything left behind – the clean steel curve of a letter opener, the spent battery of a smoke alarm – felt like the debris of a blast site.

Yasmin registered what she'd said and raised her hands defensively, as if warding off an attack. 'I'm sorry,' she said. 'I just . . . you set all these impossible standards and I screwed up and I hate that you're judging me.'

Leila couldn't speak, unable to metabolise her sister's cruelty.

'It was only one time and I was drunk and I was selfish. So what? You don't need to judge me.'

Leila stared at her. 'I wasn't judging you,' she repeated.

'You dropped your drink and ran off like a fifties housewife. *God*, you're so puritanical.'

'It wasn't that.'

'Then what was it?'

The two of them stared at each other. Leila held her breath, feeling the swell of pressure in her chest.

Yasmin's patience broke. 'Well, it must be nice to always be the most perfect person in the room.'

'I don't think that.'

'You *do*,' sneered Yasmin. 'You always think you know best; always telling me what to do. Maybe you need to back off and let me make mistakes. *You* made a pretty fucking big one.'

And there it was: *blame*. In the months that followed the verdict, Yasmin had never explicitly blamed Leila for what had happened to Max. There was sadness, grief and horror, but the *blame* was left unsaid. Now, it pulsed brightly between them. All this time, Leila had thought herself a martyr who had sacrificed something sacred for her sister. Now, held in the glare of naked blame, she was choked by the fact that she fully deserved it.

'You're right,' she said. 'I'm sorry.'

'Yeah, we're all sorry,' said Yasmin bitterly. 'All my life I've lived in your shadow. I've seen you soar and succeed, giving my husband secret handouts.' She saw the look on Leila's face and sneered. 'Oh, yes, I know all about them. This may surprise you, Leila, but I'm not a fucking idiot. I saw the transfers from your account to his.'

'I was trying to help.'

'Yeah, well, maybe I don't need your fucking help anymore!' Yasmin looked at her as if she were something revolting: a node of pus in a wound, a clot blotting a tampon. The corner of her mouth pinched cruelly. 'Maybe, Leila, you need to find something else to fill the yawning void in your life.' She bared her teeth in a smile. 'Get yourself a fucking hobby.' With that, she turned and stormed out, leaving the door swinging on its hinges.

Leila felt the space vibrate around her, like the rumble of a distant lorry that shakes the ground beneath your feet. She slid down to the bottom stair – not collapsing but a gentle sinking to the earth. A memory rose unbidden. Max at the age of two, plopping himself in her lap. He glanced up at her and smiled.

'What?' Leila asked.

He smiled. 'Just want a hug.'

She had snuggled him to her and held him tight. The absence of him was a solid thing. Leila would never watch him grow up, would never see him fret about a crush, would never be drinking one evening with Yasmin and notice how his arms looked a man's when he lifted something heavy. Leila had wiped him from the world. The knowledge of it was like a rotting inside. If she left it untended, it would eat her alive.

*

Shep waited until his colleagues left the kitchen before he ventured in. He loathed Monday morning small talk. There were always the same questions and the same banal answers. *How was your weekend? Fine, thanks. What'd you get up to? Oh, not much.* Shep's answer was always the same. *Went for a run around Fairlop Waters. Beautiful this time of year.* In his thirties, he would conjure marathon nights out with fictitious friends. 'You know the sort,' he would say with a casual lift of the shoulder. 'It starts out in some trendy bar in Shoreditch and ends up with you drunk as a skunk on top of the Shard.' He would roll his eyes with a little chuckle. For years, he crafted an image of the footloose bachelor, but what might have once been envy morphed undeniably into pity. He eventually realised that he sounded pathetic and stopped engaging altogether. The truth was far more predictable: evenings alone with Netflix. Meal times were the worst. The vacant seats around the table brought his loneliness into focus. He refused to migrate to the sofa though; clung to this vestige of civility.

He drained the coffee pot and set another brewing for the next desperate customer. He retreated to his desk and groaned at the sight of his inbox. Fifty-three new emails. It was a wonder he ever got anything done. Just as he clicked into the first one, a shadow fell over his screen.

'Did you just get in?' asked Heather Witter from the front desk. *Witter by name, witter by nature* the others joked about her.

'Yes. Why?'

'Have you seen your walk-in?' She saw his quizzical look

315

and huffed. 'Steve was meant to catch you on your way in. The lady's been waiting an hour. Said she needed to talk to you.'

Shep frowned. 'What does she look like?'

'Thin, pretty, bitchy resting face.'

He reached for his coffee mug.

'Asian,' Heather added.

His fingers froze on the tip of the handle. *Leila Syed*. He shot up from his chair, heart motoring in his chest. 'Why didn't anyone try me on my mobile?'

She shrugged. 'You never asked us to.'

Shep was already walking away, out to reception. It was a blocky, austere space and the only dash of colour was the dull shine of the dark blue floor. 'Is there someone here waiting for me?'

'Oh, yes,' said the custody officer. He raised a finger towards the corner. 'She's just there.' He glanced up and saw the empty chair. 'Oh. She must have got tired of waiting.'

'Did she give you a name?'

'Just yours.'

Shep swore. He strode down the corridor to see if she was hovering by the noticeboard. 'Did you see where she went?'

The officer screwed up his lips in a show of contrition. 'Afraid not. Sorry.'

'How did she seem? Stressed? Panicked? Calm?'

'She was calm and polite. She arrived at eight. I told her you were normally in at nine, but she said she wanted to wait.'

Shep glanced at the clock. It was ten past nine. 'You didn't see when she left?'

'No. But she was still here at five to nine. I know because

she got up and was peering through the door as if she wanted to greet you in person.'

Shep looked out and saw that it had begun to snow. Clearly, she had left before it set in. 'Well, thanks for your help,' he tossed at the officer.

He looked up with a grin, ignoring Shep's sarcasm. 'Any time,' he said with a wink.

*

Yasmin watched the snow fall in her back garden, a soft carpet setting over the central path. She wanted to go out there and lie in it and make a snow angel as Leila had taught her when she was five years old. Her sister would always let her have the last patch of unbroken snow beneath the apple tree. In the face of all that followed, it amazed her that they had *ever* had a tree. Their spartan flat in Frinton Mews barely had functional windows let alone a garden. Whatever space they did have was stuffed full of books, picked up for pennies at the second-hand shop. Leila had got it into her head that the path to social mobility was paved with big books and would press them onto Yasmin with all the zeal of a tiger mother.

She smiled as she recalled their vastly different tastes. Yasmin would curl up with Danielle Steel and Jackie Collins while Leila opted for business tomes: *The Greed Merchants, The Battle for the Soul of Capitalism, Disneywar: The Battle for the Magic Kingdom*. It was no wonder that, for Leila, life was one big competition.

Yasmin bristled with guilt when she remembered their confrontation. She had said cruel, nasty things that wouldn't easily fade with time. But surely Leila would forgive her. She always did.

Yasmin heard the doorbell: one long note followed by a short. She glanced at the clock. It couldn't be Leila. It was ten past nine on a Monday and she would already be at work. The bell rang again and she hurried down the hall to answer it.

'Will?' she asked in surprise. 'What are you doing here?'

'Can I come in?'

She glanced at the hall behind her, then opened the door wider. 'I've just made some tea.' In the kitchen, she poured two cups and then gestured towards the garden. 'Shall we go out and look at the snow?'

He smiled. 'That would be nice.'

She pulled on a thick woollen cardigan and stepped outside. Both of them hovered at the edge of the decking.

'How are you?' he asked.

'I'm okay.' She glanced at him sideways. 'Is this about the book?' She had texted him last week to seek his advice on the publishing deal.

He set his cup on the garden table. 'Not really.'

'Then?'

He toed the edge of the grass. 'I was hoping to talk to you. About what happened.'

She pulled her cardigan tighter. 'I'm all talked out, Will.'

He was quiet for a moment. 'Then maybe I could talk and you could listen?' He cringed a little at the high-pitched note of hope in his voice.

Yasmin sighed. 'I can't be your therapist, Will.'

He looked at her. 'I'm not asking you to be my therapist, Yasmin. I just want to talk.'

She angled her head in cool bemusement. 'Then get a therapist. Surely you can afford one?' She thought that she'd forgiven Will for writing about Max, but it was clear there was still resentment.

'Why are you being like this?'

'Like what?'

'Look, I understand if you don't want to talk, but you could at least reply to my texts.'

'Why? I've *told* you not to text me.'

'You know what, Yasmin? You're not the only one who lost him.' Will levelled his gaze on her. 'Max was *my* son too.'

'Yeah and maybe we *deserved* what happened,' she said.

'Don't say things like that. Please.'

'I almost told Leila the truth last night.' She lobbed the words like a weapon.

He stared at her. 'You know you can't do that.'

'Yes, I'm aware of that,' she said in a sneer.

'Stop playing games then.' His patience ebbed. 'What *did* you tell her?'

'She thinks I slept with Jason. She still doesn't know that you came to the party.' Yasmin remembered that night vividly. Leila had cancelled last minute, but Will didn't get her message in time. He turned up in full black tie and proceeded to search the crowd. By the time he saw the text, Yasmin was draped across his arm, bitter and tipsy, in desperate need of release. They hadn't even discussed it; just headed to the hotel opposite for angry, cathartic sex as if it were predetermined. 'What we did that night was unforgivable.'

'We were drunk,' he said, quick as a reflex.

'And that makes it okay?'

'Of course not, but it was one mistake. We were drunk and angry and—'

'Oh, spare me, Will. We did what we did because we were selfish. "One mistake," you call it? Well, that's easy for you to say. I had to face it every single day. Maybe you couldn't see it, but Max looked more and more like you: the same cheekbones, the same smile. I was terrified that Leila would see it one day.' Her lips twisted in an airless smile. 'Do you know what crossed my mind when I heard that Max was gone? Some disgusting part of me thought, "Well, Leila's back where she wants to be: firmly in the lead." What kind of person thinks something like that?'

Will grimaced. 'That's all you, Yasmin. *Your* insecurity. *Your* paranoia. Leila has never competed with you. She's always put you first. Always wanted you to win.'

'Jesus. You come here to talk about Max and end up singing Leila's praises.'

'I don't want you to misjudge her. Leila would do anything for you.'

Yasmin tensed defensively. 'I never asked her to.'

'So, what then? You'd rather have entered the system? Be punted from stranger to stranger? I still don't think you know what she did for you. Look at her, Yasmin. Look at what she's achieved. What else could she have done if she didn't have an eleven-year-old child to look after when she was eighteen?' He paused as if expecting an answer. 'It's time to move on. We may never stop grieving, but don't ever doubt how much you mean to Leila.'

Yasmin was quiet, chastened by the truth. Her voice quivered when she spoke. 'I've been so unkind to her.'

Will smiled sadly. 'We can make it up to her.' He caught a snowflake in his right palm. 'All we have left is time.'

*

Leila watched him watch the snowfall, a faraway look in his eyes. He turned and said something snippy to the desk officer, who volleyed something back. For a moment, their actions seemed to slow. Sound took on a distorted timbre: the trickle of melting snow on the window, the toil of ancient heating, the tap of his brogues on the epoxy flooring, a material that Leila refused to work with. It would be so easy to let him leave.

'Detective?' she called, her voice strange and echoing.

Detective Shepherd spun and fixed her with his cool blue eyes. 'Ms Syed.' His voice clicked all sound back to its natural grooving. He straightened his tie and approached her. 'How may I help you?'

She had imagined this moment a dozen times. She had worried that she might backtrack and reach for an excuse. In one scenario, she panicked and said, *I'd like to ask you out to dinner.* In another, she simply turned and fled, overwhelmed by the prospect of telling the truth. She was terrified of what would happen. She pictured a thicket of journalists charting her every move. Tabloid headlines freighted with pointed language – childless, motherless, barren – would turn a nation against her. She was chilled by the thought of incarceration; imagined the feel of prison on her skin: cold and wet and close, like damp sliding to rot.

She had grappled with the logic of coming clean, for Andrew would be caught in the fallout, but she knew she couldn't carry this guilt for the length of a lifetime. If only Yasmin had told her the truth when Max was born – or not told her the truth at all. She could maintain the illusion that what she did was merciful.

It's the bravest, most selfless thing anyone has ever done for me and my family, Andrew had told her – but they were both mistaken. Leila had killed Max and the only way to live with that was to tell the truth.

She held the detective's gaze. 'I would like to confess,' she said, her voice labouring beneath her courage.

Shep studied her for a moment with a real sadness in his eyes. He nodded once, wearily, as if he had been expecting her. 'Please come with me,' he said, his fatherly tone an unexpected comfort in this harsh place of recompense. She swallowed and followed him along the plastic flooring down to the abyss.

Acknowledgements

Thank you to my very own superwomen Jessica Faust and Manpreet Grewal for making everything possible. I would not have a career without you.

Thank you to Lisa Milton and the brilliant team at HQ: Janet Aspey, Sian Baldwin, Claire Brett, Dawn Burnett, Sophie Calder, Lily Capewell, Laura Daley, Rebecca Fortuin, Georgina Green, Melanie Hayes, Becca Joyce, Melissa Kelly, Imie Kent-Muller, Fliss Porter, Lucy Richardson, Joanna Rose, Darren Shoffren, Katrina Smedley, Isabel Smith, Joe Thomas, Angela Thomson, Georgina Ugen, Kelly Webster, Harriet Williams and of course the fantastic design and production teams. Thank you, also, to Peter Borcsok and the team at HarperCollins Canada who backed me from the beginning.

Thank you to Mary Alice Kier for all your work on super top secret projects, and to James McGowan and the BookEnds team.

Thank you to all those who so generously lent me their expertise: Matthew Butt QC, Dr Richard Shepherd, Graham Bartlett, Nadine Matheson, Melissa Jaquez, Dr Claire Windeatt, Dr Daniel Wilbor, Kevin Wong, Amit Dhand, Sara

Crofts, Dina Begum, Hawa Choudhury, Hiren Joshi and Lee Adams. As ever, I hope you will forgive me for any errors I've made or creative licence I've taken with your meticulous advice.

Thank you to The Society of Authors, the Author's Foundation and all my fellow authors who have championed my work. I appreciate your generosity so very much.

A special thank you to all the booksellers, librarians, reviewers and bloggers that have pushed my book (now books!) into the hands of readers. You are the lifeblood of our industry and I am profoundly grateful to you all.

Thank you to my sisters Reena, Jay, Shiri, Forida and Shafia. I'm lucky to have a group of five soldiers to call on when I need.

And, Peter, you know the drill by now.

Turn the page for an exclusive sneak
peek at the upcoming new courtroom
drama from Kia Abdullah

THOSE PEOPLE NEXT DOOR

Coming in 2023

Chapter One

Salma had always sworn that she would never end up in a place like this. 'It's a bit like purgatory,' she had joked when they first came to see the house in a harried half hour before work one morning. The estate agent, a hawkish woman with a watchful gaze, had herded them from room to room and Salma had murmured with approval, even commenting on this or that 'lovely feature' as she and Bilal locked eyes, amusement passing between them.

They had agreed to see it only because there was a gap between their other viewings and the agent had pushed this property. It was in a neat cul de sac on the eastern reaches of the central line. It was built seven years ago, said the agent, and still had the bright, bland feel of a new development. There was a dizzying amount of brickwork and even its name, the mononymous 'Blenheim', felt like an artless attempt at class, like petrol stop perfume or 'Guccci' shades. Upstairs, out of the agent's earshot, they had giggled about the perfect lawn.

'Do you think Neighbourhood Watch will knock down your door if the lawn gets above two inches?' said Bilal.

Salma fought a smile. 'We're being snobby,' she said but with laughter in her voice.

The agent walked in and the two of them sprang apart like children caught red-handed. 'It's lovely, isn't it?' She nodded at the window, her silver-brown bob swaying with the motion.

'Lovely,' Salma agreed.

That was six months ago and after close to forty viewings, they had grown weary. Nothing else matched Blenheim for price, condition, space and safety and so they talked each other into it. *Four double bedrooms*, said Bilal. *And it's still on the Central Line*, said Salma. *The neat streets and quiet neighbours.* If they could set aside their vanity, they could be very happy at Blenheim and so they had put in an offer – and here they were, their first week in their new home.

They hadn't yet met their neighbours but, yesterday, a square of white card appeared on their doormat inviting them to a May Bank Holiday Barbecue. *No need to RSVP. Just turn up!* it said in jaunty letters. Salma had read it wearily. She wasn't an introvert by any means but did find parties tiring. She far preferred to meet new people on a one-to-one basis. Still, they were new here and had to make an effort. Salma had prepared some potato salad and told her son, Zain, that he had no choice but to join them. They approached 13 Blenheim like a trio of soldiers heading into battle. Salma paused outside and assessed her husband and son. As she straightened one of Bilal's crooked collars, he caught her hand in his and kissed it.

'Here goes,' she said. She rang the bell but no one answered. Music bled from the garden and Salma counted to twenty before she rang again. Zain ventured to the side of the house and pointed at the open side gate. They walked through in single file and hovered at the edge of the gathering. There were about thirty people of varying ages, laughing and milling around.

There were cheers around the barbecue as the first tranche of meat was dished up, filling the air with a pleasantly smoky smell.

A woman spotted them and her eyes lit up. 'You must be the new arrivals!' she called. She detached herself from the group and pulled Salma into a matronly hug. 'I'm Linda Turner, the hostess.'

'Oh hello! I'm Salma. Thank you so much for inviting us.'

'Bilal,' said her husband. He caught the crease of Linda's brow and promptly added, 'Call me Bil.'

She brightened. 'Bill! How wonderful to have new neighbours.' She turned to Zain. 'And this must be your son. My, what a handsome boy!'

Zain smiled politely. 'How do you do?'

She made a whoop of delight. 'And such manners too!' She looked at the glass bowl in his hands. 'You didn't have to bring anything! But thank you.' She took the bowl and ushered them into the party. 'What can I get you to drink? We have wine, beer, cider.' She paused. 'Or we have fresh lemonade and fruit juice.'

Bil smiled. 'A lemonade would be lovely – thank you.'

'Make that three,' said Salma.

She beamed. 'Wonderful!' She left them with their next-door neighbour. 'This is Tom Hutton. He can give you a lowdown on everyone here.'

Tom greeted them warmly. He was in his mid-forties, broad-shouldered and muscular with thick dark hair splayed beneath an orange cap. As she spoke, a young bull terrier bounded up to him. 'Her name is Lola,' he said, bending down to pet her. He looked up at Salma. 'She was a showgirl,' he added in a deadpan.

Salma broke into laughter and Tom nodded in approval as if she had passed some test. Lola snuffed at Salma's feet.

'You don't mind, do you?' said Tom.

'No, not at all. We have a dog too, a Lab called Molly.'

'Oh, that's great. This is such a dog-friendly neighbourhood. You're going to love it.'

Linda cut in to hand out drinks. Bil volunteered to help with the barbecue and she happily whisked him away while Zain retired to a corner of the garden to busy himself on his phone.

'So what do you do?' asked Tom.

'I'm a teacher,' said Salma. 'Geography at a secondary school,' she added, pre-empting his follow-up questions. 'What about you?'

'I work in advertising. At Sartre & Sartre.'

'Oh wow. That must be glamorous.'

'It can be,' he said with a grin, clearly enjoying the compliment. 'And what about Bil?'

Salma tensed. 'He's a restaurateur,' she said, thinking of Jakoni's, Bil's beloved restaurant that had shut down in January after a horrendous year for hospitality. Now, it sat empty despite their best efforts to sell it.

'Restaurateur?' Tom puckered his lips in a show of approval. 'You must be doing alright then, no?'

Salma looked bemused. 'I mean, we're doing okay.'

'Sorry if that's rude. I was just wondering how come you got this place then?' He nodded in the direction of their house.

Salma relaxed, relieved to find that he too was skeptical of Blenheim. She smiled playfully. 'It's not so bad, is it? Where else would I find such a pristine collection of lawns?'

Tom frowned. 'It's just that I would've thought you were above the threshold.'

'What threshold?'

'Well, for the social housing,' he said matter-of-factly.

Salma blinked. 'Oh,' she said, realising what Tom had meant – not *you're wealthy so why would you choose to live here* but *you're wealthy so why did you get social housing?* She shifted uneasily. 'We bought it privately.'

Tom's jaw fell open. 'Oh! I'm sorry. I didn't mean to assume. In fact, I *wasn't* assuming. I was certain that the house next to us was social housing.' He cringed. 'Obviously, I was mistaken.'

Salma waved in a show of nonchalance. 'Ah, if only! It might have saved us a pretty penny.' Her voice laboured with the effort to put him at ease. She reached for something else to say.

'So what school do you teach at?' asked Tom.

'Ilford Academy in Seven Kings.'

'Oh, right. Do you enjoy it?'

Salma could feel the conversation slipping away from her but was keen to keep the momentum. If they parted now, it would surely make things more awkward the next time they met. 'Yes,' she replied. 'It's especially nice in *August*.' She laughed at her own joke but it had an obvious, forced quality to it. She didn't understand why she was being this way. She was normally poised and confident, perfectly versed in small talk. She reached for a question but was cut short by a woman who slid up next to Tom. Salma stared for a second. She was tall and willowy with white-blonde hair, delicate cheekbones and a tiny gap between her front teeth that seemed to only add to her beauty.

She held out an elegant hand. 'Willa,' she said. 'Like the writer.'

Salma shook it and pretended to know which writer she meant. 'Are you a model?' she asked out of genuine curiosity.

Willa made a snap of laughter. 'You're sweet, but no. I run our home.'

'Sorry,' said Salma. 'I assumed you could be. You must get that all the time.'

Willa rolled her eyes. 'Thank you, but it's fucking embarrassing. I'm like an Aryan wet dream.'

Salma nearly spat out her lemonade. She was unsure if Willa was blithely outspoken or if she actually rather enjoyed Salma's display of shock. She looked across at Tom who didn't respond, only slid an arm around Willa's waist. Salma cleared her throat. 'How did you both meet?' she asked, steering them into safer territory.

'I know what you're thinking,' said Tom. 'How did a brute like me end up with a girl like her?'

'Tom used to be a firefighter,' Willa cut in. 'Believe it or not, he ran into a burning building and saved me. I was twenty-one. He was twenty-seven and that was that.'

Salma looked from one to the other. 'Is that true?'

Willa gazed at Tom adoringly. 'One hundred per cent.'

'Oh my god. That's incredible.'

Willa burst out laughing. 'I'm just fucking with you!'

Salma grew still. Then, she smiled and pretended she was in on the joke and not at the butt of it.

'Of *course* that's not what happened,' said Willa, 'but the real story is almost as cute.'

Salma waited but Willa was speaking to Tom now.

'Do you remember how you chased me for six months? Sending me flowers and chocolates. God, wasn't there even that H. Samuel bracelet?'

Tom looked at Salma sheepishly. 'Willa's family are rich,'

he explained. 'So here I am sending her Milk Tray and a five quid bunch of flowers while she's used to,' he looked over at her, 'what's that poncey brand you like?'

'Charbonnel et Walker,' she said smoothly, then turned back to Salma. 'He wasn't a firefighter but,' she winked, 'he did let me ride his pole.'

Salma chuckled politely. She, like most people, did a sub-conscious thing when she met someone new. She assessed whether or not they were part of her 'tribe'. Tom and Willa with their strange, abrasive humour were most certainly not. Normally, Salma wouldn't mind and simply get on with her day, but this was a new neighbourhood and she had to make an effort. 'You mentioned that you run the home,' she said to Willa. 'Do have kids?'

'Yes. A son, Jamie. He's seventeen.' She must have caught the surprise on Salma's face because she added, 'I had him young; at twenty-one.'

Salma calculated that Willa was thirty-nine, five years younger than her. 'That works out well for me,' she said. 'My son, Zain, is eighteen and I'm sure he'd love to meet Jamie.'

'That would be lovely. Jamie needs to make a few friends.'

They talked for a while longer and Salma scanned the crowd for Bil. She saw that he was cornered by Linda and excused herself to join them.

'What is that delicious nutty flavour in the potato salad?' Linda was asking.

'Fried pine nuts,' said Salma.

'Ah, well, thank you for indulging us. For reference, I can handle my spice so if you ever want to bring something with a bit more zing, you'd be more than welcome to.'

Salma smiled. 'Of course. I'll bear that in mind.'

Linda clapped her hands, twice like an excited child. 'I look forward to it.' She looked over Salma's shoulder. 'Well, I should mingle. Please help yourself to the food and drink. There's so much to get through.' She beamed and then left in a cloud of activity.

Bil looked at Salma. 'How long do you reckon before it's okay to leave?'

'Stop it,' she chided. 'We have to make an effort.' She fixed on a fresh smile and led him back to the fray.

Salma felt herself uncoil, the tension leaving her muscles as soon as they left the barbecue. Blenheim looked uncanny without any streetlamps. The local council insisted that lights would spoil the character of the local area and so it lay in darkness. Bil gripped her hand and they walked home in silence, needing total privacy before they could relax. They approached their lawn, still a consistent one-inch tall. Their neighbour Tom had mowed it while the house was being sold. Salma stepped onto the blue-black of it and felt her shoe flatten the spongy grass. She kicked a few pebbles back onto the path and picked up a palm-sized banner that Zain had stuck in a plant pot. She dug it back in place and followed Bil inside.

'Zain?' she called. He had left the barbecue half an hour earlier and was no doubt on his computer.

'Hi, Mum,' he called back.

'Did you eat enough?'

'Yes, Mum,' he said in a wry singsong.

She turned to Bil and exhaled.

He laughed a little. 'You okay?'

'Yeah, I'm fine.' She smiled wickedly. 'Shall I take Linda a naga dish next time?'

'Well, she *can* handle her spice.'

Salma covered her face and groaned.

'It's okay,' he said. 'It was just a lot in one go.'

She nodded vigorously in an attempt to convince herself. She uncovered her face. 'Are *you* okay?'

'Yeah. I'm fine.' He reached for her and she fit herself against him.

'We'll be okay, right?' she asked.

'Yes,' he replied, and she felt it boom in his chest.

'We haven't made a mistake?'

There was the tiniest pause before he spoke. 'No.'

'Okay. Good.' She kissed his cheek. 'I'm going to take a shower.' She pulled off her hairband and headed upstairs. She paused briefly on the landing to listen to the click of Zain's keyboard in the attic. She peeled off her socks and tossed them in the laundry bin. In the shower, she realised that she could hear voices on the other side: the deep murmur of Tom's voice and the lighter pitch of Willa's. She pressed her ear to the wall but couldn't make out any words. She listened to see if their conversation had the tightness of an argument or the lightness of a joke. Were they discussing her family, just as she and Bil would discuss theirs?

Tom's words returned to her: *I would've thought you were above the threshold.* She flushed with indignation and hoped once again that they had made the right decision. If they had known that Jakoni's would shut its doors, they would almost certainly have stayed in their tiny flat in Seven Kings. By the time it happened, however, they had already spent money on the survey and convinced themself to take the leap. Five months later, they still hadn't sold Jakoni's.

Her stomach clenched with unease; a sudden conviction that they'd made a mistake. But they didn't have a choice, she reminded herself. Not after what happened with Zain. She didn't have the luxury of doubt. This was the safest place that they could afford and they would make the most of it. It was true that missed her old neighbourhood – the big, messy families and rows of crowded houses – but here Zain had room to breathe: a large bedroom, his own bathroom, a balcony and a garden too. There would be a period of adjustment, of course, but they were sure to fit in before long. They had to. They had nowhere else to go.

Zain blew out a lungful of smoke, fanning it as he did so. If his mum found out that he smoked, well, then there'd be hell to pay. Her father had died from lung cancer and she was a full-on fundamentalist when it came to smoking. It annoyed him, but it could be worse, he supposed. His peers were like double agents: sweet, respectful, *seedha saadha* with their parents, then totally fucking wild behind the scenes. At least his mum knew what was what and allowed him certain liberties if he didn't take the piss. He never really appreciated it 'til he saw how others lived.

He took another draw and felt it burn in his chest, then exhaled slowly. He thought of the barbecue and the repetition of that dreaded question: *what do you do?*

I'm a student, he had told them, hating himself for the lie. In truth, he'd been kicked out of college last year, which meant he couldn't sit his A Levels, couldn't go to uni, couldn't get a decent job and was living with his parents like a deadbeat, spending his Friday nights on Twitch, live streaming his coding. That's one thing he could do, but most tech jobs asked for degrees. The startups that claimed to overlook formal education, relied on other cues – accents and expensive accessories – that Zain lacked too. Trying too hard felt worse than not trying at all and so he gave up looking.

He leaned over the balcony wall and took another puff. He heard a cough next door and quickly stubbed out his cigarette. For a panicked moment, he thought he was back on Selborne Estate with his mum's room next to his. He relaxed when he saw a boy lean out towards him around the thick column of brick separating the two houses.

'Shit, sorry, mate,' said Zain, fanning the smoke.

'Oh, I wasn't dropping a hint,' said the boy. He was close to Zain's age, white, and looked like he belonged in a boyband: thick brown hair styled stiff with gel, a touch of K-pop in his delicate chin.

'Nah, it's alright,' said Zain. 'I was done anyway.'

'It's handy to have the top room, huh?' said the boy.

Zain noticed a quirk in his speech: the 's' dropped from 'it's. *It handy to have the top room, huh?* 'Yeah, it is,' he replied.

The boy stretched across the column, so far that Zain worried he might fall. 'I'm Jamie.'

'Zain.' He shook Jamie's hand and was surprised by its firm grip. He smiled. There was nothing he hated more than a limp handshake.

'So...' Jamie lifted his chin at the garden. 'What brought you to paradise?'

'The search for a better life,' said Zain, matching Jamie's tone.

'Ha! Prepare to be disappointed.'

Zain laughed. 'How long have you lived here?'

'We moved here when I was ten, so seven years now.'

'What's it like?'

'It's alright.'

Zain noticed that he dropped his 's' again – *it alright* – and wondered if he had a speech impediment. He felt a drop of affection and for a moment, was hit with a yearning for siblings. Relatives often joked that Zain was an old soul. They didn't understand that, as an only child, you ate most of your meals with adults. You listened to adult conversation, adult concerns, and it was natural to inherit them. He remembered using the word 'inquisition' soon after starting secondary school and being teased no end. After that, he deliberately dumbed down his vocabulary. Sometimes, he stammered not because he couldn't find a word but because he was trying to swap it for a shorter one. That was the thing about Selborne Estate. It gave you a sense of community, but it held you back as well. Zain had seen this play out with his friend Amin. He had secured a good job straight after school: IT support for a medical research centre in the city. Every day, his old school friends would see him leave in the frayed brown suit he'd inherited, a satchel slung over his shoulder, and tease him for being a *boroh sahib*. A big man. *He's too important for us now*, they'd say. *Rah, look how he's ignoring us.*

One day, Amin turned up in a grey hoodie and jeans.

'Ey yo, what's going on, man?' asked Zain.

'You won't believe it, mate. They fired me.'

'Wait, what?'

'They said I stole from the petty cash.'

Zain narrowed his gaze on him. 'Did you?'

'Nah, course I didn't.'

'Then they can't do that!' Zain got so riled up but mid-rant he registered Amin's nonchalance. He watched him for a moment, hit with the cold suspicion that Amin had done it on purpose; had got himself fired because he was tired of being othered, not by his colleagues at his fancy office but his friends right here at home. Selborne Estate was a safety net but one with a ceiling you couldn't escape.

It's partly why when his parents suggested the move, beneath his initial resistance, he felt a seed of relief. He hadn't known that they'd end up in this wasteland of a street.

'Seriously though, I can't wait to leave,' Jamie cut in.

'Where'd you go? Uni?'

Jamie shrugged a shoulder. 'Start my own company maybe.'

Zain laughed but then caught a look of hurt. 'Sorry, I just... it's not that easy, is it?'

Jamie ducked a little, embarrassed. 'No, you're right. It's stupid.'

'Nah, man,' Zain backtracked guiltily. 'It's not stupid. It's better than working for someone else.'

'I've applied for some funding from Google's startup fund.'

This piqued his interest. 'Oh, yeah? So you have an idea?'

'Kind of.' He paused. 'Well, yeah.'

Zain arched his brows to show the younger boy that he was impressed. 'What is it?'

Jamie withdrew, suddenly shy. 'Well... Hang on.' He retreated into his room and returned a few seconds later.

He handed Zain a stack of paper. On it were mockups of an iPhone screen. 'It's an app,' said Jamie. 'To help deaf people communicate with hearing people.'

'How does it work?'

Jamie reached to take the papers back and talked him through the mockups. He explained the purpose of the app – a real-time sign-to-speech translator – and talked him through the designs.

'How come you're interested in this?' asked Zain.

Jamie set down the papers on the brick wall. 'Well, I don't know if you can tell, but I'm partially deaf. I was born three months premature, but they didn't realise there was anything different until I was about four. By then, certain sounds had escaped me. I've seen a speech therapist but even now, I sometimes miss letters. It's kind of like talking in a different accent, you know? You always have to be concentrating so eventually I decided, so what? What's normal anyway?'

Zain nodded. 'Good on you, man.'

Jamie flushed. 'Thanks. I just need to find someone who can build the damn thing now.'

Zain fixed his gaze on him. 'You know I code, right?'

Jamie did a double take. 'Really?' He hesitated. 'Would you... would you be interested?'

Zain considered this. 'I mean, maybe.' He leafed through the designs again, then quizzed Jamie a little bit more. He puckered his lips in thought, then said, 'Okay, why not?'

'Seriously?'

'Yeah, seriously.'

Jamie beamed. 'Fuck, man. That would be fantastic.' He reached out his hand again.

Zain shook it and felt a warm feeling: a sense of purpose and comradeship.

There was a call from inside Jamie's house. 'Shit, that's Mum. I better go. Here, take my number.'

Zain keyed it into his phone and listened to Jamie scurry inside. He looked out over the inky grass, feeling a new thrill of hope.

Salma groaned as she examined her profile in the mirror, noting the paunch around her midriff.

'No one tells you that, after forty, you basically can't eat bread,' she said.

Bil laughed. 'You don't look a day over twenty-five.' He leaned in and nuzzled her neck.

'Get orf,' she said, mimicking the boys from the eighties Accrington Stanley milk advert.

'Oh my god, are you trying to do a Scouse accent?'

She frowned. 'Were they Scouse? I thought they were Geordie.'

'God, you Londoners,' He threw up his hands in surrender. 'You're all hopeless.'

She rolled her eyes and watched him pull on a T-shirt.

'Will you have time for breakfast?' he asked.

'Sorry. Not today.' She felt a mix of guilt and gratitude. When his restaurant shut down, Bil was devastated but went straight back into work, taking a job far beneath his skill level at a curry house in Newbury Park. He was on gruelling split shifts, but still woke up every morning to make her breakfast. She kissed him goodbye, grabbed her bag and headed downstairs. They had moved two miles farther out, but her commute was still easy: the 169 bus nearly all the way to her school.

Outside, she noticed that Zain's banner was on the floor again. She picked it up and fingered the flimsy fabric. *Black Lives Matter*, it said, printed in black on a pink background. She had protested when Zain first displayed it.

'I think we should meet the neighbours first before we put up something like that,' she'd said.

Zain had looked at her scornfully. 'Because *that* will inform whether or not black lives matter?' he'd asked.

She'd sighed. 'Just put it somewhere not too in your face.'

It was strange how certain hang-ups stayed with you. When she was eleven, she got caught up in the excitement of a World Cup match – 1990 she thinks it was – and mocked up a St George's Cross, which she taped to their living room window. When her dad came home from work, he ripped it down with an urgency she'd never seen before.

'Don't ever do that again,' he said. 'We'll get a brick through our window.'

The ferocity in his tone frightened her and though she didn't understand it, she didn't question him further. Even now, as an adult, she didn't understand if he thought that the danger lay in her claiming the flag as her own, or because he simply associated it with violence. It broke her heart that her father, who couldn't read English words, recognised danger in that single image.

She shook off the memory and stuck the pink banner back into the plant pot. She headed towards the bus stop and heard a beep to her left. Her neighbour, Tom, was in his car and she raised a hand to wave. He rolled down his window and beckoned her closer.

'Morning, Salma.'

'Hi Tom. How are you?'

'Good, good.' He took off his sunglasses. 'Listen, can I ask you a favour?'

'Of course.'

He grimaced as if this pained him. 'Can you guys try to park in front of your house?'

Salma looked at her car, which overshot their house by a foot. 'Oh, sorry! I didn't realise there was designated parking.'

'No, no. There isn't. It's just we have two cars so if you overshoot, we can't get both of ours in.'

'Oh, right.' Salma frowned. 'It's just that sometimes people park outside ours, so we roll forward a bit so our car will fit.'

'Ah. Maybe you could find out who's doing it and have a word?'

'Um, I mean, sometimes it's different cars.'

'Okay, well...' He tapped the steering wheel as if trying to think of a solution. 'If you can't figure out who it is, then that's fine obviously, but it *is* a bit of a pain for us to park around the corner.'

'Of course,' said Salma evenly. 'I'm sure it is. We'll try our best.'

'Thank you,' he said with an apologetic smile.

Salma readied to move off, but he stopped her.

'Sorry, while I'm being annoying, I should say that the fence between our gardens has a loose board. We fixed it last time and then again when the house was empty, so maybe you guys could have a look at it?'

Salma smiled. 'Of course.'

'Great.' He beamed. 'Thank you for being so understanding. Have a good morning.'

'You too,' she said, her cheeks burning hot. Surely, it wasn't reasonable to claim a section of the road just because it passed your home? She wished she hadn't agreed so easily. Or that she'd at least made a pointed joke to show him this wasn't okay. She dwelled on it all the way to work, so that instead of nestling in her favourite seat – the top right-hand corner – she stood and watched the landscape, her frown etched deep.

She shook it off as she approached her school, a large, flat building in a godless corner of Ilford. She passed through the security gates and headed up to her classroom. There, she felt at ease. Unlike many teachers she knew, Salma loved her job. She enjoyed the constant hum and activity and thrived on being busy. It didn't even bother her when people made snarky comments about *all that time off*. Very few people could do what she did as effectively as she did, and that fact made her proud.

She settled into the room, a small rectangular space dripping with maps and trinkets. Salma took comfort in crowded places. Perhaps that's why she struggled with Blenheim: all clean lines and large, wide spaces. She stowed her bag and prepared for her tutor group. A knock on the door broke her focus.

'Miss, can you help me?' It was Haroon, a shy, rake-thin boy in her class. He hovered at the threshold.

'Yes.'

He came in and sat by her desk. 'Miss, I've been trying to fill this in, but I can't work it out.' He held out an A4 form.

She glanced over the first page and saw that it was a housing benefit application. 'Can it wait 'til clinic tomorrow?' she asked.

'If I don't send it before the post today, there'll be a gap in our payments.'

Salma nodded. 'Right, okay, well, the class is coming in, but can you drop by here at break? We can go through it then.'

'Can we finish it in twenty minutes though?' His eyes were wide with worry.

'Should do. If not, I'll call them and ask for an extension.'

This made him relax a little. 'Thanks, Miss.' He headed to his desk at the back of the classroom.

The 'clinic' Salma referred to was her labour of love. She had pitched it as 'a Citizens Advice Bureau for pupils' but met resistance from the head.

'It plays into stereotypes,' George had said, 'that B-A-M-E people can't help themselves.'

'But what if they *can't*?' she'd asked, frustrated.

'Then it's not our place to help them.'

Salma couldn't bite her tongue. 'This is where your leftie sensibilities actually interfere, George,' she'd told her.

The head had acquiesced. 'Fine. But if the press get wind of this, they'll make a meal of it.'

'It's volunteer run!'

'On school premises.'

'Are you in or out?'

'Fine,' she'd relented. 'I'm in.'

And of course there *was* a need for it because despite what George had said, there were plenty of pupils who needed help. Children like Haroon with parents who couldn't speak English had to navigate labyrinthine systems like HMRC, the NHS and DWP.

Last week, a pupil came by the clinic and asked her to

explain a home test kit for bowel cancer so that he could translate it for his mother. Salma watched the young boy redden as she explained it step by step. Eventually, she asked if he would prefer one of the Urdu-speaking female teachers to call his mum and explain. The boy had agreed with great relief.

Haroon took his seat and the rest of the pupils filtered in. They were a lively group, but after four years in Salma's form class, easy to control. She had enjoyed watching them mature: Patrick who had started off a nightmare but was now a fine young man; Ritesh who was far too serious but bloomed into a comedian. Some kids, like Haroon, stayed the same and others went the opposite way. Tara, a studious, gawky kid had discovered boys and makeup, and let her grades plummet.

Salma hoped that she had got the balance right. When she first became a teacher, to her 'making a difference' meant creating doctors and lawyers, fulfilling parents' dreams and funnelling pupils to top-tier unis. She slowly accepted that this wasn't possible – not with the budget and restrictions they had. Then, she realised, that 'making a difference' didn't have to be so grand. It could be as simple as helping Haroon with paperwork so he that could rest easy today, or telling Faisal that he needn't explain to his mum an embarrassing medical test. It was taking the web of a million worries that made up adolescence and unpicking a little corner of it.

The bell rang to signal the start of teaching hours. 'Alright, settle down please,' called Salma. She opened the register and started a new school day.

*

Willa beeped the car horn once, then again, more prolonged to make sure that Jamie heard. He came hurtling out the door and hurried into the car.

'I haven't got all day, mate,' she said.

'Oh, really? Women's bake sale pressing, is it?'

She tapped his arm in a light rebuke. She and Jamie were more like friends than mother and son. She had had him at twenty-one, far before she was ready. There was a tax on motherhood – a yielding of a part of yourself – and she did not want to pay it, so acted more like a friend. It had worked though. Her son had become a fine young man.

She glanced over at him now. 'Remember what I told you?' she asked.

'I won't tell Dad,' he promised.

'Good.' She nodded towards their new neighbours' house. 'You should have come yesterday. You could have met their son, Zain.'

'What were they like?'

Willa scrunched her nose. 'Hard to say. They kind of seemed to be putting on an act.'

'Everyone does at first.'

'*I* don't,' said Willa.

Jamie made a face.

'Do I?'

'No, but you go the opposite way.'

'How so?'

He shrugged. 'I don't know, Mum.' He reached for his phone, but she stopped him.

'How so?' she pressed.

'I don't know. I can't explain it.' He freed his hand from hers and took out his phone.

She felt embarrassed by the thought of that. If her 17-year old-son thought she acted fake, did others feel the same? She decided not to grill him further. God forbid she become *that* sort of mother.

She headed off and drove the three miles to South Woodford where she parked outside what looked like a large house. She led Jamie inside and through to the waiting room, all hushed tones and plush upholstery.

Jamie's audiologist, Tania, greeted them and led them to an oblong room. At the end stood a small enclosure, almost like a photo booth, which was used to test his hearing. She had noticed lately that more and more sounds were evading him. His condition wasn't degenerative, but she worried that the amount of time he spent indoors was making him less fluent.

Tania took him through his standard raft of tests, usually done once a year. This session was additional. Jamie sat inside the booth and Tania ran through the usual spiel: if you feel anxious, then just say and we'll let you out. Jamie was asked to press a button every time he heard a sound. In another test, he was asked to repeat what he heard in his ear. Willa hated this test. It was always the one that made him lose heart.

Tania always told him, 'Even if it's a fraction of a word, try to say it. Even if it's an approximation, say it. Just say whatever you think you heard,' and Jamie would always start by trying – *oof*, *lek*, *sen* – but then dwindle into silence, embarrassed by how hard he found it. Willa tried to catch his gaze, but he studiously avoided her.

Eventually, Tania released him from the booth. 'Are you keeping up with your verbal exercises?'

He gave her a guilty look. 'When I can.'

'Jamie.' She angled her head in disapproval. 'It's really important that you keep up with this. I promise you'll see an improvement.'

Willa stepped forward hesitantly. 'Tania, could we try the Opn hearing aids again? I know we said we'd leave them, but I want to give them another try.'

Jamie frowned. 'Why?' he asked her.

'Because they help you.'

'But I don't need them.' Last time he had said the same, but she'd seen the way his eyes lit up when he put them in. He was only saying no because he knew they couldn't afford them.

'Just try them, Jamie.'

Tania rolled over to her desk and took out a pair of the premium aids. She helped Jamie try them and encouraged him to take a walk around the building. As he stepped out, Willa's voice dropped low.

'We'll take them, Tania, but can I change our billing address?'

'Of course.'

Willa read out the new details and hurried to explain why the name and address were different to hers. 'They're my dad's details,' she said. 'Do you need to speak to him?'

Tania waved away the question. 'I'm sure you're not out there stealing credit card details,' she said with a laugh.

Jamie reappeared in the doorway.

'They're yours,' said Willa.

He looked from her to Tania. 'How?'

'Grandad,' she answered. 'But don't tell your dad, okay?'

Jamie exhaled slowly. For a moment, he seemed to consider this, but then nodded. 'Okay.'

They finished with Tania and returned to Willa's car. Jamie braced himself against the dashboard.

'Are you okay?' asked Willa.

He nodded. 'It's… weird. I can hear you breathing.'

Willa grew still, quieted by emotion. She turned her gaze to the road so that Jamie wouldn't notice. She was angry with herself then, for heeding Tom for so many years. He was a proud man and refused to take money from Willa's family, so Jamie had suffered substandard care. After seeing his reaction to the Opn aids, she'd secretly asked her father for help.

'I'm proud of you, kid,' she said.

He shifted awkwardly. 'Whatevs.'

'No, hey, I *am*.'

'Thank you,' he said, looking sheepish.

She reached out and ruffled his hair. 'Come on, let's go.' She put the car in gear and headed to his sixth form. She waved him off at the gates before double-backing home.

There, she flopped onto the sofa, a seaweed-coloured Chesterfield gifted by her mother. It wasn't *leisure* that Willa had a problem with – working did not appeal to her – but that *this* wasn't leisure at all. She had imagined floating from room to room in a central London townhouse, working on her art perhaps – but then she'd met Tom.

At first, she was charmed by his insistence that he pay their way. She was thrilled by his old-fashioned gallantry but, equally, she assumed he would change his mind after they were married. They would need a nice house, good furniture, a quality education for Jamie, but Tom refused to take her family's money. He clashed with Willa's father and did not want to owe him a thing.

At first, Willa didn't care. When you had never worried abut money, you assumed you never *would*. In fact, her new low status felt good: a contrarian 'fuck you'. *Money issues*, she would say with a tinkle of a laugh as if were a rare piece of furniture, but then she realised that most people lived on forty thousand a year and really that was nothing at all. Her friends might spend that on a single event. When they realised that her money issues weren't of the *crumbling estate, old money* variety, some began to distance themselves as if poverty might be catching. Tom remained adamant that he wouldn't take her father's money and Willa had relented, but damn him for letting it affect their son.

She sat cross legged on the sofa and rubbed her belly with a palm. It would be different this time, she decided. This time, her child would get everything that Jamie had missed; everything that she, at twenty-one, hadn't been equipped to give.

For years, she and Tom had tried for a second child. Eventually, they accepted that it wasn't on the cards, so when she realised she might be pregnant, she wanted to be certain before telling Tom. This time, things would be different. Willa would be the mother she couldn't be to Jamie.

Salma loved this time of day when the students had left the building and the heat of recent bodies cooled, the hum in the air now quiet. When Zain was younger, she would rush from her school to his, peddling furiously on the relentless circuit that made up working parenthood. Now, she basked in this time: the lull between her professional and personal lives.

If pushed, she might even admit that this was her favourite room in the world. Her antique compass and the Gall-Peters map on the far wall were more powerful than art to her. She taught geography, but her subject was irrevocably twined with history: the straight lines of Africa, Britain's place in the centre, the international date line, Greenwich Mean Time. Was there any other image that spoke of so much?

When Salma was eleven, she made a list of four places she wanted to visit: Easter Island off the west coast of South America, Tristan da Cunha off the west coast of Africa, Baffin Island in Canada and continental Antarctica. These, to her, were the four corners of the earth and it saddened her now to realise that she hadn't got anywhere near them. Maybe next year if their finances were in better shape and Zain had sorted himself out, she and Bil could make some plans.

If. A tiny word that puts entire lives on hold. She shook away the thought and packed up for the day. On her way home, she popped into her local Tesco, adding up what she needed to make it to the weekend. In the end, she bought more than she intended and, on leaving the supermarket, felt her left knee grind – an old cycling injury. Sighing, she ordered an Uber. She hated to waste the money but knew that she shouldn't strain it. The car arrived within minutes and drove up Horns Road. It turned into Blenheim and parked across from her house. Salma thanked the driver and got out. As she dragged the first bag towards her, a tin of beans spilled out and rolled beyond her reach.

'Sorry!' she called to the driver. 'Can you give me a moment? It's rolled beneath the back wheel.'

'Of course, love.' He cut the engine. 'Take your time.'

Salma bent down to retrieve it. Across the street, a flicker of movement caught her eye. Tom Hutton was in his front garden, throwing a yellow tennis ball from one hand to another. Casually, he approached the fence that divided his garden from hers. He paused there and glanced up and down the street, his gaze skimming right past the Uber. He whistled nonchalantly, then raised the ball and the threw it into her garden. It knocked the banner from her plant pot and went skittering across the lawn. The whole thing was so quick that Salma nearly missed it. She blinked, not quite able to decode what she'd seen. Tom glanced up and down the street again. He tugged the hem of his blazer, then turned and went inside.

'You alright, love?' called the driver. 'Need some help?'

'No,' said Salma quickly. She snatched up the tin and stuffed it in her bag. 'No, thank you.' She retrieved her second bag, stalling until Tom's door was closed. Finally, she stepped back and the car moved off. There, alone in the open street, she felt uncomfortably exposed.

Almost immediately, she started to doubt what she'd seen. She had been crouched in an awkward position and flustered by the delay. Could she have misread his actions? But no. There had been something very deliberate in the way he had glanced up the street, then taken aim with the ball. Salma flushed with anxiety. Where the hell had she and her family moved?

Gripped by *Next of Kin*? Don't miss the explosive
and thrilling debut from Kia Abdullah

TAKE
IT
BACK

IT'S TIME TO TAKE YOUR PLACE ON THE JURY.

The victim: A sixteen-year-old girl with facial
deformities, neglected by an alcoholic mother. Who
accuses the boys of something unthinkable.

The defendants: Four handsome teenage
boys from hardworking immigrant families.
All with corroborating stories.

WHOSE SIDE WOULD YOU TAKE?

Make sure you've read the latest shocking and jaw-dropping legal thriller from Kia Abdullah

ARE YOU READY TO START THIS CONVERSATION?

Kamran Hadid feels invincible. He attends Hampton school, an elite all-boys boarding school in London, he comes from a wealthy family, and he has a place at Oxford next year. The world is at his feet. And then a night of revelry leads to a drunken encounter and he must ask himself a horrific question.

With the help of assault counsellor, Zara Kaleel, Kamran reports the incident in the hopes that will be the end of it. But it's only the beginning...

ONE PLACE. MANY STORIES

Bold, innovative and
empowering publishing.

FOLLOW US ON:

@HQStories